WATCH
ME
WATCH
YOU

Also by Lily Samson

The Switch

WATCH ME WATCH YOU

LILY SAMSON

CENTURY

CENTURY

UK | USA | Canada | Ireland | Australia
India | New Zealand | South Africa

Century is part of the Penguin Random House group of companies
whose addresses can be found at global.penguinrandomhouse.com

Penguin Random House UK,
One Embassy Gardens, 8 Viaduct Gardens, London SW11 7BW

penguin.co.uk

Penguin
Random House
UK

First published 2025
001

Copyright © Lily Samson, 2025

The moral right of the author has been asserted

Set in 13.5/16pt Garamond MT Std
Typeset by by Jouve (UK), Milton Keynes

Printed and bound in Great Britain by Clays Ltd, Elcograf S.p.A.

The authorised representative in the EEA is Penguin Random House Ireland,
Morrison Chambers, 32 Nassau Street, Dublin D02 YH68

A CIP catalogue record for this book is available from the British Library

ISBN: 978-1-529-90949-4 (hardback)
ISBN: 978-1-529-90948-7 (trade paperback)

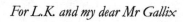

For L.K. and my dear Mr Gallix

PART I

Facebook post: Jean Winters

4 October 2024

Do you all remember my posts earlier this year about the neighbours in the flat opposite me, who I was having so much trouble with? The ones who were behaving strangely, constantly changing the locks, playing loud music suddenly (thrash metal on one occasion, top volume), making loud bangs at night, all sorts of comings & goings? They went quiet for a while but tonight is the night to end all nights! There have been screams, banging, and I think I just heard a gunshot. I've been nervous all day as it is with Edward having his op, and now this – not sure whether to get involved. Should I call the police?

Henry: I would call the police right now!

Gideon: I feel you ought to respect your neighbours' privacy. Once upon a time, the idea that an Englishman's home is his castle prevailed.

Alexa: Are you f**king kidding, Gideon? There are lives at risk and Jean is just supposed to sit there, and when you open the papers tomorrow you'll learn some poor woman's died or something & you'll know you could have stopped it. Jean, you have to call the police NOW.

CHAPTER ONE

Alice

Five Months Earlier

I wake up. It's pitch black. I can hear ragged gasps, sporadic screaming. My hand creeps across the bed, locates my phone on the bedside table. *Someone's in my flat.* Dominic? Is he hurting someone?

I tap into my phone 9 . . . 9 . . . Wait: one of those voices sounds familiar. It sounds like – my boyfriend.

I sit up, confused. Sean's currently away in Istanbul, working as a cameraman for a news channel reporting on an international conflict. But I swear I can hear his laughter echoing around my living-room.

I slide out of bed, the cold bulleting my sweat-drenched body. There's a chair jammed up beneath my door handle: my nightly routine. I remove it.

Very slowly, I turn my door handle.

My phone thumps onto the carpet as I jump.

My living-room swims in darkness, save for one square of light. My video camera sits on a tripod; a film spools from it, playing out on the wall. A couple, having sex on my sofa. The woman's throat is arched back; he buries his mouth in her neck as they reach a climax; their cries become frenzied.

It's me and Sean. We made the video two weeks back, the

5

night before he left. Our secret. Who the hell has turned on my video camera?

Now Sean and I are in post-coital sweetness, laughing softly at a joke. I press the stop button, then run to the kitchen, pull a knife from my plastic draining unit. It's still flecked red from the pepper I chopped earlier, and I know it's too blunt to do harm, but it's better than nothing.

I go from room to room, flicking on switches, opening wardrobe doors, until the whole flat is blazing with reassuring light. My pet parrots stir in their cage, looking sleepy and confused.

There's nobody here.

As I sink onto the sofa, I notice a book lying on the floor: *The Cry of the Owl* by Patricia Highsmith. Relief floods through me as I weigh it in my hands. It must have fallen from my overstuffed bookcase and hit the video camera's play button – though that's fairly far-fetched. But what else could it be?

My mobile says it's 4:34. I have a big day tomorrow and I need to be fresh and bright and my very best self. I'm starting an important internship. My trouser suit, freshly ironed, is hanging up against the wardrobe door.

I jam the chair beneath my bedroom door handle, but it's not enough. So I heave a chest of drawers over; a spider scuttles out in alarm, disappearing into a dark corner.

In bed, I send a quick WhatsApp to Sean. You'll never guess what just happened ... I attempt to turn it into a comic anecdote. I tell myself we'll soon be laughing about this, but it takes at least an hour before my rigid body finally relaxes into sleep.

CHAPTER TWO

Alice

The next morning I keep fighting yawns. I was supposed to be sharp on eight hours sleep, but instead I'm bleary on five. Crammed into a corner of the train, elbowed by commuters, I google Mina Harpenden.

She's the star editor at Principle Publishing. A legend in the industry. Her last big discovery was a number-one bestseller and was made into a hit Netflix series. She's forty years old. No children. Married to an MP: Romain Harpenden. I eye up photos of them together, at film premiers and political functions and high-society events. There's an elegance, a classiness to her beauty, reminiscent of Elizabeth Taylor. Her straight hair is cut into a dark bob, shiny as patent leather, never a strand out of place. She never smiles. Her gaze is cool; though when I look closer, enlarging each picture, I detect a strange sort of indifference.

If my internship pays off, Mina Harpenden could end up being my boss . . .

'We are now approaching London Blackfriars . . .' comes the voice through the tannoy: my stop.

The Principle Publishing offices are situated on Victoria Embankment. The late spring sun is glinting on the Thames; a few seagulls swoop and dive, making raw cries. I'm given a pass at reception and swipe into the building, exit the lift on the fifth floor, passing bookcases displaying rows of bestsellers.

I gaze across a sea of open-plan desks, feeling lost, double-checking the contact name on my phone.

'Are you okay?' A young woman with a red ponytail is approaching me, smiling.

'I'm Alice Smart – I'm the new intern. I'm supposed to connect with Sarah – Sarah Lively-Cross.'

She introduces me to Sarah. She's young, early twenties I'd guess. She has a fringe cut halfway across her forehead and sports a nose-ring and a dolphin tattoo on her wrist, but her voice is extremely posh.

'Gosh, it's so lovely to meet you.' She gives me the once-over and I detect a flicker of something – disapproval? – on her face, but then she smiles warmly.

There's an empty desk next to hers. I feel a surge of excitement as I realise which office our desks face, recognising the figure behind the glass: *Mina Harpenden*.

'. . . so I need to find you something useful to do,' Sarah is saying, as I tune back in. 'We're simply deluged with manuscripts at the moment. If you could read and write a paragraph on each one, what you liked – or didn't.'

She passes me a Kindle and I get stuck in to a submission. It's about a depressed vampire who can't stop murdering women: a kind of supernatural incel. It's awful.

In her office, Mina sits regally still. People lean towards her, anxious to please. She's shorter than I expected, and she's the only one here who wears high heels. I don't know much about designer labels but she looks impeccable in a chic navy jacket and matching skirt.

I'm finding it hard to focus. I just want to watch her. I wonder if this is my first ever girl crush.

I glance over at Sarah, who's yawning as she taps away at emails.

'Are you an editor?' I ask.

She looks flattered. 'God, no. I'm Mina's assistant. I mean, I'm hoping I might get promoted soon – I've been here three years.'

'What's she like to work for?'

I worry Sarah might not want to be interrupted, but she seems to relish the chance to gossip.

'She's not easy to impress.'

'But you must learn so much, working for such a legend.'

She rolls her eyes. 'Uh-huh.'

I try a different tack: 'Isn't her husband an MP?'

'Yes, and he's smoking hot,' she says, her eyes gleaming. 'They have such a perfect life. Did you see that *Tatler* shoot last month, of their home in Mayfair?'

I shake my head.

'It was so funny. They were trying to be down-to-earth – "we live normal lives" kind of thing, but it was hardly convincing. Their house is just the most enviable place—'

Sarah notices that Mina's tapping on her glass window, signalling for her to come in, and quickly jumps up.

At midday, Sarah goes off for lunch and I feel a little disappointed that she didn't invite me. Remembering her once-over, I glance down at my suit and spot a fraying hem, a button a little loose, and frown. Nobody else here seems to be wearing a trouser suit: everyone's in jeans or dresses.

Then my mobile pings with an email.

It's from Heather Perkins. One of my former bosses.

Dear Alice,

I'm sorry for taking so long to reply to your email. I wasn't sure how to respond. I don't feel we would be able to offer a reference for you, given the extremely troubling incidents that happened whilst you were here.

This is so annoying. I didn't even ask Heather for a reference; I wouldn't dream of doing so. I'm not an idiot. I simply asked that she take down an old photo of me on the company website. I don't want anyone digging into my past.

Panic pulses through me. I think of my wasted twenties, the jobs I jacked in, the jobs I was fired from. Gardener, personal shopper, babysitter, pet-sitter, carer: I've tried them all. My last job before this internship was looking after an elderly woman, Julia, before she passed away. We became very close. So close I often wished she was my real mother. In her worst days of sickness, when she was too tired to get out of bed, I would read to her. One day she told me, 'You know, Alice, you love reading so much, you should write a book!' I laughed and said it wasn't for me, but she'd planted a seed: working *with* books sounded like a dream career. Finally, at the age of thirty, I've found what I want to do, but how do I turn an internship into a job?

Inspiration strikes. I've seen Sarah make coffees for Mina. I head down to the Starbucks next door to our offices and buy Mina a flat white. A pinch, as I hand over the cash. This is the money I need for my dinner. Tonight I'll have to eat a baked potato with a little butter and nothing else, but the sacrifice will be worth it.

Back in the office, I notice that Sarah's long lunch break has finished. I knock on Mina's door.

I see Sarah's eyes widen. She shakes her head frantically.

I knock again. No reply. *Be bold,* I tell myself. I turn the handle and enter. Mina is just peeling a piece of paper from a notebook, dropping it into the bin, and she jumps, looking slightly furtive.

'Hi, I'm Alice Smart, your new intern. I thought you'd appreciate a coffee.' I stroll up and set it down on her desk.

Mina's face hardens. I try to hold her gaze, but as nerves mount, I drop my eyes.

'Thank you so much,' she says in a tone that suggests I've just dumped a turd on her desk. 'But I do prefer not to be interrupted.'

I exit quickly. Back at my desk, Sarah berates me: 'You must *never* interrupt – she hates it. You need training,' she adds, as though I'm a dog.

But I can see Mina's drinking my coffee. I did the right thing. I think.

At the end of the day, I linger. I've read and written a full report on the awful vampire novel, over a thousand words, even though Sarah only wanted a few lines.

Everyone's gone home. An elderly cleaner comes in, rubbing his back, and I give him a cheery wave. Whilst he's hoovering the offices at the top, I creep into Mina's office and go to the bin, fishing out the piece of paper I saw her discard.

I decide to head to the staff toilets and read it in the safety of a cubicle.

Jemima
Sexy
Age 36
Knee boots

Vegetarian
10 sexual partners
But what if psycho?

How odd, I think, intrigued. Are these notes for a date? Is Mina queer, perhaps? But isn't she married to a handsome MP? And what is that 'psycho' line all about?

I fold the stray paper and slip it into my pocket, re-entering the office. I stop short.

Mina is back.

I retreat and watch her from the edge of a bookcase. There's something cautious about the way she's heading back into her office. I observe her unlock a drawer in her desk and pull out something that looks like a small yellow kitten. As she pushes it into her elegant shoulder bag, I realise that it's a wig.

She strides out of her office and walks right towards me. I realise that it's too late to hide, it'll look too suspicious, and I just need to brazen this out, say I wanted to stay late, make a good impression—

'My bin wasn't emptied last night,' Mina says. 'If you could just . . .'

Oh great, I think indignantly. *I bought you coffee. It cost me my dinner. And I made such a memorable impression on you . . .*

I nod at her miserably and she looks flustered, as though sensing that she may have made a mistake. Then she says, 'Well, thank you,' and strides off to the lift. I can't face any more awkward conversation, so I take the stairs. I arrive in reception just in time to see her heading out of the main double doors and onto the street.

Where are you going, Mina Harpenden? I wonder. *And why do you need a disguise?* My curiosity is piqued.

She heads into Blackfriars station and swipes through the

turnstiles; I follow. I'm at the top of the escalator just as she gets off at the bottom. We're both taking the District line, heading west. The platform is crowded, so it takes a while for me to spot her. She's gazing at a Jack Daniel's advert, nervously picking at her bag strap. When she boards a train I get on at the opposite end of her carriage, turning my back on her, the wind whipping up my hair as the train screeches through stations. She changes lines at Victoria and there's such a crush of commuters, it's easy to follow her without being noticed. We board another tube; I watch her reflection as she gets off at Green Park.

I hesitate, then push my way off the train just before the doors beep shut.

Sarah told me that Mina lives in Mayfair. It's no doubt some mansion where she presides over dinner parties with celebrities and political stars, where the laughter of guests tinkles beneath chandeliers.

She hurries up the station steps, her pace more focused and impatient now, checking her watch. Piccadilly is bustling with tourists and for a moment, I lose her, then see her turn down a side street. I hurry after her and stop short—

I watch her entering an expensive boutique hotel.

Who's she meeting? Jemima?

I hesitate. I hadn't ever intended to follow her; it has just happened, spontaneously. Old habits die hard. I enter cautiously, but there's no sign of Mina. The receptionist is very coiffured and polite. I ask if I can get a drink and she points me towards the bar with a dazzling smile.

I sit on a stool before a shiny gold surface, half hidden by the elegant sprays of a pot plant. The bartender is a sexy Black guy; I ask him for a menu. The cocktail list sports drinks of various spirits and syrups and all cost £15. I can't even afford a mineral water. I pull out a small mirror from my handbag. My heart skips when I see that *Mina is entering the bar wearing the blonde wig*. She sits down on one of the luxury velvet sofas. She's changed from her crisp work clothes into a little black dress. She looks like a starlet; shades of Marilyn Monroe.

The waiter approaches her and she orders a martini.

I pretend to fiddle with a stray eyelash so I can carry on watching Mina in my mirror. When the barman asks if I want to order a drink, I say I need more time, giving him a sheepish grin.

A WhatsApp suddenly pops up on my phone from Sean: How did your first day go?

What would my boyfriend say if I replied: *Well, I just followed my new boss to a high-class hotel where I think she's about to rendez-vous with a sexy woman called Jemima . . .?*

My stomach rumbles. Mina carries on waiting. I can't skip meals; I get dizzy, irritable, so I cheekily reach for the free peanuts sitting on the bar table. The barman sets down a glass of tap water for me, giving me a wink, and I grin back at him.

'Oh my God, are you Mina Harpenden?' I hear a voice cry out.

'Oh my God,' another echoes her. 'I follow you on Instagram. Your hair looks amazing – I love your new look.'

I lift my mirror again, catch a slice of Mina's expression, the dismay that she quickly conceals.

She politely declines to have selfies taken with them.

After they've left, she pays the bill and makes a hasty exit, her martini half drunk. I wait ten minutes, finishing up all the peanuts, before I thank the barman and head off back home.

*

I get off the tube at High Street Kensington. As I turn into my road, I'm so preoccupied with Mina that I forget to be on my guard.

Then I catch sight of him and I freeze.

Dominic.

Sometimes he's standing on the opposite side of the road, arms folded, watching my flat, his stamina lasting for hours. Sometimes he's by the main entrance to the block, ready to collar me, ready to argue.

I know I shouldn't be complaining about stalkers when I've just followed Mina, but Dominic is relentless. He's in his mid-thirties, unemployed, always sports a green cagoule. Tonight he's in his usual pose: leaning against a brick wall, playing on his phone. Candy Crush is his addiction. I think about retreating to a café, lingering with a tea in the hope he'll go soon. But then he spots me – damn. I'm going to have to brave it out.

He holds his phone up, videoing me. I ignore him, but inside I'm frantic: is this his way of letting me know it was him in my flat, who set off my video?

He becomes my shadow. I punch in the code to Chesterton House. There's security here, thank God. Dominic falls back. The glass door swings shut and I glare as he carries on filming through it.

I hurry into the lift, relieved when the doors close. I tell myself indifference is the best weapon. But he has this way of getting under my skin – it's his energy. A simmering resentment, hints of violence about to erupt.

This has been going on for six months now. He thinks I owe him, and stalking is his way of putting the pressure on.

I get out on the fifth floor. My neighbour Jean, who lives opposite me, is just coming out of her flat. She's in her early sixties, with a brisk haircut and a chatty manner, but I really don't have time for pleasantries – I say, 'Hello,' and slam the door behind me, sliding the bolt across.

For a moment, I gaze around, drinking in my new place: what would Mina say if she knew I lived like this?

I check on my parrots, who live in a cage in my living-room. I got Mimi and Arthur two years ago as a gift for Julia, and I adore them – they're my feathered best friends. As I feed them mixed seeds, I become aware that there's something else wrong. My flat is unusually warm and cosy. I put the heating on for half an hour this morning as a treat, but I was so excited about Mina I forgot to turn it off. Damn: I can hardly afford the bills as it is.

For dinner I make a jacket potato. My birds fly around the flat, filling me with delight; Mimi swoops and lands lightly on my shoulder.

My eyes fall on my video camera. Has Dominic somehow got hold of a key? Maybe I should change the locks yet again.

Before bed, I check all the locks and jam the chair under my bedroom door handle.

CHAPTER THREE

Alice

I'm in Starbucks again, ordering another coffee for Mina. I've raised some extra cash by putting one of the first-edition books that Julia gifted me on eBay, which was painful.

Up in Principle Publishing, I approach Mina's office, but Sarah gives me a firm, slow shake of her head. So I bend down and leave the cup by her door. I know it opens inwards so she won't knock it over. Since following her, I feel strangely closer to her, a little less intimidated.

Sarah's on the phone, looking tense. I think Mina is telling her off. Mina works her hard, Sarah complains, and is never satisfied.

'God – that woman!' Sarah hisses, as she puts down the phone.

I give her a supportive smile, wanting to bond with her, but I suffer a pinch: *God, I'd do anything to have her job, and the chance to do it well.*

Sarah gets another call and groans: 'Peach Ingalls is here. She's our star author – only she doesn't even write her own books, her ghosts do it for her.'

She heads down to reception to collect her and bring her up to our floor. Peach struts out of the lift, swinging her glossy highlighted hair. As Mina greets her, Peach kicks over the latte I left by the door.

'Oh shit,' I murmur, watching it spill and spread, staining the carpet, wrecking her shoes.

Mina looks incensed. I help Sarah to mop up the mess, Sarah hissing, 'What the fuck? – I told you not to!' As I lay down a tissue, watching milky coffee seep into its fibres, my confidence shrinks down to the size of a pea, and I wonder how long I'm going to last in this place.

The next morning, fate brings Mina and me together.

In the toilets, I find Mina at the sink. Our eyes meet in the mirror. I feel her guard come up, a silent warning: *Don't even try speaking to me.* Since the coffee fiasco, I've kept my head down, trying to watch and learn. The only advantage is that I've finally been noticed: Mina no longer thinks I'm the cleaner, which makes me want to laugh and cry.

Mina combs her hair. She looks so strict I wonder if a strand would dare drop out of place. She applies lipstick with precision, whilst I dab my leaking eyeliner—

Out of nowhere comes a shrill, shrieking noise. Mina jumps violently. Her lipstick smears across her cheek in a red slash, like blood.

'Is there a fire?' I ask in alarm.

Mina's hand is splayed over her heart. 'It's the Wednesday test – I always forget.'

She removes her lipstick smear with a tissue. Her breath is coming hard and fast; she grips the sink and stares down into the basin.

'Are you okay?' I ask.

Is she asthmatic? I think of Julia in her final days, the breathlessness she suffered before her sickness took her, and anxiety fills me. Then I twig: Mina is having a panic attack.

I reach out and gently stroke her back, the way I used to

with Julia. Prising her hand away from the sink, I hold it and she squeezes back, so hard it hurts. 'You're okay,' I murmur. 'You're okay.' I feel astonished that Mina, so cool, so in control, could be reacting like this.

'Sorry about that,' she says briskly, though there's a slight quaver to her voice. 'That alarm was so loud.'

'Oh, I know! It hurt my ears,' I exaggerate in sympathy.

As we head out into the corridor, she turns – 'I'd be grateful if we kept this quiet.'

'Of course,' I say quickly, touching her arm, only now she flinches a little, and as she walks on, her stride becomes confident and assertive.

Back at my desk, I wonder if it was a good or a bad thing to have witnessed that. I recall the hotel I followed her into, the blonde wig, the mysterious list on the piece of paper with *Jemima* and *what if psycho?* What's going on in Mina's life to make her so stressed?

The next day, Mina is like ice. If I pass her in the corridor and say 'Hi!' her lips thin. I have five weeks left of this internship and I have to turn this around somehow – but how?

Friday dawns. This evening we've all been invited to a book launch – the first I've ever been to. I become conscious of Charles, our MD, and Mina looking over at me, speaking in low voices.

I get into the lift with her at midday.

'Hi, Alice,' she greets me, her lips approaching a smile. 'I do hope you're coming this evening.'

I'm so taken aback I can only mutter my reply.

The launch is taking place in a lovely bookshop not far from my flat, Waterstones Kensington. Mina stands at the front and makes a speech that's electric: passionate and witty in all the right places. The whole room is enthralled. Desire burns inside me: *I want to be up there, making a speech like that. I want it so badly.*

As the party winds down, Sarah slopes off early and I linger, helping to clear up sticky glasses.

'Thank you *so much*, Alice.' Mina says, beaming at me. That vertiginous feeling comes over me again. Why the sudden transformation? What did I miss? She's being so nice, it's slightly surreal.

We both end up at the bookshop entrance. When the party started a watery sun warmed us; now, with a sudden change typical of British spring weather, the rain is lashing the pavement in droves. Mina becomes irritable again, picks up her iPhone and complains: 'The Uber driver is just sitting there, ten minutes away . . . Not moving . . . What the fuck is he playing at?'

'I have an umbrella,' I offer. 'If you want to go the tube?'

Mina accepts, putting on another eerie, bright smile. But my umbrella, decorated with birds, is so – well, cheap. Tatty and thin. Within a minute, it's turned inside out and I'm fearful of poking Mina's eyes out.

As the rain becomes biblical, we shelter in a nearby doorway. My feet are soaking wet. My heart is beating. I can't make another mess of things; I have to seize this moment. I might not get an opportunity like this again.

'We could – we could go to my flat,' I burst out. 'It's not too far from here. We could – dry off – and sort out a taxi for you from there.'

Even as I say the words, I know she'll say no. She's being nicer to me, but she's not going to want to fraternise with the intern who wrecked her carpet.

'Sure,' she says, nodding. 'That's a good idea.'

'Great!' I reply, now panicked that she's said yes, anticipating the pressure ahead to impress her at every moment.

We splash out onto the pavement, Mina struggling in her heels. A worry flickers through my mind – *what if Dominic's at my flat* – but then I assure myself: not in this weather.

We hurry down Kensington High Street and I guide her into Marloes Road, to the grand Victorian mansion block framed with white pillars: Chesterton House. I type in the code and we enter, dripping and shivering. I smile at Felipe, the doorman sitting behind the elegant front desk.

We enter a lift with a plush cream carpet, and get out on the fifth floor.

I undo the double locks and let us in. Mina looks shocked.

I don't think she was expecting this.

CHAPTER FOUR

Alice

Pride plumes in my heart. I inherited this flat from Julia six months ago and every day I say a silent thank-you for her generosity. For the first few weeks I suffered imposter syndrome, waking each morning and wondering how a girl who spent some of her twenties homeless or scrimping to pay rent in a mould-infested house in Hackney shared by six people could really live here. Now I've grown more used to it, though I'm conscious of the weird paradox of my life: living in splendour whilst being cash-poor.

I guide her into the living-room. I've not got the money to put my stamp on the flat yet. It's filled with an odd mixture of antique furniture that once belonged to Julia and cheaper items I got on Freecycle. There's a chaise longue that sits next to a big squashy black leather sofa. There's several huge bookcases and a 75-inch TV belonging to Sean. A cheap coffee table; an exquisite walnut dining table with six chairs; the video camera, which still makes me shiver every time I look at it.

Mina's eyes are wide. It gives me a kick, to know I've shocked her. I hurry to the bathroom to find her a towel that's fresh and clean. When I come back, I find her at the window, gazing out at my view.

'This flat – it's simply gorgeous. How many bedrooms?'

'Um, three.'

'And you have birds . . .' Mina goes to their cage. 'They're very cute.'

My eyes fall to the coffee table and I jump in panic. Shit – *the piece of paper that I stole from her bin is lying right there.* I grab it just as she turns back to face me; I quickly crumple it up in my fist.

I offer her tea and she asks for peppermint. In the kitchen, I shove the piece of paper into a drawer. That was a close one.

As I wait for the kettle to boil, my excitement returns. *Mina Harpenden is in my flat!* Imagine Sarah's face if she saw. Then I open my cupboard and realise that all I have is a large economy-size box of PG Tips.

'I'm all out of herbal,' I apologise, taking the tea in to her.

We sit down on my big black squashy sofa. Mina takes a sip and says: 'I hope you don't think I'm rude, Alice, but Charles happened to mention that you –' she clears her throat – 'are on the internship diversity scheme.'

Why has she brought that up? Now I feel as though I'm twelve again, in the Jobcentre with my mum, my dad having lost his job yet again. The blush of shame on my mum's cheeks, the resentment in her voice.

'Yes, I am,' I say in a small voice.

'Well, I think that's splendid,' she says. 'We need more diversity. Publishing is full of posh white women. Alice, we need more people like *you.*'

She sounds as though she's speaking from a script and I feel a little cringey. So this is the reason for her sudden swerve in attitude towards me?

'I don't really want to be judged on my background though,' I say. 'I want to be judged on my work. You know – I've been reading manuscripts like mad and I think I've found a gem.

What would it take for me to be able to buy the book and become the editor on it?'

Mina laughs gently, which is kinder than the way Sarah reacted this morning when I voiced the idea. She pretty much told me that I was delusional.

'Tell you what, email it over to me and I'll read it,' she promises me.

She glances around the flat again and I sense her curiosity: *If you're working-class, how can you afford to live in a place like this?*

'A friend of mine,' Mina says, 'she was in a domestic-violence situation, and she ended up in a gorgeous flat just like this in Earl's Court owned by a women's refuge . . .' She's really fishing now. 'So, how long have you had this place?'

'Six months,' I reply.

'The rent must be high,' she says.

'Well – I actually own it . . .' I trail off.

There's a shocked silence. I feel the impact of it too: *I live in a flat worth two million.* Something I'm still getting used to.

'Is it your boyfriend's too?' she digs. 'If you have a boyfriend . . .?'

'No – it's mine. Sean lives in Hackney. It's . . .' It's so complicated, trying to explain how I came to have this flat, so I simplify it: 'I inherited it from an old woman called Julia – I met her in a local library and we became friends. The weird thing is – I'm actually broke. I can't sell it for two years, it's specified in her will, but the service fees alone are six thousand pounds. I'm surviving by selling first editions that belonged to Julia.' I nod at the big bookcase.

There's a look of genuine sympathy on her face. 'That sounds a tricky situation. Have you thought of AirBnB?'

'I did,' I agree. 'I feel a bit weird about having strangers to stay . . . but yes, I should try it.'

'You could . . .'

I sit up; she's thinking up some plan, but then she just trails off and the silence hangs between us.

'I could . . .?' I nudge her.

But Mina's distracted by her phone, which keeps buzzing. As she reads a message, a shadow comes over her face. My curiosity is piqued: is that Jemima messaging her? Or her husband, the gorgeous MP? Maybe they're having problems of some kind. I think of her strange panic attack in the toilets, her reaction to the fire alarm.

'D'you have any wine?' Mina suddenly asks.

I'm about to say no, when I remember that Sean bought a bottle a few weeks back, for us to open on his return. It's an expensive one, but I can replace it (somehow). I have to keep my boss happy.

As I come out of the kitchen with the bottle and two glasses, I notice Mina is eyeing up in my video camera in fascination.

'Do you like making movies?' she asks.

'Well – not so much me – my boyfriend is—'

Oh shit. Mina's just pressed the play button. Up on the wall the film streams again: me and Sean, having sex on my sofa, our cries of pleasure ringing out—

'Oh gosh, I'm so sorry,' Mina says, pressing buttons desperately.

I quickly switch it off, but the noise and image hang in the air like an afterburn.

I feel very self-conscious, but I catch Mina smiling to herself, as though she's amused by the *faux pas*.

'So how long have you been with your boyfriend – Sean? That's his name?'

'Yes. I met him twelve years ago,' I say, my cheeks still

warm. 'But we were together six years, then we had a long time apart before getting back together.'

'So it's serious . . .?'

'Yes,' I assert. In fact, Sean wants it to be serious, but I'm trying to keep things light.

'Hmm. Anyone in the office you find attractive?'

I nearly spit out my wine and Mina laughs. It's the first time I've ever heard the sound, seen joy on her face; it makes her look radiant, beautiful.

'Oh, come on,' she goads me. 'You must have a crush on someone.'

Suddenly Mina seems like an older sister. She's kicked off her heels and curled her feet up on the sofa.

'George in marketing is pretty sexy,' I muse, because everyone flutters around him in the office; he looks like Harry Styles.

'Oh yes, George is a pretty boy,' Mina says, a little dismissive.

'Charles is quite hot, I say, exaggerating because I find him a little pompous, to be honest. 'For an older guy. He looks distinguished . . .'

'Definitely,' Mina agrees. 'He has power, and power is sexy. He used to be fun for a flirt . . .'

I raise an eyebrow. I have a feeling that she's enjoying shocking me.

'But you know how it is now.' Her face falls. 'Offices are so boring. If you flirt it's sexual harassment. Charles doesn't dare respond anymore. And it's not that I want anything to *happen*,' she says quickly. 'But what's the harm in a little frisson?'

'But doesn't it make the office a more comfortable place?' I laugh. I echo a phrase I overhead Sarah using: 'Isn't it a relief not to have to suffer the male gaze?'

Mina rolls her eyes. 'The male gaze is a wonderful thing, Alice. To have a man's eyes on you doesn't demean you, it enthrones you. If he wants you, you have all the power – he's in the palm of your hand.'

She's playing the provocateur, but I'm transfixed, imagining Mina in her heels and chic dress, surrounded by a circle of salivating, slavish men.

Buzz-buzz.

We both jump.

'What was that?' Mina asks.

Buzz-buzz.

What the fuck? I hurry to the intercom, see Dominic there in the grainy video. His thin fox-like face; the ice in his blue eyes. I was sliding into a lovely, tipsy blur but now I'm sharp and sober.

Buzz-buzz.

'Who's that?' Mina asks.

'It's nobody.'

Buzz-buzz.

Mina frowns. 'Is Mr Nobody your boyfriend?'

'Oh, no, he's – a guy who's giving me a lot of hassle,' I admit. 'He's a bit of a stalker.'

'You should call the police—' *Buzz-buzz.* 'This is intolerable.'

'I know, I know,' I reply. I can't tell her that the police would bring further complications. My heartbeat is ramping up again. The fear that he might well have a key, that he might stride in any minute and throw accusations at me in front of Mina. I hurry into the hall and double-bolt the front door.

'Isn't there security downstairs?' Mina presses. 'In a place like this, there ought to be.'

'Well, there is to a degree,' I reply awkwardly. I don't want to reveal that Dominic knows Felipe, knows all the doormen, for he's a familiar face.

'What does he want from you?' Mina asks.

'Oh, everything,' I shudder. 'Normally when my boyfriend's here he has a go and scares him off, but Dominic's picked up that he's away.' I swallow. Mina's looking quite concerned now. 'Anyway, it's all fine. I think he's left . . .' I say as the buzzing finally stops. I go to the window to check he's definitely gone.

'Well, I should be going.' Mina sets down her glass, and I curse Dom for ruining the moment.

After she's left, a compulsion comes over me. I open the door to the third bedroom. This is the room Julia died in. Usually I keep the door closed, as I need to be in the right mood to suffer all those dark and sad memories that still seem to swirl in the air.

I sit on the bed, feeling sober. I notice that bloodstain on the carpet. It's faded a little since the day she died.

Julia passed away at the age of seventy-one. For the last two years of her life, I was her carer. In the week before she died, it was just the two of us holed up in here. She'd been released from hospital, told she had little time left to live. They wheeled her in with a mask clamped to her withered face, attached to an oxygen machine that hissed and pumped all day and all night. I had been given a bag of medicines to ease her pain; every few hours I had to lower her mask and squirt morphine into her mouth with a teat pipette. I cooked her meals; brushed her hair; washed her face; a constant litany of tasks that were so exhausting they saved me from facing the reality of what was to come.

I gaze at the armchair by her bed. I'd sleep there, sometimes waking to hear her babbling nonsense in her sleep. At other times she was lucid. I'd always thought that reaching the end of your life must bring wisdom and peace: you'd reminisce, reflect, wince at mistakes, treasure the good times. But Julia's anger shocked me. She clutched my hand in her birdlike one. She told me, fiercely, that she'd wasted opportunities, missed chances, fucked up. 'You have to make something of your life, Alice,' she hissed, her nails digging into my palm until they left drops of blood.

The memory brings tears to my eyes. I know Julia would be proud of me for my internship, but I know she'd also want me to impress Mina, get a proper job. *I'll make it happen, I swear,* I tell her silently, slowly tracing the bloodstain with my foot. *I promise you Julia, I will.*

CHAPTER FIVE

Mina

Do I dare ask her?

Do I dare make this proposition to Alice?

I lie awake, the question dancing in my mind.

My husband snores in bed beside me. He sleeps like a baby. Meanwhile, I wake up every night around two, three in the morning. My sleep is one of two halves, bisected by a long period of tossing and turning and thinking and *thinking* and telling myself to stop analysing my life and raking over the past and tossing and turning some more.

Alice Smart. My first impression of her was – well, unimpressed. She looked a bit shabby. A cheap suit. Fair hair untamed like a lion's mane. She doesn't pluck her eyebrows, she bites her nails, and her posture is poor. And then she wrecked my carpet; there's still a beige stain that the cleaner can't get out.

Then Charles came into my office and berated me: 'I overheard Sarah laughing that you mistook Alice for being the cleaner. I looked her up and she's on the diversity scheme. She's *working-class*, Mina.' I had to apologise meekly and promise to look after her.

I wish we could all just move on. I made *one* mistake last year, *one* drunk tweet.

Been watching Welfare Britain. Wish I could lounge around on benefits all day eating Mother's Pride #lazywaystomakealiving #publishingishardwork

As I explained to my furious husband: in my inebriated state, I managed to convince myself people were tired of political correctness, that I'd be appreciated for my amusing honesty. Instead, I was vilified and suffered Trial by Twitter. It even made the newspapers, damaged Romain's reputation, gave us the notoriety of a couple out of touch with the masses. Since then, I've been trying to repent, to show I care about inequality in our society. I donate to food banks, give money to the homeless. But even now, sometimes I put up a post on Insta – Romain and I on holiday on the Riviera, or out to dinner – and I'll get a comment along the lines of: The other half lives the high life – the rest of us working-class types carry on snivelling in our hovels.

And so I decided to give Alice a second chance. Pay her some attention, encourage her. Show the world I'm not a snooty bitch.

I was surprised to find myself warming to her on Friday evening. She reminds me of me when I was her age: eager to please and hungry to learn. Like me, I sense, she worries far too much about whether people like her. Once upon a time, I used to dress in dull clothes, adopt sartorial conformity; I lived by a philosophy of kindness; a people-pleasing smile ached on my lips. I ended up being patronised and never taken seriously. Other people took credit for my work. I've gradually learnt how to earn respect, to project a tough exterior, to smile on the inside but resist mirroring it on the outside.

Her flat was somewhat surprising for someone who's on the diversity scheme. Can she really own it? I wonder if she's just flat-sitting and made up a story to impress me. She edged around her home as though it didn't really belong to her; there was a haunted, anxious look in her eyes.

If I were to propose that Alice rent me her flat for a night, what would she say? Would she be discreet? Romain must never find out; nobody must ever find out.

I desperately need a place. Last week I booked a hotel using a fake name, but two tourists spotted me. I don't get recognised that often, not the way Romain does, but it gave me the jitters.

After that, I lost my nerve. I had to cancel my plans; I was left feeling restless and despairing.

I close my eyes, trying to will sleep to return. A hazy memory creeps in: of the video that played out on her wall. Alice naked, legs locked around her boyfriend, climaxing. I hid how aroused I felt. Since then, I've often retreated into that memory: that video like a glimpse of a possible future, an escape I crave.

The next morning, I call Alice into my office. She looks thrilled to have been asked into my sacred space.

'Alice.' I play with a pen, keeping my cool despite my beating heart. 'I have a proposal to make to you. I – I really do need a quiet place to read manuscripts, and everything is so busy and hectic at mine . . . If you see what I mean?'

Alice nods, but I can see she hasn't quite twigged yet.

'You mentioned the possibility of renting out your flat. Well, I'd be happy to rent it for one evening. If that would suit you.'

Alice looks taken aback.

'I'd pay you one thousand pounds for the night.'

'*Wow.*' Her eyes become starry. 'That's . . . so . . . generous. I'd love that!'

'Good.' I smile. 'It's a deal then. My only concern is the stalker who was giving you so much grief last night – is that a regular occurrence? Nightly?'

'Oh God, no,' she reassures me. 'Just now and again. It's fine. I can deal with him. I can tell Felipe to keep an eye out.'

'Fine.' I smile. 'So – if I could rent it next Tuesday?'

'Sure – Sean will be back then. I can stay with him for the night.'

I glance through my office window at Sarah. I've already picked up on the rivalry between them. Sarah has been coasting here for years; and Alice is so smart and efficient and enthusiastic, Sarah feels threatened. But they're frenemies. I've seen them gossip, go for the odd lunch.

'I would be counting on your absolute discretion,' I say. 'If you mentioned this to anyone, I'd have to terminate our agreement at once.'

'Of course.' Alice looks serious, bites her nails. 'I absolutely swear I won't tell a soul.'

'Good.'

'I'll sign a contract if you like – an NDA or something?'

'There's no need.' I smile. 'And – if Sarah asks what you came into my office for, what will you tell her?' I test her.

'I'll say I've discovered a gem of a manuscript and you've seen the potential,' Alice delivers in a straight tone.

We both smile at each other and I feel an unexpected rush of affection for her.

An hour later, the office clears for lunch and I check my work phone, swallowing. There are more messages waiting for me. They're keen to meet. They think that I'm called

Jemima; I've used a photo of me that's very blurry and I'm wearing sunglasses.

I'm about to reply, to set a date, to anchor myself so I can't turn back. But then I see the message in my inbox, and bile rises in my throat.

> I know what you're doing. In order for me to let this go, you need to send £2,000 to the following account . . .

CHAPTER SIX

Alice

It's Tuesday night and I'm staying at Sean's flat in Hackney. I had to vacate my flat by eight before Mina arrived.

I can't help wondering what she's doing. Who would pay £1,000 just to sit and have a quiet space for the night? She must be meeting someone. Jemima, maybe?

Delicious smells are wafting from the kitchen: Sean's cooking. It's a rule that when I come to his, he treats me and vice versa. He's away a lot in his work as a cameraman, freelancing for various news channels. Sometimes when he's abroad, he can become abstract in my mind, and when he returns, the shock of seeing him in the flesh is a sharp pleasure: the Irish lilt to his accent, his sexy blue eyes, his grounded energy, the cute way he sings along to his iPod when he's cooking.

There's a sudden loud burst of nineties dance music from the flat upstairs. The house Sean lives in is divided into three flats. His is small and cramped; half his stuff still sits in plastic storage boxes stacked up in the corner. It all reminds me of where I lived before I inherited Julia's flat. I feel a stab of guilt, thinking of how many times Sean has asked to move in and I've said no. He's finding it hard that I want our relationship to be a paradox: committed, monogamous, but light-hearted. I tell him it's because he's away a lot filming. I tell him it's because I'm still grieving from the loss of Julia. I tell him it's because I want to focus on my career. All these things are true. But I'm not sure if he understands how raw I still feel from the years when things went so wrong between us.

At least Sean's made his flat look good. He has a flare for interior design. He decorated the dull fireplace with his own seascape tile pattern; the walls are covered with his framed photos. He has an eye for making a mundane scene look beautiful: a magpie sitting on a chimney pot, an earring dangling from its beak, the light from a sunset reflected against a trio of windows.

I think of my own flat, my stomach clenching with worry: what if it ends up being damaged or dirtied?

'So,' Sean says, coming in with two steaming plates of veggie lasagne. 'Found a series you like?'

I love our nights in together, plates on our laps, playfully fighting over what we're going to watch.

'We could watch *Love* on Netflix,' Sean suggests.

'What about *Gagged*?' When he demands a synopsis, I read from my phone: 'A crime drama about a woman kidnapped and held in a basement – will the two rival detectives find her before she's killed?'

'Sounds so feel-good.' Sean rolls his eyes, laughing as I flick him.

He always wants to be cheered up, whilst I want to savour something that sucks me in and disturbs me and tells me how dark human nature really is. He yawns; he's still exhausted from filming and scarred by the suffering he's witnessed, preserved on his camera.

I take a bite of lasagne and exclaim, 'Wow!' I'm so impressed I let him win the TV war.

We're five minutes into the comedy drama when my phone pings. A WhatsApp message from Mina. It still gives me a thrill that I've got her private number.

Do you have a corkscrew? I can't find one.

Sean pauses the show, frowning as I message back.

It's in the cabinet behind the dining table, top right drawer.

'Sorry,' I tell Sean. 'It's just my boss, checking something.'

I haven't told Sean that I'm renting the flat out to Mina. I felt I should honour my promise not to tell anyone.

'It's a bit demanding,' Sean protests, 'when you're an unpaid intern. On their oh-so-compassionate "diversity scheme".' He makes sarcastic quote marks with his fingers. 'Only they can't afford to pay you.'

'They're going to refund my travel expenses!' I protest. 'Anyway, I just want to impress her, so I can turn this into a job, and I *can* get paid.'

Sean presses play and the comedy drama skips on, but I find my attention drifting. I imagine Mina pouring wine for the mysterious Jemima.

Another buzz. I pick up my phone. Sean presses pause again. Looking murderous.

Do you happen to have a white handkerchief?

What the hell does she want that for?

Try the bottom drawer in my bedroom I reply. There are some that once belonged to Julia's husband.

I feel a little irked that Mina doesn't say thank you; at the same time, I'm pleased at the thought of being useful to her.

My phone stays quiet for the next hour. As the credits roll on the second episode, Sean turns to look at me; he's got that sexy dilated darkness in his pupils. He leans in to kiss me – when my phone buzzes again.

'Jesus!'

'I'm really sorry – just one more,' I beg him. But it's not from Mina.

It's an email. From a solicitor.

'Shit . . . Dominic – he's got a lawyer on to me,' I say, my voice trembling.

'What?' Sean reads the email over my shoulder.

Dear Ms Alice Smart,

My client, Mr Dominic Forde, is the owner of two items in your property which he has a right to reclaim:

1. An antique walnut table
2. A bookcase

I feel close to tears. I've been so fizzy about my new placement, and bonding with Mina, that I've pushed Dominic to the back of my mind. I've been fooling myself that he'll soon give up and leave me alone. And now this.

'How can he demand to take them back?' I wail. 'They weren't granted to him in the will.'

'Alice, you've got to call the police,' Sean insists. 'I keep telling you. You should be the one getting a bloody lawyer after the hassle he gives you.'

'You're right,' I say in a small voice. But I know that I can't report him. That would be far too dangerous. The police might start digging into my past. 'But I think the police might aggravate him, make things worse.'

Sean chews his lip, pondering. 'They could. I don't know – maybe being diplomatic the better option. After all, you did get the flat . . . and maybe this will shut him up for a while.'

'Or he might just move on to laying claim to everything else,' I fret.

'Julia was his mother,' Sean says. 'I guess maybe the bookcase and that – it's a consolation. It might help him to feel better and move on, maybe.'

'He never gave a toss about Julia!' I flare up. '*I'm* the one who looked after her for *two years*. He doesn't deserve anything. She told me herself.'

Sean looks a little lost. We weren't dating during the period that I befriended Julia. We'd broken up. Sean was abroad and he returned just as I discovered I'd inherited the flat; he was quite stunned by the change in my fortunes. He can't quite get a grip on Dominic either. He sometimes reasons that Dominic must have spent his life expecting to inherit the flat, so there's a motivation for his fury. But Sean doesn't really understand the situation.

He curls his arm around me, pulling me in close for a cuddle. I nestle against him, feeling a little better. When he leans in to kiss me, I see the question in his eyes, asking me to play. I nod, hungry to lose myself in him, to forget this hurt.

He sets up his iPhone by leaning it against a stack of magazines on the coffee table, pressing the record button.

This is his fetish, not mine. He once confessed that it developed when he was a teenager, when a girl across the street would watch him when he got undressed at night. At first, when he suggested it, I was wary, nervous, but I've gradually come to get a kick from it too: the thrill of being recorded, the forbidden danger of it.

As he pushes himself inside me, I see him watching us in the phone camera, watching him move and me arch back my neck, knowing our cries will be preserved. As we climax, I feel as though the pain I've been holding clenched in my heart opens up, flooding me with feeling, and I hold on to Sean tightly. If only it had never happened, this hurt between us; if only we could rewind the past and scrub out the mistakes. I know that a part of me does want Sean to be in my flat every night, to be there when I get home, to kiss me

39

good morning when I wake up, but fear holds me back: I'm too scared to trust.

As we pull apart, I gulp at the red light on the phone, which is still recording. Suddenly I feel vulnerable.

'Maybe you should delete it,' I say. This is always the problem: the risk fuels desire, but it also brings an afterburn of regret. I think of Mina in my apartment, seeing my video on the wall; I think of it playing out on that eerie night.

But Sean is already watching it back, his eyes starry. 'Look. I'm putting into the special Alice folder. It's password-protected. Even if I lost my phone, nobody could get to it.'

'I hope not . . .'

He flicks me a grin. 'Of course, if you ever leave me, I can always blackmail you with these.'

I laugh, shaking my head, and hit him with a cushion.

I check my phone again. Mina's gone quiet. I nearly reread the lawyer email again, but stop myself: *No, don't pick that scab. It's just what Dominic wants – you lying awake all night, fretting.*

We clean our teeth together; when we set our toothbrushes down, he always turns them to face each other, a romantic habit I find so cute.

Sean's bedroom is so tiny that the double bed pretty much fills it. In order to sleep on the left side, I have to clamber over it. Neon lights from a nearby curry house bleed around the curtains.

We whisper dreamy *I love you*s as our noses touch. Just as I'm sinking into sleep, fear flickers: the thought of Dominic, buzzing at my flat, wrecking Mina's evening. I just pray he stayed away.

CHAPTER SEVEN

Alice

Thank you for the favour. I have now left.

I see the message from Mina when I wake the next morning. It was sent at 3:04 a.m.

Sean gets irritable when, instead of sharing a romantic breakfast together, I hurry off saying I need to sort something for my boss.

I unlock my flat with a beating heart, dreading what I might find. Mina knows she has all the power: whatever mess she's left behind, I'll have to put up with it. But to my relief, it looks clean. My birds are happy to see me – and I'm touched to find that Mina has fed them.

I made up the second bedroom for her, but it barely looks slept in. In the kitchen I find two wine glasses. One is intact, one broken. A Post-it sits beside it, with her elegant scrawl: *So sorry about this. I added extra compensation.* An envelope of money sits next to it.

I count it out: £1,020 – I let out a whoop. Now I can pay my bills, buy some quality fruit and veg rather than damaged stuff from the supermarket discount section. I'll even have a little left over for a treat, maybe a new dress, or else some books from Waterstones. For months needing to budget has been a clamp on my heart; now peace fills it.

I don't need to go into work until eleven; I made an agreement with Mina. I sit on my sofa reading some manuscripts. Suddenly I hear a key in my door. *What the hell? Is Mina back?*

To my amazement, Sarah walks into my hallway. She's wearing a mackintosh and her hair is lightly damp with rain. She looks taken aback to see me.

'Hi.' I gape at her.

'Hi. Sorry I would have knocked but I didn't think you'd be here. Mina gave me your key.' She smiles, and then she glances around my flat, surprise etched on her face. 'This is where you live?'

Sarah looks cheated. I feel like she's about to burst out, *But you're on the diversity scheme!* but just about holds back.

'So – Mina asked me to come back because – she, er, left something important behind that she asked me to collect.'

I colour. I thought this was a secret just between Mina and me. Can she really trust Sarah? Why not ask me to collect it for her?

'Sure,' I say uneasily.

Sarah makes a beeline for the sofa, then says: 'Um, I don't think Mina wanted you to see, so . . . do you mind?'

I roll my eyes. 'I'll be in the kitchen.'

I feel irked and very curious. I'm tempted to leave the door open an inch and watch, but I can see Sarah looking, so I close the door in defeat. I imagine what the secret object might be – underwear? A contract? A gun – no, that's absurd, I'm getting carried away now.

I notice the broken wine glass again and open the fridge. There I find a half-drunk bottle of wine, a Chateau Soisy-le-Vicomte, the label patterned with a lilac logo; I think it might be from the famous French vineyard her husband owns. I take a swig, out of curiosity, and my eyes widen: it's like silk, the most beautiful thing I've ever tasted. There's something oddly intimate about savouring the wine Mina's drunk, as if whatever she enjoyed last night is seeping into me.

Sarah opens the kitchen door without knocking. She eyes the bottle in my hand: no doubt she's wondering if I'm some sort of alkie.

'I'll go now,' she says.

I make a show of seeing her out. I can see her gazing around my flat again in confusion and suspicion: *Just who are you?*

I'm jolted out of my angst when I notice that my video camera has been moved from its usual position. I frown: did Mina watch my video?

Or, perhaps, she made one of her own . . .?

At work, I struggle to concentrate. Mina strolls past my desk and I don't know what I'm expecting from her – a wink? a smile? a glint in her eye – but she just nods abruptly. Immediately, I get a flashback to the video I found on my camera. I watched it for a few seconds before guilt and conscience made me switch it off. Mina was wearing her blonde wig again. She was making love to a dark-haired man, who I'm pretty certain was her husband.

Why would Mina and Romain – Power Couple of the Year, as *Vogue* once praised them – want to rent out my flat? Do they want to spice up their marriage? I picture a role-playing scenario where Mina pretends to be Jemima.

That makes sense. After all, my flat is discreet. But I wonder what they left behind that Sarah had to collect. A sex toy? My mind buzzes with possibilities.

I ask Sarah if she wants to have lunch together, but she plays the bitch and suggests we go to the Ivy. She knows full well I can only afford to buy discount sandwiches from the local supermarket. So Sarah goes off with friends from marketing and I end up on a chilly bench overlooking the Thames, sharing my crusts with the birds.

When I head back to the office, a man sitting in reception catches my eye. I stop short.

It's Mina's husband.

It's a surreal moment: the man I've googled extensively, the man who was using my flat last night, is suddenly standing before me in the flesh. He looks a little older than the photos, his dark curls streaked with grey, but he's undeniably gorgeous.

Suddenly Mina comes out of the lift. He jumps up, then bends down – I note their difference in height – and gives her a passionate kiss.

'Oh, Alice.' Mina spots me, all smiles again. 'Romain, this is Alice – the intern I was telling you about. Alice – this is Romain, my husband.'

'Alice – so lovely to meet you!' He shakes my hand and a tingle shivers down my spine as his dark eyes hold mine: his charisma is electric. 'And you're on the diversity scheme, aren't you?'

I hold my smile, blinking. God, 'diversity scheme' is becoming my defining label.

'You should come over to dinner,' Romain says. 'We'd love to have you.'

Mina echoes him and I repress a sudden bubbly desire to laugh. Did they just ask me to dinner so they can carry on using my flat for their future rendez-vous?

Their car, waiting outside the offices, has tinted windows. Romain opens the door for his wife like an old-fashioned gentleman and Mina slides in. The car purrs away, leaving me dazzled.

*

Later, on the way home from work, I turn into Marloes Road and find Dominic there. Once again, he films me as I enter the building; another resident gives me a surprised glance.

I ought to start clearing the bookcase, prepare it for Dominic, but I'm not in the mood. I switch the TV on instead.

The video camera snags my gaze. I've already watched a little. It would be *so* unethical to watch it in full.

I should delete the file.

I go to make a tea. I only got the box of peppermint in for Mina, but now I'm starting to like it. Back in the living-room, I feel as though the video camera is taunting me. Saying *Go on, go on.*

I whisper an apology to Mina and rewind it back.

Mina's on the sofa, her dress crumpled around her waist, wearing a black lacy bra. A man's voice – which doesn't sound like Romain's – asks, 'Is this thing still filming?' Mina replies, 'It had better not be.' Now he appears in front of the camera – and I gasp. He's so young – he's mid-twenties at the most. He's also entirely naked.

He looks Mediterranean, with floppy dark hair and a gorgeous, tanned physique. He is definitely not Romain.

He returns to the sofa. Climbs on top of her. She sighs, parts her legs. He starts to caress her, but Mina freezes up – 'Are you sure that thing's off? I really don't need a record of this.' He turns, gives the camera a conspiratorial wink and assures her that it is. Their breathing becomes harsh, their kisses wild and passionate. A blush burns in my cheeks as his hand curves over her breasts, roughly pulling down her bra, sucking on a nipple as she arches her back against him. She breaks off again – 'You're sure it's off? I swear there's a light,' and he gasps, 'I'm sure, Jemima, I'm sure.' *Jemima?* Mina is . . . using a fake name? Oh: so the list she scribbled out was a persona she was creating for herself. His kisses dance up her neck; he finds her mouth again and then they start having sex, his groans leading her cries . . . Because, weirdly enough, I do get the feeling that Mina is faking it, though her face is buried in his shoulder, so perhaps this is entirely my projection. I press fast-forward, whizzing through more naked passion, until their orgasms fade. He's peeling off a condom and she sighs softly, then rises, putting on her bra and dress. He waits for her to go off to the toilet, then clicks off the video camera.

So: my boss is having an affair. With a younger man. Pretending she's called Jemima. Maybe she even pretends my apartment is hers. Why cheat on handsome, sexy, successful Romain? They seem so good together.

I delete the video.

I'm glad I watched it. Now that I know what Mina's up to, I can make sure I protect her. I won't share her secret with anyone.

CHAPTER EIGHT

Alice

Dread is churning in my stomach.

Dominic is coming over at seven to collect his furniture. We have less than an hour.

Sean dropped by after work to help. We emptied the walnut desk in the hall quite quickly, but the bookcase is taking longer than I thought. We've filled five cardboard boxes with books, and now we're stacking the remaining books against the wall.

'You have paid the gas bill, haven't you?' Sean reminds me, looking anxious.

'Don't worry, it's paid,' I reply, breaking off to give him a kiss of gratitude. When I inherited the flat, my dodgy credit rating was an issue, so Sean offered to set up the bills in his name, so long as I paid them.

Finally, the bookcase is empty. Now we just need to heave it towards the door.

'Fuck, this is heavy,' I moan. We only succeed in moving it a foot before we stop, rubbing our aching arms.

'Hey,' Sean says. 'Look at that!'

'What the hell . . .'

I lived in this flat for two years when I was looking after Julia, but I never once saw this.

There's a small door behind the bookcase, cut into the wall. It's painted white. Its handle is a faded gold. Next to it hangs a picture. It's small and drab, a dirty white frame encasing a melancholic landscape.

I don't remember Julia ever mentioning this to me.

'Shall I?' Sean asks, raising his eyebrow in a melodramatic manner as he curls his hand around the door handle.

'Go on,' I cry in excitement.

'There could be ghosts and ghouls,' Sean teases me.

'There could be a dead body,' I joke back, swallowing.

Sean pauses, milking the tension, and I give him a sharp nudge. He tries the door, but it's locked.

'Fuck,' he says. 'This is all a bit of a mystery.'

'Hey, I could check Julia's bedroom, see if I can find a key.'

As I hurry into her room, I note the time on my mobile – *only twenty minutes until Dominic is due to arrive.* I speed over to the little cabinet by her bed, pull open the drawer. It's still filled with her odds and ends; I remember seeing a key there a few weeks back, and there it is.

But when I insert it, we're disappointed to find that it doesn't fit.

'Damn.' Sean sighs. 'Maybe we can break the lock later . . .'

He turns back to the bookcase, but I stop him. 'Hey, I don't like the idea of Dominic seeing this.'

'Huh? Why not? He's just coming to get his stuff, right?' Sean points out.

'I don't trust him,' I say, my tone rising. I know he'd be enticed too. And then I'll get letters from lawyers saying: "My client has a right to see inside the room, in order that he might ascertain if any of his goods remain therein." Et cetera.

The TV is a big 75-inch one that Sean bought for us when I first moved in here. We haul it over and it conceals the door successfully.

We heave the bookcase another foot, when Sean's mobile buzzes. He pulls it from his back pocket and says, 'It's from the guy who lives next door to Dad.' I register that Sean's Irish accent is becoming more pronounced, which always happens when he's worried. His dad has dementia. His parents divorced in his mid-twenties, so his dad's all on his own. Sean shares caring duties with his sister, who takes over when he's working abroad; as soon as he's back in the country, he's expected to do his share.

'Dad's gone outside without his coat or shoes on,' Sean tells me. 'I'll just dash over and come right back.'

'But Dominic's going to be here in ten minutes!' I cry. 'And by the time you've travelled all the way over to Camden . . .'

'Can you reschedule with him?' Sean asks.

'He's on his way – it's too short notice!'

'I *will* be back asap,' Sean insists, kissing me hard on the lips. 'Look, the moment Dominic comes, call me, put me on speaker, and tell him I'm listening. If there's any funny business, I can call the police and I'll shoot right back over?'

Sean shrugs on his jacket and gives me another volley of apologetic kisses before dashing out the door.

I wanted the bookcase to be in the hall, ready to go, so that Dominic would have no excuses to linger. I press my palms to it, but despite the agonising strain in my muscles, it moves a mere inch. Sean's absence feels like a betrayal, a desertion. I know his dad needs him, but so do I. Then I tell myself off for being selfish.

The *buzz-buzz* of the doorbell makes me jump.

I go to the intercom and say, 'Come on up,' in a flat voice.

Suddenly my body is assailed with butterflies and a trembling heart and swift breaths. It doesn't matter how fiercely my sense of reason fights back, telling me he wouldn't risk

49

hurting me, that he has no right to bully me. The panic just kicks in.

I close my eyes. Julia used to advise me that if someone was upsetting me, I needed to stay centred. To remind myself that they're the one with a problem, to shield myself—

A hammering on my door.

They fill the doorframe: Dom and a tall, beefy guy with a fuzzy dark red beard, wearing a black Faster Pussycat T-shirt that strains against his gut.

'This was Mum's flat,' Dom informs the guy, as though I'm not there.

'Nice.' His gaze drinks in my home, then fixes on me, and a frown snarls his face.

'Here's the desk.' I gesture. 'We had trouble moving the bookcase – Sean and I. He's just taking a call outside, he'll be back up in a minute,' I bluff.

The beefy guy blinks, shrinking back a little.

'So I'll just wait in the kitchen,' I say, keeping my tone airy, knowing it will infuriate Dom.

'A cup of tea wouldn't go amiss,' the beefy friend says.

I ignore him, spotting that I've left out the video camera. As I carry it into the kitchen with me, I hear the guy muttering in disbelief, 'What, does she think we're going to nick it . . .?'

I wouldn't imagine Dominic would be so blatant, but I still wouldn't put it past him. Just imagine if he discovered the sex tapes, I fret, propping the tripod against the wall. I'm still suspicious that it was Dominic who set off my video camera that eerie night a few weeks ago, when I woke up to find it playing in the living-room.

I moved my birdcage in here earlier too. The birds hop and flutter about, picking up on my unease.

I hear them moving the bookcase, cycles of heaving and stopping for breath. I make myself a cup of tea, the sound of the boiling kettle like a V sign flicked at them.

'It's not going to go, Gerry.' I tune in to Dominic's voice. 'We're going to need to dismantle it.'

'There's a screwdriver in my van,' Gerry says. 'I'll go get it.'

Oh great. How long is that going to take? I hear my front door slam. Then, silence. What is Dominic doing out there?

He was such a difficult child. Julia's voice echoes in my mind. *Dominic was always falling out with his friends because he has a persecution complex.* I'd never heard the term before, but it seems apt. Dominic needs an enemy, that's for sure: and now I'm filling that role.

I lift my mug to my lips – when there's a sudden, violently loud noise from the living-room, and I spill hot liquid on my blouse. He's playing thrash metal on his phone at top volume. Mimi squawks in distress. I'm about to barge out and yell at him, when there's an abrupt silence.

'Hush, my darling, it's fine,' I soothe Mimi.

Gerry has returned. They seem to be working on the bookcase again, thank God.

I peel my blouse off and fling it onto a chair, using a tea towel to dry my skin.

'. . . There are people in this world who don't have any sense of right or wrong,' Gerry is saying. 'They find a victim, usually someone elderly, and once they get their claws in, what can you do?'

My ears burn. *Ignore them,* I tell myself, shivering as I sit down in my bra and trousers. I try to focus on reading a manuscript.

'I tried to warn Mum,' Dominic replies loudly. 'I said, this woman's forced her way into your life, she's gone from visiting to living off you, using *your* money to buy her food . . .'

For God's sake: Julia paid for my food because I was *caring* for her. Why does everyone seem to think that carers should be saints and work for free whilst starving to death? Carer's allowance was a sodding £67 a week – who could survive on that?

'She had dementia,' Dominic goes on. 'And she was partially sighted by then, virtually blind . . .'

This is not the full story.

'I didn't see what was coming,' Dominic says. 'You just don't think anyone would be that ruthless as to steal your whole livelihood . . . If Mum had been sane and normal, she'd never have let this happen.'

'She's turning in her grave,' Gerry replies. 'Fuck, you're a saint to just be walking out with the furniture. I'd fucking squat here.'

You wouldn't, I think ferociously, *because that's illegal. This is my flat.*

'Well, I've found some letters she wrote . . .' Dominic's voice lowers and I frown, listening hard. 'I'm going to be able to prove that Alice was conning her soon . . .'

I refuse to listen to any more of this bullshit. Now it's my turn for revenge: I pick a Sufjan Stevens song on Spotify and play it at top volume, drowning them out.

Finally, there's a knock on the kitchen door. I quickly grab my damp blouse, drawing it over me and crossing my arms tight as Gerry pokes his head round.

'We're done,' he says, as though he'd like to finish me off too.

'Fine,' I reply curtly.

I listen to the sound of the front door slamming shut and exhale a long, shaky breath.

From the window, I watch Dominic and Gerry loading the stuff into the back of a white van. As if sensing my gaze, Dominic looks up. I can't see his expression but I can feel the animosity blazing from him. I stumble backwards, jumping as I hear the door again: but it's only Sean, arriving far too late in the day.

CHAPTER NINE

Alice

There's an ache rippling in my wrist. I've been hoovering for an hour non-stop, sucking up dust from every neglected corner, readying the flat for Mina. She's coming this evening, so I need to be out within an hour.

It's the second time she's rented my flat; two weeks since the last time.

In the corner of the living-room, I hear a metallic clink, a rattling noise, and realise that a key is poking out of the nozzle. The carpet, which is tacked down along the edges, is slightly loose here. The key must have been tucked underneath.

I spin to face the secret door. Over the past week and a half, every time I've sat down to eat in front of the TV, the presence of that little door has mesmerised me. I've thought about calling a locksmith but the cost is too high; Sean offered to have a go, but I feared he'd damage it.

Now I slide behind the TV and put the key in the lock.
It turns.

'Wow,' I say out loud, glancing over at my birds, who peer forward as though curious too.

I push the door – it doesn't yield.

I push again, harder, and it swings open.

A cold, stale stench hits my nostrils; a cascade of cobweb sweeps down and I cry out, untangling it, sticky on my fingertips.

What is this place?

It's not big enough for a bedroom, but it's too big to be a storage closet. There's a small window that overlooks the side street, where the bins are kept, which connects to Marloes Road, the main street.

The walls are white. There's a spyhole in the wall beside the door, which gives me a view of the living-room: the edge of the TV, my black squashy sofa. When I return to the living-room, I realise that the little picture has been positioned to hang over it. The dark, drab landscape means that you can only see the hole that's been made in the canvas when you're close up.

'What did you use this for, Julia?' I murmur.

I can speculate, but Julia's gone and I feel the sadness of the mystery: I'll never know.

I remind myself: *Mina will be here in less than an half an hour.* I pull on my coat and pick up my handbag and tote, packed for an overnight stay at Sean's. Once more, I feel nervy at the thought of loaning out my flat, as though it's my child and I'm passing it on to a dubious babysitter—

Suddenly I hear voices.

A key turning in the lock. Laughter. Mina is *here.*

I seize my phone. Sure enough, there's a message from Mina warning me that she needs to come at 7:30, not 8 p.m. I'm supposed to have vacated the flat by the time she arrives. *Damn.* I was too busy cleaning to check my messages.

I freeze in panic. Her affair is supposed to be secret. If she finds me I'll never get a job working for her—

Quickly, I dart into the secret room, shutting the door quietly as a male voice says, 'Wow, this is a nice place.'

So Mina has brought over her young man again. I picture the guy from the video, young and dark-haired and virile.

'It belongs to my younger sister.'

For a moment I'm touched: I quite like the idea of Mina as a big sister. I did have a sister once, but it's been over a decade since I last saw her.

'Would you like a glass of wine?' I hear Mina saying.

'Sure. Thanks, Alice.'

I jump in confusion: Mina's told him about me? Then I cotton on.

Mina is using another fake name. She's borrowed mine – or improvised on the spot.

I peer through the peephole, unease writhing in my stomach, knowing I'm crossing a line, violating her privacy.

Mina emerges from my kitchen with two wine glasses; no doubt she's brought another bottle of Chateau from their vineyard.

She looks breathtakingly gorgeous. Her dark hair is parted in the middle and curled at the ends, bobbing against her shoulders. She's wearing a chic black dress with Bardot sleeves, only it's much shorter than her work outfits. Instead of her usual heels, she's wearing long sexy black boots, which make her look a decade younger.

As for the man – he's different from the one I saw in the video. With his blonde hair, blue eyes and tan, he looks like a young Prince William. His accent is suitably posh.

He takes a sip of his wine, then suddenly leans in and kisses her passionately; Mina responds with equal fire.

Just how many men does Mina have on the go? I draw back from the peephole, feeling heavy with knowledge I don't want to acquire. It would've been awkward for me to leave earlier, and now it's impossible. I'm going to have to sit this one out.

The ramifications sink in: I'm going to be very hungry;

I'm not going to be able to go to the loo; and I'm not going to get much sleep. I think of Sean, who's currently expecting me and cooking a lovely curry – and I realise I'm in trouble. I quickly put my phone on silent, non-vibrate mode. Then I send Sean an emergency text saying You're not going to believe this, but I'm got a HUGE work crisis. Please start without me. My stomach twists, imagining how upset he'll be.

I go back to the peephole. They're sitting very close together on the sofa, their glasses half full. I watch his eyes drink in her body. His palm slowly caresses her thigh, up and down, up and down, pausing at the hem of her dress.

'How long have you been on Feeld, Alice?' he asks.

Every time he says my name, it makes me jump.

'Oh, just a month. I've had quite a few matches . . .'

'You must have hundreds of men after you. And girls too – I mean, you're bisexual, aren't you?'

Mina is bisexual?

'You're the first guy from the site that I've met in real life.'

I have a strong suspicion that the other guy, the one who filmed them on my video camera, was her first. I bite back a smile of bemusement. Just what is my boss playing at?

'I'm flattered.' He grins, leans in, kisses her neck, but Mina shifts away. I think she wants more conversational foreplay.

'What about you, Jacob?' she asks. 'How many women have you met?'

'Three,' he replies, drinking some wine. He has a habit of fluffing up the front of his thick fringe. 'Just flings, really – I had a few dates with each one, and, er, sex with one . . .' His smile is schoolboyish. 'But to be honest, it's hard to find women who . . .'

'Who?' Mina makes him say it.

'Who just want no-strings sex,' he admits. 'Most of them

are looking for a relationship – but, like I said, I'm heading off to Oz next week, so . . .'

'Not me,' Mina confirms.

No, Mina, I reply silently. *You already have a husband.*

'Is that because you're thirty-two?'

Thirty-two? I nearly burst out laughing and quickly put my hand over my mouth. Mina can pass for thirty-two, sure, but her lies are funny.

'I'm not ready for my midlife crisis yet,' Mina replies archly.

'But aren't you at that stage in your life where you want babies and all that?'

Mina raises an eyebrow, a smile of disbelief twitching at her lips. *What a dick!* I think, but then again, he does look fairly young.

'So you're happy with a one-night stand?' he asks, pushing back a strand of hair from her face. His gestures are conducted with a smooth, manly confidence that seems at odds with his adolescent perceptions.

There's a long pause. He frowns uneasily, scared he's misunderstood. *Look at her playing him,* I think, impressed, a bit jealous, and a bit appalled by her. Mina has such a way of acquiring power over people, casting a spell.

'I'm interested in sex,' Mina says.

His eyes light up. He starts stroking her thigh again.

'But I want sex that isn't shallow,' she says. 'That doesn't mean that I want commitment, but I do want intimacy, if you see what I mean.'

'I do,' he replies, but I'm not sure that he does.

'It means that I can't just leap into bed with any handsome young man. I need courtship; I need to get to know who I'm going to bed with, to make sure this is going to work.'

'I think we'd be so compatible in bed,' he blurts out. 'I've always wanted to be with an older woman.'

'Well, let's have a few more glasses and see,' Mina says.

Shaking my head, I turn away and check my phone. Sean's reply is punctuated with a string of crying-face emojis. He's texted a pic of the dinner he's started without me. My stomach hurts with hunger. Maybe in an hour or so they'll have sex, and then head home? Or go into the bedroom? Could I creep out, tiptoe across the living-room, sneak out of the door. Could I take that risk?

I'm doing my best to leave as soon as possible I text Sean.

Immediately he replies: But what's going on???

I wish I could tell him the truth, but I'm scared of Mina's secrets slipping out. I flash-forward to tabloid newspaper headlines screaming INQUIRY INTO MP'S WIFE IN STEAMY SCANDAL. I could even end up being hacked, if the press caught a whiff of scandal: it's too dangerous to set it down in a text.

I look back through the spyhole. It's electrifying: they're staring at each other with such heat. He leans in, very slowly, seeing if she'll let him in, and she does: she opens up her lips and kisses him right back.

'Let's do it here,' he says, authoritative and mature again. 'This is a good place to fuck.' He smooths his hand over my sofa, feeling the leather bounce against his palm.

'Sure,' Mina agrees, swirling her wine.

He takes her glass and his and sets them down on my coffee table.

I ought to stop watching. But I can't help myself. They're kissing wildly; he pushes up her dress; her hand curls over his trousers. He unzips her boots and pulls down her tights, then her knickers – lacy, black, skimpy – and begins to kiss his way up her thighs. Her fingers curl into his hair, pushing him back.

'I don't like that,' Mina says, to my surprise: she seems so highly sexed.

'Thank God,' Jacob says, his tone cheerful. 'I never like giving it much – all the hairs that you get in your mouth. But I often feel obliged.'

Mina's expression reflects my dismay. Jacob quickly puts his mouth on hers and pulls her hand towards his cock. Mina caresses him attentively through his trousers, but he doesn't seem to be doing much for her. I normally prefer more of a build-up; I'm lucky that Sean is very patient and gentle. *That's enough now,* my conscience warns me, but I'm transfixed. I've always loved people-watching and nobody fascinates me more than Mina.

Then he stands up, unzipping his trousers, telling her how much he wants to fuck her, his voice ragged, and climbs on top of her.

It's all over so quickly that I think he's going to be bashful. Instead, he holds her tight and says, 'God, that was good, I loved all those sounds you made – and knowing how much I was turning you on.'

Mina makes an *mmm* noise that sounds unconvincing to me. After a little while, he kisses her hair and says, 'Shall we go again?'

Enough, I tell myself, but my eyes remain fixed on that peephole . . .

'Well,' Jacob sighs after another breathless ten minutes pass, 'that was seriously hot. But perhaps we should wrap things up now?'

I feel the shock of his words like a blow.

'You don't want to stay the night?' Mina's voice is steady, though I can't see her face.

'I've got an early start at the bank tomorrow — we have Japanese clients coming over, so . . .'

'Oh. Okay.' Mina sits up. It's odd, seeing her humiliated when only a few moments ago she had the upper hand. Isn't this the way sex always swings: they win and we lose? He pulls up his trousers, passes Mina her dress. She pulls it up her body, and turns her back to him and he flounders — 'I really think I'm spent' — and she snaps back, 'No, I meant do up my dress.'

After he's gone, Mina lies back on the sofa, and I feel my body tense with fearful anticipation: *Is she going to . . .?* Her hand begins to idle up and down her thighs; her fingers slip into her knickers. I wrench myself away, cheeks burning, gazing out into the street. I wait for her breath to break before I dare look again . . .

Her expression is dreamy and soft. *You deserve better than Jacob,* I muse. *And you deserve to be more than a fake Alice. You're better than this slutty behaviour.* Then I frown, correcting myself: I shouldn't slut-shame her.

But I suddenly wish I really was Mina's sister, that I could go out there and give her a hug and say: *Your sexy husband could take you to bed and give you an orgasm and hold you tight. I guess there's more to your marriage than I know or understand, but this doesn't seem the right way to fix it.*

Mina reaches for the TV control. I groan inwardly: last time she left around 3 a.m. What if she gets invested in a series?

She channel-hops for a while, before settling on a documentary about an abusive conman. I see her tapping away at her phone, her face fraying with stress. I hear her mutter the name Amy and wonder if this is yet another persona.

Finally, at ten, she gets up, leaves out an envelope of cash for me. *Phew.* I watch her below in the street, painted amber under a slant of light from the streetlamp, gripped by a momentary fear that she'll look up and see me, but she strides on.

I wait a few more minutes, just in case she comes back with another hot posh stud in tow. Then I push open the door, shove past the TV and run to the loo, release my aching bladder; then hurry to the kitchen, where I open a box of oatcakes and munch on several. I feel exhilarated but exhausted and hungry. I barely have the energy to go over to Sean's, but I text him Crisis is over, be there asap . . .

CHAPTER TEN

Mina

I know what you're doing. In order for me to let this go, you need to send £2,000 to the following account . . .

The email pops into my inbox. The first that I received, a few weeks ago, left me on the verge of a panic attack, until I heard a colleague gossiping about 'the scam'. Everyone at work had got one, apparently. Nobody had anything on me or knew about my trysts. I was so relieved, I nearly burst out laughing.

I delete the email and gather up my files for a meeting next door.

'You seem in a good mood,' Charles notices.

I give him an enigmatic smile.

Once upon a time, being sent a hot manuscript by an agent pitching the next big thing was a thrill; now it's a bore. I've been a high achiever for so long that the taste of success has gone stale. But this week I've had the solace of fantasy. In a tedious meeting: Jacob pushing up my dress. Sending my thirtieth email of the day: Jacob pulling down my knickers. At a lunch with an agent: Jacob thrusting his big cock inside me. And I've enjoyed that glow inside. I feel sexy, nourished, attractive: all those things I've been craving for so long.

Then Alice comes into my office. She pesters me once again about whether I've read the 'amazing' manuscript she's recommended called *Those Foolish Things*, and I say, 'Halfway through – it's really good,' when in fact I haven't read a word. She beams and I have a flashback to that video of her and her boyfriend. I think of Jacob, the sting of his abrupt departure. *Intimacy*, I realise. That was the only failure of the night.

But how can I expect that from a twenty-something who just wants a quick fuck? Unrealistic expectations are foolish.

'Shall I get you a coffee?' Alice is biting her nails, and I realise I must've been staring at her with a sour expression. It's not her fault I slept with a silly, posh schoolboy.

'Thanks,' I smile affectionately. 'I'd love a latte.'

Romain sends me a WhatsApp. Something about a crisis. My fantasises quickly recede and fear spikes me once more.

There's so much at stake, I berate myself. *What the hell are you doing? What the hell?*

The seed was planted six months ago. I was a dinner party with five other women in their forties. Leila was moaning about being premenopausal. She's usually so serene in nature, but now she was talking about being blindsided by sudden flashes of rage towards her kids and her husband. We all joked that it might not be hormonal, but the simple maturing of vision that age brings, the realisation that the patriarchy is an outrage.

As Leila went on to grumble about hot flushes and thinning hair, I suddenly saw my future. I moisturise twice a day, see off grey hair by rubbing coconut oil into my scalp, exercise, eat healthily. I know I look good for my age. But I'm in denial. The menopause feels like a withering that should happen to *older women*. That night, I imagined myself in the future, men's gazes slipping past me with disinterest. It felt like a kind of death.

A few nights on, I assuaged my insomnia by surfing a site I'd read about in the *Sunday Times*. It was called Affair.org. It was for married couples wanting safe flings.

That was too dangerous for me to risk. Not with Romain's majority slipping with each election: a scandal would finish his career. But what about a regular site? I could always say, if anyone recognised me, that my photos and identity had been stolen. I went for Feeld because it seemed such an unlikely choice for me. Using the app on my own phone felt too risky, so I downloaded it onto my work phone.

Pansexual, androsexual, demiromantic – there seemed to be so many labels on there; I kept having to google them. I created a profile for 'Venuspussycat' – a fun, sexy woman in her mid-thirties who had recently suffered a painful break-up and just wanted some fun. She was 'bi-curious' and 'sapiosexual'.

I went back to bed, fell into a deep sleep and woke feeling silly. *I'll take the profile down,* I thought, as Romain and I ate breakfast. It was lunacy. And nobody would message me anyway. Then I checked: *seventy messages.* An onslaught. Messages from men who were in their twenties, and fit, and hot, and well-toned and sexy and hungry – all wanting me. You're so gorgeous the messages cooed. You're so fit. Please message me. Please can we meet. I took all their compliments and wrapped them around me like a warm shawl. I told myself nothing more need happen.

But it seemed inevitable: later that night, in the dazed desperation of insomnia, I was back online. Setting up my first meeting. Terrified; exhilarated; hardly able to believe what I was doing.

I fight the lethargy caused by my insomnia by drinking far too much coffee, so that I head home feeling twitchy and frazzled. Romain's MP red box sits by the front door: he's home for dinner, for a change. Our housemaid, Baba, is having a day off. We're too tired to cook; we order Italian takeaway, creamy pasta and tiramisu.

As we sit at the dinner table, I gaze at the empty seats and wonder what it would be like if Aimee were here.

Romain seems quiet, tersely forking pasta into his mouth. Normally he turns to me for advice in times of crisis; he used to say I was better than any spin doctor, my compassion balanced out by a Machiavellian streak. My guilt over Jacob sharpens my urge to help him.

'My popularity ratings are down,' he tells me. 'Helen says they're at an all-time low.'

'Oh.' They've been sliding for years. And we're only one year away from a general election; Romain's very anxious he might lose his seat.

'Last year I had problems with recognition, the public didn't know my name. But now they do – and all the associations are bad. They think I'm arrogant, out of touch.' A note of accusation in his voice. 'It all stems from that tweet – the *Welfare Britain* one. Ten thousand retweets, Mina. That was quite a tweet.'

So now he's blaming *me*. I feel the sting of it. So it's my fault, not the party and their policies; not the failing NHS and closing libraries; not the public disillusionment with Brexit, but me and my silly tweet. I know Romain's up for a row, but I resist it, swallow back my pain. He's depressed. Fifteen years ago he was a star in the party and he used to grab me and kiss me and tell me he was going to be PM and how did I feel about being his 'first lady'. But it never quite happened. He made the wrong allies, the wrong enemies; never got a Cabinet post, remained a backbencher. His ambitions are unfulfilled and reality hurts. This is his mid-life crisis.

'Look,' I say, 'Corissa recommended a PR woman to me – she completely saved Fusion.' Corissa's company had a major product recall after her organic shampoo was found to have GMOs in it.

'How much does she charge?' Romain asks.

'She'll be pricy, but she'll be worth it,' I insist.

'Okay.' Romain nods, his anger diffusing. 'It's a plan.'

We smile at each other and suddenly, for the first time in a long time, I feel as though we've shifted from autopilot to connection. We always did bond when we had an enemy to unite against.

I swallow and stand up. I push his plate away. I position myself on the table before him. I part my legs. Pull up my skirt an inch. I've not had this kind of confidence in months.

I take my husband's hand and put it on the soft inside of my thigh.

His smile is awkward. His fingers remain limp.

'I have to go and check out this PR woman,' he says, all his warmth and gratitude gone. 'I have all these emails to send. This isn't appropriate right now.'

'Appropriate? What am I, a schoolgirl?' I flare up.

He flinches and we both wince, as the past comes rushing back. Me aged seventeen, at school, wide-eyed as a handsome politician strolls into the classroom to give us all an inspiring talk, his eyes lingering on me inappropriately.

'I need to follow your advice.' His voice takes on a whiny edge. 'This is important – I have to fix it.'

'Fine,' I snap. I could push him further, but I don't want to go any deeper into the issue of why my husband, who once courted me with such hunger, seems to find me about as sexy as a dishcloth.

Romain comes to bed at midnight. His snores start just minutes after his head has touched the pillow. I feel raw with rage, replaying that scene over dinner. *You should have seen how hard Jacob was for me,* I seethe at him.

Where's it gone, his desire? We've slipped out of the habit over the past two years, but tonight's rejection didn't feel as though it was about tiredness or libido or work demands. Is it his way of punishing me for wrecking his reputation?

I slip out of bed, go to my study and take my work phone out of my bag. Persephone comes in, miaowing and I pull her onto my lap.

Twenty new messages: my anger dissipates.

I tackle my inbox, Persephone's purring reflecting my mood. I sift through possible men, settle on 'hotguy108' and start up a flirtation . . .

Twenty minutes later, I set my phone down on the desk and gaze out of the window. My study overlooks the back garden via a small window with a faulty latch. I open it, savouring the night air, suddenly feeling alive and exhilarated. And something – or someone? – catches me eye, a figure darting along the back of the garden.

I squint, leaning closer, anxious now, but they seem to have gone.

PART II

WhatsApp messages of Jean Winters and Alexa McHale

4 October 2024

JEAN
I'm on my way to the police station!
Edward's driving, but the traffic is awful.
I called them after the gunshots and the
next thing I knew, the police were knocking on
my door, telling me not to come out. There was huge
commotion, noise, a gunshot and the next time
I dared take a peek, I saw a stretcher being
carried out of the flat!

ALEXA
OMG!

JEAN
Couldn't see who it was with the oxygen mask etc.
If it's that girl Alice, I will be sad. Even if
she was a bad neighbour, she doesn't
deserve this.

ALEXA
My God — are you going over as a witness?

JEAN

Yes, I've got to tell them everything I heard
and all about the background of the flat.
Bit worried as I had a spare key to the flat.
And I think I gave it to someone I shouldn't have.

ALEXA

Who? You need to tell the police this!
None of this is your fault.
You're just an innocent neighbour, FFS

CHAPTER ELEVEN

Alice

I gaze at my reflection in the mirror, propped up against my wall.

Tonight is a big night. I've been at Principle Publishing for five weeks and I'm in agony that my internship is nearly up. I kept thinking, *I can't believe that all this hard work is going to come to nothing.* Then, a ray of light: on Friday Sarah came out of a meeting in Mina's office looking irate. Mina had asked her to book me in for a dinner. 'I've never once been invited to her home,' Sarah muttered. 'God, I wish I was on the diversity scheme.'

I've also overheard Sarah telling someone that I buy my clothes in Primark, her tone dripping in derision. *Well, tonight, Sarah,* I tell her silently, *I've upgraded! I've bought a dress from Oxfam. So suck it up.* It looks classy, I think: a shimmery green dress patterned with diamonds, with a brown belt looped around it. I pile my bushy hair up on my head and attempt to pin it using an elaborate network of kirby grips.

I pick up my mobile. I'm going to be late if I don't hurry.

I reach for the envelope of cash that Mina left me. I've been so busy I've not had time to trek across London and pay it into the bank, so I've been peeling off a few notes each day to spend—

The envelope is empty.

I look behind the table, feel about the skirting board. Nothing.

I spin round. Then I spot a lone note, trapped between a window and its sill, the King's face jammed and crumpled. I open the window to grab it but the wind pulls it away and it flurries down into the communal garden. I see a figure below chase it, pluck it from the grass.

Dominic. When he came to take the bookcase – he must have got hold of my key, copied it.

Fury banshees through me. I sprint out of the flat. My neighbour, Jean, who always seems to catch me just when I least want to chat, comes out of her front door. She looks at me in surprise as I crash into the lift, muttering 'Sorry' as I jab the buttons.

Down, down, down I go. Enough is enough. He has to stop.

I burst out of the front doors of the flats, only to find—

Dominic's gone.

Back in my flat, I check my bank balance. I'm so close to my overdraft limit. There's only just enough to cover my wifi direct debit which comes out tomorrow. Plus, I need to top up my Oyster.

I drag my hands through my hair, biting my nails. In despair, I call Sean. He's away in Berlin this week and I know he's working a lot in the evenings.

He doesn't pick up. I think of the old PG Tips tin in his kitchen cupboard, the one he stores cash in, plus a spare Barclaycard in case of emergencies. I'm pretty sure he wouldn't mind if I borrowed it.

There's no time to go to his flat now. I can't be late for dinner with Mina. So I grab my Oyster card for the tube; I think I have just enough on it to get me there. As for the journey home – I'll have to pray Sean sees my message in time and transfer some funds to my account. Otherwise, I'll have to damn well walk all the way over to his flat.

Damn Dominic.

I stop short outside Mina and Romain's house. The sun is setting and it bathes the big white birthday-cake house with a pink-icing tint, glittering on the windows and on the lead tiling on the porch. I'm knocked out of my anxious stream of thought, awed by the grandeur. My flat is a blessing, I know, but this place looks as though it belongs to royalty.

Even their bell sounds posh as I ring it; a delicate *ding-dong* that echoes through their hallway. Mina greets me. She's wearing white for a change, a silky Grecian dress, and as I lean in, I breathe in a perfume that's subtle and floral and no doubt cost thousands a bottle. I get a flashback of her having sex in my flat, and hastily push the thought away.

My jacket is removed by an elderly woman with a kind, wizened face. She requests that I remove my shoes, and scurries off with those too. I follow Mina down a parquet hall; a chandelier shimmers above, casting twinkles of light across the walls.

In the dining-room, Romain greets me with a kiss on each of my cheeks, the French style. Even though it's a bit cheesy, given that he's lived in the UK for the last few decades (so Google tells me), I feel a little tingle. He's wearing a pale grey suit with a mauve silk shirt.

I've brought gifts: a bottle of wine, a box of Thorntons. They accept with a little too much praise, as though I've brought them jewels.

A cat strolls into the room, white and fluffy, with a tale as big as a fern. It sniffs me as though assessing whether I'm worthy of stroking it.

'Oh – Persephone,' Mina coos, picking it up. I've not seen this maternal streak in her before; I guess her cat must be a baby substitute, given they don't have children. 'Persephone – this is Alice . . .'

As I reach out to stroke her, Persephone claws me and Mina cries, 'See, she's *playing*. She likes you.'

I smile, letting my stinging hand fall to my side to hide the scratch mark.

We sit down at a large walnut dining table. My antique chair is hard against my back. I watch Mina unfurl her napkin, place it on her lap and I copy her. Romain opens some wine, pours it into my glass only.

'We're having a dry June,' he explains. 'But you, you go ahead and enjoy.'

I think of the wine Mina drank in my flat. I make sure I keep my lips straight: I mustn't give away the slightest clue that I've been watching her.

I do a double take when their maid comes in and actually serves us. The first course is a salad, leaves delicately draped over slices of pear and goat's cheese. I gaze at my cutlery uncertainly – only to catch Romain watching me. He winks at me, picks up the outer fork, and I grin back shyly, mirroring him.

I take a few mouthfuls, my eyes widening at how good it tastes. Romain gives me an intimate smile, as though feasting on my pleasure.

He and Mina look so good together: I wonder what's going on in their marriage that's driving Mina to cheat.

'So, I gather you've been interning for my wife,' Romain says.

'Yes,' I reply. 'It's a dream job – placement. It would be a dream job, to have.'

'How much longer will you be staying at Principle Publishing?'

'It ends on Friday,' I say, sobering up; today is Sunday. The other day Sarah asked if I was going to organise 'good-bye drinks'. Now that she knows I'm going, she's been a lot warmer towards me.

'Oh, but I think it could be extended,' Mina says lightly.

'That would be amazing,' I gush.

Oh wow, oh wow. I want to ask, to beg, how many days she'll extend it by, but I restrain myself.

'Well, this is interesting,' Romain muses. 'You actually *want* to work for my control freak of a wife?'

Mina rolls her eyes, her smile acquiring an edge.

They exchange looks. I frown, sensing an agenda I can't quite grasp. Our plates are taken away and replaced with a main course of trout and new potatoes.

'Alice, we have a proposition to make to you,' Romain asserts. 'We've both embraced social media, Mina and I. It's a good way for my constituents to connect with me. I've set up an online book group too – I want to unite people through reading, promote literacy.'

'I'm not on it,' I confess, which isn't strictly true: I have an anonymous account, so that I can follow and watch and like. But I never post. If Dominic found me on there, it would give him even more ammunition.

'Then now's the time to join,' Mina says.

'We'd love to feature you as an inspiration for others,' Romain enthuses. 'Someone who's come from a tougher background, but who's been embraced by the publishing world, given a lifeline.' His palms splay open; I notice that his gestures are very theatrical, almost Italianate. 'We could show you going on a journey with us.'

Their gaze is so intense that I take a big gulp of wine, feeling it burn down into my jittery stomach. I'm torn between feeling flattered and feeling patronised.

'It all sounds a bit *My Fair Lady*,' I say at last.

Mina and Romain look a bit panicked. I feel reassured, seeing how nervous they are too, beneath their bright grins and platitudes.

'We didn't mean . . .' Romain tries. 'We've picked you out because you seem intelligent and talented, and could go a long way, Alice.'

I can't help beaming at that.

'Just think it over,' Mina says.

I gaze at their warm expressions and the blurry thought rises: *If they knew about my past crimes, would they still want to adopt me like this?*

And then I push it away, as I always do, day after day, and return to the moment, to this beautiful, elegant room and the two stunning people before me.

The conversation flows more freely now that their agenda is out of the way. Romain pours some wine for him and Mina. Seeing me smile, he catches himself and laughs, then tells me a story about the vineyard his family owns in France. No doubt Romain is the one with the money then, because you don't earn millions as an editor in publishing. He seems flirty, holding my gaze that bit too long, gazing at my lips, but perhaps he's just on charm autopilot.

Mina, meanwhile, is amusing and sharp as always, but I can't stop feeling intimidated by her; I'm always aware of the steel in her, a barrier I come up against. With more wine, she softens, then stands and proffers her hand, 'Come upstairs with me, Alice. I've got some spare clothes I think you'd love.'

'I'll make the coffees,' Romain says. As I follow Mina, his hand brushes my back gently.

Upstairs on the second floor, Mina guides me into their bedroom: polished floorboards, lavish drapes and a king-size bed covered in a white spread, black pillows and cushions artfully scattered over it. It looks so flawless I can hardly believe anyone sleeps in it.

'I've never been in a walk-in wardrobe before,' I tell Mina, aware that I'm playing up my naivety a little. 'God – so many shoes!'

Mina smiles with pride. She's set aside a bundle of clothing for me, drawing out a chic black dress with lace panels on the shoulders and sleeves – 'Here, try this!'

I undo my belt, feeling a little self-conscious at changing in front of her. My underwear is so embarrassing: an old black bra with underwire poking out from under one cup, and once-white knickers that have faded to grey. Mina doesn't comment, just helps me into the black dress, doing up the zip, and as her fingers brush me, that flashback comes, of her in her blonde wig, making love, her fingers in his hair—

'Oh, wow, look at you,' she says, spinning me to face the mirror.

My reflection smiles back at me: a suave, sophisticated Alice that I barely recognise. The pride on Mina's face is unexpectedly affectionate, almost maternal.

I become aware of Romain in the doorway.

'Doesn't she look good?' Mina says, but now there's an edge to her voice.

'She looks gorgeous,' Romain agrees, and a look flickers between them. 'Coffee is served.'

I stare at my reflection again, their praise swimming inside me, and suddenly an emotion overwhelms me: *hope*. Every time I step into the plush lift of my apartment building, hearing the dulcet tones of my neighbours discussing portfolios and Ascot and the best local bars, I've felt serious imposter syndrome. But maybe I *can* change. Maybe I can be one of them. Maybe I can live in a Kensington flat and be an editor at Principle Publishing and I can leave the past behind me. I turn to Mina in a burst of excitement and say, 'I'll do it! I'll be part of your "journey" idea.'

'Fantastic!' Mina pulls me in for a hug.

We fall silent, gazing at our reflections. Romain is calling from downstairs, but Mina puts her hands on my shoulders.

'I was wondering, if I could perhaps rent your flat again this week?'

Is that the real impulse behind this social media journey together? I mean, I'm so desperate for the money I'm hardly going to refuse.

'Sure,' I reply. 'But – I – had a break in, so I'm going to have to get the locks changed. I can give you a new key in a couple of days . . . and I don't know if you lent Sarah the key or if she has her own?' I press her, curious to know why she sent Sarah back to my flat to get 'something'.

'Sarah?' Mina's eyebrows raise.

'Well – when you sent her back to my flat . . .'

'And she . . .?'

Is Mina testing me?

'She was very discreet,' I assure her. 'She made me wait in the kitchen whilst she – she looked around for – for whatever you sent her to get.'

Mina nods, looking thoughtful, and we hear Romain calling us again.

She draws me downstairs to the living-room, where Romain is bringing in the coffees in little blue cups.

'Alice has agreed to share her journey with us on social media!' Mina enthuses.

'Oh, I'm so pleased,' Romain says softly.

Mina changes the music from light classical to Primal Scream. She slinks onto the scarlet rug in front of the fire and starts to dance, beckoning me to join her.

My dancing style has always been stiff and too much of a side-to-side shuffle. But I'm tipsy enough to be able to swing loosely. Romain's eyes caress her, then me. I notice Mina's dancing becomes more undulating, showing off her curves, and I find myself echoing her. The atmosphere becomes sultry, sticky with lust and dangerous potential. I feel a bit weirded out; and I only realise that I'm biting my nails when Mina grabs my hands, and we do a playful fake Tango together, diffusing the atmosphere with laughter.

'I – I think I need to head back,' I say, suddenly keen to bolt.

'Let me just bring down your clothes.' Mina heads upstairs and returns with two carriers; I gush my thanks.

'So,' she asks, 'how are you getting home? An Uber?'

I check my phone in the hope that Sean might have transferred some money over. But my message is still unread.

Which means that I'll have to walk for hours over to Sean's flat in my drunk, tired state, or else climb over the barriers at the tube, which isn't a fun thought.

'I know this might sound a bit cheeky – but the money – I earned . . .' I see her eyes widen, warning me not to elaborate on the money she gave me for the flat. 'It was stolen. And I don't have enough on my Oyster to get home. Could I borrow ten pounds?'

A shadow of hesitation on her face. Unease crawls over me. She's already been so generous. Does she think I'm making up a sob story, trying to rinse her for whatever I can get?

'Of course you can,' Romain interrupts, and I realise he's been at the end of the hallway, in the shadows.

'I don't have any cash,' Mina says vaguely.

'I've got some up in my study,' Romain says firmly. 'Come on up.'

I look at Mina, as though asking for permission. 'Of course we can help you,' she agrees, but I see a glint of doubt in her eyes.

I follow Romain up the stairs, onto the second floor. When I enter the study, I let out a tipsy laugh.

Romain smiles. 'I'm the messy one.'

It's such a contrast to the rest of the house, where every surface is spotless and every picture on the wall seems hung to the exact millimetre. There are piles of books and papers strewn over his desk, an overflowing wastepaper basket. I spot a pipe and a packet of tobacco and nearly make a joke about Sherlock Holmes, but that might sound naff.

I feel a sense of shame as Romain passes two ten-pound notes over, because this doesn't feel like a friend lending cash; this feels like philanthropy that I should be grateful for. I suffer a flare of frustration: I want that power, that wealth. I want to be the one loaning, not begging.

As I take the money, his hand curls over mine. He's smiling and leaning in and suddenly his face is close, much too close, his lips brushing mine. I respond for a few seconds, and then fight my desire: *No! My boss's husband – no way!* I pull away in shock.

'I'm sorry. I'm drunk.' He scans my expression, looking panicked.

'Um, it's fine,' I murmur.

I jump as Mina suddenly appears in the doorway. What if she saw something? I want to tell her that I understand now, why she's having affairs. I understand everything.

I say goodbye, my voice falsely bright, then hurry down the stairs and out into the cool night.

I take the bus to Hackney and I'm just entering Sean's flat when his reply pings on my phone: Sorry, I only just saw your message. Dom stole your money? Alice, you HAVE to call the police.

I know, I know, I type, knowing that I can't.

You can borrow my spare Barclaycard Sean offers.

Thank God. I feel cheeky saying I'm already at his flat, so I reply with a Thank you, that's a good idea. It's nearly 1 a.m. now, so I decide to kip here for the night. As I get into bed, shoving in my earplugs, the dinner party keeps buzzing through my mind: the offer, the kiss, Sean. He'll chase me tomorrow, wanting to know if I've called the police, and what will I say?

Memories cloud my mind. Three years ago: I'm back there, in the police station. I'm being questioned by a Sergeant Pester, with glasses and a moustache, his manner casual and friendly, waiting for me to trip up . . .

What would Mina and Romain say if they knew about my past? If they knew about Julia, about Heather Perkins? If they knew that I was responsible for murdering someone?

CHAPTER TWELVE

Mina

It's 3.30 a.m. I'm in bed, having woken from a shallow sleep.

Anger pumps hot in my heart. Alice's words echo in my mind: *'She was very discreet. She made me wait in the kitchen whilst she looked around for whatever you sent her to get.'* Sarah has some cheek. I certainly didn't ask her to go to Alice's flat to fetch something, so I don't know what the hell she's playing at.

How did she find out that I rented it? It does explain why there have been a couple of odd occasions where the key to the flat seemed to have been moved. Once it was missing from the top drawer of my work desk and I thought I'd lost it, only to see it reappear the next morning. Sarah only got her job because her godfather, Roland Bentley-Jones, plays golf with Charles. I'd much prefer Alice as my assistant – but can I trust her either? Did she let something slip to Sarah?

The afterburn of our evening lingers in the air. Of laughter and dancing; of unease and lust. It was Romain's idea that we go on the Instagram journey together, repair our damaged reputations. He came up with the idea after a meeting with the PR consultant. The plan is to market Romain as a kind of Rory Stewart, championing reading, supporting Alice's publishing journey, setting up his own monthly book club online.

But I wonder if other desires colour his motivation. I

sensed that he was attracted to Alice, especially when I disrobed her of her tatty green dress and put her in a little black number. (I lied when I said the clothes were leftovers; I'd bought them new, in case she needed extra persuasion.)

Flirting with other people used to add spice to our marriage. When Romain and I got married, twenty-one years ago, I was nineteen and he was twenty-nine. I had grown up in a vicarage in Yorkshire, a dour red-brick house, poky and ivy-suffocated. The move to Romain's Mayfair mansion was a euphoric escape. I was a junior editor and Romain was standing as an MP for the first time. We were hungry and ambitious. We held dinner parties regularly; flirting with others became our game. After the guests had gone, Romain would seize me and kiss me with possessive aggression. We'd make love on the dinner table, sweeping aside glasses like something out of a movie. We'd make love on the kitchen floor, the tiles hard against my back. At the sink. Against the wall. I loved the hunger in his eyes, as though I was a drug he couldn't get enough of.

Our lovemaking expelled the poison of jealousy and fear and reassured us that we were united against the world. We seemed like the couple who had everything. Nobody was to know of the bloody secrets that had bound us in the past.

This evening, after Alice had gone, we returned to the living-room. Romain slumped on the sofa. I started dancing. I closed my eyes and spun and writhed and sashayed – to find Romain's head on his chest. He had fallen asleep.

Now I glance over at my husband, sleeping so blissfully. A faint, arid smell of tobacco oozes from him; ever since his father bought him a pipe for his last birthday, he's taken to smoking in his study. I breathe in the tobacco bitterness until I feel I'm choking—

I jump out of bed, padding downstairs to the kitchen, where I make some hot milk with poppy seeds.

Gazing out of the window, I freeze up: I could have sworn I just saw a figure, creeping along by the fence.

I move closer, frowning, but the night remains a mystery.

I jump at a presence by my legs, then hear a reassuring miaow. I pick Persephone up: there's nothing more comforting than the soft warmth of a cat.

I head upstairs, before pausing guiltily on the second floor. I know I should go back to bed. But I find myself climbing up to the third floor, to my study, white and neat with a sloping roof. I pick up my work phone. I bite my lip. If Sarah knows something, logging back in to Feeld is even more of a risk. But the fear is part of the buzz, and I log in and read through dozens of messages from young, sexy men who want me.

Matthias: he catches my eye. He's thirty-six. Moved over from Berlin three years ago. He lives in Tower Hamlets. Works in IT. Loves reading and owns a thousand books. And his photo is hot: tall, fair hair, cute Harry Potter glasses, dimples when he smiles.

Hi I write. You look interesting.

He's online, but I'm not expecting an instant message back. When I hear the alert, my heart leaps.

Hi, sexy lady he replies. How are you tonight?

Suffering from insomnia I reply.

I love your profile. I love that you're sapiosexual. I want a woman with brains.

I remind myself that this can only be a fling, but I feel the tug: towards emotional connection, towards a man who might treasure me rather than just hurry off as Jacob did.

What's your favourite book? he asks.

Lolita I reply.

No! It's mine too! Oh wow. I love Nabokov. Pale Fire is good too, but Lolita is my fav.

This is music to my ears, I reply, smiling. There is no reply for a moment, and I worry he's signed off. But then I hear another alert.

How about a video call?

My fingers trace the N and the O keys. But what if I lose him? He might think I'm refusing because I'm a catfish, that the real me doesn't match my profile.

Sure I type, but we need to be quiet, else I will wake my flatmates.

Give me five. I'll send a zoom link.

I grab my work bag and pull out my blonde wig. I used to find it itchy and strange when I first put it on, but I've grown to love it, to feel liberated by its presence. It unlocks a different me.

I'm wearing a silvery, sexy nightie with thin straps. I didn't bother to wash off my makeup properly before bed, so I grab my compact and quickly lick my finger to wipe away the dark granules that have gathered in the wrinkles around my eyes.

I open up my laptop and click on the Zoom link. I see a flash of his face on the screen. Then panic screams through me and I jab the red LEAVE MEETING button. *Shit.* How could I be so careless? Up there, on the screen, was *my name.* Just for a few seconds.

On Feeld, a message pops up: Where did you go????

I quickly change my name in the Zoom box to Serena Ferns. Then I click on the link again.

His face breaks into a smile as he sees me appear.

'Hey,' he says.

'Hi,' I whisper back.

He looks so sweet and sexy. I can see his eyes caressing

me. This feels so electric, to connect like this in the dead of night, everyone asleep, so illicit—

I hear a noise. A piercing shrill. It's the burglar alarm.

'Oh, shit,' I say. 'Sorry, that's my alarm – I'm going to need to – can we – reconnect in a sec?'

'I hope you're safe,' he says. 'Do you need to call the police?'

I'm moved by his concern but I can hear Romain getting out of bed, and I slam the laptop shut in shock. The alarm is a trigger: I can't have a panic attack, not now. I close my eyes, clamp my hands over my ears, breathe in, breathe out, and I remember how it felt when I was in the toilets, Alice putting her hand on my arm, a motherly reassurance that soothed me.

I get up, open the door quietly and pad across the hall. At the top of the stairs, I see a figure and gasp—

But it's just Romain.

He starts at the sight of me and I realise: I'm still wearing the wig.

I tear it off and Romain puts a finger to my lips. We both stand still, rigid with tension, listening to the incessant sound of the alarm. We need to get into his study, lock the door, press the panic button that will trigger a security alert.

There's someone below; I can hear the sound of chair legs grating across the kitchen floor. I think of Jo Cox, the MP who was murdered; of the death threats Romain receives, as all MPs do; of the bilious comments our Instagram posts sometimes attract, the bitterness and the envy. Who the hell is down there?

And then I hear the singing.

CHAPTER THIRTEEN

Mina

The singing voice is slurred but beautiful. She's singing a
Billie Eilish song,
something about when we all fall asleep, where do we go?
'Aimee,' I whisper.
'Oh, for fuck's sake!' Romain says. 'Right. I'll handle it.
You go back to bed.'

I ignore him, following him down the stairs. We find her in
the kitchen, by the alarm box, hopelessly punching in digits.
She's wearing ripped jeans, a leather jacket. I haven't seen
her for a year. She's twenty-two now, an adult. Her dark hair
has grown and is pulled into a ponytail, a thick DIY fringe
brushing her eyes.

'Sorry,' she slurs over the alarm. 'I couldn't remember the
code.'

Her face melts into a smile that makes me feel tender.

Romain's face tightens. He waits a few more seconds, the
noise a torture, before punching in the code, concealing it
from her with his hand. Finally: the relief of silence. He
flicks on the light. We all squint and wince.

Now I can see that Aimee's not looking great. Her puffy
eyes are underscored with heavy, bruised bags, and there's a
cut on her jawline.

I didn't realise how much I'd been craving to see her until
this moment; after all, Romain is determined that Aimee is

the devil and must be seen off at every opportunity. Sometimes even I can forget she's just a vulnerable young woman. She's the adopted child of my parents, my baby sister. The last time she came to stay, she caused such damage and chaos that Romain banned her from the house, told her never to return.

Now I pull her into a hug. She buries her head in my shoulder.

'That's enough,' Romain says, his tone hard.

As he pulls me away, the urge to punch him fires through me. Then I see the look on his face, the fear beneath his anger.

'I have nowhere to stay tonight,' Aimee says. 'Can I crash here?'

'We told you before,' Romain asserts. 'We can't have you here.'

'You only have, like, fucking ten spare bedrooms,' she cries. 'What, are they all filled with staff, like Downton Abbey?'

Romain takes my hand in his, presenting a united front. I can feel the sweat on his palm.

'I mean, I'll just sleep on the streets,' she protests. 'But I guess your government doesn't give a fuck, does it? People like me – you're legislating against us.'

'You live in a very comfortable and pleasant home in Otley,' Romain says evenly. 'Please don't exaggerate. You're supposed to check in with us before coming to London, remember? I have no doubt you have a friend here you planned to stay with.'

'It fell through,' she cries. 'I mean, come on, it's just for one night. Mina,' she appeals to me. 'Please. *Please.*'

I can't look at her. If I meet her gaze, I'll cave. So I keep my eyes fixed on our Smeg toaster, the pretty swirling blue-and-white pattern. My heart is beating very fast. I know that Romain is right. I know that if Aimee stays she'll give us sweet smiles whilst stealing from our wallets. I know she'll lie because she can't help it. When we first realised she had a problem, four years ago, we looked up all the advice available online. We read that an addict has to decide for themself when they're ready to go straight, which struck me as callous. Surely intervention was the kindest thing. We thought the solution was simple: we'd pay for rehab, the Priory; they'd cure her; problem solved. But we drove her there only to find she'd escaped the next day, and blown the extra funds we'd given her on a bender. It was then I realised that we had lost Aimee. The drugs were dictating her behaviour, ruling her routine, shaping her every thought.

'Fine,' she says. I hear the sting of my rejection in her tone. 'What a kind and loving sister you are, Mina.'

'How much?' Romain asks abruptly. Aimee's eyes flash. He taps the Lloyds banking app on his phone. 'There. Five hundred pounds in your account. You can stay at a hotel this evening, if you please.'

'Great,' Aimee says. 'I'll get room service. *Lovely*.'

I'm ready to cave, but she's already yanking open the back door, blasting us with the cold night air. She runs out, into the garden, disappearing through the trees – did she climb over the fence?

'How the hell did she get in?' Romain snaps. 'She'd better not have a key.' 'Maybe we forgot to lock up properly,' I say.

'We set the alarm.'

'We were pissed,' I remind him.

Romain locks up, resets the alarm. He rubs my shoulder and says sadly, 'We can't deal with her right now. We're only just getting things back on track with this publishing journey.'

I think of the love we're lavishing on Alice, and wonder if, in some way, she is a replacement for Aimee.

'What was that wig you were wearing?' Romain changes the subject.

'What? Oh . . .' I look him straight in the eye. 'I couldn't sleep and was thinking about dyeing my hair. I was just testing how it might look.'

'It looked great,' he smiles, and a frisson ripples through me. I'm exhausted, but eager. If he wants to make love right now, he can have me, all of me—

But he yawns, moving away, the cold air filling up the space he left, and says he has an early start tomorrow.

In bed, I can feel Romain shifting restlessly. Aimee's presence has stirred up bad memories and secrets we'd rather forget. When I finally sleep, I dream in fragments of nightmares: a teenager again, gazing at my shocked, pale face in the mirror. Romain's urgent voice: *You have to make a choice, Mina.* Desperate prayers. A stone cottage—

I wake up crying out.

The next morning is a Monday. *I need to clear up the Sarah mystery,* I think grimly, sprinkling granola into my yoghurt. Our housemaid, Baba, is loading the dishwasher. Romain is at the other end of the table, drinking espresso, on his tablet, fruitlessly googling himself. The kitchen surface is becoming cluttered with scores of plastic bottles. Romain goes through phases of reading about death-defying vitamins in the weekend supplements. He'll take them diligently for a few days and then forget to carry on.

On our spotless kitchen floor tiles, there are a few dirty blades of grass. The only evidence that Aimee was here last night. Baba spots me looking at them and quickly grabs a dustpan, sweeping them up. I smile a thank-you, papering over my sadness: who knows when I'll see her again.

I push the pain down. I've had plenty of practice at that. Onwards and upwards.

Today I'll make a video with Alice, the start of our #PublishingJourney together.

But the first thing I do when I arrive at work is call Sarah into my office. She doesn't even hear me calling her at first – she's got her AirPods in, listening to Taylor Swift's new album, no doubt.

Sarah enters. When she sees the look on my face, she looks nervous.

I get straight to the point: 'Alice told me that you visited her flat on the pretext that I asked you to collect something for me. I don't remember asking you to do that for me.'

Guilt squirms over her face before she quickly recovers herself. 'I don't know what Alice is talking about.'

I sit and stare. Let the silence become a weapon.

Sarah shifts uneasily and I think of Matthias. I messaged him this morning, apologising for the abrupt exit, and we've agreed to meet this Thursday night. The anticipation is delicious. But every fantasy is edged with fear: *What does Sarah know? How did she find out? What's her game?*

'I used Alice's flat to do a little reading,' I say. 'I can't see why you'd want to snoop about.'

'Like I say, I didn't go to her flat,' Sarah asserts, her voice sharpening. 'Alice is just trying to undermine me. I mean, God! She lies all the time – like her supposed degree from Warwick.'

I tense. Sarah's succeeded in distracting me. I should check her CV – although, given her background, maybe she felt the pressure to lie.

Sarah and I battle back and forth for a few more minutes, but her resolve toughens. In the end, I let her go. Shaking my head, I gaze out of my office into the open-plan. Alice is looking good this morning, dressed in the navy trouser suit that I gifted her. Unease ripples through me: which one of them is lying? Did Alice make up the story because she wants Sarah's job, perhaps?

Normally when I'm judging people, situations, I rely on my intuition, which whispers greater truths than my intellect. But suddenly I feel unbalanced, uncertain who to trust; and then I remind myself of the huge risks I'm taking: I can't trust anyone.

From Ruth's diary

I went to the woods today, to the place where he died. We've been waiting weeks for spring to come. Now it's here, it only made it feel all the more painful. The birds singing, the tinkle of the stream as I followed it, a squirrel scurrying by. There ought to have been grey clouds and a storm overhead.

It's still there, the oak tree his car hit. After the crash, it was half butchered, branches amputated. Someone engraved his initials into the trunk. But that was twenty years ago; now his name is gone and the branches are spread wide.

I once saw pictures of a forest where a war had taken place. Of a tree with a rifle woven into its bark, another with a hard hat halfway up its trunk. I wonder if there is a little of him left in that tree; a sliver of the broken windscreen; his hair, his skin; all preserved somewhere in the bark.

CHAPTER FOURTEEN

Alice

I watch a locksmith drilling out my front-door Yale lock. Sean kindly offered to let me use his Barclaycard to pay for this; there's still two days to go before Mina rents my flat and I get another £1,000.

My neighbour, Jean, comes out of her flat, ostensibly to walk her Yorkshire terrier, even though she never normally takes him out at this hour.

'Oh, changing the locks *again*?' she asks.

God, she's nosy. But maybe I should try to get her on side.

'Dominic's become something of a stalker,' I say quietly.

'But didn't he inherit the flat from his mother?' she asks in surprise. 'I assumed you were renting from him? The other day he asked if I had seen you and said you were behind on your rent.'

And this is the guy who has just stolen nearly a thousand pounds from me! So that's the story Dominic's spinning. I thought the doormen were just letting him in because they remembered him as Julia's son, but no: Dominic's created a whole web of lies.

'This is my flat,' I assert, looking her straight in the eye. 'Julia gave it to me.'

Jean looks quite shocked. 'Oh, sorry,' she says hastily. 'None of my business, of course.' She always says that, before she starts to dig. 'But he was moving furniture around the other day . . . As though it was his.'

I decide it's best to smile vaguely; I quickly turn back to the locksmith, asking him if he's sure it's secure, and I hear Jean tut before she shuts her door, forgetting all about walking the dog.

The next morning, I'm filled with dread. Romain comes striding into the Principle Publishing offices. I try to act busy by shuffling some papers but he stops by my desk as he walks towards Mina's office. 'Alice – lovely to see you again. How are you?'

All politeness and charm, *as though he never tried to kiss me.*

I'm terrified Mina might have seen the kiss – but she can't have, or else I'd have been fired by now.

We chit-chat about his book club before walking into Mina's office together. She sets up her iPhone in a tripod so that we can make our first #PublishingJourney video.

'Alice should stand in the middle,' Romain says. They curl their arms around me like proud parents. I'm conscious of Romain standing a little too close to me, the heat from his body caressing mine.

Later that evening, when I watch the video, I see the slight blush on my face. It's been posted on Mina's account (20k followers) and my recently created one (13 followers); I send the link to Sean.

Your boss made me laugh he messages. She sounds like the Queen.

I laugh then, because Sean's right. Mina's so smooth in real life, but behind a camera she becomes stilted and overly posh. By contrast, Romain's magnetic on-screen; he seems able to push his charisma to full volume.

The video's had 2,000 views – wow.

But some of the comments are so mean. Cruel ones about

Mina being a posh exploiter, nasty ones about me too. One leaps out:

Alice is such a faker. She looks so dumb and ugly, oh God get her out of there and get a proper intern in.

The user's name is VENOM3, followed by a snake symbol. My stomach clenches: snakes are Dominic's favourite animal. I block the user, then walk around in agitation: this is exactly why I wanted to avoid social media.

I don't sleep well, even with the chair pushed up under my door handle, and the new keys; I've stored the spares under my mattress. Sean's been sweet and sent me a silky sleeping mask; in the dark of night, I peel it off, tiptoeing across my living-room, inching back the curtain. *Oh God.*

Dominic is there. It's three-thirty in the morning. He's standing against the wall, a little square of light from his phone illuminating his face.

He's been stalking me for six months. I thought he'd tire of it by now. We've suffered a rainy June but the forecasts for sun next week have filled me with dread. The long days, the warm weather will make it all the easier for him to hang around outside.

He's playing the long game, that's for sure.

Mina is late.

I'm in the secret room, peering through the spyhole.

I've been wrestling with my conscience all day, but I finally decided to do this. I know it's wrong to be watching, but Mina's got such an enigmatic, tough professional persona. I want to see more of her night side. I want to understand that kiss with Romain better. Perhaps they have an open marriage – though how would that play out in the tabloids, if people knew?

I'm prepared this time. I've got a bottle of water, a sandwich, some snacks. I went to the toilet just before hiding out here.

As a WhatsApp message comes through from Sean, it reminds me to put my phone on silent.

When can we chat tonight? I'm really missing you.

About 10. Mina's coming over for a work meeting – she's teaching me editorial skills. It depends on how long she stays.

How can she expect you to work this late?

Be worth it if it results in a proper job.

Sean signs off with an eyeroll emoji and plenty of kisses.

Then I hear the key in the lock: Mina's here.

Mina's new prey looks nicer than the others she's brought in. With his fair hair and round glasses, there's a touch of Harry Potter about him, though his black jeans and dark shirt give him an edge.

Mina's wearing her blonde wig and a red dress with floaty sleeves. I can't help wondering: just how many one-night stands does she plan on having? Another possibility crosses my mind: is Mina moonlighting as some kind of high-class hooker? Maybe her husband holds all the wealth and she's in some kind of money trouble.

They sit on the sofa, drinking wine and chatting.

'So, Serena . . .' he asks, 'how many other guys have you met up with from Feeld?'

Mina perches on the sofa. 'One.'

She lies so well, though I sense she's relishing playing a persona, exploring another side of her personality.

'Really?'

Mina bristles. 'Yes. One. Why? Have you had many?'

'I only asked because you're so pretty. I'll be honest – I've slept with fourteen girls from Feeld.'

'Oh.' Mina arches an eyebrow and I share her surprise: Matthias looks far too innocent to be such a Don Juan. 'So, you just wanted a night with each one?'

'I did.' He grins, looks rueful. 'A lot of them wanted more.'

This guy is starting to sound like a bit of a dick, I think.

Mina rolls her eyes. 'It must be hard,' she says, 'when you have so many women who are so desperate for you.'

'I'm just saying,' he says, stroking her face, 'that it's refreshing to find a woman who's up for just sex. Your profile was so gorgeous, I was wondering if you were actually real, at first.'

Mina looks a little appeased. His thumb lingers on her lip and he muses: 'You know, you look familiar.'

Mina frowns, then quickly laughs. 'I don't think we've ever met before.'

Matthias strokes her wig soothingly, but she shudders, moving an inch away.

'You don't like that?' he asks. 'I want to know what turns you on.'

'I recently suffered some hair loss,' she improvises, 'so I don't like people stroking my hair.'

Matthias slides his hand down the back of neck instead, then gently kisses her. I wonder if Mina's still up for sex, given his crass conversation, but she seems to be responding to his caresses, which look soft and sweet. They're losing themselves in each other when his phone, sitting on the table, buzzes. They glance at it, then carry on, him unzipping her dress, rolling on top of her, his kisses becoming more passionate.

And then it all goes weird.

'What are you doing?' I hear Mina ask.

I gape in horror. Matthias's fingers are on her throat, pressing hard.

'Shh,' he tells her. 'Just go with it. You'll get an adrenaline rush, you'll enjoy it.'

'No – don't—' Mina tries to push his hands away, but he carries on pressing, relentless.

Oh my God. Is this really a sex game, or is he going to suffocate her? I could charge in there, tear him off her – but for all I know, maybe Mina set this up, maybe she wanted to experiment with a dangerous scenario.

Bending down, doing my best not to make any noise, I slide my mobile out of my handbag. Maybe I should call her and say there's an emergency. But then she'd hear my voice; I'd reveal myself – stupid idea – I'm panicked, not thinking straight.

'Stop,' I hear Mina's strangled cry. 'Please – just – stop. *Stop—*'

I don't think she's playing a role. I think Matthias is a fucking psycho.

He sits up, releasing her, and I hear Mina gasp for breath.

'I thought you'd be up for trying something new,' he says angrily. 'But it turns out you're just another bore.'

What a bastard.

'Get out.' Mina struggles to sit up, fingers on her neck. 'Get out of here!'

But he just folds his arms, as though he's not going anywhere. Rage burns inside me. I know his type. He's just like my dad. A bastard sadist.

How long would the police take to come if I called them now? Twenty minutes, or longer even? I think of my knife block in the kitchen, the four steel ones I've recently had sharpened.

Mina's pulled up her dress, holding it against her chest, her eyes flashing. 'You'd better get the hell out of here. My husband's going to be back any moment.'

'I'm sure he is.' Matthias reaches for his wine, laughing into his glass.

'I mean it,' Mina says.

They glare-stare at each other.

'Why don't we just press reset,' he says, suddenly capitulating. 'I'm sorry. I shouldn't have just – plunged in. It makes it more fun, that way, the shock of it – I've found a lot of women really like it, actually. But we don't have to do that.'

'Oh, great, we don't have to *strangle me* – how delightful,' Mina cries. Her gaze turning sour. Her dress slips. 'This isn't going to work for me, I'm afraid. I'd like you to leave.'

'Oh, would you?' His Mr Nice didn't last long. He reaches out, smirking, and I gasp as he yanks her wig off.

I put my hand over my mouth, terrified they might have heard me, but Mina's too shocked to have noticed.

'Hey!'

'Mina Harpenden. I thought I recognised you.' He picks up his phone and snaps a photo of Mina, half-topless, distraught.

Shit.

'Delete that photo,' Mina barks.

Buzz-buzz goes the doorbell. They both flinch, turn in confusion.

'That's my husband,' Mina asserts. 'Now, if you fancy a fight with him, then fine, stay here. If not, you'll delete that photo and leave. Right now.'

'So your husband's happy with you sleeping around?' he asks incredulously.

'No, he bloody well isn't. He doesn't know but now he's about to find out – and he gets *very* jealous. He has quite a temper.'

Buzz-buzz.

Matthias hovers, torn between sadism and self-preservation.

Buzz-buzz. Oh God. Nobody but Dominic perseveres at my buzzer like that.

'I can go straight to the police,' Mina blusters on. 'I'm friends with the Met chief, Sir Mike Connelly. Look him up.'

'Your husband would have a key. He wouldn't be buzzing.'

'You're lucky he's forgotten his keys. You have a chance. I'd take it.'

Oh God. Please can he just go? My heart is about to cave in from anxiety. I'm ready to burst in, shock them, even if it does mean the loss of my career—

'Fine.' He zips up his trousers sullenly. And then, just as he seems about to leave in peace, he reaches for my china sleeping cat, the one that sits on the coffee table, and hurls it at Mina. It misses her by an inch, hits the wall and shatters.

'Bye-bye,' he says in a sarcastic voice. 'Bitch.'

Finally: the slam of the door as he leaves.

Tears are pouring from my eyes. I slide down the wall, hands over my ears. *Oh God.* Bad memories are whirling; screams from the past echoing inside me. The way my dad would yell at my mum, bully her into a corner, break chairs, torment her.

I hear Mina exhale heavily. And I just want to go out there and give her a hug, but instead I stay in the room, trying to get a grip.

CHAPTER FIFTEEN

Mina

And then he's gone. Oh, thank God, he's gone.

I find a dustpan and brush, sweeping up the broken china. I just hope it wasn't expensive or had sentimental value.

The practical work calms me. Ever since I joined Feeld, that fear has been there: a sense that, sooner or later, I'd get my comeuppance. That a woman seeking sex in the way a man does just can't get away with it. It's all the TV crime dramas I've watched, where a beautiful woman is found dead in the woods and she seemed like a nice girl but really she was screwing loads of guys who could all be her killer. It's the stats in the papers. It's my father. Growing up with a vicar for a father meant I was obsessed with sex as a teenager: it was such forbidden fruit that I just wanted a bite. Even after my first kiss, I went back home convinced I'd find that the cross on my wall had fallen to the floor, or that *something bad was going to happen*. When it didn't, I only felt more uneasy, as though punishment was simply being delayed.

It's why I became an atheist when I married Romain. I don't believe in any superstition either. I think we're all responsible for our lives. *Fuck Matthias*. I'm not going to let him ruin mine. The other Feeld boys were lovely; Matthias is just a bad apple.

But I find myself trembling as I check my Instagram. Dreading that my name might be already have become a hashtag.

If he dares post the photo, I'll say it's a fake. I'll throw law-yers at him, the very best. He won't get away with this.

Buzz-buzz.

I check the intercom camera.

'It's Dominic.'

That bastard stalker. Fucking up Alice's life. God, he deserves a piece of my mind. I tell him to come on up.

I quickly check my reflection in the scratched mirror hang-ing on the wall by the door. I look a fright – I smooth down my hair, do up the zip on my dress, blot my lipstick. I'm still not wearing my knickers; I don't know what Matthias did with them.

I open the door. I'd been expecting Dominic to be taller, more aggressive. There's something oddly vulnerable about this man. He's skinny, his balled fists shoved into the pockets of a green cagoule. The look on his face, the tiredness etched deep into his skin and eyes, is that of someone who's had a hard time in life.

'Is Alice in?' he asks softly.

I'm surprised to catch an intonation of poshness, a good education, in his voice.

'She's not,' I reply. 'I'm staying here for the night.'

'And you are?' His tone becomes territorial.

'I'm her . . . aunt,' I reply.

'Alice doesn't have any relatives like that . . .' He looks bemused.

'Not by blood – by friendship,' I reply curtly. Then I decide to change tack. 'You're welcome to come in for a cup of tea if you like.'

He blinks in surprise; he was expecting a confrontation. Then he hurries in before I can change my mind.

As I make peppermint tea in the kitchen, I make sure I

watch Dominic in that gap between door and doorframe, just in case he tries to steal anything. He certainly can't sit still; he seems fascinated by the boxes of books by the wall; I'm sure there used to be a bookcase that held them. He keeps searching through them for – money? I feel enough is enough and I bring out the tea.

'Hey, I think this is yours,' Dominic says as he sits down on the sofa, passing me an earring.

'Thank you.' I accept it with a slight blush. The tea helps to soothe my churning stomach. I eye Dominic over the rim of my cup. It's tempting to berate him but perhaps it would be smarter to gather more intel. 'I gather this was your mother's flat?'

'Yeah. She died and Alice stole the flat from me.'

So this is why he's stalking Alice. He feels she's stolen his inheritance.

Dominic looks a bit indignant that I'm not giving him more of a shocked reaction.

'A lot of these are first editions that belonged to my mum. I came by because I want to take some of them back. '

'Well, I can't let you do that,' I interject hastily. 'You'll need to check with Alice.'

For a moment I'm concerned that he might become aggressive too. *It was a mistake to let him in,* I think. The shock of Matthias is stronger in the afterburn. But Dominic's expression becomes pleading.

'Maybe you can talk some sense into her about doing the right thing.'

'But if Alice inherited this flat, it was your mother's choice. Surely it's not

for you or me to judge that?'

'But how would you feel if, your whole life, you've

struggled with money, and you're due a flat, and then some woman comes along and seduces you with a long-term plan to get your inheritance. How was I to know that Alice was playing me? I fell for it.'

I frown, sitting up, conscious that Alice has told me quite a different story.

'I thought Alice made friends with Julia at the library ?'

'She did!' Dominic corrects himself. 'But Mum and I were there together. I got into a relationship with Alice first, then she got to know Julia.'

'I see,' I say, sensing this is a blurred timeline that can't really be turned into a chronology. 'But why did Julia cut you out? Why not split the flat between you both?'

'I did get some cash,' Dominic says in a sullen voice. 'It was only five grand though. This flat is worth two mil! I'm in some shithole in Golders Green! Every day I come and I look at this place and I know it's where I should be.'

His voice is rising and I can't face another fight with an angry man, so I reply soothingly: 'That is tough. But what can you do? I assume you've spoken to a lawyer about the will?'

'What I need', he says in a conspiratorial tone, 'is proof of how Mum died. Proof that Alice murdered her.'

I flinch. Now this really does sound far-fetched.

'But . . .' I force a gentle tone, recalling a chat I had with Alice the other week. 'I thought she was in her early seventies, and suffered cancer, blindness, and a little dementia?'

Dominic rubs his finger up and down the zip of his cagoule. 'I'm looking for a letter that my mum said she was going to send me, that I never got. It talks about how Alice was plotting against her. I have to find it.'

'I see. But that could have been her dementia talking.'

'Let me just check . . .' He slides off the sofa, crouching down, going through the piles of books. I feel uncomfortable; Alice didn't rent her flat to me to allow this to happen.

'I do actually have to vacate this flat shortly,' I warn him. 'So it might be better if you came back another time.'

'Vacate?' Dominic asks. 'What is this, a hotel?'

'Of course not. But I let you in, and I shouldn't have done so, though I appreciate your . . . your suffering.'

Dominic sits on his heels, eyes narrowed. 'I know you're not her aunt. You're her boss. Mina Harpenden, right? I've seen your Instagram love-ins.'

I gaze at him, unease creeping over me. 'I think you should go,' I say in a firm voice.

'You should watch her, she's manipulative,' Dominic says, standing up. 'She'll be after your job next, you'll see. Don't come crying to me when that goes down.'

'Actually,' I assert, 'Alice is really rather brilliant. It's time for you to go now.' I reach for my phone. 'I don't want to have to call the police.'

Dominic glares at me and I hold his stare, despite the memory of Matthias and that china cat whizzing past me, what might have been.

'Fine. But I'm coming back – and you can tell Alice that. You watch out for her: "Oh, Mina, let me get you a coffee,"' he says, and I'm shocked: he mimics her voice perfectly, it's uncanny.

He slams the door behind him.

God. I collapse onto the sofa. Two difficult men in succession is quite enough: my nerves are at a soprano pitch. I go into Alice's bedroom, pick up her birdcage and bring the parrots in. They delight me, cheer me up.

Was Dominic telling the truth about Alice, or was he delusional? I know when people are lying – I've spent enough of my spare time with politicians to be an expert – and his eyes kept flitting away, avoiding mine. But then again . . .

Before I go, I leave a note for Alice, apologising for the broken china cat, adding extra compensation in the envelope of money.

When I return home, I'm surprised to find Romain in the living-room; usually he's hiding out in his study.

'You're home late,' he remarks. With only a lamp on, his face is a harlequin of light and shadow; I can't see his expression clearly.

Has Matthias been in touch with him?

'I had a launch event,' I remind him in an even tone; Romain has so little interest in my career these days that he'll never check this out.

His eyes sweep over my short dress, noticing that it's a little sexier than my usual gear. He frowns. I'm half terrified, half pleased that he's finally noticed. There's a filmy scarf around my neck that I stole from Alice's drawer, hiding the bruising that's starting to appear.

He draws me down onto the sofa, curling his arm around me. Persephone jumps up and we both stroke her gently. The tenderness of being with them suddenly makes me want to break down in tears.

Later that night, I wake up in shock from a nightmare: Matthias's face snarled in fury, the rush of air by my ear as the china cat passed me. I rise up, shaken, and go into my study, opening my laptop.

No messages from him.

Yet.

*

The next morning, in the office, I learn Sarah's off sick with Covid. I'm so tired I feel delirious. I can't concentrate; like some teenager, I keep refreshing my phone every other minute in fear of the photo. I watch my colleagues coming into the office, gossiping, making tea, discussing the latest series of *Slow Horses,* our current collective TV obsession. I picture their reactions if they were to read about me in the papers. Nobody would ever look at me with respect again. I'd have to leave, if I could even get another job. All the editors these days seem younger and younger. My glory days are behind me.

I can't go on like this; I'm going to have to call my old friend Howard and ask him for help. At the thought, I feel a little better; I'm taking control of things—

As my phone buzzes, I jump. It's from Aimee: I'm broke, can you lend me £25? I sigh – typical. She only gets in touch when she wants money. But I have to acknowledge, sadly, that we trained her to be this way. It's the danger of an addict who knows too many of our secrets.

I log in to my Lloyds banking app and send her £50.

I hear a gentle knock on my open door and look up to see Alice standing there, smiling at me. I signal for her to come in and shut the door.

Dominic's accusations linger in my mind. I dispel them. Dominic is angry and delusional. Fuck Dominic, Matthias – foolish men who don't deserve our time and energy. Us women need to stick together.

'I'm so sorry about the china cat breakage,' I say. 'I just knocked my bag against it—'

'Oh, it's fine.' Alice doesn't seem fussed, to my relief. 'It was just a cheap something Sean picked up in a market. So . . .' She goes to bite her nails, then stops, giving me a sheepish grin. 'So I was just wondering, are you planning to rent the flat again?'

I pick up on the subtext: Alice needs the money. I feel awkward, because after what happened with Matthias, my Feeld days are definitely over.

'I'd love to rent soon,' I say vaguely. I find myself wondering how Alice and Aimee might get on, if introduced. Aimee might call her a bore, but Alice's good qualities might rub off on her. 'You know, my younger sister, Aimee – she sometimes needs a place to stay in London.'

'Oh, okay.' Alice doesn't look quite as enthusiastic as I'd anticipated, as if to say: *Don't hire me as a babysitter, thanks.* God knows what she'd say if she knew what I've been doing in her flat.

I give her a list of tasks to do and send her back to her desk, then I check my Instagram for the tenth time this morning. My latest #PublishingJourney video with Alice has a new comment from an account called Matthiasthebaiter. It says, Wow, looking hot, Mina 😊

I delete the comment and block him. I glance nervously round the office, then quickly log in to Feeld. He's sent me a new message:I love this photo, Mina. What do you think I should do with it? I think the world would love to see your tits.

FUCK YOU I hammer back in fury. YOU DARE TRY TO FUCK WITH ME AND I'LL DESTROY YOU! YOU JUST TRY ME.

From Ruth's diary

If Chris was still alive ... That's a branch of time I often wonder about. He'd be married, I'm sure. Even at the age of sixteen, he was a romantic. I once caught him crying at *Pride and Prejudice* on TV. He'd have kids, three, maybe four, as I think he'd have liked a big family. He'd be domestic and a good dad, but he'd probably go crazy now and then, get drunk with the lads, spend his bonus on the fruit machines or in the casino. He had that in him too. And then there's all those little moments that he's missing. Waking up to see a dawn with such divine colours that it makes your heart stop and forget about life's bind. Going for a walk in the woods, finding a bird's nest, seeing a rabbit hop through the undergrowth. Sunday-night TV, cosy on the sofa. That cup of tea in a café that makes you smile after a long day.

All of that, erased. And in the meantime, *she* gets to walk around having the time of her life. Great house, great job, money, everything. It just makes me *burn* ...

CHAPTER SIXTEEN

Alice

I peer out of my living-room window. It's not even 8 a.m. and Dominic is there. *If only he could just die,* I think in fury. *Just step into traffic, be hit by a car, a quick death, gone.* I step back, feeling guilty, as though I've hexed him.

I notice a shard of the china cat on the carpet and pick it up, shuddering. I figure that Mina isn't going to be inviting more young men here any time soon, which is going to cause a cash crisis within a few weeks. Still, maybe it's for the best, for Mina's safety – and because Dominic's realised she's a new way to target me. I knew our Insta videos would just give him ammunition.

I dreaded that Mina might take Dominic's accusations seriously, but she doesn't seem to have taken any notice. Maybe she was too shellshocked by Matthias to really take in what he said. My internship has still been officially extended.

In fact, with Sarah away sick, she's upgraded my tasks from intern to PA: emailing authors, manging her work diary. Mina makes people work hard to earn her praise, but she even lavished me with some yesterday afternoon: 'You're working three times faster than Sarah does.'

And yet. Every so often, I see a question mark in Mina's eyes. Now that I'm staying on, I'm worrying about my CV. The omissions, the things I jazzed up. But would Mina bother to check it again? I wonder if this is some self-destructive fear in me: that if things are going well, I can't believe it will last: something bad must happen.

It reminds me to check if Heather Perkins, my old employer, has taken down my old photo on her site as I requested. I'm horrified to see it's still there. I fire off another email begging her to take it down.

A sudden knock on my door makes me jump. But when I peer through the window, I see Dominic's still on the street below. It must be a delivery.

I open the door to find a girl wearing jeans and a leather jacket. She looks pretty, nervy; in her early twenties. Her hair swings in a ponytail. When she smiles, she reveals little white teeth and two vampiric canines.

'Um, are you Alice?' she asks, in a strong Yorkshire accent. 'I'm Aimee. Mina said it would be fine for me to stay.'

'She did?' I gape at her. 'But she didn't—' I break off, because actually Mina did mention that her younger sister might want to stay last week. Did I miss the date? I suppose I must have, because Mina is never vague; she's crisp and efficient.

'Right, come in,' I welcome her with a bright smile. 'So . . .' I pass Julia's bedroom, a sacred space I don't want anyone to pollute. The spare room has become a bit of a storeroom for my junk, but when I show Aimee in, she doesn't look fussed.

She dumps her black rucksack on the mattress. The gum she's chewing emits a peppermint tang.

'I'll do up the bed tonight,' I assure her. 'So – d'you want a cup of tea?'

I make some PG Tips for us both. I loathe the idea of leaving a stranger in my flat for the day. Mina's described her younger sister as 'wild' and 'unbounded'. My eyes flit to my birdcage, to my precious first editions, to the little picture that hides the secret room spyhole. I decide I'll work from home this morning, and fire off a quick email to Mina.

Aimee asks for a tissue and she removes her gum, wadding it up before she takes a sip of her tea. She's twitchy, eyes flitting around my flat, fingers toying with the hem of her jacket.

'So,' I smile at her, 'where've you travelled from?'

'Otley. That's where my mum and dad are.'

That's where Mina grew up, I recall. 'It's near the Dales, right? Brontë country,' I say, resorting to clichés, for I've never visited.

She nods, looking agitated. An awkward silence opens up between us.

'It's good to escape,' she bursts out. 'My dad's a vicar, really strict – he shoves all this God stuff down my throat. I can't breathe. He was the same with Mina.'

'Actually, I didn't know her – your – dad was a vicar.'

'As she's probably moaned to you, I'm the black sheep of the family. The wild one. Mina doesn't take me along to her *Tatler* parties or book launches – ha, no. Her reputation is everything to her.'

I wonder what Aimee would say if she knew that Mina had recently made love to three random men on this sofa.

'I recognise you from her Instagram videos. You're her pet, right?'

'I wouldn't say pet,' I object, riled.

'Hey, sorry.'

'But yes, I'm her' – I mean to say 'protégée' but the word that comes out is 'project'.

Aimee frowns. 'I thought you were supposed to be on benefits.'

'That was my parents,' I say, sighing inwardly.

'Well, I like the Insta videos,' she tells me. 'But Mina comes across as a bit of a fraud. I mean, she was brought up in the North! Where did her real accent go . . .?' Her laughter has a cruel edge and I tense.

My mobile is vibrating. I jump when I see it's Mina, as though she's somehow heard us discussing her.

'Alice, you really are needed here,' she tells me before I can even say hello. 'I'm afraid that working from home isn't an option today – I have more urgent things for you to take care of.'

'Sure, I'll come in,' I say uneasily, 'but Aimee's here.'

'Is she?' Mina sounds taken aback. 'I don't think so. Then again, I did mention your flat to her. I'm sorry if she's just turned up – that would be typical Aimee, I'm afraid.'

'She's definitely here. Do you want to . . .?' *Speak to her*, I was going to suggest, but Aimee is making frantic signals and shaking her head. When Mina asks me to put her on, Aimee darts out of the room, declaring that she needs the toilet and I tell Mina to try later.

When Aimee re-emerges, she pops a fresh stick of gum into her mouth.

'Sorry I scarpered,' she says, 'but seriously, I can't face a three-hour lecture from Mina right now.'

'Okay. Well, I'm afraid I don't have a spare key,' I lie, too anxious to give her one. 'I can get one cut today, hopefully. In the meantime, is it okay if you stay in for the day? Help yourself to whatever's in my fridge . . .'

Before I go, I leave my mobile number for her and introduce her to my birds, but she's barely interested. My bookcase seems to excite her though. I'm sure that Mina told me Aimee hasn't opened a novel in a decade. I feel so weirded out and distracted that I barely even notice Dom as I leave the flat, one worry over-layering the other. I can't help feeling a little indignant, that Mina feels my flat is hers to use whenever suits her, as though it's a hotel and I'm the housekeeper.

Then, when I get into work, I get another shock.

There's a buzz in the office. I hear Mina's name being mentioned and I worry that Matthias has outed her. But it's not scandal. It's an acquisition.

I hear the gossip from Jimoke and Beth in publicity: Mina has bought a new book, her first in ages, called *Those Foolish Things*. *The manuscript that I discovered*. The one I nagged and nagged Mina to read.

'I pulled that manuscript off the slush pile,' I cut into their conversation.

'Did you?' Jimoke's eyes are wide. 'I think Mina discovered it – and you got to read it too,' she adds patiently, as though I'm just the intern who's nurturing a delusional fantasy.

In desperate need of air, I head down to Starbucks and get a latte.

Mina has taken credit for my discovery.

I guess it is my job to help her shine. I should be grown up about it, let her savour the success. She'll be far more likely to give me a full-time job here if I do.

Back in the office, the excitement is spreading: everyone is saying how amazing *Those Foolish Things* is. Mina calls me into her office. My smile feels like a label on a bottle. I try hard not to seethe. Surely I deserve *some* credit? Mina starts listing what she needs me to do today and my pen cuts into the page as I write down the mundane tasks, emails that need sending, and things to follow up on.

And then Mina throws me a curveball.

'By the way,' she says, 'I called Aimee, and she's not at your flat.'

I gape. Aimee must be lying – and I don't know her well

enough to cover for her. I don't want to get tangled up in a family drama.

'Look, she's at my flat. I made her a cup of tea.'

Mina gives me a long look. 'I just had a quick call with her, to check what was going on. She's in Kent for the day.'

Now I feel pissed off. Is she gaslighting me? First the acquisition, now Aimee?

Then she flashes me the photo on her phone. A young woman with dark hair – Aimee – is on a station platform, by a sign that says EDENBRIDGE.

'You don't need to – fabricate – anything, Alice. You're doing good work here, and I'm grateful for the fact you have allowed me to use your place.'

She smiles then, sweetly and I manage to grin back at her, but inside I'm panicking. *Whoever I've let into my flat, it can't be the girl in who's in that photo. So who the hell is in there?*

For the next hour, I clock-watch. My lunch hour begins at midday, and I can't just run out of the office before then, as Mina has asked me to greet an author in reception. As soon as I've done my duty, I run a Google search for pictures of Mina's sister. Maybe Mina has worked hard to keep her out of the limelight, because I only find one picture, a blurry one from a Billie Eilish concert. I enlarge the photo, comparing it with my memory of the stranger in my flat. They do look very similar; both sport thick, choppily cut fringes and ponytails. But then I notice that Aimee doesn't have sharp vampire teeth – that's the giveaway.

Mina is right: the person in my flat is pretending to be Aimee. Which is just surreal.

Midday comes. I run to Blackfriars station and take the tube to High Street Kensington.

I hurry up the stairs, dart out of the station, past shoppers and yummy mummies, and turn off down Marloes Road. I flit past Dom, giving him the finger as I go, because I'm starting to put two and two together and it wouldn't surprise me if he had something to do with all this. It could be an elaborate plan to get back into my flat.

Outside my front door, I halt, suddenly cautious. If Sean were here, he'd be telling me to call the police. I put the key into the lock, let the door open a few inches. Then I take my keys and slot them between my fingers as a weapon. I push the door open gently—

Something comes swooping towards me and I let out a scream—

But it's just Mimi, my darling bird. How come she's out of her cage?

My mouth feels dry. My heart is frantic.

'Aimee?' I call. '*Aimee?*'

With Mimi on my shoulder, I enter the living-room and stop short. My books are all over the place, on the table, on the sofa, the floor. Many are open, as though she's been searching through them. Maybe she's acting for Dom, trying to find this dangerous letter from Julia. I'm relieved to see that Arthur is in the cage and I let Mimi join him, locking it up. I go into my kitchen, grab a knife from the block and then head towards the bedrooms.

Empty.

The bathroom is empty too.

I hurry back to my bedroom and reach under my mattress with dread, certain that my spare keys and my cash will be gone – but my fingers curl around the envelope. Everything's still there.

Phew. But what the hell did she want, if she didn't want to steal from me?

I go back into the spare bedroom, glancing round. No sign of her rucksack: she's definitely gone.

On the bedside table, I spot a newspaper headline, torn from a photocopy, and a twirl of paper, from her packet of gum.

SEVENTEEN-YEAR-OLD BOY DIES IN HORROR CRASH! reads the headline.

This has been left out for me to see – but what does it have to do with me?

As I head back to the office on the tube, I think of Mina's so-called acquisition and something kicks inside me. *It's so unfair.* But I have to just grin and bear it and make some video for her Instagram saying I'm so thrilled to be an intern. The fake Aimee would have laughed at that, I muse, recalling how she confided in me. She seemed so sincere. I felt moved and disturbed by all the things she said and now I know that none of them can be true.

CHAPTER SEVENTEEN

Mina

I'm in the middle of a dinner party when the phone call comes through from Howard.

We've got six guests: three couples, all close friends. We're at that stage of the evening when we've moved past polite life updates and competitive status brags to drunken playfulness and laughter and illicit cigarettes and downing shots like teenagers. It's the most fun I've had in ages; a relief from everything bad that has happened recently. Every day this past week I've woken up with a terrible sense of foreboding, and I've grabbed my phone to check if my life has crashed and burned overnight.

Now I slip out through the French windows, padding through the garden, past the fountain, the gnarled ceanothus oozing blossoms; past the willows, until the chatter and music fade to a low hum. I sit on our bench, gaze up at the half-moon, and call Howard back.

Howard is one of the few people I really trust. Back in the days when we lived in Otley, Howard was Romain's best friend and drinking buddy, a local policeman who became a PI. When we moved to London, we stayed in touch. Howard would help Romain if there was ever any trouble, or if we needed a background check on someone. I haven't disclosed too much about Matthias, just that he's a stalker giving me hassle.

'I've looked into Matthias,' Howard tells me. 'He's in a financial mess. He set up a business consultancy that made a loss, went under. He owes HMRC twenty K in unpaid taxes.'

'Thank you,' I breathe out. Knowledge is power. This is ammunition. I must find a way to use it, somehow.

'Is it okay if this is our secret?' I cajole him. Back in the day, Howard used to flirt with me and he still calls Romain 'a lucky guy' to have 'nabbed' me.

'Sure,' Howard agrees, sounding flattered, if a little curious. 'If you need any more advice, feel free to call me any time. I'm here for you.'

I see a figure on the lawn and whisper that I'll call him back.

It's Leila. Her dark curls flow over her shoulders as she plonks herself on the bench next to me. She nestles her head against my shoulder, happy and hazy with drunkenness.

'You okay?' She's wondering why I'm preoccupied, a little distant, I suspect. Normally I'm much louder at parties.

'I'm good,' I manage.

'Your garden is stunning,' she sighs, her voice rich with envy.

Even at night, it's beautiful. Twenty years ago, it was a mess of earth and weeds. I was the one who designed it. It's taken years for the ceanothus – my favourite – to flower. I remember when Romain and I brought it back from the garden centre and it was just a little spindle of a plant that we fretted over like a baby we weren't sure would survive.

A chill comes over me. 'Oh God,' I say.

'Mina?' Leila draws back hair from my face. 'What's the matter? I could tell something was wrong.'

I turn to her. 'I just have this – irrational fear – that I'm about to lose everything,' I whisper.

'But why? What's going on?'

'I don't know,' I backtrack. 'My insomnia, it makes me feel so tired half the time, and then I drink too much coffee, and then I go into hyper-anxiety mode . . .'

'You have everything,' she reminds me, with that mix of generosity and envy I've grown used to in our friendship. 'You don't even have a mortgage.' Leila has really been suffering recently, since interest rates have gone up.

'I know, I know,' I say. 'It's just . . . silly.' I press my hand to my heart.

'Is it Romain? He would *never* cheat on you,' Leila assures me. 'I've seen women flirt with him – he doesn't give them an inch.'

Which only makes me feel a hundred times worse. I've seen powerful men splashed across the papers, felled by scandal and seduction, suffering a huge divorce bill on top of embarrassment and I used to think, *What a dick, why couldn't you just practise some self-control?* Now I know. *I can't bear it,* I think. *I can't bear to lose all this, this lovely house, my garden, to end up in a tiny flat, alone, all our friends forced to take sides, Romain's career finally burnt to ashes.*

I have to stop Matthias, somehow.

It's the dead of the night. Romain is asleep upstairs and I'm down in the kitchen with a pen and notebook. The guests have gone, leaving a sparkle in the air, an energy the house has lacked in months. Even Romain went to bed in a good mood.

Leila suggested I compose a gratitude list. She said it helped her get through the tricky 'midlife' period. I write:

Persephone
A Mayfair home.
An enviable job

The trouble is, everything I write makes me feel comforted and happy, shadowed by a fear that it could be taken away from me.

CHAPTER EIGHTEEN

Alice

It's 7:30 on a Friday night. I come in from work so tired I don't even make it to my kitchen for a much-needed cup of tea. I just lie on the sofa, face-down on the leather.

Mina is working me so hard. That said, she looked exhausted too today. I know she suffers from insomnia. She had another panic attack this morning; it was early, no one else in, and I guided her to the toilets. She held my hand tightly and when her breathing had softened, I pulled her into a tight hug, whispering, 'There, there,' as though our ages were reversed. God knows what triggered it; she'd been looking at her phone.

Finally, I drag myself up and release my birds. As Mimi flies out, she cries, 'Murderer!'

I freeze. The word makes my blood run cold.

'Where did you learn that?' I ask quietly.

'Murderer! Murderer!'

Mimi picks up words from time to time, from the TV, from a phone call, but usually she has to be trained, a word repeated over and over, before she learns it.

I gaze around my flat uneasily. Has someone been in here? Dominic? But I changed the locks. Has Mina given my key to anyone? Sarah, maybe? I head over to my new bookcase, which I just picked up on Freecycle, a lovely oak affair which a local posh family were giving away before moving to Spain.

Wasn't *The Cry of the Owl* originally on the top shelf? Or I am just being paranoid?

Home is supposed to be a refuge of peace and comfort. When will I ever be able to settle into this place?

I boil some spaghetti and stir in a tin of discounted tomatoes, and sit with it on my lap in front of the TV.

My mobile buzzes and I hope it might be Sean—

Hi, it's Aimee, how are you?

Oh. It's . . . the fake Aimee. The mystery girl who turned up at my flat.

Hi I reply crossly. You left my flat in a bit of a state!

Really sorry about that – I meant to clear up but my dad called with an emergency.

I'm about to type back *I know you're not Aimee* but I hesitate. I think Dominic might have sent her to look for the 'murder' letter he's convinced Julia wrote. If I play along, she might let something slip.

No worries I type back. How is everything?

I'm great.

I'm about to reply, when I see little bubbles appearing.

Actually, I'm not OK. I'm feeling sad.

I get you I reply, faking empathy. Life is hard for me too right now. Well, there's the good and the bad. I pause. What's your bad?

Everything. The unfairness of life. I just wish there was a system of justice. That life was like the Marvel movies and the bad really did get punished. Or even if karma existed . . .

I feel sick with unease. Is she ventriloquising Dominic? I imagine him sitting next to her, expelling his anger through her. I wait for her to start up about inheritances and stolen flats, but instead she says: I went into the woods last month. I saw where he died.

Now I'm confused. I think back to the article she left

behind, the scrap of headline curled on the bedside table. I tried googling it but I couldn't find out anything, and just assumed it was litter she wanted me to dispose of.

Who? I type.

Chris Jones.

Who's he? What happened to Chris?

There's the truth and there's the propaganda. You must know that.

I hesitate, scrambling through memories, trying to understand how I might know him. I can't think of anyone I've ever met by that name.

Please explain . . .

There's a long pause.

I try again: How did Chris die?

He was murdered.

I type How? then delete it and write: Who murdered him?

As I wait, the dread mounts, but then my WhatsApp shows her new status: Last seen today at 20:03. Maybe she lost reception . . .

Five minutes goes by, then ten, and I realise she's gone.

Now I feel completely lost. Is this all some elaborate story Dominic's concocted to wind me up?

I shake my head at Mimi. 'Just what the hell was all that about?'

And Mimi replies: 'Murderer!'

CHAPTER NINETEEN

Mina

Where's Romain?

He's already ten minutes late. I decide I'll order wine, even though it's normally Romain's prerogative; he tends to fuss for ages over the menu, asking the waiter questions to show off his expertise. I pick a bottle of Vin de Constance. I'm in the mood to celebrate.

I've won the war.

Matthias has been defeated. He's not going to post that photo. He's not coming after me. The Feeld chapter in my life is closed. I'm sure I'll look back on it in a few years with fondness, disbelief, maybe treasure it as a wild adventure, but for now it feels as if I've narrowly avoided a car crash.

Tonight signifies a fresh start. Leila was right about making a gratitude list. My life is overflowing with wonderful gifts: an enviable job as a publisher, a beautiful house worth millions, a gorgeous cat, a husband who's – well, we have some issues to work out, but so do all couples. We've been together over twenty years.

Leila suggested putting aside one night a week for a date night was a good idea, so that's what I've planned tonight.

Where are you? I message Romain. I send him a photo of the bottle of wine, as a provocation.

When my phone buzzes, I smile in relief. But it's not my husband, it's Aimee.

She wants money, another £100. I sigh, tucking her message away for later.

A message from Romain, at last: Sorry, Mi, can we cancel dinner? I've got a crisis.

I bite my lip as the waiter comes up, and order a salad for my starter, telling him my guest is a little late.

I glance around the restaurant. At couples and groups of friends eating together, laughing together; I sip more wine, suddenly feeling very alone. *Be grateful*, I remind myself, *that you can afford to feel lonely in a place this expensive—*

Fuck it.

Fuck gratitude.

Sometimes you can't manifest things. Sometimes you can't force life to bend the way you want. Sometimes you have to face harsh reality.

Do you fancy coming out tonight for dinner? I message Leila. Sorry such short notice.

She replies five minutes later: So sorry hon I'd have loved to but just putting the kids to bed and Ian's not back till late this eve xxx

I pour more wine and scroll through my contacts . . . Alice. I sit up. I've socialised with her a few times and enjoyed it, but since we work together, I don't want to get too chummy. But a recklessness is coming over me, that familiar feeling that propelled me to go on Feeld on the first place. And so I text her.

She replies almost immediately: Love to!

By the time Alice arrives, twenty minutes later, I've eaten little of my salad and drunk far too much of the wine. She greets me with a hug and a big smile and as she sits down, I feel glad I've invited her. The feeling is compounded when her eyes moon at the menu. I tell her it's all on me, savouring her breathless excitement. Alice, I observe with envy, really does have gratitude.

'Are you okay?' Alice asks, picking up on my mood.

'Yes.' I try to force a smile, but it wilts. Suddenly I'm tired of trying to maintain an act. I want to confide in Alice, connect with her. 'No.' I let out a sigh. 'Romain and I – we're going through a difficult patch in our marriage.'

For a moment I worry that Alice is far too young to empathise with midlife marital crises, but then I realise I'm just patronising her.

'Relationships are hard,' Alice says. 'Me and Sean – we're good, but at the same time, we're not good.'

I grin, for she's summed up my marriage too.

Someone in my eyeline makes me start: a fair-haired man leading a woman to a table. He looks familiar: is that . . . *Jacob?* I reassure myself: *It's not him, it's just your guilt talking,* and turn back to Alice.

'Sorry – I just thought I saw someone I know. So how did you and Sean meet?' I ask, leaning forward.

'When I was only eighteen,' says Alice. 'He was working in a bar in Mile End and he served me Guiness all night, and he took my number.' She smiles fondly at the memory. 'We moved in together, at his parents' house in Guildford. We couldn't afford to rent our own place. We were happy together for six years. It was all going really well – and then one night he said he needed to talk. I actually thought he was going to propose. Instead, he dumped me.'

She laughs, shaking her head, but I sense how much it hurt her.

'The bastard,' I say.

'Well, we were young,' Alice says.

'I was young when I met Romain,' I say. 'I was only seventeen.'

'Really?' Alice looks fascinated.

'He was an MP. He came to our sixth form to give a talk about politics, inspire more women to get involved. I was at a girls' school and the entire class was swooning over him.'

'But . . . isn't that – a bit like – grooming?' Alice looks concerned.

'Not at all,' I smile. 'I was the one who chased him. I knew what I wanted. He had a wife, though.' I chew my lip. 'It was all a bit of a mess. What about you and Sean – how did you get back together?'

'Sean went to Spain for a few years,' Alice says. 'He met a guy out there and they moved in together. He thought he was gay – but eventually realised he was bi. When it came to an end, Sean moved back to London, and he got in touch – it was just after Julia had died and he really helped me work through the grief. He's grown up a lot, and now he says he wants us to be serious – but the trust was broken before, and I don't know if I can . . .'

'I understand.' I nod, drinking more wine, filling her glass too.

'Has Romain ever . . .?'

'Oh God, no,' I say. Our main courses arrive, trout for me, a goat's cheese tart for her. –

I become aware that the Jacob lookalike is approaching. He starts at the sight of me. Oh God. It's him.

'Uh, hi – um, Alice,' he says, fishing for the fake name I gave him.

I glare at him. 'I think you must be mistaken,' I assert.

'No – I think we – had that date in your friend's flat . . . but your hair was a different . . . colour.'

'I have no idea what you're talking about.'

'Right,' he agrees, his face flushed. 'Well, sorry about the misunderstanding.' And he hurries away to the gents'.

I turn back to Alice, shaking my head. 'How weird.'

'Who was he?' Alice asks softly.

'He . . . just . . .' I realise Alice isn't going to be fooled by any bullshit excuses. And suddenly I'm overwhelmed by an urge to confide in her, a driving pressure to release all this anguish and shame and confusion; my intellect tells me to shut up and save it for someone I know better, like Leila.

But I know that Leila will judge me. Leila believes utterly in monogamy, til death do us part. Maybe the wine is making me foolish, but I have a feeling that Alice will understand.

'He's an ex,' I say. 'I'm the one who's cheated. On Romain.' I almost relish the shocked look on her face. 'With a younger man.'

'What happened?' she asks slowly. 'You just met someone . . .?'

'I just wanted to feel – I wanted someone young and alive and full of hope, who'd make me feel good about myself. It wasn't just one younger man, it was a few – a few flings here and there.' I stop short, worried Alice might be disgusted.

'Good for you,' she says. 'I think you did the right thing.'

And to my surprise, she chinks her glass against mine.

'They were in hotels,' I say, suddenly concerned she'll realise the real reason I rented her flat. 'And I had trouble with one man, Matthias – he actually took a photo of me. I only just stopped him posting it.'

'Fuck, that's scary.'

Without naming Howard, I tell her that I found out Matthias owed taxes. 'I called him up, pretending to be from HMRC, telling him his payment plan was void and he had to pay it all back at once. He eventually guessed it was me, but it was enough for him to be freaked. I hit him where it hurts. He backed off, sent me the photo, promised he'd deleted it and apologised. I told him that if he still had it, if he ever dared to post it, I'd use my contacts and ensure he ended up bankrupt.'

'You're brilliant!' Alice laughs, her eyes bright. 'That's so smart. God, I wish I could get rid of my stalker with that style.'

'I can always give you access to my lawyer,' I offer her, a little puzzled by her inability to handle it. 'I also have a contact in the force, Mike Connelly. I could put in a call to him.'

'Thank you,' she says, sounding a little vague. 'So, are you going to keep taking revenge on Romain?'

Revenge – a weird choice of word, I think blurrily, sipping more wine. 'Oh, no, it's over now. The guilt was getting to me. I wanted to compartmentalise it, the way men do, but . . . I couldn't quite.'

'But maybe Romain is just as bad . . .'

'He isn't,' I insist firmly. 'He wouldn't cheat on me.'

There's a funny sort of pause and I frown uneasily, sensing Alice is about to say something I don't want to hear. I try to signal to the waiter, to interrupt the moment, but she blurts out: 'He tried to kiss me, when I was at your house for dinner. I needed to borrow money to get home, if you remember? I stopped him, I swear, but . . .'

I feel as though she's shot a bullet into my heart. This doesn't sound like Romain.

'I think you're mistaken,' I hear my voice rising. 'Romain just wouldn't do that. Not just for me – but for his career. He is scrupulous about not making mistakes.'

'I'm really sorry.' Alice takes a big, frantic glug of wine. I narrow my eyes. She did look as though she was nurturing a crush on him, that time that she came to dinner.

'Maybe I was mistaken,' she goes on. 'I mean, he was very drunk.'

There's a long silence and then I hear myself saying that it's time to get the bill.

Monday morning and Sarah's returned after her bout of Covid. As she sets down my coffee on my desk, I feel relieved to have her back.

Sarah might be a little lazy at times, and that business with Alice's flat was odd. But I know who she is. Her godfather, Roland, was my first boss. When I glance through my office window at Alice, I suffer a sense of vertigo, disorientation.

Romain and I had a busy weekend. He wanted to make up for missing our dinner and whisked me out for a lovely breakfast at the Ivy. My mood thawed; I even managed a flash of gratitude. Then we met with his parents for lunch and a walk on Box Hill. On Saturday evening, we went to the theatre to see *Hamlet*; we had front-row seats, and both of us were moved to tears by the end.

On the way home, in the Uber, I gathered the courage to ask him upfront: 'Did you kiss Alice, when she came to dinner?'

He jumped and then laughed, curling his arm around me. 'Of course not – if anything she was the one who seemed to be flirting with me all night – I gave her the money and she tried to kiss me. I stopped her, she apologised and said she was drunk. And that was that.'

I felt relief course through me, followed by the sting of shame. Here was Romain, fending off young women; here was me, indulging in one-night stands with young men. That said, we didn't make love that night, as I'd hoped. But we cuddled up tight and he told me he loved me for the first time in months.

Now, as I watch Alice sitting reading her Kindle, I feel confused, and foolish. Why the hell did I open up to her? It was the drink that did it, and my vulnerable mood. I watch Sarah watching her too, her expression seething with jealousy. I still haven't got to the bottom of why Sarah went to her flat, and what she was looking for.

'What do you think of her?' I ask.

'She's lovely,' Sarah says, looking down. 'Working-class. Great.'

'Yes, yes,' I roll my eyes. 'But what do you think of *her*? Be honest.'

'She lies,' Sarah says eventually. 'There's that degree she claims she got from Warwick.'

Yes, I think, *and that time she claimed Aimee came to her flat, which was odd.*

'Plus, she boasted to a few people here that she discovered *Those Foolish Things,* trying to take credit for your work.'

I feel a little sheepish about that one. I've been so desperate to have a hit that I did steal her discovery, but it happened to me too when I was an intern.

Once Sarah's out of the office, I call Warwick University.

And I discover that there was no Alice Smart who graduated with a 2:1 in English in the year 2015.

It takes me around twenty minutes of hunting before I find an old photo of her, about ten pages into Google Images, looking younger and fresh-faced. She's wearing a green jumper and a woolly hat and is wielding a spade; I can see it once existed on Green-Fingered Gardeners, a company listed in Surrey.

I call them up. I make up a story that Alice has put them down as a reference.

Heather Perkins promises to call back within a short while, but she needs to check some details first as Alice worked there five years ago.

My heart is beating; my intuition is telling me that something is wrong. I check my Instagram. We've put up three videos now; each has had about 3,000 views. When we first set up our #PublishingJourney Romain had wanted to run more checks on Alice, but I vouched for her. My usual judgement has been wobbly; I've been hazed by insomnia, distracted by affairs, by my issues with Romain, and Alice seemed the perfect protégée.

A call on my phone. It's Heather.

'To be honest, I'm surprised that Alice put us down as a reference . . .'

I bite my lip, recalling that I made that up to justify my digging.

'. . . because she was dismissed for theft. I'm afraid that we had to contact the police, but we decided not to press charges in the end. However, we did let her go.'

'Oh,' I say, in shock. 'I see.'

'The theft wasn't a one-off – it took place over a period of time. However, given the fact that Alice is a rather vulnerable individual . . .' Heather trails off.

I jump: Alice is hovering outside my door, carrying a latte from Starbucks as though it's the Crown Jewels.

I shout, 'Come in,' and she places it down with a beaming smile.

I smile back, feeling lost. Normally I'm a good judge of character, but Alice has blindsided me.

Who is she?

CHAPTER TWENTY

Alice

Five Years Earlier

We've chosen a night when the moon has waned to a sliver, ready to renew itself in a few days' time. Tonight is my test, a chance to show him that I'm worth his investment. It's nearly midnight. We walk down the alleyway together, the one that bisects lines of suburban houses in Sutton; we walk hand-in-hand, as he says that it's a good cover story: a couple in their twenties, on their way home from the pub after seeing a movie, happy, a bit tipsy.

Number 38 is right at the end of the street. It's detached, cut off from the others by a tall, unkempt hedge and an over-grown oak in the front garden. My heart is beating violently: this is it, it's finally happening.

He gives my hand a squeeze: a silent *good luck*. Then he strolls back to the alley, where he'll have a smoke and call up a friend, chatting casually as he waits for me.

I approach the house, cross the litter-strewn front garden, follow the path round, click open the back gate.

I pause outside the back door, glancing around at the neighbours' houses, the odd square of light. My hair is tied back in a ponytail and I'm wearing jeans, a black jumper; I look nondescript. He wouldn't even let me wear any makeup.

If anyone comes, I'll say I heard a noise and thought I should be a good Samaritan and check all was okay.

The back door doesn't budge. Fuck – it's supposed to be unlocked. Maybe we can abort: relief washes over me. Then I try again, giving it a shove and the stiff door suddenly bursts open and I nearly fall into the kitchen.

I close the door, glancing around, making out a kettle, a sink, a draining board. There's a lot of clocks in the house: I can hear overlapping ticking, incessant, like mechanical insects, making me nervous. Why bother with them when you can just use your mobile?

I tiptoe down the hallway, turn off into the living-room. There's light pollution from a street-lamp, which illuminates the row of books on the shelves. *Great Expectations* . . . *Persuasion* . . . Here it is – *Jane Eyre*. I pull it out. A green cover, boards nearly coming off the spine, and it seems so shabby I wonder if it can be the right copy. But I check the shelves. There are no other *Jane Eyre*s.

I think I've completed my first task.

The second one is the harder one.

I go into the hall, carrying my book, and climb the stairs, very slowly, one at a time.

On the upstairs landing, I stop. Two bedrooms. A bathroom. A separate toilet. Dave told me that she uses the toilet regularly. And so I do as instructed: I go into the bathroom and wait behind the door. It's so old-fashioned: a bath, no shower, an old pea-green mat on the floor. I wait five minutes, my heart finally calming – and then I hear her.

The creak of the bed. Her shuffle on the carpet. The toilet door closing. The squeak of her thighs on the toilet seat.

This is my moment. I cross the hallway, into her bedroom, and slip under the bed. The carpet is old and threadbare. I feel an itch come over me, ignore fears of bugs and bites. I press my hands against the thin mattress, unable to see, only feel. I can hear her coming out of the toilet, the noise of the sink as she washes her hands. I begin to feel frantic – I can't find anything and I need to hurry, she'll be back any moment.

Then my hands hit something. Paper. Notes. *The money*. I pull out a fat bundle from the slats, triumph beating in my chest – I found it. I passed the second test.

Now I just need to get out of here—

I'm too late. The woman is shuffling back into the room. She climbs into bed with a faint moan; I feel the mattress bulge through the slats against my body.

It's then I realise. It all falls into place – the clocks, her slow gait. Dave never told me that she was elderly. He claimed she was a cheat, that she deserved to have money stolen – but God, she must be nearly eighty, and if I take this, she might not be able to heat her house this winter.

Sweat pricks my eyelids. My breathing sounds so loud and shaky in my ears. I just pray that she's deaf and falls asleep fast.

One of my hands is aching, thick with the book I'm holding. The other is curled around the wadge of notes.

I can't take this money, but how will Dave react? How long will he let me stay with him if I don't come back with the goods? I've seen flashes of his temper, more and more recently. He always says sorry, that he gets frustrated easily, but they scare me. And now he's out there, waiting in that alley, getting cold, impatient. This was supposed to take fifteen minutes max.

A few minutes pass and I hear a snore.

I shuffle my body out from under the bed and, very slowly, I get to my feet.

And then I make the mistake of banging the book against something – something wooden, which clatters to the floor.

Her eyelids flutter open.

I gasp.

I freeze.

She reaches for her walking stick, swings it at me—

My fist is full of notes. I release them, scattering them over her, over the bed, and I hear her gasp in confusion, and I grab the moment, and I run.

Down the stairs, down the hall, out through the back door, wrenching it shut.

I slam through the back gate, and across the lawn—

And I see the houses and I remember that Dave said, 'Don't run, don't panic, that will just draw attention to yourself.'

And so I walk as fast as I dare, past the parked cars and neat lawns, back to the alley, gasping his name.

He flings down his cigarette, and grabs the book from me, shoving it into his rucksack. 'Just stay calm,' he whispers, and we walk up, over the bridge to the station, where we join a few people on the platform, getting the last train back into London. I hear the distant sound of sirens, and I tense up, but Dave shakes his head sharply.

On the train, we chat about the film we've supposedly seen, and Dave says it was so frustrating to see the kids throwing popcorn, and that Cruise never seems to age, and I nod in agreement as my sweat dries on my skin.

We have to approach our home the same way that I did the woman's house, going round through the back. Dave says this place is owned by a Russian businessman who just bought it and then fucked off and doesn't care. We broke in three weeks ago. We live day by day, never knowing how long we have. It's luxurious but we can't get the boiler to work.

The moment we get inside, he demands the full story.

'I couldn't get the money,' I cry. I tell him I only found a few notes, that she threatened me with her stick and I dropped them in panic. His eyes are narrowed, and then his hands slide over my body. I'm terrified, but then I realise this is not about sex: he thinks I'm hiding it. He makes me strip to my underwear to prove I have nothing before he'll believe me.

Thank God for the book: as I get dressed, I see him pull it out of his rucksack and handle it lovingly, his eyes glowing.

'So it's worth a lot?' I ask, wanting him to reassure me that yes, I passed the test. He shrugs, and I sense I'm on probation.

Later that night, I slip into bed, and he gets into his sleeping bag on the floor beside me. He says he can't sleep on a bed: he grew up sleeping on boards and that's what he's used to. I listen to him snoring and stay awake, fretting. I have to impress Dave, but I'm furious that he tricked me; he must have known that if he'd mentioned she was elderly I would never have gone through with it. And yet, and yet: only a few months ago, I was suffering long, freezing, frightening nights on the streets, and I can't ever go back to that. Even prison would be preferable. At least there would be a roof over my head, a bed, hot meals.

When I'm sure that he's fallen asleep, I climb out of bed, go downstairs and I check his cagoule, draped over a kitchen chair. I've been daring myself to do this for weeks; now I feel bold from the theft. I pull out his wallet, check his ID, discover his real name: not Dave, but Dominic.

Dominic Forde.

CHAPTER TWENTY-ONE

Alice

I love commuting in the mornings, being part of the middle-class herd. It affirms to me that Dominic and I have taken different paths as I leave him behind to linger by my flat, playing Candy Crush. Once we were partners in crime; it was Julia's death that separated us. I'm building a real life now. Trying to make amends.

But there are times when I gaze around the office and think, *These are exactly the sort of people I once watched in cafés, whose houses I invaded and stole from.* The ones Dom and I once derided as posh cunts, with easy lives. Now I can see they're decent human beings, and come with their own frailties. Nearly everyone in the office seems to be suffering from some kind of trauma beneath their shiny personas. Beth suffered from anorexia as a teenager and is still struggling to put on weight. Jimoke developed OCD during the pandemic, and hair loss, and is having EMDR treatments to recover. Jerry is trans and has suffered online abuse. Half the office is in therapy. I wonder if I should try it too – if I could ever afford it – but I feel a certain terror at the thought of cracking open those painful areas, letting all the darkness come seeping out.

PTSD is a word they'd probably used to describe my mental state after Dominic. From his abuse, from the person he made me, from the poverty and the hunger, from the crime, the theft. And the murder that I was forced to commit. I have to face up to that. I wept for days for the person I killed. And yet flashbacks will jump out at me suddenly: as I go into the office kitchen and make a coffee, see my fingers curled around the mug, I'll suddenly see them splayed out across her neck, feeling the pulse of life underneath, remembering how I crushed it out of her. Every time I hear a police siren, when I'm in the office, on the street, I feel a fear twist inside me, and a relief when it fades.

That life, the sins I've committed, belongs to the old me. Now I'm the new Alice, in a flat worth £2 million, ready to become a rising star in publishing.

Except: there's something wrong with Mina.

'Hello, Mina,' I say brightly. It's Monday morning and I was the first in the office as always.

'Hi.' She grimaces, her voice like ice.

'Hey,' Sarah greets me. I watch her go into Mina's office. I feel pain in my gut. Mina's gone so cold on me.

When I told her that her husband had tried to kiss me, her reaction was calm and measured, though I did see something flash in her eyes. I just felt she deserved to know the truth. We were both drunk, both confessing.

Now I regret it.

I'm wearing the very suit she gifted me a month back; suddenly it feels scratchy and uncomfortable. Is this just about Romain? Am I a toy she's got tired of? Is it because our #PublishingJourney videos are starting to become a little embarrassing? Our fans have divided into #TeamMina and #TeamAlice, and it's turned into an online class war: if you're a *Daily Telegraph* reader and shop at Fortnum & Mason you support Mina; if you're a worker bee struggling with the cost of living you support me.

Panic fills me. I'm always first in the office, I work the hardest, yet I'm a ghost without a salary. What do I have to do to secure a job? What am I missing?

I stare down at the bundle of leaflets in our main office space. *OPEN MIC*, it says. *A night of poems, readings, music and fun!* It's tonight.

I can't go, I reason, hope dying inside me. Sean is back tonight after weeks away in Berlin. It's our precious reunion.

And then I watch Sarah leave Mina's office and return with a coffee. I glance back at the leaflet, a plan forming in my mind.

'Can I have a tap water?' I ask the man serving at the bar. I couldn't ask Sean to lend me any money. We had a row before I left the flat for the open mic night. All I have is £3 in my pocket.

The barman gives me such a sarcastic look that I relent and ask for a Coke.

The open mic is being held at a pub in Shoreditch. The compere gets up on stage. He's called Gary Kit and he's one of those extravert types who relish being in the spotlight, cracking bad jokes every other sentence. But he does a good job of bigging up the performers.

On comes a poet, bespectacled and foppish, wearing a trendy tie.

'My poem tonight will be about a time when I was so depressed, I no longer felt like washing . . .' He clears his throat.

Oh God. I groan inwardly. I fought with my boyfriend for this? Our row ended with a compromise: I'd go for an hour max. Sean was hurt that I was so ready to desert him on his first night back; he complained I was putting my career first. I swore it wasn't the case, but deep down I fear he's right: as much as I love Sean, it is my number-one concern right now.

A guy bangs into me, splashing my Coke onto my jeans.

'Oh God, I'm sorry,' he says.

'Don't worry,' I say tersely. Audience members look over, distracted from the reading. The poet pauses. I blush.

'Really, really sorry,' he whispers. He has a slight accent; it reminds me of Romain. He grabs a napkin, passes it to me.

'It's fine.' I'm slightly mollified by the fact that he's so good-looking. He's got thick black hair that licks over his forehead, hazel-green eyes and a big, warm smile.

As we listen to the next few acts, I feel conscious of his presence next to me. Every time someone does a bad reading we roll our eyes in a surreptitious pact of embarrassment.

In the break, he says, 'Look, let me buy you a drink, after I ruined your jeans.'

'Thank you! Just a Coke . . .' He raises an eyebrow, and I say impulsively: 'Okay, I'll go wild. Add some rum.'

He gets us drinks and guides me into an intimate corner.

'I'm Lucas, by the way,' he says.

'I'm Alice.' His handshake lingers, deliciously.

'Are you reading tonight?'

His eyes are so dark, I notice. He's one of those people who holds your gaze instead of looking away.

'Oh, no,' I reply. 'I'm actually a junior editor at Principle Publishing, so I'm seeking new authors.' Just a slight exaggeration.

'Wow.' His eyes moon. 'I'm reading this evening, actually . . .'

'Oh, that's great,' I enthuse.

I take a sip from my drink, aware of his eyes caressing

my lips. There's a frown on his face and he hesitates before speaking.

'Actually,' he blurts out, 'your imprint rejected me, about six months ago. It was a standard email.'

'Ah.' I feel disappointed.

As the break ends and the second half begins, the compere bounds up: 'And now for Lucas Chamila, reading the opening of his novel-in-progress.'

Lucas flashes me a nervous smile and, on impulse, I give him a hug of support. 'Good luck!'

He stands behind the mic, leonine under the golden spotlight. He has such presence . . . but I'm convinced that I'll soon be cringing.

'So, tonight I'd like to read from my novel, *Playthings*. I've been working on it for five years. It's a kind of crime novel about a man who decides to kill his lover, not realising she's already decided to kill him.' He gives a little shrug, grinning at the smattering of applause. 'Okay. Here goes . . .'

And then the magic happens.

I listen, spellbound, tingling all over.

Two hours later, I come out of High Street Kensington station on a high. Sean's already messaged saying that my 'crazy stalker' is hanging around the building, so he'll meet me and walk me back home.

As I come up the escalator, I spot him with his hands in his pockets, tanned and stubbled. He looks tired, grim, a little sad. And I realise how glad I am to have him back after a fortnight apart, how much he *does* matter to me. I fling my arms around him and feel his body melt against mine as we compete to hold each other the tightest.

'Sean, the most amazing thing's happened!' I gabble as we

walk onto the high street. I want him to know that delaying our reunion was worth it. I explain that I just discovered an amazing new talent. 'He's emailing me his book. I told him a bit of a white lie – he thinks I'm an editor at Principle.'

I wait for Sean to tease me, but he looks worried. 'You need to be careful of your boss, though – what if she nicks your work again?'

'Yeah, you're right – I need to come up with a plan,' I agree, a little disappointed. I know Sean feels jealous of my passion for my new job, but his takes him away all the time and I've had to learn to put up with that.

As we turn onto Marloes Road, the street-lamp illuminates a harlequin silhouette of amber and shadow. Dominic's leaning against the wall, waiting.

'What is it with him?' Sean asks, slowing down. 'How many months has he been doing this now? Before I went to Berlin, you promised me you were going to report him to the police.'

'I know, I know, I've just been so busy with work and—'

'Alice! This is out of control. I mean – is it just about the flat? Is he obsessed with you romantically or something?'

'God no,' I protest. 'He just . . .' I lower my voice as we get closer to Dominic.

As we walk past, he makes sex noises and a blush sweeps over my face. I guess the subtext: he's seen the video of me and Sean making love. I think he was the one who switched it on that night, before I first started as an intern, and I feel a rise of anger, at the fear, the loss of sleep I suffered.

'Fuck off,' Sean says to him.

Dominic just carries on.

'I said *fuck off*.' Sean turns on him. Sean rarely loses his temper, but when he does, it's a sudden, shocking combustion.

It all happens so quickly I can't digest it: Sean's fist swinging, the *thwack* of bone against bone, Dom's nose bleeding, flecks raining down on his cagoule.

'You cunt!' Dominic yells, his fingers on his nose, blood soon smeared everywhere. 'You bloody punched *me*? Your girlfriend *murdered* my mum – and now I'm homeless, and you want to own the fucking streets?'

We're attracting attention. This isn't the sort of consternation that occurs on this sort of street. I recognise a woman from one of the flats below mine walking past me with her cockapoo, giving me a look that's half horrified, half reproachful, as if to say: *Must you bring this here?*

I tug at Sean and hiss, 'Let's just leave him alone and get out of here.'

Sean is breathing hard and looking shocked. I drag him into Chesterton House, Dominic's insults hurled at our backs.

Up in my flat, I make cups of tea, adding extra sugar. I keep flitting to the window. Dominic's disappeared, but I dread the arrival of a police car, officers knocking at the door.

Sean's sitting on the sofa, rubbing his knuckles, which look raw and flayed. I pass him his tea and then gulp mine, burning my tongue.

'We should go to the police.' Sean puts down his mug, splashing droplets across the table. 'We should go right now.'

No, my heart screams in protest. *No.* I can't have them digging into my past, my history, what happened with Julia.

'They could charge you with assault! That's the last thing we should do,' I argue.

'I was protecting you,' Sean fires back, but he looks meek. He knows that my father was an aggressive man, that any sort of male violence leaves me sick and shaken. He grabs my hand, massaging my fingers. 'I'll be staying tonight – I can stay the week if necessary . . . He'll back off then.'

I love Sean for being protective, but I'm already fretting. *What do I do if Mina wants to rent my flat?*

We settle down with old episodes of *Fawlty Towers* in an attempt to laugh away our stress. I let my birds out; Mimi loves Sean, whom she seems to have bonded with since first setting her avian eyes on him. She sits on his shoulder, sometimes mimicking his laugh or a stray phrase, which tickles us both.

'Murderer!' Mimi chants. 'Murderer!'

'Where did she pick that up?' Sean asks.

'A crime show, I think,' I reply nervously.

'Murderer!' Sean chants back at her, making it all a joke. But from time to time I see him rubbing his red knuckles. There are still a few flecks of Dominic's blood on them.

As Sean switches off the TV, I can feel the energy between us. We haven't made love for two weeks; we can't let Dominic ruin the night. I lie back on the sofa as he sets up the video camera, the red light blinking. I can feel the tremble in his kisses, the aftershock of the fight still rippling through us: the sound of that punch, the blood. Kissing me, whispering that he loves me, he unzips my trousers, pulls them down. I feel more self-conscious than usual of the camera, as though it's a spyhole and we're being watched. I picture Dominic behind the lens and shudder, then close my eyes, forcing the image away, as Sean's kisses whisper down my body, and then he's moving inside me, and I lose myself in him.

When Sean goes to the bathroom to shower, I check my emails and see that Lucas has already emailed his book over to me. His email is signed off with Lucas xx Settling on the sofa, I open the manuscript on my Kindle, hoping and praying that the book's going to live up to the promise of those first few pages.

But before I can even start there's the sudden sound of a siren and my body grows taut with fear, my heartbeat flurrying as it comes closer and closer – and then it passes, quietens, and I let out a shaky breath and start reading.

PART III

Police Report: Interview with Jean Winters

4 October 2024

DS Matthews: Can you tell us about any previous incidents with Alice Smart?

Jean Winters: Well, the number of times I saw *men* going in and out – and the sounds of – *you know* – I did even wonder if Alice was a – *you know*. But apparently she worked in publishing.

DS Matthews: But were there any other strange happenings, looking back?

Jean Winters: Well, that's why I think he decided to investigate, you know. He was concerned. He was upright, a good man. That's why I gave him a key. Maybe I shouldn't have.

DS Matthews: I'm a little confused . . .

Jean Winters: Sorry, my head's all of a muddle.

DS Matthews: Can you clarify who you gave the key to?

CHAPTER TWENTY-TWO

Mina

I'm not looking forward to firing Alice. Normally I don't mind letting someone go, if it's necessary: it's business. But I do feel a wrench. I've grown so fond of her. I'm nervous too, given that I've confided my secrets in her. But I think I've come up with a way to keep her quiet.

Romain's not happy either. We're standing in the Terrace bar at the House of Commons, sipping drinks, quiet and terse. The #PublishingJourney was really starting to pay off; Romain's popularity ratings are picking up. Now he's scared that we'll be seen as ruthless and capricious, picking Alice up and dropping her. But if we keep her on, she could become a liability: we can't win.

'I think I'll head home,' I say, setting down my glass with a bang.

'I'll stay a little longer,' Romain says.

'Fine.'

He leans in to kiss me, to keep up the public show – MP with his devoted wife – but I turn away abruptly and walk out.

I stand opposite Westminster Abbey in the twilight, waiting for my Uber and arguing with Romain in my head: *I don't know why I'm always to blame for everything . . .*

An uneasy feeling comes over me. I turn and see a glint of fair hair, someone in the shadows. It's Alice.

'Hi.'

'Hi – wow, it's good to bump into you!'

I frown at her show of theatrical surprise. Westminster seems such an unlikely place for us to bump into each other.

'Did you follow me?' I ask her outright. My Uber has pulled up and I wave at the driver, who looks impatient. 'Alice, it's ten at night. I'm heading home.'

'I'm sorry. I just – I overheard you telling Charles you were drinking at the House of Commons tonight. I didn't realise the security would be so tight . . .' She nods over at the queue of people waiting to be let in with a pass.

She looks so contrite that I feel a tug of empathy and remind myself sharply she can't be trusted.

'Look – come back with me,' I relent. 'Let's talk back at mine.'

We sit in the back of the Uber in silence. I tell myself this is a good thing. It will force me to tell her she's fired.

At home, Persephone greets me and I guide Alice into the kitchen, making a fresh mint tea for us both. As I open the cupboard, I spot a box of Fortnum & Mason chocolates that someone gifted me and which have been sitting there since Christmas. I offer one her, then sit down next to her.

'Alice—'

'Mina – the reason I wanted to talk to you is because I've discovered the most *incredible* author,' she bursts out. 'He's called Lucas Chamila. I discovered him at an open mic and his novel's the best thing I've ever read. I want us to buy him. I want to edit him.'

'Alice,' I object in horror, then trail off. Fuck. I think of how brilliant the first book that she discovered was. So now what? Do I fire her and steal the book? How the hell would that look on our #Publishingjourney?

As if sensing my turmoil, Alice argues: 'We have a rapport.

He says he wants me to edit him. He won't sign with you if you get rid of me.'

There's a long, awkward pause.

'Are you . . .' Alice's voice drops. 'Are you planning to get rid of me? Is it Sarah? Has she said something?'

'Alice . . .' I take a sip of tea, burn my mouth. God, this is excruciating; trying to get my words out is like a tooth extraction. 'Alice, I spoke to Heather Perkins. She told me about the theft . . . and I'm afraid it's not going to work out for you at Principle Publishing.'

There, I've said it. I don't feel any relief, just a deeper pain.

Alice slumps. I push the chocolates towards her; she laughs incredulously and pushes them back.

'I've arranged for a possible one-week internship with Roland Bentley-Jones,' I say.

'Sarah's godfather? She says he's in his sixties and is the biggest chauvinist ever and his indie is failing. I don't want to go there.'

I'd been hoping Alice would be grateful to have any lifeline, and that she would swear to keep my affairs secret in return for me organising this.

'What if I go on Instagram?' she flares up. 'What if I tell the world just how great my publishing journey has ended up, all because I'm from the wrong class?'

Now anger flares inside me. 'Alice, we've done a lot for you.'

'You've had me as your unpaid slave. I've worked *so* hard. You only want me as your working-class victim if I'm all shiny and perfect – if I turn out to be human, to have had problems, well, that's no good—' Her voice catches with tears and I swallow. 'Hasn't it occurred to you that it's *because* of my background that I stole, and not out of choice, but because I couldn't pay my rent, because Heather was exploiting us all, paying less than the minimum wage, and my internet, my gas were about to be cut off, so I borrowed money from the till. Regularly. I was putting it back, but I know it's wrong. But I was desperate. You have *no* idea,' she carries on in passion. 'You have a security net. You have power, money. You can snap your fingers and make things go away. I had no net. Nothing. After Heather "let me go", I ended up homeless.'

I feel anger flaring up again, if only because her words sting so much: I know that her accusations are true.

'The fact that you took Heather's story on board says it all. You never even asked for my side. You trusted her because she's the woman with the nice accent, whereas you've always been suspicious of me, right from the start, like you've been waiting for me to fail . . .'

'Alice, that's not true!' I protest. But I fear Alice's accusations are accurate, that I'm riddled with prejudice. 'Tell me more – tell me about how you grew up. I want to understand.'

'You want some Dickensian story of poverty, all romanticised. I can't give you that.'

'I know, I know. Tell me your story as you want to tell me.'

Alice draws out her wallet, and lays a few crumpled photos on the table. They look like shots from a Ken Loach drama. In one, Alice looks about thirteen; her blonde hair flows over her bony shoulders. Her younger sister is holding a bike with a missing wheel. Next to them stands her mother, sunburnt in a sundress, a tense smile on her face; and her father, with wavy fair hair, his arms folded, his expression like that of a boxer anticipating his next fight. The backdrop – the huge, horrible building, and the ragged grass – looks like a council estate.

And then Alice tells me her story.

She tells me how she grew up in a cramped flat on the Angell Town Estate. Her dad was in and out of work as a sample box maker, a taxi driver, an odd-job man. When he was out, he'd drink, and the drinking led to fits of frustrated anger, and soon Alice's mum was covering up bruises with excuses and makeup.

Alice was doing well at school, but when she reached the top of her class, it made her father angry. He'd been denied an education by his father. He warned her that if she came home with another A, he'd beat her.

So her grades slid. Alice would cry herself to sleep at night. She turned sixteen; her future looked bleak. Then, in a backlash of fury, she decided to revise like mad for her final exams. She got top marks, and her father put her in hospital – with a black eye that got infected. It was there, staying overnight, that her mother gave her an envelope of cash.

She'd been saving for months. She told Alice she had to change history. She hugged her and cried. She told Alice she'd arranged for her to stay with an old schoolfriend's family, Frieda's. Alice would change schools. Her father wouldn't know. He'd just assume she'd run away.

And so Alice had a fresh start. She missed her mum like mad, but they spoke on a burner phone once a week. Frieda's family grew tired of having her, however. After her A levels, she slid into homelessness, and eventually joined a scheme by Heather Perkins to help homeless people work in her gardens. Heather, she explained, had good intentions, but was disconnected from reality; she barely paid the minimum wage, not realising it wasn't enough to survive on, and became angry when they begged her for a pay rise. 'She wanted to promote herself on Instagram,' Alice said, 'but she didn't really care much for us.'

I blush at that remark.

Alice fell into rent arrears. She borrowed from the till, put it back at the end of the week when she could. But someone else had seen her, reported her to Heather. Heather, who was growing tired of her scheme, dismissed her without pay or notice. Which left Alice homeless again.

Alice looks exhausted by the confession. Suddenly I feel as though I'm on the verge of tears. I reach for her and she looks surprised when I pull her into a tight hug.

When I draw away, she looks awkward and very young. I dab my eyes with a napkin.

'So – can I stay on and edit Lucas? You'll give me a job?'

'Let me talk to Charles,' I say. 'I'll tell him everything. I think it is only fair that you should get a permanent job and edit Lucas – though I'd like to read it first.'

Hope lights up her face, so radiant that I want to hug her again. A rosy glow comes over me. I'm going to give Alice another chance. I'm going to make her my star. I can't let her end up like Aimee. For the first time in a long time, I'm doing some good in the world. When Romain first became an MP, I was full of idealism, keen to support him and care for our constituents, only to discover how hard it is to make a difference when you're a cog in the machine of politics, of power games and hierarchies and rivals and big interests and corporate sponsors. Tonight, I've been humbled. I want to make a difference.

I hear Romain's car pulling into the drive. I frown. I wanted to get Alice out of here before Romain returned.

Staring her straight in the eye, I say in a neutral tone, 'Look, if you're going to work for me, then you'll have to be careful around Romain. He said that you tried to kiss him.'

'*What?*' Alice looks genuinely shocked. 'No! Not at all. *He* tried to kiss *me.*'

I realise that she's telling the truth.

And that, on some level, it doesn't surprise me.

'Forget it,' I say quickly. 'Let's not ruin the moment.'

Alice nods, blinking hard, her face tense as we hear the sound of Romain's key in the lock.

He comes into the kitchen and Alice gives him a polite hello.

'Good evening,' he says smoothly. I picture him trying to kiss Alice. *Bastard.*

'Alice and I had a long chat,' I say. 'And I think we'd like to continue on the publishing journey, wouldn't we, Alice?'

I know that Romain will be furious that I've done this without discussing it with him first; I see the shadow on his face. He always wants the last word on every decision. But he tells us it's a great idea.

'I can give Alice a lift home,' he offers.

I gaze at Alice, checking if she's comfortable with the idea. She gives a small nod.

'Great,' I say brightly.

Jealousy flares, but I push it away, determined not to wreck the moment. This can be a test: if he returns and anything's happened, I'll know. It'll be all over his face and Alice will tell me.

'Bye, Alice,' I say, hugging her tightly.

After they've gone, I regret it. Was Alice telling the truth? I think of them in the car together and a sudden, wild urge comes over me, to hurry upstairs and log in to Feeld—

Madness, I tell myself. I think of Aimee, of the therapist who said impulse control is low in addicts. The ability to resist temptation is a crucial part of getting ahead in life.

I pick up my phone. There's a new email notification that looks like spam, when I notice the subject line: I KNOW WHAT YOU'VE BEEN UP TO WITH THOSE BOYS FROM FEELD, MINA.

A feeling of sick dread comes over me as I read it. I sink down onto a chair, rereading it over and over.

This is a serious blackmail email. They know all about my affairs with younger men.

They want £2,000 by Sunday.

CHAPTER TWENTY-THREE

Alice

I want to whoop and scream at the world, *I've got a job*. But I can't quite believe it. I just hope Mina means it, that she isn't playing me. I crave time to digest the news. As we head out, I tell Romain I'll get the tube.

'Don't be silly,' he insists. 'There's hardly any traffic about at this hour.'

I go to get into the back seat, then realise it makes Romain look like a cab driver, so I walk round to the front. He backs out of the drive, tells me to put on my seatbelt.

'I already have,' I say, crossing my arms.

A silence builds between us. I was wondering if he might offer up an apology, given that Mina is now officially my boss. But no: nothing. I glare over at him. Neon London lights pass over his face, highlighting his chiselled good looks, the high cheekbones, full mouth, dark brows, the sweep of his wavy dark hair. He's so attractive, to an infuriating degree. I feel wrung out from my emotional session with Mina, and over-sensitive, as though my skin's been rubbed raw. My anger rises and, as we stop at traffic lights, I reach out and slap his cheek.

'Hey!' He turns in outrage. My hand is hovering in the air – I'm shaken by my impulsive behaviour – and he grabs it, holding me tight, ignoring my attempts to pull away. He stares at me and I stare at him and the air burns. For one shocked moment, I think he might kiss me again—

Cars toot behind us.

He lets me go. I fold my fingers in my lap, pressing them between my knees.

'You lied to your wife,' I say. 'Apparently, *I* tried to kiss you.'

'It was selfish, I know,' says Romain, his voice calm. 'I wanted to protect her. We've been married for over twenty years. She would never cheat on me. I didn't want to hurt her.'

I want to laugh in his face at that, but in order to protect Mina, I give him a sullen nod. It's touching that they're both convinced the other would never cheat, or perhaps it's a sign of their vanity.

Romain pulls into Kensington High Street. I'm about to berate him for nearly wrecking my career, when he starts speaking:

'I've been an MP for two decades. I know what you imagine me to be. You think I have power and that I'm a sleaze, that I prey on women. In fact, I've never cheated on Mina in all this time. Seriously – you would know if I had. I'm a public figure.' The click of his indicator as he turns into Marloes Road; Chesterton House looms in the darkness. 'The fact is you have an effect on me that I haven't felt in a very long time. I thought I had – I thought I had lost my – I just – I want you so very badly.' His voice breaks. 'I think about kissing you all the time. I dream about you. I'm besotted.'

He's pulled over outside my block and I sit there, stunned.

'I . . .' I trail off. Romain turns and smiles at me, his eyes sad.

'I didn't mean to make you feel uncomfortable. I wish I

could find the antidote. My father taught me that self-control is everything.'

He slowly runs the tip of his finger down my cheek. A trembling heat shivers over me. Then he draws away, grips the steering wheel. 'I should go back to Mina.'

'I have a boyfriend,' I say in a small, shaky voice.

Neither of us move. I feel as though he's just presented me with an exquisite gift, but I don't want to unwrap it; I can only hold it heavy in my hands. The shadows shift and I suddenly realise that Dominic is outside my flat, watching us.

'Is he your stalker?' Romain asks. 'Mina told me that he was giving you grief.'

I nod. Before I can protest, Romain has got out of the car and strides over to him. I watch as they exchange words. I wait for Dominic to jeer, to taunt, but to my amazement, he walks off. What one earth did he say to pull that off? Romain comes back and opens up my car door like a gentleman. I'm so touched that he got rid of Dominic, I almost want to hug him, but he smiles and says: 'Goodnight, Alice.'

That was all so fucked up, I think. I should be dancing with joy. I'd planned to call up Sean and scream the news down the phone. Now I feel all distracted and churned up. I thought I hated Romain, yet tonight his vulnerability moved me. I'm sure he's fallen for a fantasy version of me, but it's impossible not to feel flattered – unless, of course, he *is* a sleaze and uses that same story with every woman. But he sounded so heartfelt. I stroke my cheek where he caressed me. I rewind to the traffic lights, picture us kissing hard, his hands on my thighs, pushing up my skirt . . .

I don't like Romain but I want to fuck him. He's arrogant and privileged and irritating; the perverse thing is, like a bad romance, this only accentuates my desire. Plus, I have a weakness for father figures, and the way he saw Dominic off was heroic and sexy.

Only a few days ago, I was crushing on Lucas. I remind myself that I'm with Sean, and guilt crawls over me. I don't want to betray Mina, either. She did seem to believe me when I told her that Romain had been the one who tried to kiss me. She's given me a chance and I have to do my very best with it.

I've got a job! I message Sean in the lift to my floor. Mina finally came round!

No reply yet . . .

There's an envelope lying on my doormat, which I pick up as I enter the flat. I tear it open.

A newspaper article drops out.

It's from a local paper, the *Yorkshire News*. It's dated 2001. It reports on the death of Chris Jones, a seventeen-year-old boy who died in a car crash.

What the fuck?

I sink onto my sofa.

Suddenly my new job is forgotten. I think this must have been sent by the fake Aimee. It echoes her texts. But is it an accusation or a cry for help? Is this a story concocted by Dominic to wind me up or have I wronged a real person?

When I google the accident, I can't find anything. I can't recall ever meeting a Chris Jones. That's the trouble with Dominic, with our past: the ripple effect, the pain and chaos we caused. Maybe we robbed Chris. Maybe it triggered a heart attack, a breakdown; maybe he lived for weeks in fear that mounted and mounted until he took a wrong turn and crashed that car. And now this woman, whoever she is, is haunting me.

What will come next? I have a feeling she might want compensation, demand money. She's seen this flat. She'll have debated whether I deserve it. And maybe I don't, I consider, on the verge of tears.

Just when I thought I had something to celebrate, this happens.

I go to bed haunted by memories of the Alice I used to be.

CHAPTER TWENTY-FOUR

Alice

Three Years Earlier

'Tobias? Oh God, please . . . Oh God – *help me*—'

'Jessica? Jessica? What is it, darling?'

'There's been a fire at the offices. When everyone surged out I fell and I'm hurt. Darling, please – please come—'

'What the hell? Oh God, right, I'm coming. Right now. How badly are you hurt?'

Dominic rings off. He fingers the burner phone. The way that he mimicked Jessica's plummy accent is incredible. I punch his shoulder and whisper that he deserves an Oscar.

We discovered Jessica a few weeks ago. A yummy mummy in Hampstead, who lives a perfect life with her husband and their nine-year-old son and teenage daughter in a four-bedroomed house. We followed her to a number of coffee shops, where we sat and listened in as she chatted with her yummy mummy friend, Karen; Dom even recorded her a few times on his mobile. Back at our squat, he'd 'get into character' for an evening, speaking in her voice for several hours.

I suffer a momentary sadness that Dominic isn't on stage, enthralling an audience; that instead we're watching a middle-aged man come running out of his house, jump into his Porsche and drive off at top speed. As he passes, I see tears running down his face, and I feel dirty and mean.

His house has a sweeping gravel drive fringed with a magnolia tree. We find that he's left the back door unlocked in his panic – perfect.

We act quickly. I hurry upstairs; Dom tackles the downstairs. In their double bedroom, I find a dressing table with a jewellery box. I yank out all the bracelets, rings, earrings, throwing them into an Asda carrier.

The next room I enter belongs to their teenage girl. I stop short, gazing at her gorgeous turquoise bedspread, the plump pillows, her walk-in wardrobe—

I hear a car pulling up on the gravel driveway at the same time as Dominic calls my name.

Shit. Tobias is back way too soon. Which means he must have phoned Zoe again, got through and found her completely calm and wondering what the hell her panicked husband was ranting on about.

I tumble down the stairs. At the bottom, I bang my ankle against the bannisters and scream, rubbing the flayed skin.

'Just get the fuck out of here!' Dominic hisses—

In the diamond-patterned windows of the front door, we see a blurred figure approaching, and we both speed to the back door, slam it shut, run down the long length of the garden.

We've done our prep. There's a panel of loose fencing right at the back, from a storm that blew a few days ago, toppled trees, caused a day of train cancellations. We escape through it, out onto a street, and then walk casually, the Asda bag bumping against my thighs.

Three days later we wander through a town in Surrey called Woking.

We've been doing this for two weeks now. Under dark

clouds, under moonlight, under shadows, under rain. We pick a different place each night. We walk and talk in low voices. We look at houses. Quick, casual glances. Places with bushes around them that would shield us as we entered, or old double-glazed windows with beading on the frames, that can easily be prised open, or couples who leave their front door regularly on the latch.

We're starting to trust each other with our pasts. I've told Dominic about my parents, about how I wish I'd had a chance to go to university.

Our mood drifts, becomes dreamy. We start discussing fantasy homes.

'I'd love to live there,' I say, as we pass a detached house with Tudor beams, and a long garden with an apple tree.

Dominic rolls his eyes, scoffing. I explain that it reminds me of Frieda's family, who took me in after I had to leave home as a teenager. A lingering wistfulness for that year: home-cooked family meals, early nights and jolly breakfasts, homework at the kitchen table. Until I was asked to leave, because they claimed that I stole from them.

'They would've chucked you out no matter what you did, you know,' he says, with generosity and condemnation. 'People like that, they love the *idea* of being do-gooders, and philanthropy, and all that, but as soon as they realise it takes money and effort and sacrifice, then they soon lose interest. Easier to run a charity luncheon, right, than actually take care of someone.'

'Yeah,' I say, despondently. Having to leave has left a permanent scar on my heart: it set up the fear that anything good won't last, that if life blesses me, then soon curses will fall.

'So you grew up in West London?' I ask him. I'm picturing

a council flat in Shepherd's Bush. 'Were your parents on benefits too?'

I've been probing for weeks. Suddenly he stops, grabs my hands. I tense up. I've been worried, wondering, what Dominic wants from me, and trying to work out how I feel about him. We sleep in the same room together, we eat together, we steal together. I care for him like a brother. He calls me his partner in crime – but does he desire more?

Then I realise he's inviting me to feel some scars that are riven beneath his hair.

'My mum's responsible for those,' he says casually, and I gape at him in horror. He shrugs. 'I'd rather not go into it . . .' Then he nods at a house. 'Look at that.' He lets out a whistle and I feel a nervous, guilty thrill: we've found our next mark . . .

Back at the squat, I assume that we'll spend the next few days on Google Maps, analysing the street, the neighbours.

In the afternoon, however, Dominic suggests that we go to 'the library'.

'Okay,' I agree in surprise. Dominic's always declared that he hates reading, and the only interest he seems to have in books is selling stolen first editions.

I feel frustrated that he still doesn't trust me enough to tell me more. I never get his plans in full – just pieces of the puzzle.

We get out of the tube at High Street Kensington. We're hungry. We haven't sold the jewellery on yet – Dominic prefers to wait a while, as an immediate sale is risky. It takes half an hour of hanging outside a McDonalds for a dieting teen to come out with a bag of fries, barely eaten, and toss them into a bin. Dom pulls the bag out. A passing woman in a navy coat eyes us in disgust. Her daughter looks puzzled, as though trying to work out why we're monsters whom her mother clearly loathes.

'Posh cunts,' Dominic declares loudly. The woman tugs her daughter on. I gave the little girl a reassuring smile. Dominic's sheer misanthropy still comes as a shock to me. People-watching is our game, but he'll find something bad to say about anyone and everyone – they're fat, they're thin, they're a feminist, they're an idiot. He hates everyone in the world – except me. It's our bond: us versus the universe.

Kensington Library is a fancy place. Dominic leads me to a seat tucked away by a window, and then he points out an old woman sitting at a table.

'Go and make friends with her,' he says.

'We said no elderly people.'

I wait for his sneer. Whenever I argue that they're 'vulnerable', he simply bats it back at me – *so are we*.

'We're not going to steal from her,' he says. 'This is just . . . a test.'

'Okay,' I say uneasily.

On days like today, when our funds are running low and cold chips are churning in my stomach, and I'm still hungry, and thinking of the pies Mum used to make – I feel so desperate, so beaten back by life, that morality seems a luxury. Something I can't indulge in, because life, as Dominic keeps saying, is a survival of the smartest. I think of the way that woman just looked at us, as though we were less than human, and something hardens inside me.

I drift over to the old lady's table, eyeing the pile next to her.

'I must have read *Oliver Twist* six times,' I remark, sitting down next to her.

I'd been expecting her to be grateful for company. But

she looks me over with shrewd eyes. Then she sighs. 'I'm just starting on audiobooks. I much prefer reading, but these days, my eyes . . .'

'What about large print?'

'I've tried it, but it's still not enough.'

'They ought to do huge print,' I empathise, and she suddenly laughs.

'I think it's sad,' I go on, 'that there so many library cuts at the moment.' I just overheard two people with posh voices discussing the subject, so I figure it must be a middle-class concern.

'It's awful.' She shudders in agreement. 'We'll soon be a country of illiterate philistines.'

I glance over at the bookcase Dominic is hiding behind, listening in. He's taught me that when it comes to a con, less is more.

'Well, I should get going,' I get up, pleased to see the disappointment in her eyes.

She looks me up and down. 'I can buy you a cup of tea, if you like,' she says, and her tone irritates me a little, as though she's doing me the favour of a lifetime.

I smile. 'I'm fine.'

Her face drops. She's keen. *Good*: I can hear Dominic's voice of approval in my mind.

'I'll be back tomorrow,' I say. I'm surprised by how grateful her smile is, and it's then that I realise the depths of her loneliness, how this might have been the longest conversation she's had in days.

'Lovely, let's chat then . . .'

'I'm – I'm Alice.' I blurt out my real name in a moment of weakness.

'I'm Julia,' she says. 'Julia Forde.'

I quickly conceal my shock and give her a breezy wave. Outside, I turn on Dominic.

'You could have told me . . . She's your Mum?' I ask.

'Yeah. Shh. Come here.' He pulls back, into a shop, and we watch as Julia shuffles past, then follow her at a distance.

I frown, thinking of the scars I felt on Dominic's skull, a map of abuse. As Julia enters a block of flats, Dominic's eyes gleam.

'Now *there's* a fantasy home,' he says. 'It's where I grew up.'

'But that's . . . that's *posh*.' I use his favourite word. I'm completely confused. 'How come?'

'As a matter of fact, I went to boarding school.'

'You're kidding!'

Dominic's fury for anyone 'loaded' or 'posh' or 'privileged' seems to spew from a raw wound inside him. I'd assumed it came from anger about how the other half live, not because he belonged to that other half.

'Boarding schools are for rich people who can't be bothered to look after their kids. There was this prefect who had it in for me, used to beat me – the masters turned a blind eye.' His chameleon accent is becoming more refined, as though he's back there. 'But I swear, school was better than the abuse I got at home. That's why I ran away, at eighteen.' Now there's a dash of Cockney again.

'I'm sorry,' I say, with feeling. A mistake, I realise, seeing his jaw tighten. Dominic doesn't like pity.

'Imagine . . .' He nods at the grand building. 'Imagine living there together.'

What's he suggesting? I wonder, with a shiver. That we murder her or something?

'The trouble is, I'm not in her will. We've not spoken in years now. And even though she's the fucking abuser, I'm the one who's suffering, because – she's ashamed. I'm a living reminder of what she did. I've got the scars to prove it. But you – you, Alice, you can befriend her. A lonely old woman is an easy target. And then, you'll tell her how family matters, how important it is to make amends, and she'll let me back in . . . She's seventy-one and her health's shit. She'll be gone in a few years. And that flat could be *ours*.'

We stand there for a while, letting the idea take root in us, blossoming fear and excitement.

CHAPTER TWENTY-FIVE

Alice

The *Bookseller* announcement goes up online on Friday morning.

> Newly promoted editorial assistant Alice Smart has bought *Playthings* by Lucas Chamila in a two-book deal for Principle Publishing.

As I dance around my flat, my birds caw and swoop, celebrating with me.

'I did it! I did it!' I cry, pausing to catch my breath. I go into Julia's bedroom, touch the photo of her on the dresser. She would have been so proud of me. I suddenly feel teary with an ache for her to be alive again; I picture us chinking teacups, drinking and laughing together.

Ever since the offer was made to Lucas, I've woken up every morning convinced that Mina is going to call me into her office, and laugh: *You didn't really think I'd let you buy a book, did you?*

But now it's official. I had to have a lengthy interview with Mina's boss, Charles, which she helped me to prep for. I have a six-month contract as an editorial assistant – and if that goes well, it'll be followed by a permanent contract. A salary. And Mina is going to oversee me editing my first title.

I'm working from home this morning. Mina suggested it after I told her I was having trouble concentrating in the office. I'm no longer a ghost there, and everyone has been stopping by my desk to congratulate me. Mina laughed and said it was a nice problem to have.

A worry, tickling my mind: I've had a few more messages recently from the fake Aimee but I haven't replied, too busy with all the excitement of my new job. And I'm scared, too, that life's good, and I don't want to be pulled back into my past. I'm hoping that if I ignore her, she might just disappear.

Now I've got a celebratory lunch at a posh restaurant in Covent Garden with Mina and Lucas.

It's a gorgeous sunny day: little clouds like ice cream scoops in a bright blue sky. I enter High Street Kensington tube, heading for the eastbound District line when some instinct makes me turn and look up.

Dominic.

He's on the escalator above me. Instead of his usual cagoule and jeans he's wearing a smart suit; he looks as though he could work in a bank. I'm so freaked out that as my escalator scales to the bottom, I nearly trip up.

He's following me.

This is a new development. Normally he just holds vigil outside my flat or *buzz-buzz*es my doorbell.

This is not a good day for his games. Of course he'd have an antenna for that.

There are delays, so I have to weave through dense crowds, muttering, 'Excuse me, sorry,' until I'm right at the end of the platform. I can't see any sign of Dominic. The platform fills up, a swirl of jostling commuters. I'm wearing a lacy white summer dress, one that Mina gifted me; I've even straightened my hair with an old pair of tongs that I dug out from Julia's bedroom—

A pressure behind me, suddenly. Someone too close, his breath hot against the back of my neck. In the paralysis of fear, I can't look back. I hear the rumble of the incoming train, the screech of wheels against the track, hypnotised by the flashing light emerging from the tunnel—

—and suddenly the pressure shoves me forward and I stumble, past the white safety line, the tracks coming up to meet me and I want to scream: *Dominic, you can't do this to me, you can't—*

A man grabs my arm. Pulls me back. The train whizzes past us, terrifyingly close.

'Are you okay? That was scary,' he says, over the noise of the train.

'Thank you,' I manage to reply in shock, as the doors open and people spill out, my body tender to touch, shuddering with each brush and shove against me. The impatient crowd carries me onto the train. My heart is still wild, my hands trembling. I look for Dominic this way, that way, crane my neck, glancing down the carriage; a woman notices me and frowns, so I glance away.

And then I spot him. Through the small window that looks into the next carriage. Quickly, I turn my back. It could have been him then, sidling up behind me – *fuck*.

It's not as though he would get the flat if I died. No, he's got desperate. He's giving up and he doesn't care. He wants revenge now.

As sweat dries on me, I start to shiver with cold shock. Maybe it is time to accept that this game is too dangerous. Maybe I should find a way to break the conditions of Julia's will, sell up, silence him with a share; I could still live in a beautiful place somewhere else. But then fury surges inside me: *I'm finally getting the life I want. A great flat, a dream job. I've suffered for over a decade. Why should I have to give it up when I've only just got it all?* It's not my fault that Julia favoured me, not after what happened. He's making me the scapegoat, but he created his own disaster.

'You look good,' Mina greets me warmly as I enter the restaurant.

'Thank you!' I glance back at the door. I didn't see any sign of Dominic following me from the station, thank God.

'You okay?' she asks, noticing my hand trembling as I reach for a glass of water. 'Nervous?' She misinterprets.

'Yes,' I say, my smile feeling wobbly. 'A little!'

'Don't be. Lucas will be even more nervous, I guarantee, and it's our job to put him at ease and explain the process that lies ahead.'

Mina's dressed to impress too, I notice, in a sleek black dress with a silver buckle. As she talks away, giving me advice on how to handle Lucas, I feel reassured, righted in her presence. I'm so grateful for the support she's given me, if a little self-conscious. I'm not used to telling people about my past. I held a lot back – there were things I couldn't tell her that I knew would be too much, like the house thefts, the murder – but she knows more of my secrets than anyone since . . . since Dominic, I reflect.

Her eyes light up as Lucas enters the restaurant. He gives us each a kiss on both cheeks, the French way, which makes me blush, though I guess it's normal for Mina.

Lucas sits opposite us both, grinning away, and I realise how much this means to him. Joy surges inside me: *I bought his book! I made this happen!*

'Did you have far to travel, Lucas?' Mina asks.

'From Mayfair – not too bad,' Lucas says. A moment's

awkward pause, and then he enthuses: 'I love your Instagram videos, by the way. I was watching over the weekend. Team Alice, Team Mina – it's so funny.'

Mina tenses a little; #TeamAlice is still faring slightly better.

'You should be in our next video,' I say, and Mina nods.

'I think it's great that you're making publishing more diverse,' Lucas says. 'But I'm afraid I'm terribly privileged, so I might as well get that out of the way right now. My mother is a German aristocrat, my father is Sri Lankan and Finnish, and he owns a property empire across Europe.'

'No need to apologise,' I assure him, but he and Mina exchange guilty looks, which makes me feel left out.

'Alice told me you're spending half your time in Paris at the moment?'

'I am, yes,' he replies. 'Though it's not as glamorous as it sounds – I stay in a *chambre de bonne* in Pigalle.'

'What's that like?' I interject.

'It's the tiny room at the top of the building, where the maid used to stay,' Lucas explains. 'But it's romantic too, like a writer's garret.'

'I once stayed in *chambre de bonne* for a month,' Mina says. 'In the Latin Quarter. My husband is half French, you see. We used to enjoy spending summers there.'

Lucas's face lights up and they're away, talking about the best places to stay. The last time I was in France was on a school trip when I was fourteen, and I felt embarrassed because the school had to cover my fee, when all my friends' parents could pay for them.

'We're just so excited about publishing your book, Lucas,' I cut in.

His eyes shine. He really does have such beautiful eyes:

somewhere between green and brown, thickly fringed with lashes.

Suddenly I notice Dominic entering the restaurant—

What the fuck? Still, there's no way he's going to be able to get a table. This place is usually booked up for weeks.

I gape as the waiter checks the diary, shows Dominic to a small table. Dominic sits with his back to us. He orders wine.

'Alice?'

I become aware that Mina is nudging me.

'Sorry, I zoned out,' I say quickly. 'I just need the loo.'

In the toilet mirror, I tell my reflection to stay cool. What can he try in a crowded restaurant – come at me with a knife and fork? But, as I rinse my hands, the terrifying thought hits me: he could just go and tell them all about Julia, about the real story, and use embarrassment as his weapon. And then there's that letter he keeps going on about. I wrench paper towels out of the dispenser, throw them in the bin, hurtle up the stairs and back into the restaurant.

I see Lucas and Mina talking intimately, and undisturbed, thank goodness. As I head over, I see Dominic is now tucking in to a rare steak. How the hell can he afford that? With the cash he stole from me, no doubt.

As I sit down, I notice they're speaking in French and I feel a little lost as they burst into laughter. Then Lucas turns and gives me a super-watt smile.

'*Mon éditrice*,' he says and it's so sexy I feel a shiver as he holds my gaze. 'It took me five years to write *Playthings*, so I hope you will be kind to me in the edits.' He gives Mina a sly look. 'My manuscript was actually rejected by you, when I sent it in last year.'

Mina looks alarmed. 'That would have been Sarah,' she says quickly, scapegoating her assistant.

I'm aware of Dominic in the periphery of my gaze, ordering more wine, course after course. We get our desserts and Lucas playfully teaches me a little French when I profess to know none. I can't help but notice how close his leg is to mine under the table. I think of that open mic night, of how we bonded so intimately over drinks, then push the thought away. This is my first chance to be a proper editor: I have to keep things professional.

The meal comes to an end and I'm almost relieved. I feel resentful that Dominic's presence overshadowed my first big author meeting.

Mina pays on the company card and we head out. They've just exited, when the waiter politely approaches me.

'The gentleman here says that you have agreed to pay his bill.'

'Me?' I glare at Dominic incredulously.

I don't like his smug smile. Or the way that he's opening his rucksack and drawing out a letter. I take a nervous step forward. I recognise that black ink, that handwriting: it's Julia's.

Surely this can't be it. The elusive letter that he claimed to Mina that he was searching for.

'I'm not paying your bill,' I hiss at him.

'Shall I read it out loud?' he says in a jovial tone. Then he adopts Julia's voice, capturing just how she sounded at the end of her life, gravelly and quavering, so spot-on that I'm shocked. '"I can't trust Alice anymore. I'm scared of the soups she makes me, I'm scared when she guides me to the toilet that she's trying to trip me up so that I fall."'

How the hell did he find it? Did he get into my flat? Find it in an old book, as he warned Mina?

'It's a fake,' I assert, though I know Dominic couldn't pull that off.

'A handwriting expert could verify it.'

'What do you want?'

'As I said, the bill, for starters.' He glances at Lucas and Mina. They're looking in through the glass, trying to work out what's going on. I give them a quick wave.

'I can always show this letter to your boss. Or the police.'

'Fine.' I turn to the hovering waiter, who's looking slightly bewildered. He presents the bill. £256.76. I pull out my card. I have just enough to cover it. My first salary payment won't come in for another three weeks; Sean's lending me daily funds at present. I type in my pin. Dominic grins away, smug as hell, and I want to run over and grab his fork and stick it into him. But I just nod politely at the waiter, who's probably a little pissed that I haven't the funds to tip him, then I turn and walk out.

'Sorry,' I say to Lucas and Mina. 'The waiter thought he knew me! But it turns out it was just a mistake.'

Lucas exclaims in amusement, but Mina looks disturbed. As we head off, she leans in and says, 'You need to sort your stalker situation out, Alice,' before turning back to Lucas and telling him how 'truly wonderful' our lunch has been.

CHAPTER TWENTY-SIX

Mina

It's nearly midnight and I'm sitting at my kitchen table, Pachelbel playing as a calming backdrop. I'm making a list of potential blackmailers.

Matthias.

He seemed the most obvious culprit, at first.

With Romain's profession and the increasing turbulence in the world, we get threats on a regular basis. I've had blackmail emails in the past that were really just attempts to fish, from tabloid journalists at *The Sun* or the *Mirror,* hoping I'd panic and reply. If I responded in fear, they'd know I was guilty of *something*; Romain has trained me never to react. And let's face it, my Feeld affairs aren't the worst sin – I've other secrets from my past. I recall Alice's face when I told her about how Romain and I had got together when I was only seventeen. I edited my history carefully. She doesn't know the half of it.

But this blackmail threat is different. It lists details. The day it came through, I was filled with fear and rage and ready to call up Matthias, but I told myself to play it calm and logical.

I called Howard again. He told me that Matthias was in St George's Hospital, undergoing surgery after an accident. Howard doubts he could have sent it.

Sarah, I add to the list.

She's fuming about Alice's promotion. And I think back to

the mystery of why Sarah went back to Alice's flat to check up on me, which is still unexplained.

Alice.

It feels painful to write her name.

I cross it out.

And then I remember the lunch we had yesterday.

Alice.

She bombards me with emails asking for support and guidance. I love mothering and mentoring her, but I think of how twitchy she was yesterday. Of how her stalker suddenly turned up – to taunt me? A silent way of letting me know it was him sending the demands?

Dominic, I add to the list.

Alice seems reluctant to report her stalker to the police and I don't understand why.

I add more names – *Jon, Roland, Alison*. Old work colleagues, ex-friends. As the decades have gone by, there are inevitably dozens of people who have grudges against me, which I'd assumed were minor but might have put down roots.

Oh God.

This feeling of sitting here, right now, and knowing that someone out there is full of such hatred towards me, is laughing at me, watching me, makes my skin crawl. I just want to know *who* and I want to know *why*.

In a fit of despair, I screw up the ball and reread the email.

Two thousand pounds. The deadline is tomorrow, 11 a.m. I can afford it. But I know the narrative that will follow: they'll ask for more, and then more, and then more—

A rap on the kitchen door; I jump. It's Aimee.

I know what I'm supposed to do now. Romain has set the protocol. I stand firm, I tell her to leave, I give her money, if necessary. I don't let her manipulate me.

But as I stare at her, out in the cold and dark, I picture Romain kissing Alice, feel the sting of his betrayal. And I think, *Is this what I really want? To keep rejecting her, year after year?*

What if she stops coming back?

I press a finger to my lips and she mimics me.

I unlock the door and try to hug her, but Aimee steps back, shoving her hands in her pockets, suddenly sulky and defensive. I bury my hurt and examine her face. Her pupils aren't dilated; the whites look clear.

'Let's go for a drive,' I whisper. 'Otherwise Romain could—'

'Yeah, good idea,' she says. 'I'll wait by the car.'

I tiptoe upstairs in a hurry, pulling on a jumper and my green gardening trousers over my nightie, shoving on my driving shoes. Out on our driveway, I unlock the Jaguar. I remind Aimee to put on her seatbelt and she sighs, clicking it into place. I steel myself: this could all turn sour, or strange, and I have to be prepared for that. You never know with Aimee.

On Piccadilly, we pass tourists and buses and post-clubbing girls and boys in drunken groups.

'So, how's college?' I ask. After a few years off whilst Aimee struggled with her addiction, she's gone back to a college in Otley to retake her A levels. She's on her half-term break now. 'Are the exams are coming up?'

'Uh-huh.'

'What universities are you going for?'

'Oh, Oxford.'

For a beat I believe her, and smile in joyful pride. She rolls her eyes.

'You could go there if you put your mind to it,' I say, sharply.

'I'm trying for London. I just want to escape *them*.'

I feel for her, then. My parents are so strict. We're more similar than she knows. I went through the same transition, from being the good girl who went to church, to rebellion and bad-sheep status. I never went down the drugs route though, and it breaks my heart that it's where Aimee has ended up. In marrying Romain, I grew up; Aimee's addiction feels like a frozen childhood, a determined refusal to mature.

She reaches into her handbag and lights up a cigarette. I tell myself not to berate her, alienate her. But then I smell a whiff of weed; it's going to stink out the car.

'*Aimee!* Oh, for fuck's sake!'

'I guess this would fuck up your image, wouldn't it?' Aimee says. 'I wouldn't look good in your Instagram *journey*.'

I feel briefly touched that she's watched the videos, before wondering if she's the one who left hurtful comments.

We carry on chatting tersely as I drive out of London, heading towards Surrey, craving quieter roads. I want to lecture her to stop throwing her life away, but I bite the words back. If you try telling Aimee what to do, she embraces the opposite.

'Do you have a boyfriend?'

'Yes. He's called Michael. He works in London.' She sounds excited. 'He's quite a bit older than me.'

'How much?'

'Fifteen years.'

My dismay must show on my face, because she says: 'Romain was ten years older – you can't judge me.'

'I'm not,' I insist. I manage a smile. 'I'd love to meet him.'

Maybe he could be her saving grace, a motivation to get clean. Something, someone, to live for.

Country smells drift through the windows. Aimee flicks her lighter on, off, on, off, and I tell her to stop.

'Aimee.' I take a breath. 'I need to ask you something, and you mustn't get upset, or offended. Just be honest with me.'

'What?'

'Someone is sending me blackmail emails. Is it you? A joke, maybe?'

Even as I say the words, I realise the mistake. I hear the outrage, the hurt in her laughter, and my heart sinks.

'Jesus Christ.' Aimee flares up the lighter again. 'Of course I fucking didn't. You guys are constantly buying my silence so I don't ruin your perfect image – why would I bother?'

It's such a painful truth that I feel tears in my eyes.

'Why the fuck are you being blackmailed?' Her lighter flicks on-off-on-off, veering too close. Her voice rises, becomes hysterical. 'Are you having some affair with your lesbo assistant—'

She screams, and I'm aware that there's a smell of burning, and Aimee crying, 'Your hair!' I look down and see a front lock of my hair licked by yellow. I hear myself cry out. I put on the brakes, halt right in the middle of the road. Water – there's a bottle of Evian, half-drunk, in the seat compartment, and I use it. A hiss; a burning smell. *What the fuck?* I can hear Romain's voice in my mind, reprimanding me, saying I should never have come, with Aimee it always turns out this way.

Aimee flicks the lighter and I yell: 'Just put the bloody lighter away!'

She starts to laugh. I sense it comes from nerves, but I suddenly feel murderous.

This was all such a silly idea. I scan the moon, the trees, the fields, and suffer a sense of déjà vu, of being a teenager again, back in Otley, in a car with friends, laughing and drinking. I push it back, start up the car, do a U-turn. There's still a burning smell in the car and my top is damp. I glance down at my hair again, relive the shock. I'll have to go to the hairdressers tomorrow, get it evened out. I press my foot down on the accelerator. I want to get back home quickly now, to be back on the streets of London, blasted by city neon. My breathing is coming faster and faster and I tell my body, *No, not now, you can't do this.* I can hear Aimee asking what's wrong, and I put my foot down again. My breath is a piston, my heart is shrieking, my hands clammy—

A car comes round the corner with a blinding flash of lights, honking its horn, and I swerve, skid up a bank, hit the edge of a fence. Cows moo in alarm. I hear Aimee crying in fear. 'What is it, what's happening, are you sick?'

'Just . . . a . . . panic . . . attack . . .' I bury my face in my arms, resting on the steering wheel. The words of my therapist soothe me: I picture myself in a dark cave, all quiet, all peaceful, and I hear Aimee saying, 'Mum, Mum, are you okay?' and despite all my fears, it's the first time in years she's called me that, and it's beautiful to hear.

The next morning, I sit in the living-room, strands of my hair falling to the newspaper on the floor. It's a Sunday but my darling hairdresser, Henrique, still drove over when I made an emergency call. Now he's feathering in layers at the front.

Romain watches, frowning. I told him that I accidentally set alight to it last night when brewing up some hot milk, half asleep.

It's 9 a.m. according to my mobile. I have two hours before my blackmail deadline ends.

We drive over to Leila's in Hampstead. She's having a

garden party for ten or so friends. Romain and I sit in silence, Radio 4 burbling away. I feel the distance between us, of the new life I am now living without him: one of seeing our daughter, one of secret affairs, one of blackmail threats.

'Auntie Mina!' Leila's children, Cara and Bartholomew, throw themselves at me. I play with them more than any other adult here; and I feel the heartbreak of a lost motherhood. I'm pretending that Cara is Aimee. I'm trying to live out the experiences I never had, of plaiting her hair and dribbling a football between makeshift goals.

I look over at Romain, standing by the trestle table, biting into a sausage roll, and feel a surge of anger. *You're too young to be a mother.* Those were his words, when I was eighteen. Echoing my mother, reinforcing the narrative around me that I, Mina, was inept and young and foolish and couldn't cope. I make a mistake. I let my baby go and it's all his fault.

Ten minutes, my phone reminds me.

Ten minutes to decide if I pay the blackmail threat, or run the risk . . .

CHAPTER TWENTY-SEVEN

Alice

This is weird: I'm gazing out of my living-room window, watching parents with pushchairs and posh joggers in designer yoga gear, and there's no Dominic.

He's been gone for three days now.

His absence doesn't reassure me. It just makes me more nervous – what's he plotting? Sean's returned from his latest work assignment and I can hear him humming in the shower, the murmur of Radio 4 in the background. When I told him how Dominic had tried to shove me under a tube train, he looked shell-shocked. Last night he suffered a nightmare that Dominic had succeeded and woke up crying, thinking he'd lost me. We held each other tight and went back to sleep nose-to-nose.

I ache to tell Sean everything: to confide in him about the letter Dominic's threatening to send to the police. But how can I? I'd have to explain everything that happened with Julia. Sean grew up in a nice, middle-class household. When he dumped me and travelled abroad to Spain, his parents lent' him money, whilst I slid into poverty. It marked a shift in our fortunes, a forking of our destinies. He was drinking cocktails on a sun-soaked terrace whilst I was rummaging in bins. I'm scared that if I tell him the truth, he'll walk away and never come back.

'Victory!' Sean exclaims, coming up behind me, a towel

around his waist. He smells all fresh and citrusy from his shower; he circles a damp arm around me. 'That bastard won't be coming back. I fixed it for you.'

'You have?' I have awful visions of Sean beating Dominic to a pulp.

'I called the police,' Sean explains. As I freeze, his eyes widen. 'Alice, we can't go on like this. He nearly fucking *killed you*. I had to do something. By the way, I gave your number to the police. They'll follow up with a call.'

'But . . . but . . . *Oh God*. You shouldn't have done that! He'll just retaliate,' I cry, pushing him away. I run my hands through my hair. *Shit*.

Sean's eyes flash with hurt.

'You should let me help you,' he argues. 'I can keep you safe.'

'But you've only made it worse! I can handle Dom by myself.'

'Fine. If this is the shit I get for helping you, then I'll be off.'

'But—'

'Because if you don't want to get rid of that weirdo, if you *want* him there when he's tried to push you under a tube, then there's something seriously wrong, something you're not telling me.'

'Please stay . . .'

'You want me to stay. But you don't want to move in, do you?' Sean presses me again.

'I . . . don't know,' I say weakly.

Sean storms off. I listen to the sounds of him dressing and packing, followed by the slam of the door. I sit down, tears in my eyes, resisting the urge to run after him and hold him tight and tell him I've changed my mind.

But Sean doesn't understand. I dig my fingers into a

cushion, hit by a flashback of the day Julia had me arrested. Sergeant Pester with his cool blue eyes and his casual questions, waiting for me to trip up.

I gave your number to the police. They'll follow up with a call. Sean's words fill me with dread. If they do, I won't take their call.

The next morning, I wake up filled with regret and sadness. I pick up my phone to send Sean an apology, then stop. I think of that night when we were sitting on his bed in his parents' house in Guildford. How he told me thought things had 'fizzled out' between us. Moving out, moving into a box room in a house in Hackney with six other people, crying myself to sleep every night whilst music thumped through the walls.

I know Sean has grown up a lot since then, but I'm scared his behaviour wasn't just due to immaturity. Sean loves to travel; he has a restless streak. He wants me now because I'm holding back; I'm scared that if I commit, we'll grow stagnant and he'll lose interest again.

I head out to work. The tube feels too much of a risk; I favour the bus instead. It takes an age as we trundle through London traffic, caught in endless jams. I get to work late and Mina looks unimpressed.

I watch her glide into her office, so self-possessed, so in control of her life. I think of how she handled Matthias. I relive that moment when Dominic pushed me, when the track came rushing up towards me; I picture alternative horrors, the District line tube train smashing against my body, my blood spraying against posters for beauty products and West End musicals. I shudder in horror.

Mina wouldn't let Dominic get away with this. Nobody

fucks with Mina. She'd break his balls. I have to follow her example. I have to turn the tables.

It's not long before Dominic resumes his vigil outside my flat. The following night I sit by my window, watching him watch me.

He waits two hours. It's nearly eight when I see him slope off. I jump up, grab my bag, lock my door, hurry into the lift and head after him.

I follow Dominic to High Street Kensington station. I hang back until he boards, then jump into the next carriage, risking quick glances at him as he flicks through a copy of the *Metro*. At Embankment, he changes for the Northern line, walking at a fast pace, hands shoved into his cagoule, and I hurry after him at a safe distance.

He gets off at Golders Green. Twilight is falling as we emerge from the station. I follow him down a main street filled with tatty shops, the pavement strewn with litter, towards a dreary, seventies-style graffiti-sprayed block. He enters and a light goes on in the left ground-floor flat. I hide out by a trio of ash trees, their bark tattooed with penknife carvings and burn marks. Dom's a night owl. If he's going to vacate his flat, it'll be within the next few hours.

A buzz on my phone. I hope it's Sean – but it's an email from Lucas about his author photoshoot. I smile, sending a quick reply – I still get such a kick to think I have my own author.

When I shove my phone back into my bag, I think of Principle Publishing colleagues, at home in their flats, watching TV they'll gossip about tomorrow, and wonder if I'm being crazy, hanging out here. This is not my life anymore. I'm tired and I need my sleep to be up for work tomorrow.

I turn to go, but the thought of the letter snags me again. If I can just get hold of it, then maybe this whole stupid farce can end—

Dominic is coming out of the block of flats.

I wait until he's disappeared into the distance, and then I seize my chance.

I push open the door to his block. In the hallway, I face four grey doors; the buzzer list by the main entrance lists DOMINIC FORDE at number 3.

I know how to break into a flat; Dominic spent months training me. So long as he hasn't double-locked it, I can do this.

I glance around nervously. I have some more open mic leaflets in my handbag which I grabbed from the office. If any residents appear, I can pretend I'm leafleting. I jiggle the lock using tweezers, then I slide an old credit card between the lock and the doorframe.

I hear a noise and jump as a guy in a baseball cap comes out of his flat. I'm scared I've got guilt written all over my face, but he scans my smart suit and slick ponytail, and I can see his thought process play out: *Nicely dressed middle-class woman, can't be doing any wrong.* He gives me a friendly nod, then leaves the building.

I turn back to the door. I'm out of practise. Shit, I've lost the knack. It's not going to work.

One last try—

There's a satisfying click and the door opens with a whine.

The very scent of his place – of damp, unwashed clothes, Chinese takeaway that needs to be thrown out, fruity vape smoke – is so inherently Dominic that I suffer a flood of memories. I shake them off, refusing to be dragged back to my old self.

194

It's a tiny flat. There's an air of abandonment about it, as though it's a place he doesn't feel he deserves to be condemned to, so he can't be bothered to keep it nice. The main area is a lounge and kitchen combined: trainers and crumpled cans on the floor, an old sofa, a desk with an Apple Mac sitting on it, the keyboard submerged by a slew of papers. In the midst of it all is a huge flatscreen TV, lovingly polished clean and free of the dust that lines everything else.

I quickly check the two other rooms: a bathroom with a shower and toilet squeezed in tight together. A bedroom carpeted in clothes. The bed is covered with a smooth sheet; a sleeping bag is crumpled on the floor. Dom still can't sleep on a mattress then.

A pinstriped suit catches my eye. It's hanging on the back of a chair, along with a snazzy tie. It's the one he wore on the day he tried to push me under the tube, and as anger fills me, I consider finding a knife, slashing the sleeves—

And then I catch sight of his phone.

It's on the floor, peeking out from under the bed.

I pick it up. That Dom's left it behind makes me nervous, because he could come back for it any minute. Unless . . . he's gone out with a burner, so he can't be tracked.

I know his old passcode, just as he once knew mine. I type it in: 24319. My heart leaps: *it works.*

I have so little time – I hardly know where to begin. I check his Gmail account. But I'm shut out, I need a password – damn.

On his WhatsApp, I find a string of messages with Gerry, the one who helped Dominic move his furniture out of my flat. Another with someone called Snake. Her profile picture is an icon of a red snake, tail looping into its mouth, and I frown. Isn't that the same picture as the user who keeps leaving such vicious comments on our #PublishingJourney videos?

The messages are broken fragments, more emojis than words. They seem to be flirty and it makes me wonder if he's grooming another young woman, training her as he once did me—

My name leaps out from the chat.

Now that cunt Alice has reported me to the police, need you to go tonight.

I went to her flat. Couldn't see Alice.

OK, no worries 👍

Another message has a picture of me attached, a blurry figure entering my building, the time and date recorded.

I feel sick. So they're watching me. Recording when I go in, when I go out. Building up a pattern of my routine. The messages are interspersed with Dominic's usual misanthropy:

Just saw a man who was so fat u wouldn't believe it! I mean, they should put all the fatties on the Isle of Wight & let em sink it with a laughing emoji reply from Snake.

I scroll down to older messages.

Oh – look, here we are. Snake has attached a photo of Mina, entering my flat – shit. There's a lot of people going in and out of her flat all the time – weird?!

What are they using the flat for? Alice is def up to SOMETHING.

Maybe Mina & Alice are lesbian lovers?

I laugh in shock. Their other speculations are just as ludicrous – they imagine that I'm sourcing cocaine and passing it on to Mina.

Or Mina is having an affair with someone else in the building.

I squirm: that's closer to the truth.

And Alice is bribing her, so that's why she had that cash. It was way too much for just a rental.

So they *did* steal my cash last month – though I still don't know how they got the key.

Maybe . . .

Fucking mystery isnt it?

Isn't it, I correct silently.

I worry that I'm wasting time. I need to focus on finding the letter. I put his phone back, hurry into the lounge to his computer desk. I flip through papers: floor plans, estate agents' brochures, intel on properties of the rich, places he's clearly staking out for future burglaries, until I hit a bundle of white sheets of paper. On the top is a half-composed letter from Julia – *shit.*

> *Dear Mr Wentworth,*
>
> *I feel I must write to you, as my lawyer, to express my concerns about Alice and her suspicious, strange behaviour . . .*

The last sentence is repeated over and over and it's then I realise, laughing in shock: Dominic is practising her writing.

The letter is a fake. He wrote it himself.

My relief is short-lived. He could still show his fabrication to the police. How could I prove it was a fake? I raise my phone to take a photo, a frightened voice reminding me that if I ever did show this, the police would know I'd broken in—

Out of the corner of my eye, a figure catches my attention. I look up, to see Dominic striding back towards the flats.

I run to his front door, but it's too late. I hear the voice of his neighbour, asking him to keep the noise down.

Dominic's reply is sullen, careless.

The front door starts to open.

CHAPTER TWENTY-EIGHT

Alice

Panic screams through me. I run into the bedroom. The only other furniture in here is the wardrobe. I fling open the doors, ready to hide – but it's stuffed with clothes, old rucksacks, an army uniform. I crouch down to slip under the bed – only to find it's crammed with suitcases.

There's nowhere to hide.

I press myself against the wall right behind the door, and stand there, trembling, as Dominic enters the flat.

I hear the sound of water. The hiss of a kettle. I sniff in trails of smoke from his vape, laced with a sickly cherry flavour. It irritates my throat, and I swallow hard. A sneeze tickles my nose and I force it back, feeling it fizz silently. My eyes wander over his belongings, trying to see anything I could use as a weapon.

But there's nothing, save that snazzy tie, and I end up picturing Dominic twisting it around *my* throat, squeezing hard . . .

I hear his voice, suddenly.

'Those places are fucked up, they're for rich people who can't be bothered to look after their kids.'

Is he on a call?

'There was this prefect who had it in for me, used to beat me – the masters turned a blind eye,' he says.

I realise that this is a confession he once made to me. And

now he's . . . rehearsing it. He's playing it back on his phone, listening, I think, and then he picks out certain phrases, refines them, repeats them over and over.

I feel very strange. When he confided in me about his past, it hadn't occurred to me that it was a fabrication. Julia confirmed that he had gone to private school – did he make up the stories about being bullied?

And then I hear his voice break with tears. He sobs for a few minutes. I shudder, confused and lost. I don't remember ever seeing Dominic cry. Maybe this is an act of catharsis, a way of banishing his past by speaking it aloud?

'Come on,' he mutters to himself. 'Pull yourself together. Dominic's going to kill you if you don't get this right.'

Is Dominic hearing voices, splitting himself into fragments?

Suddenly he stops rehearsing. As I hear him heading towards me, I tense up, sweat slithering down my spine . . .

And then there's a bang close by. I jump, hear the hiss of water. *Oh thank God!* He's in the shower.

Now's my moment.

I tiptoe into the living-room, open the front door with a mild click, shut it gently and then make a run for it.

Outside, the night air is warm and balmy. I dodge a crowd of drunks, and don't stop running until I've reached the tube. Passengers look up as I jump onto the train, breathless, eyes streaming, red-faced. As I sit down, digesting everything that I saw and heard, I feel gutted that I didn't have time to take a photo of the letter. But it would've been too risky to linger: God knows what Dominic would have done if he'd found me.

Even though it's been a relief to confirm that the letter was a fake, I've only ended up with a fresh set of worries. Who is this person he's got helping him? I think of the fake

Aimee. Could it be her? The strange rehearsal of his past; the sobbing. I don't know how to put all the pieces together.

Back home, I'm snagged by Jean outside my flat, and I don't even mind when she subjects me to a five-minute monologue about her new cactus; it's grounding, normalising.

Inside, I greet my birds, then scroll down my WhatsApp thread with 'Aimee'.

The last message she sent me was over a week ago. I was relieved she'd gone silent; now I feel frustrated. If she's based in Otley, how can she be watching my flat? Or did she just make that up as part of her facade?

Maybe the best solution is not to get mad, but to make contact. If she is his helper, then I know exactly what this woman is going through. Once upon a time Dominic preyed on me, made me his sidekick. Despite everything, I do actually feel for her, if she's become my replacement. Maybe I can find out Dominic's plan *and* persuade her to steer clear of him.

Hey I message her. How are you?

I don't have to wait long before she replies: Not bad, how are you?

Have you been in London recently?

Sadly no. Stuck in Otley.

Hmm, I think, then type: I thought I saw you outside my flat the other day.

Not me.

There's no point in trying to accuse her, however confused and riled I feel – she's not going to confess to anything.

I've been wondering if you might want to meet up. If you're ever back in London.

I'd like to. Has Mina been in touch about me staying at yours?

I frown, picturing her and Dominic sniggering as they imagine me for falling for their ruse. But maybe it's best to keep playing along for now.

Sorry, I can't have anyone to stay – my boyfriend is here.

A pause, and I worry I've upset her.

Do I know you? I type. Maybe from the past?

No, she types back, of course not.

Finally, I take the plunge:

I know you're not Aimee. So – can we meet to discuss?

I gulp as the minutes ago by. Shit, maybe I've lost her—

I'm sorry I lied. I'll explain everything.

Okay I type back, my heart hammering. When? Next week?

I'll try. I'll book a coach to London. Need to borrow some money for somewhere to stay. Will let you know the date asap.

From Ruth's diary

I got my diagnosis today. I sat in a state of shock in the GP's surgery. You hear the stats, you know someone who's fought it, someone who's been killed by it, you know that 1 in 3 of us are going to get it. But you never really think you'll be one of them. Cancer: fuck. A tumour in my kidney. I came back home and found everyone the same as ever. Laure was depressed over not finding work, Jim was drinking beer and about to watch the football. I snapped at them both, told them to make more of their lives, and they looked bewildered.

I couldn't tell them the truth. I couldn't get the words out.

I woke up in the night feeling scared that I won't be able to avenge Chris in time. I've let it all slide for years, and now I've read through my diaries again, and the newspaper pieces, and I feel mad that justice was never done. Maybe now it's going to be too late.

CHAPTER TWENTY-NINE

Alice

It starts to set in about a week after our break-up: an ache for Sean. I keep picking up my phone and expecting to see a photo of his new location; a silly joke; a link to a video of a crazy cat or a rare bird species. I find myself checking when he was last online. I wonder who else he might be messaging. I start typing a message to say sorry, then delete it.

I wish he was around so I could confide in him about the fake Aimee. She sent a date for our meeting this weekend, along with a link to a bizarre video about the 1 per cent all being part of some elite cabal. It looks like a loony conspiracy video, to be honest. I'm still suspicious that she's the one watching my flat for Dominic. I keep looking out of my window, suspicious of passing strangers, trying to spot them.

Editing Lucas's book is the perfect therapy. I work on it over a three-day period in a frenzy, losing myself in his dark tale of murder and pain and revenge. I stay late in the office; I feel safer there than I do in my flat.

I send it over to Lucas, feeling drained but satisfied. Fulfilment bubbles up inside me. *I love this job.* I glance over at Mina, ensconced in her office, and I feel like running in and gushing thank-yous and hugging her again, but of course, she'd just think I was crazy.

Instead, I head out to meet Lucas for his photoshoot. Originally Sean was booked to do it, but since our break-up I had to find a quick replacement: a photographer called Mary Chang.

We meet on the South Bank. A strong sun glints on the Thames and the trees with their butchered arms. Mary's smart and efficient, with short grey hair and tattoos spiralling over her arms. On my mobile, I film her positioning Lucas so that the river is his roiling backdrop; I can add it to our #PublishingJourney Instagram thread.

Lucas is dressed in a black T-shirt and jeans; his black hair is styled back from his face in a leonine quiff. A sexy frown creases his forehead; the final photos are going to have a touch of James Dean.

After Mary finishes up, I offer to buy him a drink and we head to the BFI, sitting down at an outside table.

'You looked fantastic,' I enthuse. 'Those pics are going to be stunning.'

Do I sound as though I'm flirting? But Lucas just looks pleased and I hear Mina's voice in my mind, reminding me to relax and be confident – just as my phone buzzes with a call from her.

'Alice, I know this is short notice, but I wonder if I might rent your flat in two nights' time?'

I hesitate, anxious, wondering how I might warn her about Dominic. But I've no excuses prepared, and so I agree, and she hangs up briskly.

'That was just Mina,' I tell him.

'As a matter of fact, I saw her last night,' Lucas says. 'I was at a launch party at Daunt's.'

'You did?' I ask, with a flash of FOMO, wondering why she didn't take me.

'She's so grand, isn't she?' he says, an intimidated look on his face.

'She certainly is,' I agree, 'but she's a pussycat underneath. I think she likes to project a queenly ego. No – scratch that, she has got a big ego –' we both laugh '– but she's earned the right to it.'

'She emailed me a copy of *Those Foolish Things* – it's amazing,' he says, referring to the book I discovered, and I bite my lip.

I ought to be wrapping up and getting back to the office, but there's something so seductive about being in Lucas's presence. Tourists are drifting by, snapping selfies of the Thames and the bridges and St Paul's, but it feels as though we're in our own private bubble. He holds my gaze a little longer than necessary, cocks his head to one side when I'm speaking as though fascinated. I agree to get another round of drinks.

I tell him that when I was editing his book, I got shivers every time I read the scene where the killer stalked his ex-girlfriend.

'I actually bought a gun to research it,' he says.

'No – you're serious?'

'Really, I did. It's a French pistol. I had to get a licence. I see it as my good luck talisman now. Hey, you should come over to my flat and I'll show it to you.'

'I'd like that,' I say, smiling, trying not to stare at his lips.

His mobile buzzes and he suddenly frowns, tells me he has to go.

'Sure,' I reply, worried I've kept him too long. *This is a professional relationship,* I remind myself. But as we say goodbye, Lucas leans in and kisses each of my flaming cheeks, and I sail back to my flat on such a high I don't even care when Dominic films me.

*

Two nights later, I come home from work early and prep my flat for Mina's arrival. I pull the curtains closed; I don't want Dominic snapping embracing silhouettes. Then I slip behind my TV and unlock my secret room. My birds are twittering away, like a Greek chorus that voices my conscience: *You shouldn't, you shouldn't.*

I shouldn't be watching Mina, but ever since Matthias threatened her, I feel protective of her. She's telling everyone at work I'm her protégée; she's beamed a bright spotlight of success on me. Still, I do feel a bit pervy and guilty as I shut the door behind me.

Whilst I'm waiting, I check my email. Earlier today, Lucas forwarded photos from the shoot. There's one that I keep enlarging, of his profile against the sky: Roman nose, full lips, strong jaw. Each time I look at it, my stomach does a somersault.

Sean's WhatsApp status shows he was online thirty minutes ago. Suddenly I feel sad and guilty that I have a new crush, that Sean doesn't know and maybe wouldn't care.

Mina's key in the lock. Voices. I peer through the peephole.

Mina enters, looking as sexy as always, wearing a red dress. The young man behind her makes me start. What the hell: it's Lucas! I was expecting some Feeld toyboy, but – *Lucas*?

CHAPTER THIRTY

Alice

Lucas is wearing exactly the same outfit that he chose for his photoshoot. The same dark T-shirt, and jeans, the ones that make him look so sexy.

They sit side-by-side on the sofa. When Mina offers him some wine, Lucas replies, 'I'll just have a tea, thanks.' Mina looks disappointed, so he quickly changes his mind: 'Sure, some wine would be nice.'

'So this is your "reading" flat?' Lucas asks.

'It's not mine,' Mina replies. 'I'm lucky – this is on loan from a generous friend who's away. I do relish having a quiet place to read and think.'

What bullshit! I'm so incredulous I want to laugh. Indignation spikes me too: Lucas is gazing round in admiration. I want him to know that this is *my* place.

'It's beautiful.' Lucas puts down his glass, goes to the window and pulls back the curtain. 'Amazing view, and such a good location.' When he returns, he sits a little closer on the sofa: Mina and I both notice it. 'So, we can go through your manuscript together . . .'

I gape as Mina reaches for her navy satchel and pulls out a leafy manuscript.

'I know you had some concerns . . .' Mina says.

Concerns? Only this morning, Lucas replied saying that he thought my edit was 'fantastic'.

'The thing is,' Mina says, 'Alice has done some very good work here . . .'

My head is spinning: is Mina betraying me or defending me? She did take credit for her first acquisition. What if she's stealing my author from me behind my back?

'I know, I know, Alice is great,' Lucas says, fingering a tassel on one of my cushions. 'But she thinks my sex scenes are gratuitous. I think they're so important to my characters.'

'I found them very erotic, beautifully done,' Mina says. 'You can always push back, you know.'

Lucas sighs. 'I like Alice, but maybe she's a puritan.'

'I don't think so. She once tried to kiss my husband,' Mina blurts out.

I flush. Dear God, did she have to bring that up?

'*Alice once tried to kiss your husband?*' Lucas says in shock. 'Wow. And you still kept her as your assistant?'

'Well, she claims *he* tried to kiss her.' Mina looks sad. 'And I don't know. Maybe that is the truth.' She sighs. 'In the end, I had to stop speculating, for my own sanity. Anyhow, I think it was just a one-off.'

Lucas blinks, uneasy, and I want to wrench open the door and tell Mina that he doesn't want to hear any of our private issues.

'But she's your assistant,' he repeats. He laughs, shakes his head. 'You keep your enemies close, right?'

'Oh, Alice isn't my enemy,' Mina says, to my relief. 'I'm really very fond of her. Anyhow . . .' she begins. 'We should get back to—'

'So do you and your husband have an open relationship?' Lucas asks her. 'Have you ever kissed anyone else?'

'Oh, no,' Mina lies. 'We're not open – we're not anything, really . . .' She trails off.

'I'm sorry if I shouldn't be asking you these questions,' Lucas says.

'Well, perhaps we ought to get back to business,' Mina replies briskly. She pats the sofa next to her, wielding her elegant navy pen. 'Come.'

Lucas shuffles up so that he's right next to her, the manuscript now balanced on her right knee and his left one. As she flips through, she murmurs things like, 'I think Alice has made a good observation here' and 'Is this bit clear?'

Then I hear her tut.

'There are quite a few spelling mistakes in her comments.'

'Well, yes, I didn't want to make a big deal out of that,' Lucas says.

Mina sighs. 'I asked Sarah to proof the edit and she clearly didn't bother.'

Now I feel humiliated. I did run a spellcheck on the document, but it didn't catch everything. And I don't have a grand BA in English like everyone else in the department.

My hand flies up and I hear Mina's voice cajoling me – *Don't bite your nails.*

Fuck it, I think, tearing away at them savagely.

They flick on through the book, until they come to the finale pages. Mina's pen goes *tap!*

'You know, you could do more with this ending. It's only just struck me, but it's really not satisfying to solve the crisis with a *deux ex machina.* Characters should resolve problems through their own ingenuity.'

As her words sink in, I feel sick. Yes: I'd had an intuition that the ending didn't quite work but I'd been too proud to ask Mina for her thoughts, worried she was getting impatient about all the time she has to spend guiding me.

'You're right – that will really improve it.'

Mina is gazing at him, her smile soft and seductive. She reaches out and gently rearranges a lock of hair, brushing it back from his forehead.

'There,' she whispers.

Lucas turns. I can't read his expression, but I'll bet he's horrified.

He leans in and kisses her passionately.

My mouth is an O.

They kiss and kiss. Lucas's hand curls around Mina's head, pulling her in, opening up her mouth with his. I can't believe it. It's one thing for Mina to prey on young men, but to pounce on an author – *my* author – *no, no, NO!*

Mina draws back, blinking.

'I'm sorry,' Lucas says.

'It's fine,' Mina says. 'It was just – unexpected.'

Is she for real?

'But a good surprise,' she adds.

Lucas sets his glass down on the floor and caresses her face with his fingertips.

'You're so beautiful,' he says. 'When we were in Daunt's the other day, I just wanted to . . .'

I quell inside, suddenly close to tears and feeling like such an idiot. So much for the chemistry between us: it must have been a product of my feverish imagination.

'I felt it too.' Her voice is small with vulnerability. 'It was instant, yes . . . although at the time I wasn't sure if perhaps you liked Alice.'

'Alice is very sweet,' he says. 'But you – you're a real woman.'

I can't go on. I step away from the peephole, gaze out through the window into the side alley.

A few minutes pass, and I can't hear much. Swallowing, I turn back to the peephole, newly self-conscious.

They're kissing again, hands roaming passionately, clawing hair, caressing skin, tugging at clothing. I want to die inside, though a part of me is also aroused, for it's a mirror of the fantasies I've started to have about Lucas. She untucks his T-shirt from his jeans, her palms caressing his chest; Lucas's hands curl around hers, stopping her.

Mina frowns.

'You're really special,' he says. 'We should take this more slowly.'

'I only have this flat for one night . . .'

'But we can meet again, right? At mine . . . at a hotel, if we need to . . .'

'Hotels are not a good idea. This is much safer. It's very important that we're discreet,' Mina holds his hands in hers, looking vulnerable. 'I could get into so much trouble.'

'Because I'm your author?'

But you're my author, Lucas.

'Yes. There's that. And there's the matter of . . .'

Your husband, I finish off in my head.

'This has to be our secret, okay?'

'I get it.' Lucas looks a little upset, but he gives her a tender kiss. 'I just – I want to get to know you. You're special.'

'I'm a lot older than you.' No doubt Mina's conscious that she can't fake her age this time.

'Who cares about age?' Lucas asks. He sighs. 'I . . . actually have to go. My father's in town. He's come over from Berlin, and I did actually think this was an editorial meeting, so . . .'

'It is,' Mina interjects. 'We just . . .'

'Yes. We did.'

They stand up. Lucas wraps his arms around her and gives her one last lingering kiss before whispering something in her ear that I'd die to hear.

After he leaves, Mina sinks down onto the sofa. She looks dreamy, euphoric; I watch her pick up Lucas's manuscript delicately, as though it's a rare and precious thing. As she leafs through it again, slowly, I feel anger rising up inside me; I swear she's lingering on his sex scenes. Finally, she finishes off her wine and leaves.

I wait for five minutes, then come out. Their energy is still lively in the air: scents of aftershave and perfume, of wine and kisses. I notice that Mina hasn't even left me any money and I hear myself let out a small scream.

It's then I notice how little Lucas drank. I take a swallow from his glass, savouring his taste. Then I tell myself off for being a saddo, and I despondently take the glasses into the kitchen to wash up.

I lie in bed, chair under the handle. Sleep is impossible. I feel just as hurt by Mina's betrayal as I do the loss of Lucas. I've grown to love her as I once did Julia. Now I've learnt that her moral compass is nonexistent. Trust: a word she's always bandying about, and I've had to work so hard to earn hers, but she's not willing to repay it.

The more I replay the scene, the more I wonder on it. Sarah's always going on about power dynamics and privilege and MeToo. And let's face it, in any scenario between Mina and Lucas, she has all the power and he's vulnerable. If the genders were reversed, everyone would see this as a MeToo story, because the underlying subtext could easily be seen as: *I'm publishing you, so if I want to kiss you, you can't object. I give you royalties; you give me sexual favours.* Maybe Lucas flirted with her because he felt obliged to flatter her. Maybe when she swept that lock of hair from his forehead, Lucas felt he had to go along with it. When she tried to undress him, he stopped her, with the excuse of wanting to take his time – or maybe he just leapt at the opportunity to escape. And let's not forget that Mina's favourite novel is *Lolita*, which says it all.

Alice is very sweet. His words keep singing inside me. *But you're a real woman.* All of his words were ambiguous, slippery: the more I analyse them, the less I'm clear of their meaning.

I'm scared. Once upon a time, Mina seemed to be making my career; now she's threatening to blow it apart. If Lucas is her latest toy, she might discard him, leave him scarred, leave me to pick up the pieces.

CHAPTER THIRTY-ONE

Alice

It's Saturday morning and I wake up feeling nervous: I'm meeting the fake Aimee today. I pull on jeans and a blue-and-white striped top that Sean gifted me. I feel a pang that he's not around to come with me. He was due back from Malta yesterday, but he's not been in touch.

There's no sign of Dominic, so I risk the tube. I'm glad not to be at work today. I feel odd about Mina, now I know she's preying on my author. I've sent Lucas several emails asking if he's happy with his edit and I'm nervous for his reply on Monday.

Mina – who has a great habit of contacting me just when I'm thinking of her – pings me a message as I get off the tube.

Could we please film another video, with Romain? We need to keep our #PublishingJourney going.

Oh God. My stomach twists at the thought. I put my phone away, pushing away my anger.

We're meeting in the Pret nearest to Pimlico. The fake Aimee – as I can't help but think of her – is sitting at a window table, a can of Coke before her. As she soon as I enter, she jumps up, waving.

'Hi,' she says. Her accent still has a Yorkshire twang so perhaps that is authentic.

I grab a tea and sit down. She looks different from last

214

time; no leather jacket and jeans in imitation of Aimee. No ponytail; her hair flows over her shoulders. With her face made up, she looks in her early twenties. The only constant is the gum she's chewing, just as she was before.

'So, you work for Mina?' There's an edge to her voice, as though I've admitted to working for an oil company who pollutes the sea.

'I do.' Despite all of her recent betrayals, I feel defensive. 'You obviously know her pretty well, if you're able to impersonate her sister . . . How did you know about me, about Aimee? Have you been watching my flat, hacking our phones or something?'

'No! Of course not. I've known Aimee a few years,' she says. 'We live in the same town. We've partied, got drunk, hung out.'

'Does Aimee know about you pretending to be her?'

'As a matter of fact, the first time, Aimee suggested it herself as a joke,' she says. 'We've both got dark hair – she said I'd look good if I wore it like hers. I got a fringe cut. Aimee is such a narcissist, she *loved* someone mimicking her. She told me Mina had suggested she could stay at yours, so . . . I figured – well, it was an opportunity.'

This is unexpected. I was certain this was all Dominic's plan, unless she's protecting him.

'An opportunity for *what*?' I ask, ruffled.

'It's not what you think,' she says, her voice softening. 'I wasn't out to steal your stuff or do any harm . . .'

'Well, can you start off by telling me your real name?'

'It's Laure,' she says. 'Laure Jones.'

'How old are you?'

'Twenty.'

Silence.

'And why did you target me?' My hands curl tighter around my paper cup.

She hesitates. 'I watched your #PublishingJourney videos. I could see in your eyes that a part of you thought they were bullshit. And I just thought I could trust you. I mean, they're just using you, the pair of them, Mina and Romain – anyone can see that.'

Coming the day after I've heard my boss tell my author that I tried to kiss her husband, her words hit hard. But I keep my voice steady, refuse to get into a fight.

'So you are working for Dominic?'

'Dominic?' She looks surprised, or maybe she's just a very good actress. 'I don't know any Dominics . . .'

I try another tack.

'You sent me an article, about someone called Chris Jones – who died? What's it got to do with me?'

A dread fills me. That I'm about to learn of some action in my past that led to terrible consequences. That she wants revenge.

'He was my uncle,' she says, swallowing. 'He died before I was born.' Her voice is quieter; she's lost her antagonistic edge.

She flicks through some photos on her phone and shows me one of two teenagers side-by-side, with fair hair, a lush green woodland behind them. The boy in a T-shirt, wielding a stick and a cheeky grin; the girl has two plaits and a white sundress.

'They were twins – Chris and my mum, Ruth,' she says, her voice catching. 'They're dead now. Mina's to blame.'

Mina? I realise, with a jolt of shock, that I'm not the one Laure's angry with.

'Why Mina?'

'Do you know how rich her husband is?' Laure's tone becomes vicious again. 'He's a multi-millionaire, with that vineyard, but does he pay any tax? Oh, no. It's all offshore, of course.'

'Okay, but what about—'

'Typical bloody one per cent,' she says, and there's something in her tone that reminds me of Dominic and his rants. 'They have all the privilege and what do they do with it? They destroy the rest of us. Their carbon emissions are bigger than sixty-six per cent of the poorest, you know . . .'

'But can we get back to Mina?' I ask.

'I'm getting there,' she snaps. She blows out a breath, rubs the nub of her palm against her forehead, her expression haggard. 'I'm sorry, it's just – this whole situation . . . Nobody's ever going to believe me. When I tell you, I know you're just going to think it's bullshit. Because your job is at stake.'

'I – I do like working for Mina, but . . .' I want to rant, *I think Mina is untrustworthy, and back-stabbing, and she's now trying to play Humbert Humbert with my author.* But it wouldn't surprise me if Laure was secretly taping this conversation, so I speak with care: 'But . . . I know she's not perfect.'

'She's dangerous, that's what she is!' Laure says. 'She and Chris, they were dating at the start of sixth form.'

'But I thought she met her husband when she was a teenager . . .'

'Exactly. Chris was her boyfriend when Romain first turned up at her school. My mum wrote about it in her diary.'

To my surprise, Laure pushes her phone towards me again. I eye up a photograph of a diary entry, written in looping blue biro.

The sexy MP came today to give his talk. He said we all have the power to change our lives and the lives of everyone around us. Mina sat at the front for once. She kept asking questions. She acted as though he was a god. Afterwards Chris turned up and wanted to walk her home and she acted like she barely knew him. What a bitch!

I told Chris not to bother with her anymore but he just chases after her like a puppy following his master.

Last night Chris borrowed Dad's car when Mum and Dad were out. He gave me £1 not to tell

The rest of the entry is cut off.

I glance up at Laure. There is something powerful and moving about diving into this entry – if it's authentic. I remind myself to stay on my guard.

'What has Mina got to do with Chris's death?'

'I think she persuaded him to borrow the car,' Laure says. 'I think they went joy-riding. My mum suspected Mina was in the car that night.'

'But that's not Mina's fault – if he crashed. I mean, even if she fled—'

'But I found another entry.' Laure becomes passionate. 'Describing how Mina loved the adrenaline rush, was always telling Chris to go faster, faster. And sometimes she would drive too, even though she didn't have a provisional license, nothing – Chris was 'teaching' her. It wouldn't surprise me if *she* was the one behind the wheel when it crashed, if she dragged Chris's dying body into the driver's seat and then fled, saving herself.'

'Wouldn't the police have analysed the car?' I ask, shocked.

'By the time they arrived, it was on fire and Chris's body

was already a charred wreck. Which makes me wonder if Mina set it alight herself, to cover up what she did.'

'God, that's a pretty strong accusation . . .'

'Listen: Mum writes that Mina lay low afterwards, and acted weirdly. She didn't even go to Chris's funeral. Can you imagine? By then she was too busy fucking Romain, and pretending she and Chris had never even dated. Her class hated her, she had to take time off school, never finished her A levels. My mum lost her twin brother. And it broke her.' Laure's eyes film with tears. 'They'd been so close. Mum was suicidal. I didn't know all this till – she died . . .'

'How did your mum . . .' I trail off, feeling her pain, thinking of my mum, still lost to me.

'She died last year – lung cancer. I never really understood why my mum's life went off the rails as a teenager. When I was going through her stuff, I found her diaries – then I understood everything. The grief and the rage – Mum was so mad that Mina had got away with it. Mina fled Otley, went to live in Scotland for a while, and then to London with Romain. She stole him from his wife.'

'Romain was married?' I ask.

'Yep. She got to live a charmed life and enjoy her fancy job in publishing. My mum ended up having a breakdown, dropping out of her A levels, needing therapy, medication. She never really got her life back on track – I mean, seventeen is that age where your decisions define your adulthood. She lived a life of quiet desperation.'

A long silence. Laure looks exhausted. She reaches for some gum, removes the silver, pops it into her mouth.

'Thank you for sharing this with me – I really appreciate it.' I realise I sound oddly formal, like Mina and come back to myself: 'But – why me? I mean, I'm a nobody, just an assistant.' *And I'm the last person the police would ever believe.*

'But you're close to her.' Laure's eyes flash. 'This is why I had to pretend to be Aimee – I hope you get that now. If I had contacted you out of the blue, you wouldn't be here now. I'd be some weirdo who you blocked on Instagram. I had to get you thinking, wondering . . . And then I needed to meet you for myself, to see if I could trust you.' Her voice becomes urgent.

I have to admit that she's right: it worked, but she has no idea of the nights of worry and turmoil she's caused me. I'm still digesting her words, trying to work out how I feel about her story.

'If you're friends with Aimee, couldn't she help?'

'Aimee's an addict.' Laure sighs. 'You can't rely on her for anything.'

'Oh. I didn't realise that . . .'

'Plus, Mina and Romain bankroll her lifestyle – she's got this flash car recently, all these designer clothes. She hates them but she's not going to bite the hand that feeds her. But you – you can get into Mina's house. You can investigate. You can get her drunk, get her talking about the past. See if anything comes up.'

'I could do,' I reply, thinking, *No way. I'm not about to jeopardise my job.*

'Don't you see? Laure presses me. 'This is happening all over the world. The richest one per cent can do any crime they like; the rest of us suffer the consequences . . .'

I frown. It's not that I disagree with her words, but she sounds fanatical again, as though she's channelled a private anger into a political cause.

'Look, I have to go,' I say, checking the time; I set up another coffee with a friend, so that I had an excuse to leave. Now I feel a certain regret. 'How long are you in London for?'

'Only four more days,' Laure asserts.

'Well – look, how about we meet on Monday?' I ask her, and her eyes light up.

'That'd be good,' she says. 'Seriously, I have so much more to tell you.'

CHAPTER THIRTY-TWO

Mina

It's 8.30 a.m. Romain and I slide into the back of our Jaguar, ready for work.

'Go via Piccadilly and Northumberland Avenue,' Romain instructs our driver.

'But it ends up slower that way – there's always so much traffic,' I object.

The driver looks at me, then my husband, and Romain reiterates his plan, and that's that: as always, Romain has to win every argument.

Normally I'd sit and stew in irritation but this morning I don't really care. I'm bathed in euphoria; I keep replaying the kiss with Lucas. A WhatsApp from him flashes up on my screen and I flick Romain a quick glance, but he's engrossed in Instagram. Yesterday I caught him in his study, rewatching a #PublishingJourney video that featured Alice, his expression rapt, eyes starry with lust.

Can we meet? The other night was so amazing.

I bite back a smile of relief and joy. Lucas wants more.

I try to stay sober. I remind myself of the blackmail threats that I've received – three to date. I've paid them all. A new one in my inbox this morning, demanding £2,500 by the end of the week. As I predicted, the demands keep rising.

This is just about the worst possible time to begin an affair.

Let alone one with my author. People at work are starting to wonder if I've lost my touch. In a way, my biggest recent discovery has been Alice; I'm her queenmaker, reflecting off her new shiny glory.

And yet: I close my eyes, replaying that kiss, swooning inside. I sought out Feeld with a belief that playing it trivial would offset my guilt: just a bit of silly fun. I thought I could compartmentalise those first affairs, indulge, and go back to my normal life with greater endurance. Instead, I realise, they've been the first stepping stones away from my marriage, and now I'm venturing further and further out. Lucas promises something far more intimate, but in turn far more dangerous.

At work, I bump into Alice in the lift.

'Hey.' I grin at her.

Her 'hello' seems a little sullen. I feel guilt crawling over me – but then I tell myself that she can't possibly know what went on the other night. I do feel bad that I told Lucas about the kiss between her and Romain; I needed to confide in someone, but it was unfair.

'Um, I've been thinking about the edit that I did for Lucas,' Alice says. 'I feel we could do better on the ending. It was keeping me awake last night.'

'Why not just send an email, suggesting you both brainstorm the ending?' I suggest, my guilt intensifying.

'Great,' Alice says in a flat voice. 'I'll get on to that. By the way, you didn't leave any money for renting the other night . . . so . . .'

'Oh God, I'm so sorry,' I say in horror. 'I'll arrange a transfer at once.'

'Wonderful,' she replies, as the lift doors open.

Does she know? I fret, watching her walk away. *What if Lucas has confided in her?*

The funny thing, I wish I *could* open up to Alice about what's happened. But I can imagine the shock and disgust on her face, given how professional she likes to be: this is her first acquisition and I'd be besmirching it.

My affair with Lucas wasn't planned. Looking back, it was our celebratory lunch that started it.

When Alice went off to the toilet, leaving Lucas and me on our own, his eyes fell to my wedding ring. He asked me how long I'd been married. I said drily, 'Far too long,' and he laughed. I asked him, lightly, if he had a partner. As he replied in the negative, he held my gaze. He asked me what I'd loved about my husband so much that I'd wanted to marry him. I'd been a little taken aback, but Lucas had assured me that he'd just been interested in terms of a character he was working on for a new novel. 'I really can't remember,' I confessed. 'I suppose it was all about illusions, as it is when you're young.' I joked that I was trapped in my marriage but Lucas didn't laugh. He looked intrigued, asked what I meant. I tried to be vague but our conversation felt as intimate as a post-coital chat. When Alice returned, we quickly went back to discussing his debut, but Lucas held my gaze, camaraderie flickering in his eyes, as though we now shared a secret.

The next time we met was a launch party for a book edited by a mutual friend. Lucas guided me to the very back of the bookshop, to show me a copy of *The Lion, the Witch and the Wardrobe*. I was so moved when he told me that his mother had read it to him when he was a boy. She had died of a heart attack when he was twelve; today was the anniversary of her death. He asked if we could have a meeting about his edits.

I agreed, Alice's flat in my mind: it would be a lovely, quiet place to have a discussion. I hadn't expected to end up kissing my author, although, looking back, that was rather naive: something in my gut kept whispering that this was no ordinary meeting.

I sit down my desk, sobering up as I reread the blackmail threat email. At the moment, they only know about Feeld, but how long will it be before they find out about Lucas?

I need to figure out who's doing this.

CHAPTER THIRTY-THREE

Alice

I'm meeting Laure again this evening, after work, and an uneasy anticipation flutters inside me all day.

After our last chat, I googled everything she told me. I managed to verify a lot. Yes, Mina did go to Otley Grammar for Girls; I find the detail in a local paper feature. Yes, Ruth, her mother, did die last year: I discover an old Facebook charity appeal from someone trying to raise money for Cancer Research.

I'm still doubtful about whether to trust Laure, but I'm hungry to know more. Every time Mina calls me into her office, I picture her seducing Lucas, and I marvel at her ruthlessness. She's come crashing off her pedestal: her past seems as murky as mine. I keep reminding myself: *Who am I to judge her?* Maybe she has murdered someone – but so have I. She's become a complete enigma: I want to grasp who my boss really is.

I meet Laure in the same branch of Pret as before. It's more crowded today, jostling with office workers, and Laure is looking tired; she tells me she's staying in a hostel.

'I've been reading through more diary entries,' Laure says. 'I keep coming back to the fact that Mina disappeared off to Scotland so soon after the crash.'

Laure's repeating herself from our last meeting and I feel a little frustrated.

'Well, Mina just invited me to a party on Friday,' I say. 'I'll see if I can get her talking . . .'

'That's great,' Laure enthuses. 'I need the loo, but look – you watch this video, whilst I'm in there, it'll explain everything. I was like you, at first. I was naive, I thought the world was a fair place . . .'

I want to tell her that boy, I know the world isn't fair, but Laure is already pressing her phone into my hands, getting up to go.

I wait for the YouTube ads on Grammarly to finish and then the video begins: 'The richest people in the world are pulling the strings . . .' Blah . . . blah . . .

A message notification pops up: How did the meeting with Alice go?

The message is from someone called Matthias.

Matthias?

I nearly drop the phone. What the fuck? He was that Feeld psycho. I remember the way he pinned Mina down on the sofa in my flat, his hands on her throat.

I'm being played.

That bastard Matthias is behind all this; it's some kind of sick revenge. They must have thought I'd be easy to manipulate: the working-class intern who feels like an outsider, spinning me stories about inequality and injustice.

I grab my bag. I don't even want to hang around to hear Laure's next round of lies and excuses. I hurry out of café, speed down the road. *Enough.*

Back home, I compose a WhatsApp for Sean: How was Malta?

I add a kiss, delete the kiss, add the kiss, delete, and finally I just press send.

Laure's messages are piling up, eight in total, but I'm not

reading them for now. Whatever trouble Mina is in, I don't need to protect her or save her. I don't want to get involved.

Fifteen minutes pass. I check my message to Sean, craving one tick to become two. I realise just how badly I'm missing him. Missing his Irish lilt, his playful sense of humour. Missing our banter, the videos we make, Sean playing with Mimi.

And I want to confide in him about everything that's happened today.

I lie on my sofa, thinking back to the first day we met. I was eighteen. I'd been staying with my friend Frieda, but her parents had asked me to leave after her brother had pretended I was stealing from them. Frieda was tearful, on my side. She let me stay in the garage a night or two, lent me a sleeping bag, but it was still freezing in there and I woke with a sore back. In classes I found myself still shivering, falling asleep. *What next?* During lunch breaks at school, all I could do was sit on a bench in a dazed terror and picture myself homeless. Would I end up on drugs, raped, beaten up? And then I knew what I had to do, the only thing I could do: go back home to Mum and my sister and my dad. Even if I was risking violence, it was better than the streets.

My mum hadn't been in touch for a month. I'd messaged her about the theft accusation – no reply. She'd always believed in me but I was scared she thought I was guilty. Back at our block of flats in Brixton, I was shocked at how grimy it was. Frieda's posh house in Hampstead had spoilt me; I was used to fancy cars, gleaming windows with drapes. I climbed the stairs, knocked on the door in dread and hope. I wanted to hug my mum; I wanted to punch my dad. When there was no answer, I crumpled in a ball by the door, waiting for them to come home – only to find a strange woman with a shorn head appearing.

She told me she was now living in the flat. My family had moved away three weeks ago.

'They didn't leave a forwarding address,' she said, passing me a bundle of post. 'Or a number or anything . . .'

I went to a bar that night. In the toilets, I held back tears, telling myself over and over, *Mum hasn't been in touch because she wants to protect you. That was always the plan.* I plastered on the makeup, positioned myself at the bar, smiled at the sexy barman with fair hair. I needed a bed for the night. My plan was to pretend I'd passed out from alcohol, hope someone took me home. It was dangerous, but I felt desperate. I couldn't face the streets.

The barman bought me a beer. I hated the taste, the yeasty smell, but made myself drink it. I wasn't used to alcohol, became drunk quickly, and soon I was telling him my story. He looked alarmed, sympathetic. That night, he let me come home with him to his flat in Hackney. He slept on the sofa like a gentleman, didn't lay a finger on me. In the morning, he told me his name was Sean and made me breakfast. I was wearing nothing but an oversized T-shirt I'd borrowed from him; his eyes travelled over me despite himself. I recognised hope; escape; a new life. I put down my spoon and sat on his lap and pressed my lips to his.

That was how our relationship began. I saw Sean as my hero, my white knight, the man who saved me. Our relationship was always unbalanced that way. I loved him more. When he ended it with me six years on, he wanted adventure, travel.

Now it's the reverse. Sean wants stability and he wants me and I have the big flat. It's been a weird power shift.

But now, I realise, I do want him. I want him here with me. Thinking about it all makes me yearn for my mother.

Twelve years – and I still haven't heard from her. When I inherited this flat, I searched for her on social media, dreaming of rescuing her, but I still couldn't find her. She's gone, my sister's gone; if they're still alive, even.

My phone rings: it's Laure. When I ignore it, she texts me.

I know you saw the Matthias message. I worked it out. But I'm not with him. Everything I have said is true, I swear.

CHAPTER THIRTY-FOUR

Mina

I'm not paying them.

Maybe it's my affair with Lucas, but I'm suddenly feeling reckless, careless. I'm tired of this stupid game. I doubt the blackmailers have anything concrete on me; I'm going to let the deadline slip by and stop giving them all the power.

Tonight Lucas and I are going to a party together. We've invited Alice along so that it doesn't look too suspicious. I spot her reading in her lunch hour, a grammar primer – Lynne Truss's *Eats, Shoots & Leaves*. This is a relief: I hadn't been relishing the thought of having to humiliate her with a lecture on improving her grammar.

Lucas has said he'll pick us up en route. Alice and I wait outside our offices at 6 p.m. A silvery Uber pulls up.

I'm about to slide into the back next to Lucas, when Alice suddenly darts ahead, sitting between us. I have to make do with greeting Lucas across her. God, his smile is sexy; I love the way it lifts on one side; I love the playful spark in his hazel-green eyes. The urge to kiss him becomes feverish.

Alice looks very tense. 'Where are we going tonight?'

'It's a party at the house of a friend of mine, Michel Lambert,' Lucas says. 'It's in Primrose Hill.'

Excitement fizzes inside me. This is what I find so attractive about Lucas: his spirit of adventure, of unpredictability. He's a hedonist, I sense, and I find that so sexy.

The Uber turns into a sweeping gravel driveway flanked by stone lions. A dance beat vibrates from a grand mansion; laughter and voices float out.

A maid opens the door to us, takes our names. We're ushered through a hallway decorated in pinstriped Paul Smith wallpaper, into a vast white kitchen. Outside, about thirty people are drinking, smoking, dancing, chatting on a patio framing a swimming pool.

'Hey!' A man with a shorn head, wearing a linen shirt, comes bounding up, and greets Lucas with an ecstatic hug. 'Lucas, Lucas, Lucas!'

'Michel!' Lucas introduces us: 'This is Mina, and this is Alice.'

'*Enchanté.*' He kisses our hands theatrically. His eyes flit from me to Lucas and back again: has Lucas told him we're a couple?

'Is Mina your . . . *mère*?'

Mother?!

Alice's laughter is cold and glassy. Lucas looks irked. 'Michel,' he says in a warning voice. 'Mina and Alice – they are my editors.'

'I seem to be making all the faux pas tonight.' Michel laughs, looking entirely unrepentant. I get the feeling he was deliberately being an ageist dick with that '*mère*' question, but as we head into the party, I feel dull and dumpy in my work clothes, wishing I'd had time to change before coming out. I applied extra makeup in the work toilets, but I suspect this grey dress still makes me look more serious than sexy. Out by the pool, I notice several guests eyeing up Alice. She's wearing a dress that looks similar to the one I wore to our lunch with Lucas, black with a gold belt. Everyone looks at least fifteen years younger than me.

Lucas is swamped by friends. He shoots me an apologetic look, but then gets waylaid by a woman.

I chit-chat with a German filmmaker, who pitches his novel to me, followed by a marquise, who's quite sweet and pitches her cookbook to me. I overhear Michel offering to make Alice a cocktail, but she says she's tired, wants to leave early, and disappears without even saying a proper goodbye.

What's up with her? I wonder. She's been very subdued this week.

My third cocktail is finished; I'm drunk and tired and grouchy, and various guests are stripping to their underwear and jumping into the pool. I wander down into the peace of a rose garden.

My phone buzzes.

It's another blackmail email.

I missed the deadline and now they're coming after me.

I tell myself to read it later, but my depression makes me weak, makes me open it and drink in the poison:

You didn't pay us today, so we've upped the fee, Mina. You have until 9 a.m. tomorrow morning and now you owe us £3,000.

Shit. I should have fucking paid them.

The email has sobered me. I feel as though I've stepped out of the present flow of madness and seen myself from above. *You're older and wiser than anyone at this party. The kiss with Lucas was fun but he'll be no different to the other Feeld boys: you have no hope of a future together. You don't have to people-please. Just go home.*

I'm scrolling for an Uber, when the call comes through.

'Aimee?' I ask in a low voice.

Her voice is snotty, choked with sobs. 'I can't pay. They

say they're going to call the police – I'm really stuck, I don't have any money on me. It's not my fault, I swear. Michael said the bill was on him and then he walked out.'

'Okay,' I break through her stream of panic. 'Please just tell me where you are and I'll come get you.'

'Sanderson's bar, in Leicester Square. Thank you, thank you.'

I search for a nearby Uber, when another worry hits me: do I have enough to cover a big bar bill *and* this blackmail fee? Shit. My salary goes into my own current account. Pocket money, Romain has called it, for he pays all the main bills. My salary's always been plentiful, but I've blown so much on renting Alice's flat recently that for the first time in decades my balance is low. I bite my lip. I can text Romain to transfer extra, but he's so tight with money and I'll have to come up with an excuse—

'Hey.' It's Lucas. His eyes are bloodshot. Lucas is a hedonist; he won't want this sort of hassle. It's not his scene.

'I need to go,' I say curtly. 'My sister's in trouble.'

'Then I'll come with you,' he asserts, surprising me.

'It's fine—'

'I'm coming. I'll get us an Uber, now. Tell me where we need to go. We can fix this together.'

Sanderson's bar is classy, all glass tables and cocktails served by swish, impeccably dressed staff. I spot Aimee at a table on her own. As we approach her, Lucas hears my intake of breath and touches my hand.

Aimee's wearing a little black dress, the straps slipping down her shoulders, her chestnut hair unravelling from a tortoiseshell clip, mascara tears streaking her cheeks.

'Darling, what happened?' I touch her face. 'This is Lucas. We're here to help you.'

'Lucas — oh, thank you, Lucas, my knight in shining armour!' Aimee grabs Lucas's wrist, handcuffing it, and he laughs awkwardly.

I prise her fingers away and she curls them in her lap, crying again. 'We had a row, me and Michael. He said I was looking at other men, at the waiter — I wasn't doing anything. He just walked out and I don't have any money. I'm really sorry.'

'It's fine,' I reply, keeping my tone brisk when I feel like sobbing myself. 'We'll pay.'

Then she passes the black box, and I fish the bill out of it and gape: oysters . . . champagne . . . mojitos . . . It's over £400.

'God, Aimee!'

There's something theatrical about the sheepish expression she adopts and I feel a flash of suspicion, scanning the room. I wouldn't put it past Aimee that this Michael is sitting at another table, smirking as we pick up his bill. I narrow my eyes, noticing white crumbs around her nose, her lips.

'Look at this,' I cry, brushing them away. 'Look at the state of you!'

We glare at each other, the mood souring. Lucas quickly hails a waiter and before I can protest, he's got his card out and is typing his pin into the machine.

'You didn't have to do that,' I protest weakly.

'Thank you, Lucas, you're my hero,' Aimee says in a baby voice, and I silently warn her: *Don't you dare go near him. He's mine.*

The bill paid, we head out into the warm evening.

'I don't know where I'm going to stay tonight,' Aimee sobs afresh. When Lucas offers up a spare room at his, I slap the idea down at once.

I give Alice a call. The reception isn't great, and when she says no, Aimee can't stay, she's too tired after the party, I feel the rejection like a punch in the gut. I've come to think of her flat as a bit of a second home. I actually feel shocked that she'd reject me in a crisis.

Lucas calls up a trusted friend who has a spare room and who used to have addiction issues of his own; he's willing to keep an eye on her. We drop her off in Clapham and then, after a long night, we Uber back to Mayfair.

Lucas lays his hand down on the seat next to me, letting our little fingers brush against each other. He's been so supportive this evening; I'm surprised and touched by his behaviour.

'Is Aimee . . .' Lucas trails off, looking confused. 'Is she your daughter?'

'No. I love her like a daughter, but no, she's not mine.' Telling that lie for the thousandth time stings like salt, and I suddenly feel the urge to spill everything. I tell myself fiercely not to be stupid: I hardly know Lucas. Yet I feel as though an unexpected intimacy has occurred tonight, that we've bonded through his helping me.

At the bottom of my road, I ask the Uber to drop me off, as though I'm some teenager sneaking home.

'Wait.' Lucas seizes my hand, his eyes filled with longing. 'Can we meet in the reading flat again? Soon?'

'I'd like that,' I agree. As he leans in, daring me to risk a kiss, it takes all my self-control to pull back, to slide out of the car and walk away, longing howling inside of me.

Inside, I go to my study and pay the blackmailer, nearly emptying my account. I can't even pay Alice for the use of her flat – I'll have to ask her to wait. This is getting out of control: I have to find out who's responsible and end this nightmare.

CHAPTER THIRTY-FIVE

Alice

I hear the twist of the key in the lock. I stand up and stare through the spyhole.

It's two nights since we all went to the party at the house of Lucas's friend. Mina asked to rent the flat again, at short notice, so I agreed. But I'm definitely justified in watching them this time: I'm concerned about their power imbalance and what Lucas might feel obliged to do. I want to look out for him.

Lucas enters. He's looking gorgeous in a crisp white shirt. But: how come he has a key? Did Mina give it to him? Did she make a copy?

He sits down on the sofa, fingers tapping on his mobile.

He stands up.

Walks in agitated circles.

He makes a call, leaves a message: 'Mina, it's me. I don't know – I mean – you have to believe me. That email you got wasn't from me. Why the hell would I want to blackmail you? I mean – I'm not in need of money, I don't want to play games with you' – he emits a stressed laugh – 'I just want to be with you. Just . . . can you please get over here? Can we talk?'

He slumps on the sofa, burying his face in his hands. I frown – Mina is being *blackmailed*? I wish I could unlock this door and ask what's going on.

Lucas keeps on obsessively checking his phone. I think uneasily of the messages I saw on Dominic's phone, the photographs they've been taking. I didn't spot him before I locked myself in, but his accomplice could be out there – whoever she is – blending in, unnoticed. Then there's Laure and Matthias and whatever their game is. Maybe it was wrong of me to rent it out, however badly Mina's behaving: without telling her what I know, I'm putting her in even more danger.

Lucas calls her up again: 'Mina, I'm going to wait ten more minutes and then—'

Buzz-buzz. He runs to the intercom, a smile of relief erupting on his face.

Mina enters, her face looks taut with fear.

'What the hell's going on?' Lucas asks. 'You ask *me* to meet, then you don't turn up and say you've received some email with my name on it? I mean – is this really about blackmail or is it your husband? Because we don't have to do this, I thought you wanted—'

'This has nothing to do with Romain,' Mina says quietly.

She sinks onto the sofa, looking exhausted. Lucas sits beside her at a cautious distance, biting his lip. Then he reaches out and takes her hand.

'I'm sorry,' he says. 'I'm just scared I'm going to lose you before we've even had a chance. I don't get – why do you think it's *me*?'

'I realise – it's not you . . . But the email, it means they know about you, you see?'

'What do you mean?'

'They sent an email from a new address. It came into my inbox as Lucas Chamila. See?' She pulls out her phone and shows him.

'I never sent that!' Lucas cries. 'I don't have a Yahoo

email. But Mina – it's just some scam, someone's winding you up . . .'

'No,' she says, shaking her head. 'It's serious. They've been sending threats for weeks and I've been paying. It started with two thousand, then three, and now they want four. And they're watching me. They know, somehow, what I'm doing – and now they're letting me know that they've seen you're with me.'

'But what can they have seen? So I've entered this flat. It's Alice's, right?'

So Mina's told him the truth – that this is my place.

'And she's my editor, so this is work. And you're her boss. It's not weird for us to be here. I mean – there are no cameras in this place, right?' Lucas scans the room and I pull back instinctively, feeling self-conscious. 'They haven't sent any photos, any evidence?'

'No . . . no,' she replies. 'But maybe we should change the location. I mean, what if they're coming from Alice?'

I freeze.

'But I can't see Alice doing that,' Lucas protests, much to my relief. 'You've given her a job – she's grateful, I can see that. She really looks up to you.'

'Does she? I think she did. But she's very cool with me these days.' There's a hurt in her voice that surprises me. 'But you're right. Maybe it could be Dominic, that awful ex of hers.'

My ex? Then I remember the night that Dominic dropped by the flat and spoke to Mina, made claims that we'd been together.

'Alice is simply failing to deal with him,' Mina says. 'And I'm very concerned.'

'You need to get these emails analysed,' Lucas says. 'You

need to find out where they're from, and you need to stop paying. I mean, would it be so bad if people found out we're together? You can't be the first *editrice* to fall for their author?'

'But Romain is an MP and there's an election next year . . .' Mina trails off. 'And we've only just – started this . . . whatever this is . . .' She looks pale, twists her wedding ring, and I can see Lucas is brooding. Then a smile tweaks her lips.

'You're jealous,' she remarks.

'Of course,' he snaps.

Her victory is my sadness: I have to acknowledge that if he's this possessive of her, it's not a one-sided love affair being forced on him by her.

As they start kissing, Lucas unzips her dress and she undoes his shirt. They look . . . *good* together. Despite the age gap. She lies back on the sofa and Lucas starts to kiss his way down her body; I feel aroused at his slow and gentle pace, at the way his lips brush her breast, linger on her stomach, smiling as he tickles her, and then slide up her thighs . . .

And then she stops him. Just as she did with Jacob, I realise.

Lucas straddles her waist, gazing down at her. He brushes her lips with his fingertips. 'How come you don't want me? I just know you're going to taste so good . . .'

'Romain never liked giving it,' Mina says quietly. 'It's not his thing . . .'

'*What?*' Lucas is theatrical in his determination to rival him. 'He's crazy. He's selfish. You deserve this pleasure . . .'

I shiver. I was never aroused when I watched Mina with her Feeld boys, but this is different: longing floods through me. I ache for Sean, silently check my phone, but he still hasn't replied to my message.

*

The next day, I'm exhausted. I ended up in the little room *all night*, my head nestled on the carpet, freezing cold, pain in my bladder. Mina didn't cut the evening short as she normally would: she and Lucas went off to the spare bedroom together. Every few hours, my nightmares would be broken by the sound of their cries of pleasure, the bed rocking against the wall.

They didn't leave until eight this morning, getting dressed together and making toast and coffee as though they were a married couple who'd been living in my flat for years.

The moment they'd gone, I dashed out, used the loo and tried to wake myself up with a cold shower. I drank coffee and ate toast too, their post-coital energy still swirling in the air, intimate and sexy.

When I get to work I dump my bag on my desk and head to the loos, so desperate to grab just a few minutes of sleep that I rest my head against the cubicle wall. Drifting off, I slide and bang my head against the sanitary bin, jumping to my feet in shame. As I wash my hands, I cringe over the fact that I spent most of last week on the verge of going to HR to complain about Mina abusing Lucas, completely overwhelmed by righteous indignation. Now I feel a paradox of emotion: miserably happy for her. It was clear from watching them again last night that Lucas adores her. Maybe I shouldn't hold a grudge. She shouldn't have told Lucas about the kiss with Romain, but I guess she's pretty mixed up right now.

I go for lunch with Cathryn, an agent who's sent me a hot debut novel on an exclusive. The strain of presenting a lively front to her against a backdrop of exhaustion forms a headache in my temples. I head back into the office – and stop short.

Sarah's using my laptop. When she sees me, she jumps, looking guilty.

'Sorry,' she says quickly. 'Mine just froze up and I wanted to check some publication dates.'

It's the first time in a while that we haven't spoken in cold monosyllables. 'OK,' I say, 'but I need to use it now.' I pause. 'How's it all going?'

Sarah rolls her eyes. 'I can't get anything right these days. Today Mina's going on about how I forget to put the apostrophe in "isn't".'

I give her a sympathetic glance and Sarah calls someone from IT, who comes up and says there's nothing wrong with her machine. I gaze over at Mina's office. She looks odd today, both euphoric – bathed in post-coital dewiness – and also hyper-anxious, and I wonder who on earth might be blackmailing her.

CHAPTER THIRTY-SIX

Alice

Buzz-buzz. It's early in the morning and I'm looking forward to getting into work. Yesterday I put in a bid on a book for £25,000. I love the fact that my job can be like gambling; it strikes me that this is a middle-class risk, framed as creative and positive, with a safety net underneath, whereas once, for me and Dom, it would have been fruit machines and breaking into houses.

Buzz-buzz. I check the intercom camera – it's Laure. *Shit.* I thought she was supposed to have gone back to Otley.

I ignore her and she disappears, thank God. I pack my tote bag, feed my birds, ready to go – when I hear a loud knock on my front door.

Oh, great. Someone else must have let her into the building.

When I open the front door, I find her looking frail and anxious, chewing gum.

'What happened? One minute you were in Pret with me and the next—'

'I realised that I couldn't help you,' I say, trying to close the door. 'I'm really sorry, but I do have to go to work—'

'Wait!' Laure presses her palm against it. 'Can we at least talk? I know – I think – you saw a message from a guy called Matthias on my phone – was that it? I've been wracking my brains, it was all I could think of.'

Jean comes out of her flat, looking over at us nosily. I'm keen for her not to overhear anything, so I usher Laure in.

We sit on opposite ends of the sofa. My phone says it's 8:11. I'll give her until 8:20, then insist she leaves.

'I should never have got Matthias involved.' Laure's gaze is intense, her speech rapid and nervous. 'It was just a coincidence. I knew him from Bristol Uni – he came over from Berlin on an exchange. He ended up moving to the UK, and we met up for a drink a few months back and he was showing me all these girls on Feeld he was hoping to bed. And then . . . I saw Mina's profile. I mean, I thought it was a fake. It couldn't really be her, right? But then Matthias thought it *was* her after they had a Zoom, and he went along to meet her . . .'

Anger flares inside me. Mina might not be my favourite person right now, but I haven't forgotten how horrific that night was . . .

'So you didn't know that Matthias was going to be violent?'

'What d'you mean, violent?' Laure looks genuinely shocked.

'Oh, so he neglected to tell you that he tried to strangle her, for fetishistic fun? And you're the one who set this up?'

'No, not that like,' Laure objects.

'You weren't trying to punish her?' I fire on. 'For being part of the one per cent, part of the evil cabal ruling the world—'

'Fuck off,' Laure cries, her voice breaking. Tears film her eyes. 'I just wanted information. Matthias was supposed to ask her about Chris, get to know her. That's all. All he told me was that they had sex and Mina got rid of him before he had a chance to dig . . .'

Laure rubs her eyes, looking embarrassed to have shown

emotion. Despite everything, I feel sorry for her. And I believe her. I think.

'Well, what's done is done,' I say. 'I think you have to drop this thing – if you can't, then I can't get involved. I'm sorry, but it's not my battle.' *I have enough battles of my own to fight,* I add silently.

'Look, I've got a new lead. A woman that my mum used to work with in Otley: Sue. She knew Mina too, when they were teenagers. And this – this is really a breakthrough – she was with Mina the night that Chris died. She could tell us more about whether Mina had injuries that might prove she was driving the car.'

'Okay.' I sit up. I must admit, I am intrigued now. Even if Laure's got involved with dodgy folk like Matthias, she is sincere: I can see that.

'Plus, I keep coming back to the weirdness of Mina disappearing off to Scotland for a year right after the crash.'

'It is pretty odd,' I agree, 'but she was probably traumatised – maybe her parents just wanted her to have time to heal.'

'Listen: Sue visited her. My mum wrote in her diary that Sue came back with secrets, but refused to disclose them . . .'

'That's interesting.'

'It is!' Laure looks thrilled that I'm coming round to her story. 'I mean – it's right after her GCSEs. She had to forgo her A levels. Why do that? Unless you're really messed up, because you were responsible for someone dying *and* you've got a secret to hide. I've got in touch with Sue and she's willing to speak to us . . .'

Us makes me nervous, but I have to admit, I'm tempted. 'So is she coming to London . . .'

'No. That's the trouble – Sue's up in Otley. But we could travel there together!'

'You want me to go all the way up to Otley!' I cry in disbelief.

'It's two hours to Leeds on the train. It's not like we're flying to Australia. It's a day trip,' Laure argues. 'It's nothing. And you can work on the train. Look – when I spoke to Sue she implied there were things she didn't want to put in an email, that she would only disclose in person.'

'Let me think about it,' I say uncertainly.

'The only reason I extended my stay here down south was to make sure you came back up with me—'

'Seriously, I do have to get to work.'

'Okay. Fine. But given that you go in to work every day, and you're running after Mina, and making her coffee . . .' Laure sees me wince as her voice grows bitter with sarcasm. 'Okay, I know you like her, but don't you want to know who she is? Who Mrs Glossy is underneath all those jewels and fancy clothes and her la-di-da voice?'

I hesitate and Laure leans forward, sensing she's hit a weak spot: I'm fascinated by Mina's past, by who she really is.

'Let me think about it,' I say, but before she leaves, I see a look of triumph on her face: she knows she's got me thinking.

CHAPTER THIRTY-SEVEN

Mina

Romain drops the bombshell at breakfast on a Thursday morning: we're in financial trouble.

For one scary, surreal moment I fear that somehow he's found out about the blackmail threats. But then he starts speaking about the vineyard. There's been a catastrophe: the crop has been blighted by phylloxera. This year the losses will be deep; the vineyard might even go under, with outstanding debts, which means all our assets, even our house, are in danger. I listen in shock. The vineyard has been our source of wealth for decades: the foundation of our financial stability. I don't know all of the ins and outs; Romain's always been the one in charge of the money.

'I'm going to book a flight at the weekend. I need to speak to Anaïs,' he says, referring to the manager over in Bordeaux. 'And we need to start economising. It's time for austerity.' He sounds as though he's introducing a government policy into our household.

Then he adds that if I could transfer some of my publishing earnings into our joint account, that will help with cash flow and bills. I maintain my poker face whilst thinking, *Shit, shit.* I have virtually nothing in it. Romain has never bothered to check or analyse my spending, which he's called my 'pocket money'.

I go into work feeling shellshocked. Alice chases up the

money I owe her for the rental with Lucas and I assure her: 'God, I'm so sorry – it's slipped my mind. I'll transfer over later today. And your salary payments should start tomorrow.'

That certainly cheers Alice, who looks brighter as she leaves the office.

I don't have enough to pay Alice, though Lucas has offered to help. I keep refusing him, feeling too proud, but maybe I'm going to have to turn to him. I can't get my head round it all: I haven't been broke since I was a teenager.

Back home, I find the kitchen in a mess. Dishes piled in the sink, Romain's dirty laundry in a wire basket, crumbs on the tables. When Romain comes home and enlightens me: he's 'suspended' Baba, as another attempt to budget.

The whole energy of the house feels different without her motherly warmth and calm. Now it's cold and chaotic. After cooking an abysmal dinner that Romain barely eats, I end up at the sink, rubber gloves on and Fairy liquid squirted in the bowl, feeling tired at having to do all this after a day at work. I remind myself that this is normal, that I've been spoilt for so long . . .

I ask Romain if we can plunder our savings, but he points out: 'We don't know if this bad year is a one-off. I need to see how blighted the crop is. We might be in the same situation this time next year.'

'What about Aimee?' I ask, thinking of how she'd react if we stopped her payments. Then I consider what she spends the money on. 'It might force her to get clean . . .'

'No,' Romain says crisply. 'Those are a necessity. We can't risk her spinning out of control right now.'

I nod, stunned, play the dutiful wife on autopilot. I help pack his suitcase for his trip to Bordeaux.

In the bathroom, I sit on the edge of the bath and read

a new message from Lucas. I think I'd be going insane right now if it weren't for him, if I didn't have him to look forward to . . .

The evening after Romain leaves, I travel over to Alice's flat. We debated whether to meet at my house, but I felt too nervous about the CCTV installed everywhere. Lucas insisted that he pay the fee.

We arrange for me to enter the flat first and Lucas to turn up an hour later, to avoid too much suspicion. I sit on the sofa, reading but hardly able to concentrate. At six, the doorbell rings. I have to still the urge to run over in excitement like a teenage girl, forcing myself to walk with cool dignity and open the door. Lucas is wearing linen trousers, sunglasses, his hands in his pockets. He looks cool and beautiful and my heart whispers, *I'm falling in love with him.*

I close the door and draw him into the living-room; there, with the curtains safely closed, I let him kiss me.

'I've missed you,' he whispers, holding me tight, and I tell him I've missed him too.

I offer him wine, suddenly feeling heavy with subterfuge. I love the fantasy nature of our affair, yet a part of me craves honesty, a necessary step for real intimacy. I wonder if Lucas would still want me if he knew I was a mother, if his fantasises of me might be replaced by images of me breastfeeding or changing nappies. I can't face losing him, not right now; I feel so raw and vulnerable, everything collapsing around me.

Soon he's kissing me hungrily. He pulls down my sleeve, slips his finger under my bra strap.

'Before Romain went away, did you make love? Good-bye sex?'

'I've told you a dozen times,' I say, holding his face in mine. 'Romain and I never have sex.'

'You're sure it's not just a line . . .' Lucas always looks a little dubious when I tell him this.

'It's the truth.'

'Then he is an idiot,' Lucas asserts, drawing me for a deep kiss.

I love his jealousy. After years of Romain's indifference it's an aphrodisiac.

And then we're on the sofa, making love, lost in hot bare skin and sweet pleasure. As Lucas enters me, he stops to gaze down at me, his eyes soft: 'I love you, Mina.'

I gaze up at him, the words stuck in my throat. My heart is beating very fast but I can't say it, I can't.

Afterwards, we go into the kitchen and Lucas insists that he cook dinner. We laugh and cook together, dissecting fat tomatoes for a pasta dash, sprinkling in oregano, softening the spaghetti with olive oil. As we sit down to eat, he lights a candle and places it in the centre.

'I wish we could be like this every night,' he says, a little provocative now. It's even more dangerous than *I love you*.

'I wish we could too,' I say at last, and I see happiness break on his face.

Oh God, what am I getting into? This can only be an affair. It needs to be controlled and kept in its place.

After dinner, we share a bottle of Chateau Soisy-le-Vicomte and curl up on the sofa together, sharing one glass back and forth between kisses.

'How is Aimee doing?' Lucas asks.

'She's ignoring my messages,' I say sadly. 'She tends to go through cycles – I hear from her a lot, and then something happens, like that night at Sanderson's, and she wants to be rescued but she's also embarrassed and angry that she's been rescued. So then she goes silent . . . I want to build a relationship with her, but it's hard.'

'If there's a twenty-two-year age gap, then I guess you never really shared bunk beds or played together,' Lucas muses.

'No, we didn't,' I say.

A silence.

'She's – she's my daughter,' I burst out.

Even as I say it, I can't believe I've broken the pact Romain and I made twenty-two years ago.

In all that time, I've never told anyone.

Until tonight.

'It doesn't surprise me,' Lucas says. 'When you were together, I picked up on it . . .'

'I was so very young,' I say, unable to look at him. 'I wanted her, but I couldn't cope. My parents adopted her, took her on as their own.'

'Shit.' Lucas sits up, taking the glass away from me, setting it on the table. 'So – she's your daughter? But . . . right. Wow. You keep it quiet?'

'Aimee didn't even know herself, until a few years ago,' I admit.

I watch Lucas's expression, and I'm relieved to see curiosity rather than judgement. I refuse to be ashamed; I spent my entire childhood being trained into that.

'Tell me everything,' he says.

I explain to Lucas what it was like, being brought up in such a strict household. Throughout my early teens, I embraced their Christian faith. I wore a chastity ring to broadcast that I was waiting for marriage. But as I grew up, I started to wonder, and I started to question. How the whole of humankind's downfall could hinge on just one curious bite of an apple. And why it all had to be blamed on a woman. I had a teenage boyfriend called Chris when I began my affair with Romain. When I met Romain for secret liaisons in the back of his Volvo I felt so powerful, fascinated by his inner battle, his voice telling me that *this is the last time, this can't happen again*, whilst the fever in his eyes showed that men were just as capable of being tempted. Of falling. The chastity ring I wore was an aphrodisiac; the more forbidden the fruit, the more heightened the taste, I realised.

'Romain was always jealous of Chris,' I explain to Lucas. 'But Chris had been my first love – though he was like any seventeen-year-old boy. He'd be cold, he'd be hot, he'd ignore me with his friends. And then – then I did the pregnancy test. I mean – I had just got my GCSEs, I was starting A levels – and . . .'

'But the baby was Chris's?'

'No – Chris and I, we weren't having sex. We were both so young, I told him I wasn't ready. No, it was only Romain I was sleeping with . . .'

My father's shock was satisfying. He even broke down weeping in the middle of a sermon. My mother told me I'd never be able to cope with a baby. I was too flighty, she declared, too wild. Romain's reaction was heartbreaking. I had thought it would force him to leave his wife. Instead, he demanded I have an abortion.

'Bastard,' Lucas says, tightening his arms around me.

'Then there was the accident . . . Chris and I got drunk one night, in the graveyard behind the vicarage. He decided to drive home. He ignored me telling him it was too danger-ous. He loved borrowing his parents' car, going too fast. And he crashed the car – in the woods. He died that night.' Tears sting my eyes at the memory.

'Oh God,' Lucas says. 'Mina, what a thing to go through.'

'I decided to keep my baby. My parents were terrified of the scandal. They made me swear not to tell anyone. Looking back, I think they'd already started planning that they would adopt her. My mum had always wanted another child. They arranged for me to stay in a cottage in Scotland that once belonged to my grandmother. I was holed up there for a year. I had Aimee in that cottage. I'd post secret letters to Romain, because I was still in love with him, still in love with Chris's ghost. It was a crazy time.'

'That's a lot when you're seventeen,' Lucas says. 'I couldn't have handled anything like that.'

I feel sad when I tell Lucas how I came to losing Aimee. My heart would burst with infinite love as I watched my child sleeping, when I gazed down at her and saw the exact shade of my eyes reflected back at me, when her pudgy little fingers curled around mine. But I was struggling. My mother was constantly criticising me, making out I was a bad mother if I slept through Aimee crying, or forgot to sterilise a bottle in my exhaustion. I fell into a depression. Finally, six months after she was born, I relented. I agreed to let my parents legally adopt Aimee. We went back to Otley. The cover story was that I'd had a break abroad, that my parents had adopted and I had a new baby sister.

'Now that I was free of "baggage", Romain finally left his wife,' I said. 'It was a bit of a scandal – I was still so young, only eighteen. And I just wanted to escape everything. So we moved to London, where he was selected for a new, more highly prized constituency. It was a fresh start for us both. I was able to finally take my A levels, get a degree, begin publishing internships . . .'

I rarely saw Aimee. And that ache for her grew over the

years. My mother, who had grown bitter in middle age, blossomed as she took care of her, sending me photos and videos of Aimee growing, developing teeth, hair, calling her Mummy for the first time, gaining braces, losing braces, becoming beautiful. I wanted to see her, but often Romain would demand that I cancel plans to travel north, citing an important social event that was crucial to his career, reinforcing my mother's conviction that I was a neglectful parent.

'But he should have been a proud father,' Lucas protests. 'If I was a father, I'd love my kid – I wouldn't behave like that. How can he?'

'I know, I've said the same so many times. But he just didn't want to face it somehow. For a while, he tried to insist that Chris was the father, even though it's not possible. I said, "Do a DNA test," but he wouldn't.'

Lucas falls silent. I can sense him digesting it all. Romain has been the caricature bad husband until now and suddenly he's realising how complex everything is.

And I haven't even told him everything. There's so much I've held back, but it's enough for now.

'And Aimee found out?' Lucas asks.

'I . . . That's a story for another day,' I say, suddenly feeling exhausted.

'But I want to hear everything,' Lucas begs. 'Don't hold back.'

'I'm just too – too drained.'

Lucas holds me tight, but I'm scared. I'm scared he's judging me.

'You must be thinking what a terrible mother I am,' I say in a small voice.

'No,' Lucas protests. 'I'm not, not at all. I'm thinking that nobody has let you be the mother you wanted to be. And that's pretty sad. You've been moved like a pawn by your parents, by your husband.'

'You think I'm weak,' I flare up.

'You were so young,' Lucas says. 'Who can make those kinds of decisions then?'

'It's always been Romain who called the shots,' I tell him in a shaking voice. 'It was only in my early thirties that I began to gain perspective on the situation. I had gone from a controlling father to a controlling husband; I hadn't broken free but was experiencing life on repeat.'

Lucas is quiet. I feel sad, because I want him to tell him that I can escape, free myself. But it's too late. Romain has me trapped. He knows the very worst of me, the secrets I can't even share with Lucas. Romain owns me.

And now I've just handed another man a weapon: my past. If our affair ever went sour, Lucas could destroy me too.

Then I look up, into Lucas's beautiful eyes. And I see something in him that Romain lacks: a kindness.

I lean in and kiss him . . .

After we've made love, we lie in a dreamy post-coital mode for a while, kissing, exchanging whispers, when suddenly something catches my eye.

'Look – that picture on the wall, the one by the TV – it looks weird.'

'What d'you mean, weird?'

'I noticed it last time and thought then it didn't look right . . .'

I get up and walk over, peering at the picture. Is that a *hole* in it? A . . . spyhole?

Lucas helps me to shift the TV and I'm shocked to see a

door behind it. I had no idea there was a room here – and why is it hidden away? I rattle the handle; it's locked.

Then I look through the peephole in the picture. The room is small. It has a threadbare carpet, a window – and nothing else. I twist my neck, but I can't get a full view of the room.

'It's empty,' I say in relief.

'Let me see,' Lucas says. 'It looks like a store cupboard.'

'Yes – I guess it is. I'm surprised Alice didn't mention it . . .' Whenever I suggest to Lucas that Alice might be the one blackmailing me, he thinks I'm being paranoid. But this has made me feel jumpy. 'Can we go into the bedroom . . .?'

CHAPTER THIRTY-EIGHT

Alice

Three Years Earlier

I'm in Kensington Gardens when I spot some purple crocuses. I pick a few. A woman's voice chides me: 'It's illegal to
pick those, you know.'

I freeze: I'm being accused of criminal activity, just for
taking a few flowers? I can hardly put them back. I hurry
away, clutching them tight.

Outside Julia's flat, I see Dom across the road. He hangs
out there day after day, leaning against the wall, playing Candy
Crush and vaping. It's his way of 'keeping an eye on things'.
It's begun to irk me: I'm the one doing all the hard work. We
argued about it the other day.

In the lobby, I smile at the doorman, who gives me a cool
nod. I'm still the new girl. He's more friendly with the other residents, who've been here for years, like that bossy woman Jean.

I unlock the door to Julia's flat with a spurt of pride; she's
just entrusted me with my own key.

She's asleep in her favourite cosy armchair, nestled against
her stork-embroidered cushions. Her stick lies by her feet; an
audiobook narrator is adopting the breathless voice of Jane
Eyre. Her white hair flops over her forehead; she's recently
had a black streak dyed into it, which she jokes is her Cruella
de Vil look.

Waking up, she looks bewildered. I sense how I might look to her, through her partially sighted vision: perhaps like the pictures in the book about Monet that she showed me the other day, more dots and blurs of colour than lines or sharp edges.

'Look.' I bring the flowers close so that she can smell them. Her face lights up. 'I actually got into trouble,' I say, as I get a crystal vase. 'A random woman accused me of stealing them.'

'Sod her!' Julia laughs. 'Now, it is time for tea?'

'I think it is,' I reply. It's become a refrain between us, every mid-afternoon. I go to the kitchen, spoon Darjeeling leaves into her little brown teapot, put delicate cups onto a tray.

It's been three months since I first met Julia in the library. I began helping her with her Waitrose shopping. I would linger, offer to cook her meals. Dominic had to help train me, back in in the house we were squatting in; we shoplifted some Mary Berry cookbooks from a local Waterstones and poured over them. After six weeks, I started staying one night a week, because Julia was going through a phase of nightmares and disorientation. Then two nights, three nights. I love sleeping here: the luxury of a smooth mattress, of crisp sheets that smell of clean citrus.

In my anxiety I spill a little tea.

'What is it?' Julia asks, curling her hand around mine. 'Something's upset you.'

I don't want to tell her the truth, so I focus on the incident with the flowers. 'The woman who told me off, she was so . . .' I break off, for Julia's been teaching me not to swear. 'She was so pious. It reminded me of how, when I was a teenager, I was staying with my friend, Frieda, and her family. They accused me of stealing.'

Julia's pale eyes are sympathetic with interest.

'The ridiculous thing was, I was trying *so* hard to fit in. I did the washing-up after every meal. Frieda thought I was a boring square. Her parents were so compassionate. They ran a homeless charity; they saw me as a project. But her older brother, Mark, didn't like the fact I'd taken the bedroom he wanted. There were nights when I had to put a chair under the handle of my bedroom door because he was trying to get in. After that, his dad's watch suddenly went missing – and it was found in my room. Mark had planted it. So then they asked me to leave. They weren't going to choose me over their son, after all.' I take a breath. 'The weird thing is, once I had to leave, the fact they'd thought I was a thief burned in me. And later, when I *did* steal, from Heather Perkins, it was as though I was . . . I was doing what they'd finally predicted I would do all along. Like I couldn't be any better.'

'As though they'd carved out a role for you,' Julia muses.

'I don't know why they took me in in the first place.'

'Oh, middle-class guilt, I imagine.'

'Oh, right,' I say, interested, as she elaborates. This is what I love about Julia. I find the world a confusing place, and I'm constantly churned up with the injustice of it all. But she knows how to translate my feelings into words, gives me terms and phrases that anchor them into context: class, society, first-world problems.

Julia goes off for her afternoon nap at four. I eye up the bookcase. I don't want to do this, but Dominic is insisting I do.

I remove a copy of *Oliver Twist*.

It's a first edition. Dominic says it's his due, but I still feel miserable: Julia is too lovely to deserve this.

I'm also scared that Julia's going to notice. It's the third valuable rare book that I've stolen in the space of eight weeks. She might be partially sighted and a little muddled, but there's still a sharp beadiness in her.

Dominic and I argued last night. We met in the McDonald's on Kensington High Street and shared a Coke, shoving it back and forth as the ice melted.

'I can't eat if you don't steal a book,' Dominic insisted. 'We need the funds. You're getting too emotional, too attached. She did this to me, remember?' He parted his hair, showing me the twist of a scar, the raw white skin.

'I know.' I shrink back, because I find it so hard to imagine Julia doing that, but homelessness has taught me that anyone can turn out to be capable of anything.

So now I follow Dominic's orders, against my will, my gut instinct.

I slide *Oliver Twist* into my rucksack.

Julia wakes up from her nap in a crabby mood.

I can't seem to get anything right. I've brought her the wrong slippers; the tea I've made is too strong; the tea I've made is too weak; I've bought her a copy of the *Daily Mail*, when I should have got *The Times*.

'But you always ask for the *Mail*,' I say brightly, wondering if this is a sign of impending dementia, which Dominic wants me to note daily. 'Look – it's got Kate and William in it,' I add, for Julia is a passionate royalist.

'So it does,' she says, leafing through, but an impatient frown lingers on her face.

Perhaps this is who Julia really is, I muse sadly. Perhaps she's starting to show her true colours, as Dom predicted.

Buzz-buzz.

We both jump; Julia rarely has any visitors. I check the intercom camera and double-take.

'It's your son,' I say nervously.

'Dominic?' Her expression becomes vulnerable. She takes a very big gulp of tea. 'I see.'

I'm just as panicked. We were supposed to wait another three months before bringing Dominic back into her life. I was supposed to bump into him by accident, drop hints to Julia that he wanted a reconciliation.

Buzz-buzz.

'Let's see what he has to say for himself.' Julia's hand curls tight around her stick. Her eyes are fixed hard on the door.

When I open the door Dom is chatting with Jean, the neighbour. His accent is already posher: he can really switch it on when he wants to.

I flash my eyes at him: *What's going on?* But he barges past me.

Dominic always wants to be the one in control. It's never *our* plan, but *his*. Once I loved the fact that he was in charge, that he was so savvy, that he knew how to pick a lock or spot a plainclothes. Now I just feel pissed off. He's the one who's being emotional, I reckon. It's been going so well with Julia and I'm scared he's going to blow it.

'Hi, Mum.' Dominic kisses her cheek. Her lips remain thin.

He sits down and pours himself some tea, heaping in four sugars, then natters away for a while, whilst Julia eyes him up dubiously. Then he nods at me.

'So who's this you've got working for you?'

Julia's face brightens. 'This is Alice. She's my carer. She's becoming like the daughter I always wished for,' she needles him.

Pride blossoms in my heart, but I feel awkward. I don't want to become ammunition in their family war.

'She sounds far too good to be true,' Dominic remarks, refusing to look at me.

'It's been so long since you last visited,' Julia remarks, hurt in her voice.

'I've been travelling,' Dominic improvises. 'I was in Spain, France, all over really.'

'I see.' She stares at him over the rim of her cup, hawkish. 'Run out of money, have you?'

Dominic pauses for too long.

'You know, I've decided to change my will recently . . .' she says, testing him, and Dominic sits up. 'I'm giving it all to the Cats Protection League!' she cackles, slapping her knee, and her stick falls, clattering down by her feet.

'Great idea,' I declare, glaring at Dominic.

'What about me? What about some compensation for you murdering my dad?' Dominic asks.

Julia just laughs some more. Then she shoots me a glance. 'When I told you what he was like, I doubt you really believed me. But – here he is.'

Dominic looks so pained that for the first time I wonder if Julia did abuse him, if the doubt I harbour is unfair. I decide to retreat to the kitchen. I refill the teapot, angry that three months of good work is about to go down the drain.

When I go back in, they're both looking even more tense.

'So – where did you find this Alice?' Dominic asks.

'In Kensington Library,' Julia says.

'What, you didn't get her from a proper agency? No reference?'

What the hell is he playing at?

'See, I was watching Alice just now and I'm sure she put something of yours in her rucksack. I think you should check it. Just to be sure.'

I freeze. My heartbeat starts to speed up as I realise what Dominic is doing.

'No need.' Julia rolls her eyes. 'Alice might steal crocuses, but that's as far as she goes.'

'You've got to watch out,' Dominic says. 'I was reading in the *Mail* this morning about how the care system is rife with con artists. If she's got nothing to hide, than she'll be fine to show you . . .'

I'm trying to scrabble together excuses, but it's too late. I didn't recognise how far our relationship had fallen apart. And now Julia is asking me to open up my rucksack, her eyes bright with faith in me. I'm probably the first person she's trusted in years.

'I'll check then.' Dominic reaches for the rucksack and I consider making a run for it, but it's too late: he's already showing his mother the *Oliver Twist* inside. 'This looks familiar, doesn't it?'

An hour later, I find myself in an interrogation room in Kensington Police Station.

When Julia called them, I went crazy. I told her that Dominic had planted me, but I'd grown to care for her. I begged. I used the word *love*. Dominic tried to deny any involvement, but Julia was suspicious. At least I have that one small victory. But he just got told to get the hell out of her flat, whilst I got ushered into a police car by Sergeant Pester.

I've avoided ever ending up in a station for so many years. I've come close, so many times. Now I feel defeated, ruined.

'How did you come to defraud Julia Forde?' Pester asks.

'Julia is starting to show signs of dementia. She said that I could borrow the book and her son wanted to accuse me, because – well, he's a nasty man. It's all a misunderstanding.'

'I see.' I can tell he's not buying it.

'Dominic got jealous. He wanted to be remembered in her will.'

'Oh?' He catches me. 'And did you want to be remembered too?'

I fall silent, wondering if, right from the start, I should have just adopted the standard 'No comment' defence, like criminals do on TV. Pester keeps his eyes on me like a spotlight, and the pressure grows, and I trace the table with my finger, panic mounting—

A rap on the door. Sergeant Pester rises, addresses a female PC in a low voice. He turns looking furious. Now what am I being accused of? Sweat seeps through my thighs, sticking my trousers to the plastic chair.

'You can go,' he sighs, shaking his head.

At first, I think I've misheard him.

'Julia Forde decided to drop the charges.' He waves his hand at me as though I'm a stray animal. 'Go on then – get out of here!'

I jump up, knocking over the chair, and exit in a daze. Outside the police station, the sky is grey, cars are shooting past, and London is carrying on as usual. But my world has been reconfigured. In the space of a few hours, I've lost my allies, Dominic, and now Julia; I've lost my home and a safe place to sleep at night. I walk down the road, with no idea of where to go now, and suddenly I feel very alone.

CHAPTER THIRTY-NINE

Alice

On the day I'm due to meet Laure, my alarm fails to wake me and I oversleep. When I finally stir, I see it's ten past nine and freak out. I pull on my clothes, grab an apple from my fruit bowl, and pound all the way to High Street Kensington tube station, perspiring under the glare of the sun.

I meet Laure at King's Cross and we run down platform 9, jumping onto the train for Leeds just before the doors beep closed.

We find some seats and catch our breaths. Laure breaks off from chewing gum to give me a nervous smile. She's carrying a rucksack; her return to Otley will end her stay in London. She looks pent up. She asks me if I've been able to spy on Mina.

I give a vague reply. I don't tell her that two nights ago, Mina rented my flat again, but I couldn't face another night of fractured sleep in the secret room. Instead, I booked a room in a Premier Inn. I stayed up late watching TV and resisting the temptation to message Sean and beg him to get back together, then spent most of the night tossing and turning on the scratchy white sheet. Laure would go mad if she knew I'd missed an opportunity to spy. I regret it too: I keep wondering what whether Mina and Lucas are still together, what secrets she might be sharing with him.

'So, what about the woman we're meeting?' I ask. 'Can you tell me more about her?'

Laure looks excited, speaks in a gush:

'Sue and my mum worked together in a gift shop. Mum said she was quiet, really nice. Like I said, she's mentioned in the diary. Sue was close to Mina and Mum was convinced she knew something. And there's more – I managed to chat to—'

'Sorry – maybe I should take this,' I interrupt, as a call comes through on my phone. It's from an unknown number. I'm scared it might be the police, following up on Sean's complaint.

I decide to answer too late, just as they ring off.

'So I met up with Aimee whilst she was in London,' Laure picks up her story. 'And we got pissed. In the early hours of the morning, she got all weepy and I asked her about Mina going to Falkirk when she was a teenager. Aimee said something about a baby . . . when I tried to push for any more, she passed out.'

'What?' I try to moderate my shock. 'Aimee's an addict. If she was drunk she could say anything. You said yourself she wasn't a good source.'

'But I think Aimee let the truth slip because it makes sense, don't you see?' Laure becomes impassioned. 'This whole mystery of why Mina disappeared off for a year to Scotland – it's been going round and round in my mind. If, say, she was pregnant with Chris's baby, then maybe she had to get rid of it.'

'You mean she had an abortion?' I ask, fearing Laure might mean something more dramatic and horrific.

'Yeah, maybe that. Her parents were so hyper-religious, though, that they'd have said no to an abortion – they'd probably have made her give it away. I mean, they adopted themselves, so they'd know all about the procedures . . . And if Mina *was* responsible for Chris's death, then she probably wanted nothing more to do with the baby.'

Laure keeps on speculating for a while, and she's so intense that I'm relieved when she goes off to the buffet car to get teas for us. I gaze at my reflection: ghost fragments on the green countryside blurring past. I can't quite digest her words: I feel convinced one minute, doubtful the next. Maybe I'm scared that if we do find out that Mina was responsible for the death of a seventeen-year-old boy, I'm not sure how we'll proceed. It's not as though Chris's death is even considered an unsolved case. It was ruled an accident. Would the police really listen or care? I picture officers striding into our offices, Mina being escorted out in her heels: it's surreal.

At Leeds, we change for Weeton. Sue's house is a bus ride away and we get off and walk down a sunny lane to a stone cottage sporting window baskets, fiery with geraniums in pink and scarlet.

The doorbell chimes a snatch of nursery rhyme and Sue opens the door. Though she's the same age as Mina, she looks older. She's small and sprightly, her blonde hair streaked with grey; her manner is warm and welcoming.

Sue ushers us in. Her living-room is cluttered and cosy, with green sprays of ferns everywhere and ivy curling from a pot, framing an oil painting over her mantelpiece.

After we've had a chit-chat, her tone becomes more formal. She flicks her hair behind her ears with her long, polished nails, and asks: 'So, Laure, what did you want to talk to me about?'

Do I detect impatience in her tone? As though she's dealt with Laure before?

'I hope you don't mind me coming back,' Laure says, the

'back' making me uneasy. 'So, Alice here works with Mina at her publishing house.'

'Oh!' Sue raises her eyebrows, looks a fraction less sceptical. 'And how do you find that?'

'She says it's hard going,' Laure cuts in, before I can reply.

Sue purses her lips, nodding. I realise then that Laure's brought me here in part to bolster her credibility, to prove that she isn't just an obsessive with a vendetta against Mina. I'm supposed to back her up.

'Alice also feels Mina is a very troubled person,' Laure goes on. 'And then I recently found a diary, from my mum.' She pulls it out of her rucksack, opening it up.

As Laure passes it over, Sue smooths the page and says, more gently: 'I can imagine this must mean a lot to you, to find this.'

'Please,' Laure begs her. 'Please just read the entry.'

Sue reaches for her reading glasses, her face furrowing into a frown. She takes an age to read. The background tick of the clock seems to grow louder and louder.

'Well, I know it says here that Ruth thought I might be acting strangely,' Sue says, her tone still gentle to the point of patronising, 'but I wasn't covering up anything. You see, as I said before, Mina was at my house on the night of the crash. We were doing homework together. I remember her trying to call Chris and he wouldn't pick up.'

'But *before* she came to see you, she might have been in the car with Chris – maybe even driving. Did you see any injuries on her?'

'None,' Sue asserts. 'And the police interviewed her too. They'd have seen if she had any scratches. Besides, she was with me from seven in the evening onwards. It just doesn't make sense – Chris crashed much later in the evening.'

Laure falls silent, crushed by disappointment.

'Look, when I was at school with Mina, she could definitely be a bitch from time to time. But it was all a bit of an act. Underneath that, she could be very generous. I remember I had a hamster who died and I was heartbroken, and the next morning Mina went off to the pet shop, used all her pocket money to get me another. Mina would never harm another person.'

'Well, okay,' Laure protests, her voice shrill. 'But can we stick to the facts? There's a timeline that occurred after Chris's death. Mina suddenly went to Falkirk, Scotland. She was about to do her A levels, she had everything ahead of her – and she just jacked it all in, disappeared for a year.' Laure takes the diary back. She's so agitated as she searches for the entry that she tears a page and winces.

I catch eyes with Sue; she looks both sympathetic and dubious, as though she's a therapist and I've brought her a troubled patient.

Laure regains control. 'Here, I've got it. It says here that you went off to Scotland to see Mina. Her mum was up there with her.'

'Laure.' Sue's voice becomes firmer. 'Mina was devastated by Chris's death. And there was a lot of gossip flying about that her parents didn't like. Like you, people thought she might have been involved, in the car with him that night. And then there was her affair with Romain – he was newly married and his wife was finding out. Imagine dealing with all of that at the age of seventeen! They took her to Scotland to try to smooth things out, save her reputation.'

'But I heard from a reliable source that Mina might have been pregnant,' Laure says.

'What source?' Sue frowns.

'From Aimee . . .' Laure trails off.

'Aimee? Mina's younger sister? But she's an addict,' Sue voices my thoughts. 'Look . . .' She hesitates. 'I visited her in Falkirk and . . .'

'And what?' Laure presses her, sitting forward.

'I'm not saying that Mina was delusional. But she'd had this big shock. At school, she used to sometimes pretend she was pregnant – she'd say it to cause gossip, to get attention, she liked the idea of it. And this time round, it was the same lie. But I visited her at three months in, and there was no bump. She was not pregnant. She was just broken. There was no baby, my dear.'

Silence, as the words sink in.

We're interrupted by the click of the front door. A man in the doorway: middle-aged, wearing jeans and a leather jacket, with salt-and-pepper hair.

'Howard!' Sue looks a bit testy. 'Laure was just sharing some more memories of Ruth.'

Howard frowns, but then nods: 'Well, I'll leave you ladies to it.'

We stay a little longer, until our cups have grown cold and the biscuit tray is cleared and I see Sue drumming her fingers against her chair, whilst Laure circles the same questions again and again. Finally, I cut in: 'I think we should go.'

Sue looks relieved and jumps up. We say our goodbyes and Laure sets off down the road at a furious pace; I have to run to catch up.

'If only I'd discovered her diary when Mum was still alive, if only—' Laure voice breaks. 'If only I'd made the effort, got to know her then, I could ask her all about this and I'd *know*—'

She breaks down sobbing. I feel awkward, then put my arms around her and comfort her with a hug. I tell her that I think I understand. She wants to know her mum – not just as the person who raised her, but as a fully rounded human. It's a way of keeping her alive; a way of stopping memories from fading to sepia. I was the same after Julia died. I stared at photos obsessively, replayed a video of the time I gave her the parrots as a present, Julia laughing as they swooped around the room. There were letters that I read so many times I knew them by heart. It's the same with my real mother, too; sometimes I can't even quite remember her tone of voice, the way she said my name.

Laure and I go to a nearby café for another drink. We chat briefly and then I see it's three o'clock.

'I guess I should go. '

Laure nods sadly. She looks pale, hollowed out, from having reached a dead end, but I fear that in a few weeks' time I'll receive another call about another clue. At least I understand now how deeply she's driven by grief.

We say goodbye and I make my way back to the station. On the train, I buy a sandwich from the buffet and find a window seat. I'm feeling a little guilty. I've spent the last few weeks determined to demonise Mina. Now I have visions of her as a traumatised teenager, locked in a Scottish retreat with an overbearing mother. No wonder she married young. She was probably desperate to escape it all. And it's clear that she had nothing to do with Chris's death, despite Laure's desperate search for someone to lay blame on. My only regret – and I know this is crazy – is that I'd actually found some comfort in the idea of Mina as a murderer; then we'd be two of a kind.

A call comes through on my phone.

'Hi, it's DS Matthews here, calling from Kensington Police Station.'

I tense.

'I'm just doing a follow-up. I called your partner, Sean Kelly, and he suggested I should speak to you directly.'

'Oh, right, yes,' I say gaily. 'Right.' At least Sean hasn't told them about our break-up, which gives me faint hope.

'Mr Kelly has explained to me that Dominic Forde has been intimidating you by waiting outside your flat day and night.'

'Well – I think – to be honest, it's no big deal, and Dominic's stopped now anyhow, so . . .'

Silence. Now the police have my name, will it go onto an official file?

Her voice cloys with sympathy: 'If you're feeling intimidated, then we can protect you, you know. You can let me know what's really going on.'

I want to laugh. Once upon a time, when I was homeless, the police were constantly moving me on. They had very little sympathy for me. Once, a sergeant drove me to a shelter as a favour, but then pulled up in a car park and tried to rape me. I managed to scream and get away, but that was just before Dominic discovered me.

'Thank you,' I say at last. 'I do appreciate your – your support – but I don't want to file a complaint . . .'

'Well, we have spoken to Mr Forde.'

'You have? What did he say?' My voice is high.

'He denied that he'd ever been near your flat. He claims that you'd been harassing him – he showed us photos of you.'

'Photos?' I whisper, terrified they might show me breaking into Dominic's flat.

'Of the time you were together, in the past . . .' she says. 'So this might account for his harassment now, I should imagine: he's jealous that you've moved on and now have a new partner?'

'Yes – exactly, that's right,' I say, astonished by her sympathy.

She tells me that I can put in another complaint if his behaviour starts up again, and then gives me the phone numbers of several domestic abuse helplines, which I pretend to write down dutifully.

I hang up, surprise singing inside me. It's hard to get my head round the idea of the police being my ally after years of seeing them as the enemy.

If Dominic is now on file as a weird stalker, then even if he did produce a letter, would they take it seriously? Maybe he can't retaliate. Maybe all he can do is exchange lame WhatsApp messages about me. And if he dared follow me down to the tube again – well, it would all be on camera. Surely he wouldn't risk it, would he?

So much of my fear has revolved around the belief that the police would never believe me, because in the past that was always the case. But that was before I had status, money, a job, a flat: things are different now. Which means I'm safe: they won't start investigating my past.

And to think I broke up with Sean over this. I've berated him, cursed him, when he really was helping me.

By the time I arrive back at my flat, it's early evening. I turn into my road, butterflies frenetic in my stomach, my fear returning. Dominic might be poised, ready to retaliate—

But there's no sign of him.

I head up into my flat. I check again from the window.

273

Dominic is gone.

Does this mean I've won?

The peacefulness of my flat is lovely, but it's also lonely. I pick up my phone, swallow my pride and, even though Sean hasn't replied to my last two messages, I type:

The police called. They're sorting out Dominic. A big thank you . . .

I let my birds out and sit down in front of the TV. Something feels wrong, and I wonder if I'm so used to being on edge, buffeted by threat, that I can't adjust to calm.

But, no – there *is* something awry. My bookcase, I realise.

My books look wrong. I get up, examine them. They've been reordered.

The titles have been arranged so that the first letter of each one spells something out. *Middlemarch*, followed by *Under Milk Wood,* followed by *Rebecca.* My eye traces it down, until the word forms:

MURDERER

PART IV

WhatsApp messages of Jean Winters and Alexa McHale

4 October 2024

JEAN

Nearly at the station and Rupert,
from the third floor, just texted!
Apparently it's worse than I thought –
he's seen a body bag being carried out of the flat.

ALEXA
OMG!

CHAPTER FORTY

Alice

I stand in Mina's garden, clutching a manuscript of *Playthings,* a breeze rippling the pages. Mina's iPhone sits on a tripod facing me. It's the end of summer. A dying bee zizzes lazily past me; roses bleed the last of their perfumes.

Mina looks tense. She asked me to come over to hers as it's ages since we last made a #PublishingJourney video.

'I'm so happy to have just finished my first ever edit on a book . . .' I gush about Lucas's novel. 'And it's all thanks to Mina Harpenden. She's been the most amazing mentor to work for and I'll never forget it.'

Mina looks surprised and genuinely touched. I feel the urge to hug her, but I know Mina isn't tactile in that sort of way.

'Would you like some tea?' she asks me as we finish up.

As she walks across the grass, I picture Mina as a teenage girl, shipped off to Scotland with a strict mother, and feel a wave of empathy towards her. I've been feeling bad recently about how I vilified her. I suppose I was jealous of her and Lucas, especially when I'd just lost Sean. And there was Laure, with her crazy conspiracy theories that came to nothing. Over the last month, I've made an effort to connect with Mina again, to work hard for her, to go for coffees, film videos. We've really started to bond.

Mina comes back from the kitchen carrying a tray; I wonder what happened to her housemaid, Baba.

'Alice, I was wondering if I might ask a favour,' Mina asks, sitting down. 'I'd love to rent your flat again one evening this week. I'm afraid that I could only offer a nominal fee. We – Romain and I – we've been having a difficult year with our vineyard – we've had issues with a damaged crop, so . . .'

'I'm really sorry to hear that,' I say, in shock. I've always seen Mina's wealth as infallible, too vast for her to ever be in danger of sinking.

'So – the flat . . .?'

I pause, weighing up the dangers: Dominic has finally left me alone, so there's no chance that he'd be watching the flat. But there's always his mystery female accomplice . . .

'You see, it really is difficult with the vineyard,' Mina repeats, misunderstanding my reticence.

'The money isn't a problem,' I say. Finally, I'm on a salary. Money is no longer a tick-tock of anxiety in the background. 'I mean – don't worry about it. You can have it for free.'

I want to be generous, but Mina looks irked, lifting her chin proudly.

'Oh, let me pay a nominal fee,' she insists, and I realise she doesn't want to be seen as a charity case.

And I won't watch you this time, I promise her silently.

And yet.

Just before Mina is due to arrive, I find myself in the secret room. The thought of renting a Premier Inn room again fills me with such loneliness: sitting up watching TV in the impersonal bed, a dreary view, windows I can't open, the fug of strangers come and gone.

Mina and Lucas are like a real-life soap. I want the next episode, and I want it because I care about her. My curiosity tingles through me every time we're at work and I glance over at her office: how is she going to resolve this affair? Is Mina just toying with him or is she thinking of leaving Romain? And what about the threats she's receiving? It must be hard, dealing with that when she's in financial trouble—

I hear a key in the door and realise *Mina's here.*

I quickly lock the door.

Lucas takes an envelope out of the inner pocket of his black velvet jacket, counts out the money nervously, and then leaves it on the dining table.

Then he sits down on my sofa. He pours some wine. He looks anxious.

I hear a key the front door: Mina's here. But, wait: I only gave Mina one key. She's had a second one cut, without even asking my permission.

Lucas draws her in for a long, deep kiss, before Mina pulls away.

'Did anyone see you come in?' Her voice is tense.

'Nobody – I didn't see that guy – what's he called? Dominic?'

'Good. I didn't see him either.'

Mina's eyes flit across to the peephole in the wall and I catch my breath.

'I checked the spy room,' Lucas says, his lie surprising me. 'Nobody there.'

Shit. So they've discovered the room? Did they come across it when they were last here, when I left them unwatched? What if they check it again? Thank God I've locked the door. And if they were to look through the spyhole – well, the view is limited. I could stand flat against the wall; they wouldn't see me.

I need to keep watching; I need to be ready if they decide to check.

They're perched on the sofa, taking sips of wine. Mina looks tense and rigid. Lucas keeps interrupting their small talk with kisses on her lips, her cheeks, her hair. It's as though Mina is a hard block of sculpture and Lucas is softening her, reshaping her, until her tight smiles become sighs and soft laughter. He finds the side zip on her red dress and tugs it down. His kisses skim over her breasts, over her stomach, lingering at the rim of her knickers. It looks as though Lucas has converted my boss to oral sex then.

I listen to her orgasm reaching a crescendo, my cheeks staining red. Lucas rises and gives her a passionate kiss. 'I want to be inside you,' he tells her. They start making love. Lucas stops in the middle, gazing down at her and whispering something about her being beautiful. She whispers back, 'I love you.' They stare at each other in rapture. It's so swoony, so gorgeous to watch, that I feel quite touched.

Afterwards, they lie on the sofa together, Lucas's fingertips circling her spine.

'Mina, if I tell you something, do you promise you won't freak out?'

'What?' Mina tenses.

'Aimee got in touch with me yesterday, out of the blue, asking for money. I sent her twenty pounds. I mean, it's just twenty pounds, right?'

'You shouldn't have!' Mina exclaims. 'Oh God, I'm really sorry.' She sounds hurt. 'I don't know why she didn't come to me. She's been ignoring my texts for weeks.'

'There's something else . . .' Lucas says. 'You know when Aimee stayed with a friend of mine? Well, I had left my gun in his flat – and it's gone missing. It went missing the day after she stayed. He only just told me about it.'

'Oh God,' Mina looks distraught. 'I'll ask her about it. I'm so sorry.'

Lucas strokes her hair. 'You promised to tell me more about her.'

'I don't know where to begin,' Mina says quietly.

'You were saying before that when Aimee was eighteen, she wanted to know who her real parents were . . .'

I sit up, intrigued; neither Mina nor Laure ever mentioned any details of Aimee's adoption.

'She did,' Mina says sadly. 'She started contacting agencies, doing research. My parents were torn as to whether to tell her the truth. Romain was furious. He thought it was better that we make up a story. In the end, after a row, I travelled up to Otley without him. My parents and I – we told Aimee everything.'

Everything? What truth? If Romain was furious, then – was he the father? If he was seeing Mina as a teenager, then maybe he preyed on other girls. Mina definitely can't have been pregnant; Laure's contact, Sue, confirmed that.

'I thought that finally knowing would help Aimee. God, I was naive. The fantasy she'd had was of two loving parents, forced to give her up out of poverty, aching to be reunited with her. Her sense of self collapsed. She'd been inclined to drink too much, and now she went completely off the rails. Worse, Romain's solution to everything is money – he started bribing her to stay quiet by buying her presents, sending her money whenever she asked. That's why she feels she can turn to you – as an extension – and just get what she wants. But having that money meant she could afford an addiction.'

So Romain has got something to hide, I muse. It seems he is Aimee's father. God, what a bastard he is, if he doesn't want to recognise her.

Then I remind myself that I only know a fragment of the truth, not the whole story.

I frown, suddenly feeling a tickle my throat, swallowing it down hard.

'Now, whenever I see Aimee lost to drink and drugs, I feel as though it's our fault. My heart breaks.'

Mina's on the verge of tears. Lucas puts his arm around her, shushing her, kissing her temple, assuring her that she's done the best she could do in a nightmare situation.

The tickle in my throat worsens. I step back, swallow hard, several times, but it persists.

I look round. Normally I keep a bottle of mineral water, but I forgot to bring one in.

When I look back through the peephole, I watch Lucas going into the kitchen. The tickle thickens, my chest heaving, tears streaming from my eyes. I can hear the kettle brewing and as it gets louder, I try to time the release of a short cough. The relief is only temporary before the tickle is back, snagging my breath and—

'Who's there?' Mina cries.

I freeze.

The door to the secret room rattles violently.

'Hey, what's up?' I hear Lucas's voice close by.

'Someone's in there – I heard them cough! This is locked! They must be inside.'

Oh my God.

The thin door vibrates with heavy banging.

'Come out, please!' Lucas says in an authoritative, formal tone. 'We want to know who you are.'

Mina cries, 'I swear I can see someone in there!' and I press myself flat against the wall.

The door rattles again. 'Is that Dominic?'

Fuck, fuck, fuck.

I gaze at the window. The drop would be far too high; I'd break a limb, risk death. Could I climb down into another flat, knock on a window? *No: I'm not James Bond,* I think, hysteria bubbling inside me.

Could I just wait this out? If I face them, this is the end of my career. There's a horrible feeling lurking in my stomach, a sense that I was always destined to end up at this point.

Then I hear Lucas saying that they should search for tools in the flat. That they can break the door down.

I'm had.

Oh Mina, I pray, *please forgive me.*

'I'm coming out,' I hear myself croak. 'I'm coming.'

'Who's that?' Mina's voice is a whip.

I freeze at the door, the key in my hand, but I can't bear to put it in the lock and face them, I can't bear to.

'It's me. It's Alice.'

Silence. I force myself to insert the key. My hand is shaking so much it takes several goes. I twist it.

'I'm really sorry,' I say, through the door. 'I just ...' I lean my head against it, feel wood against my nose. 'I was just – you came in – I was behind – I was stuck – I couldn't just – show myself and walk out in the middle – of it all.'

Silence. The handle turns; I see Lucas. His expression is sympathetic. I step out. We're all crammed into a huddle, far too close, and Lucas is still topless and barefoot.

Mina's expression is one of outrage. Her nostrils are flaring, her arms folded over her dress, which hangs loosely on her, half-zipped. My fear is so potent, I transcend the emotion. Adrenaline pumps through me, telling me I need to just walk this tightrope. I have to keep my job. I have to bullshit.

'I'm sorry. Like I said, I got stuck – I didn't watch, or see anything . . .' Sweat on my forehead, trickling down my back.

Mina is staring at me with a look of complete shock and betrayal.

But Lucas manages an embarrassed smile.

'Well, it sounds like an unfortunate mistake, like a crazy French farce – doesn't it, Mina?'

Mina hisses: 'There's a fucking peephole in that room. If you weren't watching, what the hell is that thing for?'

'That's – it was the previous owner's, Julia's – I'd forgotten it was even there. There are probably others—'

'Others watching?' Mina's nearly shouting.

'No – of course not! I'm just saying that I have no idea why it's there. I was just cleaning the flat, I got trapped, I felt embarrassed.'

'What about cameras? Were you filming us? Was this for some kind of blackmail?'

'Of course not!' I cry.

'Let me see your phone,' Mina demands.

I have to go back into the room, which doesn't help my case. I pick it up from the floor, put in the passcode, hand it over, show her the button for photos—

'I can find videos, I'm not stupid,' she snaps, whilst Lucas gives me a slightly awkward smile.

She sifts through them. There's nothing there. I've recorded Dom a few times, waiting by my flat, made a few of my birds calling and being cute. My face feels raw with heat as she passes it back.

'Well . . .' she says.

'It all seems to be a misunderstanding,' Lucas asserts. 'But – we'd appreciate it if you kept everything that you've seen secret.'

Mina shakes her head. 'I don't believe a word she's said. She knew we were coming.' She turns back to me, her eyes hollow. 'Are you the one who's been blackmailing me? Because our vineyard's collapsing, I have no money – Lucas is paying the demands . . .'

'Of course I'm not,' I cry. 'I have a salary now and I'm so grateful to you for my job.' Terror pounds in my heart: do I still have a job, after this?

'Maybe you just want to fillet me for all you can,' Mina cries.

'God, I would never do that.'

I plead to her with my eyes, but she glares back with such intensity that I have to look down.

She strides to the sofa, gathers up her clothes, yanks up her zip, breaking it in her fury – '*Shit!*'

'You can borrow a dress from me,' I offer.

'We're leaving,' she announces. She goes to the table, picks up the envelope of cash, and goes to pocket it, but Lucas eases it out of her hands and passes it to me with a nod, before they turn and exit.

CHAPTER FORTY-ONE

Mina

I gaze through my office window into the open-plan area. I watch Charles stop by Alice's desk. She tugs down the hem of her dress, and shyly accepts his handshake. She's all the rage in the office this morning. She's won a book auction for a debut novel called *Lordship*. Everyone in the office is predicting it will be a big hit.

I'm the only one who hasn't congratulated her. My door is closed; my office is my cave.

As if reading my thoughts, Alice turns towards my office window. I duck my head, pretending to be staring intently at my computer screen.

I'm still stinging from the revelation that she watched us. So is Lucas. This morning he sent me a message declaring, I want you to be my editor. Can I fire Alice?

I'm glad he's feeling angry. That night, after we discovered her spying on us, we went for a drink on Kensington High Street at an elegant cocktail bar called Amaro. I was numb with shock. I was wishing I'd interrogated her more, but my first instinct had been to get out of there as fast as we could. The questions were still swirling through my mind – *how many times had she watched us?* I kept jumping at the thought of all those tell-tale signals that had told me something was wrong. How I thought I'd heard a gasp the night Matthias tried to attack me; that time that we'd spotted the spyhole;

how, on another occasion I'd been convinced I could hear breathing, but had dismissed it as paranoia. Lucas's response to the situation was to down a glass of red and burst into sporadic laughter – 'My editor's got a fetish! She's a voyeur!' or 'I should put this in a novel.' I wasn't amused. For the first time since our affair had begun, I felt alienated from him, Alice like a wedge of embarrassment between us.

I've spent the weekend feeling raw, exposed. Alice knows I'm a private person. That I find it hard to trust. Yet she's seen sides to me that I'd wouldn't even reveal to close friends. She's stolen my secrets. She's heard my orgasms. She's seen me naked. My overweight tummy; my cellulite; my bush! God! She's seen Lucas put himself inside me and she's watched him taste me. I feel diluted, as though my life is not my own, as though I've built up layers of experience like a house and discovered Alice is squatting in the basement.

And then there's the issue of Aimee. I don't think I ever did confess that I'm her mother. But what if she's guessed? What if she actually was there the night I told Lucas? If Alice is the one blackmailing me, then I've given her all the ammunition she needs.

After all I've done for her: that's the main refrain that keeps repeating in my mind. A while back, just after I got together with Lucas, she went through a phase of being very offhand. Sometimes I saw a look on her face that reminded me of Aimee, like a teenager who's in the process of discovering her parents are human beings, and is immensely disappointed by this revelation. But then it all changed again. The shine of admiration back in her eyes; her energy and enthusiasm for making the videos; we were working well together. Unless it was all an act—

Charles is at my office door.

'Hullo!' he greets me. These days, he increasingly reminds me of a Tory MP, with his patrician sweep of grey hair, his navy suit with a handkerchief poking out of the top pocket. 'Marvellous news about Alice.'

'Yes.' I try to sound genuinely enthusiastic.

'You did such a great job, bringing her in,' he says, apparently forgetting all his prior concerns about hiring her, how I had to persuade him.

I glance into the open-plan office again. The dress Alice is wearing is black and simple, the type I usually favour.

'I did,' I say.

The moment I found out about the theft at Heather Perkins's business, the weird CV, I should have cut her loose. I should have seen she can't be trusted.

'Though she's still got a lot to learn,' I add.

'Well . . .' Charles picks up a paperweight from my desk and plays with it. 'That rather brings me to my next point. Perhaps *we* can all learn from her. The thing is, Mina . . . you've only acquired one book in the past four months, and that is rather – well, slight, compared to . . .'

'Actually, Cathryn pitched *Lordship* to me first, and I suggested she send it to Alice,' I say. An out-and-out lie, which I regret as soon as I say it. 'I wanted to give her a chance . . .'

'Oh,' Charles says. 'I see. But . . .'

This is appalling: *he's here to tell me off.* It's surreal. My protégée is out there, a liar, a thief, and God knows what else, and she's the star and I'm being told, implicitly, that I'm on probation.

'If you could – take on a few more acquisitions of your own . . .'

'Of course,' I reply smoothly. 'Although, as it happens,

Lucas has asked if I could take over as his editor. Alice is still very green – it's his request.'

'Oh.' Charles looks a little dismayed, as though wondering just how much of a bitch I am. 'What about the #PublishingJourney story? She's a star in the making – let's nurture her, rather than undermine her, at this rather delicate stage.'

'Absolutely.' I flash him a beam. 'I've been sent some very promising submissions, so I'm sure I'll be acquiring more soon.'

'Good.' Charles puts down the paperweight, claps his hands together. 'We should all have lunch together – you, me, Alice.'

After he's gone, I can feel the ache in my cheeks from so many forced smiles. My throat feels dry; I reach for my bottle of Volvic.

I go through my inbox. It's damning. I've let everything slide, so anxious over the bribery threats, so distracted by my affairs and by Lucas, and now, so concerned by Aimee.

I have to get my act together.

I flick back to my last blackmail email.

Tough having to pay a tax for your sins isnt it?

I glance out at Sarah's desk, notice that she's chatting with Alice. I consider how frequently Sarah makes lazy grammatical errors like *'isnt'*, and how much she loathes me these days: another relationship I've sacrificed for the sake of Alice. I've heard on the grapevine she's applying for other jobs. Could it be both of them – Sarah and Alice in cahoots, perhaps?

At the end of the day, I'm the last person left in the office. I work and work, and I find it's a relief to drown myself, to shut out the pain.

The cleaner has just come in, and I'm feeling hungry and ready to go, when I notice a flurry of WhatsApp messages. All from Alice.

16:04: I'm really, really sorry, Mina.

17:30: I want to make it up to you.

17:45: I'm really sorry. Could we go for a drink, perhaps, and talk it all through?

I'm about to message back and tell her where to go, when an idea tickles my mind. A way to test Alice. A way to make her pay.

It's time I took control of my life. Everything is falling apart around me and I have to come back out on top.

Sure, I reply, let's go for a drink tonight. How about the Amaro bar on Kensington High St. 8?

CHAPTER FORTY-TWO

Mina

Alice is waiting for me in the bar when I arrive exactly on time. She's at a table by the window, biting her nails. At the sight of her, anger flares inside me. I was supposed to be seeing Lucas right now. I've postponed him until later tonight. I know he'd only try to talk me out of my plan if I shared it, and I feel furious with him too, for not taking her betrayal seriously enough, for suggesting I should forgive her.

There's a sense of exhilaration behind my rage. Recently my usual backdrop has been one of panic, but now there's a bright, pulsing adrenaline.

'Hello,' I hear myself say as I sit down opposite her. Alice sits up, as though to attention. A waitress rocks up with two menus and lights the tea candle on our table.

'A mineral water,' Alice requests.

'You should have alcohol,' I push her.

'Um . . .' She winds her hair around a finger. She probably wants to get home early and sober and read her subs and discover the next bloody Booker winner. 'OK – a peach bellini.'

'I'll have a large white wine,' I say, smiling sweetly. I'm planning to let Alice pay the bill.

'I – I owe you an apology,' she says once the waitress has left. 'I didn't get stuck in the room like I said. I suspected there might be something going on with Lucas and I wanted to confirm it.'

I feel my hackles rise: what kind of apology is that supposed to be?

'Oh, I'm sorry, I didn't realise you were the morality police,' I fire at her.

'I'm not.' Her eyes are flitting all over the place. As the drinks arrive, she plays with her straw, crushing down the ice in her drink. 'But you shouldn't – you shouldn't be having an affair with an author. It's unethical.'

I splutter in shock, dabbing wine from my chin.

'Alice, I am not Harvey fucking Weinstein! Our relationship is consensual – as you saw.' I see her flush. 'Author–editor relationships are – well, they're frowned on, but they're certainly not *illegal*. I'm not the first this has happened to. The fact is Lucas wants to be with me. I make him happy.'

Alice shifts uneasily.

'Whereas, if I were to go and tell Charles Goddard about your CV and the theft – well, I don't know if he'd keep you on.'

Alice freezes, fear flashing in her eyes.

'He came into my office earlier today. He said he feels you've taken a gamble by paying such a huge advance for *Lordship*.'

'Really?' Alice looks sulky. 'He congratulated me.'

'Imagine if I were to tell Charles about Heather Perkins and the fact you have a stalker who claims that you killed an old woman to gain your flat. That I have no idea who you really are, and that now I've found you spying on me, watching me having sex.'

Alice seems to be in a state of shock. I lean back against my seat. All these thoughts have been churning inside me, until they've coalesced into the conviction that I've hired a lying sociopath. But now she's here in front of me, I remember Alice is human. I remember her confession about her mother, her childhood. How vulnerable she is, as Lucas keeps reminding me. I bite my lip.

'I'm – I'm sorry,' she says at last. She blinks back tears. 'I can't tell you how much this job means to me – and I know I've betrayed your trust, but please – just let me rebuild things. I should never have watched you. It just – it became an addiction. You were so amazing, you were my boss – so enigmatic. I wanted to – see you . . .' She trails off.

I freeze.

'How many times did you watch?'

'Um . . .' She fiddles with her straw again. 'From your date with Jacob . . .'

I'm stunned. I'd thought she'd just seen me with Lucas – it made me wonder if perhaps she had a secret crush on him. But this means she saw me with Jacob, with Matthias, saw them kiss me, caress me, undress me. The pulse between my legs distracts me, and I try to repress it. Despite my anger, my shame, I feel oddly flattered that my love life was exciting enough that a young woman would want to watch me.

But this is a dangerous situation: what if she were to tell Romain?

'What can I do?' Alice interjects. 'How can I make it up to you? I can find you another book to buy – you can have all the credit,' she offers, pushing her hair behind her ears.

'I'm perfectly capable of finding my own books!' I berate her furiously.

'Yes – of course,' she says.

I swirl my wine. Making her wait. The punishment I've come up with has felt so satisfying in my head, but I know that once I voice it, I'll have set something in motion that I might not be able to control or come back from.

'I want you to seduce my husband,' I instruct her.

'*What?*'

'You'll ask Romain and me to dinner. I'll make a last-minute excuse that I can't make it. I'll be in the secret room. And it will be *my* turn to watch you.'

'But – I can't. I have a boyfriend, Sean . . .'

'You told me you'd broken up.'

'Well, yes, we have . . . kind of . . .'

'It will be our secret,' I assure her, enjoying her panic. 'Look: I know you're attracted to Romain. All women are. He's a very handsome man, and I'm gifting him to you.'

Alice stares into her cocktail. And I see something pass over her face, a look that scares me. 'And what if I were to make a bargain with you?' she says wildly. 'You forget about my big mistake, and we carry on – and I don't make a #PublishingJourney video where I tell the world that you tried to force me to be with Romain.'

'You wouldn't dare,' I cry. 'Nobody would believe you. I've been in this industry almost twenty years. I can take your job away just like that.' I snap my fingers.

Alice is already starting to crumple.

'Okay, but I just feel that to be with Romain is . . . I just . . .'

We're interrupted by the waitress, asking if we want more drinks. I ask for the bill, then push it in Alice's direction. As she draws out her purse to pay, though, I only feel humiliated. Imagine not even being able to pick up a drinks bill.

Alice taps her Monzo card on the machine; the waitress thanks her for a generous tip.

Silence. Deadlock. My heart is hammering. What else might she try? How much did she hear about Aimee? What if she uses that as a bargaining tool?

But she's looking lost and defeated.

'Okay,' she says at last. She gets up, slides off her seat. 'Um – I need to go, but yeah, sure, I'll do it.'

'Alice—'

But she's already gone, hurrying out of the bar. I roll my eyes. Then I see her rushing past the window, and I realise that's why she left: she didn't want to cry in front of me. A moment of sanity hits me: *Just what are you doing?* I shake it off. Alice deserves this.

'So, did you make up?' Lucas asks me, when he picks me up twenty minutes later.

I haven't told him of my plans for Alice. 'Yes. Sort of.'

Lucas kisses me, looking pleased. He's still of the mindset that Alice didn't mean any harm.

Our Uber snakes through lines of traffic until we finally arrive in Mayfair. We pull up outside a large Edwardian block with red brick and white sash windows; inside, we climb a narrow staircase to the second floor. It's the first time I've seen his flat.

As we enter, he seizes my hand, transferring a nervous film of sweat to my palm. It's much smaller than I'd imagined it: because of his love for Paris, and his wealthy father, I'd been picturing high white ceilings, ornate cornices. It's just a studio, very plain, with floorboards and no rugs. I notice things poking out from under his bed, which makes me smile, wondering if he pushed all his mess under there at the last minute.

'Well?' Lucas looks at me. There's a subtext to all this: *This is where we might live together, one day, if you wanted to . . .*

'I love it,' I manage.

'You don't.' Lucas sighs. 'I know you don't.'

'I do, I really do. '

'*Nein*. You can't fool me.' He kneels down before me, pushing up my dress, tearing down my knickers. I'm shocked and aroused by the audacity of it, not even bothering to kiss me first, just launching in and tasting me. We make love on the floor and it's beautiful and wild and passionate but the boards are rough against my back. Afterwards, we lie in a tender haze of soft kisses and endearments, and the thought troubles me: *Can a passion like this really last?* And then what, if it were to slip away, over the years: would there be enough left? I wonder if this flat is too small for Persephone, and she'd miss having a garden to frolic in, chasing bees and insects, eating grass for her furballs.

We get dressed, shower, cuddle sleepily on the sofa. He asks if I've heard from Aimee. I tell him she's still quiet, remote.

I try to picture Aimee visiting. The first image that springs to mind is of her flirting with Lucas. He wouldn't respond now – but what about in ten years' time? And when I'm sixty, Lucas will be starting his midlife crisis, whilst I'll be struggling with grey hair and a post-menopausal moustache. I love Aimee but she never fits anywhere, that's the trouble. She's a puzzle piece with jagged edges.

'Tell me what you're thinking,' Lucas says.

'All's well,' I say, kissing him. 'I'm starting to like it here.'

'Oh, sure,' he teases me before going over to the fridge to get some wine. I think he's playing the cynical, flippant card to hide how vulnerable he feels, and it scares me, knowing his happiness lies in my hands. I care for him so much, but I know how fleeting romantic illusions can be. Once upon a time, I looked upon Romain as a god.

I pull up my feet, trying to get comfy on the hard grey

sofa. The drink with Alice replays in my mind; I think of the proposition I made her. I'm forcing a situation that will implode my life, free me, but a fear comes over me, my eyes dancing around my future home: what if I lose more than I gain?

CHAPTER FORTY-THREE

Alice

Mina's in my secret room. She arrived at my flat, punctual at six. When I unlocked the little room for her, she gazed around, examining it as though it were the scene of a crime, then demanded that I give her a glass of wine.

In ten minutes' time, her husband will be here. I'm wearing a classy black dress Mina picked out for me, the one she once gifted me when I was just an intern. Her face was cold when she helped me to do the buttons up. I don't understand what game she's playing. Is this a punishment or a test? I asked if I was supposed to be a honey trap, testing to see if Romain might be unfaithful.

But Mina refused to explain.

'It's up to you how you want to play it, Alice,' she said icily, closing the door to the room.

Maybe she wants to even the scales. She's having an affair, so if he has one, she can feel less guilty.

I deserve to be punished. She took a chance on me, nurtured me, and I've messed everything up. I can't throw my precious job away; I have to do as she asks. But I don't understand: is this an act of revenge or masochism? Maybe she's torn between her husband and Lucas, is wondering which way the scales might tip—

Buzz-buzz.

Romain is here.

I swallow, biting my nails, aware of Mina's gaze, which must be fixed on me as I head towards the front door.

Romain is dressed in a dark suit, looking far too handsome and sexy. He seems less polished than usual; his white shirt is open at the neck and looks rumpled and unironed. His stubble grates my skin as he leans in, kissing each cheek, so close to my lips.

He's brought a small bunch of white roses.

'Mina's texted to say she's running late,' he says. 'She told me to come up, have a drink.'

'Oh, right, sure,' I say. I worry my voice sounds false and artificial. Once upon a time, Dominic and I used to do this for a living: playing the con. I'd thought those days were behind me.

Romain pulls a bottle of wine from his briefcase, telling me it's an '87, one of his vineyard's best years. As he passes it to me, our fingers brush. He runs his eyes over my dress.

The chemistry between us is still there: charged and dangerous.

I pour the wine and take a big gulp.

'We haven't made any #PublishingJourney videos for a while.' Romain's voice is a caress, as though he's talking about a sex video. 'Why don't we make one now, you and me, chatting about – I don't know – the latest books we've read and enjoyed?'

'Um, okay,' I agree.

He holds up his iPhone, and we both switch on smiles and say 'Hi' to the camera. He effuses about a new biography of the PM, I go on about *Bear* by Marian Engel, and then we wave goodbye until next time.

'That was great,' Romain enthuses, uploading it. *God, if the people watching knew what was going on tonight,* I muse, and gulp down a load more wine.

His eyes flick over me again. 'That green dress you wore, when you first came to dinner at ours – do you still have it?'

'Yes . . .'

'Could you put it on for me?' he asks softly.

It's a weird request, but Romain has a dominating way about him: as though it would be unreasonable for me to refuse.

In my bedroom, I change and eye up my reflection. Several months ago, I'd put this dress on thinking I looked sophisticated. But it's just embarrassing. It's gauche and tatty and girlish.

I head out feeling self-conscious, but Romain gives me a nod of appreciation.

He walks up to me, and – just as he did in the car after giving me a lift home – he runs his finger down my cheek. Heat simmers under my skin. It's such an intimate, familiar gesture that I shudder– what if Mina thinks we're having an ongoing affair? I step back jerkily, ruining the moment.

'Mina might be here any minute,' I point out.

'Of course,' he replies, businesslike again, and I go to the kitchen to check on dinner. I pull on oven gloves, draw a lasagne out of the oven, leave it to cool down a little. I arrange some garlic bread on a tray, turn up the gas mark a notch, and put that in.

My head is swimming. Something is going to happen between us, I can feel it in my gut.

I want to press pause. Slow down.

When I come out, Romain is looking cheerful.

'Mina's just messaged. She's cancelled for this evening – a work crisis, an author who's trying to break his contract.'

Hmm, I think, picturing Mina behind the door just a few feet from us.

'So it's just you and me,' he says, walking up to me, predatory. He stands close, then a little closer, his suit brushing me. 'Have you thought about what I said in the car?'

I flush again. Mina is *so* going to think we're having an affair.

'I don't know what you're talking about,' I lie.

Romain looks angry. He grabs my wrist.

'I know you haven't forgotten, and neither have I.' He leans in, his voice lower: 'We could just have one night together, and nobody would ever know.'

'What about your wife?' I murmur. I can't even look at him; I fix my eyes on his shirt.

'Mina wouldn't care,' he sighs. 'Believe me.'

He slips his fingers under my chin, tipping up my face so that I have to meet his gaze. My mind is telling me to walk away, make an excuse, but my body disagrees. He hears me draw in a ragged breath and he smiles, leans in closer, our breaths becoming shallow. He's drawing out the anticipation now, pulling back teasingly as I lean in; and then he breaks, pressing his mouth to mine. We kiss hungrily. His hand smooths up and down my spine. His tongue is fierce in my mouth. My desire overwhelms me, and then I think, *Fuck, Mina is watching.* Romain gathers up my hair, pulls it into a bun.

'This is how it was when you came to dinner,' he whispers. 'You had it up and all the pins were slipping out.' He lets my hair down, unzips my dress, and it slithers to the floor in a green pool. I let out a cry as he picks me up by the waist; he sets me on the table, next to the three places that Mina helped me to lay earlier. I'm in my underwear; he's still in his suit, but when I reach for him, he pushes my hands away, trailing kisses over my collarbone. He undoes my bra, cupping my breasts, telling me how *belle* I am. The only clothing of his own that he removes is his jacket; his shirt kisses my body as he climbs on top of me. I am painfully conscious of Mina watching as he caresses me, but as desire builds, a switch flips inside me. *You created this,* I rage at her silently as he tears down my knickers. *You made it happen. Your husband wants me and you have to watch and it's your fault.* I feel Romain's mouth back on mine, him unzipping his trousers, opening up to him as he thrusts inside me. Cutlery falls to the floor as we make love in a frenzy, building to a climax.

Oh God, I think, as I open my eyes. *What have we done?*

I become aware of a blaring sound. It's from the kitchen. The fire alarm. The garlic bread! I left it in the oven.

Romain draws out of me, dazed, and I hurry into the kitchen. I open the oven and smoke tendrils out. The garlic breads are black husks. I reach blindly for the tray and burn my fingertips. *Stupid,* I think, running for the cold tap.

'Are you okay?' Romain comes in.

'I burnt my fingers.' I'm almost hysterical with laughter and pain. I point at the oven. He reaches out too, in a daze, and I yell, 'Gloves!' at him. He starts, then puts them on. I stand on a chair and switch the fire alarm off.

When I climb down, we look at each other and then we laugh and laugh. Romain gently pulls me into his arms, stroking my hair and whispering, 'That was gorgeous.'

In the living-room, I get dressed, serve the lasagne, and sit opposite him, my body still tingling with orgasm and my fingers red and sore. I don't care about Mina anymore. I've done it now. She's seen it all. Romain shifts back into MP mode and entertains me with political stories. Maybe it's just his autopilot manner when he's at dinner. I'm already tipsy from drinking to calm my nerves before he made his move. As he pours glass after glass, I realise I'm sliding into drunkenness.

Maybe it's the best state to be in. Once Romain leaves, I'm going to have to face Mina.

I get up to make tea. I'm unsteady and Romain grabs me, his hand on my cheek.

'I'll go make tea,' I say firmly, pulling away. We can't do this again. Once was sinful enough.

Tea will dilute the alcohol, sober us up.

I carry our drinks into the living-room to find Romain on the sofa. He pulls me onto his lap.

'Are your fingers okay?' he asks.

'They're throbbing a bit,' I say, smiling as he kisses them. Then, as he leans in, I pull back. 'I feel guilty. I mean, you said you'd never cheated on Mina before and now I'm the first . . .'

'And I meant it,' Roman says, his breath warm on my lips. 'But Mina is having an affair.'

I pull back in shock. 'You—' I very nearly burst out, *You know about it*, but even in my inebriated state, I manage to save myself from disaster. 'Really? Are you sure?'
Romain's face becomes raw with pain.

'I don't know who – maybe it's someone at work. Have you seen her flirting with anyone?'

I shake my head. 'No, she's so professional – but how come you're so sure?'

'It's money. Money can always tell you a lot about what's going on, Alice.' His voice is sharp with hurt. 'Her current account has been buoyant for years. Now it's nearly empty. She's spending like mad, keeping some toy boy happy.'

'But that's a big leap. You don't know what she's spending it all on . . .'

His fingers curl around my arm, yield a pressure. 'Do you know who it might be?'

'Maybe it's nothing to do with a man. Maybe it's because she's panic spending, because of your financial crisis – maybe it's the vineyard,' I say.

Romain laughs. 'The vineyard is going to be fine. There was a minor crop issue, but it'll bounce back.'

'Oh, right,' I say, confused. 'I thought Mina said . . . you might have to sell up . . .'

'I might have exaggerated somewhat to Mina . . . We're fine, financially,' Romain asserts, and I wonder if he just can't bear to admit that he might be on the verge of losing everything.

Our lips meet again. That fire licks up between us, and I'm scared we're going to make love, right on the sofa in front of his wife – when his phone vibrates in his pocket. Romain breaks off, apologising, checks the caller. 'Sorry, I have to take this.'

He keeps me on his lap, stroking my hair and face whilst he listens. Then his hand stills, his expression sobers. I sense he's getting bad news.

'I have to go,' he says. 'I'm sorry, my darling Alice. It's a crisis at the Commons.' I get up and as he stands, he grabs the sofa. 'God, I'm in no fit state.'

We both laugh uneasily.

'I'll see you down,' I say.

In the lift, he curls his arm around me and we start kissing again. As the doors open and we enter the lobby, Romain moves away from me, conscious of the public space.

We head out into the cold night air. Whilst we wait for the

Uber, I start to shiver and Romain puts his arm around my waist. I look for Dominic in fear, but there's no sign of him. As the Uber pulls up, I turn and say a bright goodbye, and Romain cups my face in his hands. He checks the streets, which looks empty: the coast is clear.

'You're so lovely,' he says, and as I go to kiss his cheeks the French way, he plants a kiss right on my lips. I'm aware of a flash nearby; Romain jumps, prickled, scanning the scene anxiously.

'Can you see anyone?'

'No . . . I think we're okay.'

'I'd better go. We'll speak soon.' He seems more sober now, jumpy, hurrying into the car.

It's only as the Uber pulls away that I see a dark figure, hiding by the bins. Their face is covered by a scarf – Dominic? Did they take a photo?

Before I say anything, they hurry away. *I'm probably just being drunk and paranoid,* I assure myself.

As I go back into the lift, panic fills me. I imagine having to face Mina, the recriminations, the tears, her fury. This was her stupid, insane idea. I should never have played along. I should have gone to Charles, complained, begged for help.

'Mina?' I call her name as I enter my flat.

I call her name several more times, but there's no reply. When I open the door to the secret room, I find that it's empty.

CHAPTER FORTY-FOUR

Alice

I'm at work when the message comes through from Sean:
Fancy meeting up for a drink? I'm in London tonight . . .
I do a double take of surprise. I'd been sitting at my desk,
trying not to stare at Mina's office, trying to forget that night
with Romain, to stop it repeating over and over in my mind.
I'd given up on Sean ever getting back in touch, but here he
is, right of the blue.

Right now, it feels like a lifeline.

I'd love to, I want to type back in joy, but then my hurt resur-
faces: it's taken months for him to reply properly. I'll delay
responding for a day or two.

'Alice!' Mina emerges from her office. 'Have you booked
lunch for twelve at the Ivy as requested?'

'I have,' I reply, switching on a smile. It's been a week since
she watched me and her husband have sex. Whenever I've
tried to talk to her about what happened, she shuts the subject down. I'm trying to kill her with polite kindness, hoping
we can get through this phase. But on bad days like this, I
wonder. Her middle-class guilt has evolved into middle-class
disdain. I've seen this happen before, with Frieda's family,
with Heather Perkins. Now I'm a convenient scapegoat.

Mina returns to her office but comes out a minute later.
'Can you go down and meet my guest? Bring him up to my
office.'

I go down to the lobby and freeze up in horror.

It's Romain.

At the sight of me, he looks distinctly uncomfortable too; only a week ago, he was inside me on my dining-room table. *How did it feel for her to watch?* I keep wondering. Was it sexy? Painful? Shocking?

'Mina's waiting for you upstairs,' I say, gesturing to the lift, before hurrying out of the building. I decide I'll escape for an early lunch break.

I buy a sandwich and sit on a bench, pulling my new iPhone out of my bag. I treated myself with my new salary, though now I'm already regretting splashing out: I'm starting to wonder if I will still have a salary next month, the way things are going. Maybe I should follow Sarah's example and start applying for new jobs.

I read Sean's message again. I wanted to play it cool. But I'm feeling so shaken up that I reach out to him: I can meet tonight, that'd be great.

I should get back to the office, else Mina will berate me, but I linger. I'm still wondering about Aimee, Mina's sister. I flick through Google, searching for pictures of her. The only one I can find is that blurry one of her at a Billy Eilish concert. I zoom in close, trying to see the ghost of Romain in her features. Could he really be her father?

Then I put my phone down, biting my lip. I need to forget Mina and Romain, revert to a businesslike relationship. Their private affairs are none of my business.

At seven that evening, I get off the tube at Vauxhall and head for Nolan's pub.

My phone buzzes as I'm about to enter. It's a message from Laure and I skim the preview that pops up: WTF? Are you serious? Since our trip to Otley, she's gone quiet, but now my phone fills up with a flurry of notifications.

God know what that's about. I shove my phone back into my bag. I don't have time for one of Laure's mad outbursts; I need some relief after a bruising day at work.

I enter the noisy, buzzy atmosphere of the pub. Sean's sitting on a stool by the bar. My heart stops. I feel as though I'm seeing him for the very first time. He's so very tanned from his trip abroad, his fair hair streaked by the sun. When he turns, his blue eyes light up and all I can think is: *He's gorgeous.*

As we greet each other, there's an awkward moment where we lean in, the way we have a hundred times before as a couple, and then aim for each other's cheeks, our noses bumping. We apologise and laugh.

'What would you like to drink?' he asks.

'Um, just a Coke,' I reply and Sean raises an eyebrow. I can hardly tell him that I'm off alcohol. That I have been ever since that night with Romain, when I awoke the next morning with a hangover from hell and guilt and self-loathing crawling over me.

Sean has a Guinness. We chink glasses, catching eyes. I repress the urge to throw my arms around him and tell him how much I've missed him.

For all I know, Sean might be about to tell me that he met a sexy someone on his travels, that he's in a new relationship, and I'll have to pretend I'm happy for him.

'So, how's life?' he asks me.

'My job is great but awful,' I say. 'My boss really hates me.'

'Because you're outshining her?' Sean asks.

'Not exactly. I did something to really put her off me.'

'What?' Sean asks, and I'm distracted by his dimples and

how cute they are, and how buzzy his sideburns are and how blue his eyes shine.

'I feel like I need to be a lot drunker to tell you,' I confess.

'Ha-ha – well, on that Coke, you'll soon be away,' Sean laughs.

I'm aware of my phone buzzing away in my bag. Either Laure is obsessed or there's a work crisis. I decide to just be in there here and now with Sean.

So I get a new round of drinks, opting for some rum in my Coke this time, and I ask Sean about his work trips abroad; he tells me about the riots he filmed in Paris.

'So, now you're an editorial superstar, are you dating someone glam in publishing?' Sean asks.

I bite my lip, shake my head.

'No one-night stands?' Sean asks, teasing, digging, a little jealous.

'I . . .'

'What?' Sean presses me.

'I pissed my boss off because I watched her having sex with a younger guy.'

'What?' Sean splutters.

I lean in. 'You have to keep this secret, but you know that secret room we found in my flat? Well, Mina asked to rent my flat for the night and as I needed the extra money, I said yes, but then – well, I got stuck in that room, she came early, and so I ended up . . . watching. But then she found out. Oh God, she found out.'

'Alice, this is all so kinky! I love it!' Sean revels in it, making light of it, and I feel the heavy weight of the last week lift a little. 'I guess this episode won't be featuring in your next #PublishingJourney video?'

'Um, I think they'll be on hiatus for now.' I laugh sheepishly.

Sean asks if I want another round of drinks. As I go to the toilet, I nearly trip on my handbag strap, which has got caught on my stool; he catches me, and I feel a shiver of heat between us.

The toilets are grungy and tiny, with a scratchy mirror. The drier doesn't work, so I find a tissue in my pocket to dry my hands. I'm tipsy now, but conscious that my phone is *still* buzzing away with calls and notifications. I pull it out, suddenly sober and sharp, sensing this might be serious. The crazy thought that runs through my mind – that haunts me from time to time – is that I'm going to be told Mum has died, and the police have tracked me down to inform me.

Then I see the messages are from work colleagues and friends. There's one from Jimoke:WTF?

Beneath this, there's a link to an article on the *Daily Mail* website.

I click on it. I can't see anything much, except celeb gossip, Katy Perry's new single – and then a headline on the sidebar catches my eye.

MP ROMAIN DUPONT CAUGHT IN AN EMBRACE WITH WIFE'S PA!

'Fuck!'

I drop my phone in shock. When I pick it up, I find the screen cracked in the corner – my brand-new phone.

Fuck, fuck, fuck.

I scan the article in shock. Words leap out at me: *Romain and Alice Smart were caught kissing . . . outside her block . . . illicit rendez-vous . . . embattled wife Mina Harpenden made the mistake of employing her as part of a diversity scheme . . .*

Another buzz. I nearly drop my phone again. I see it's from Sean.

I'm terrified he's seen the article, but his message is just a playful What the hell are you doing in that toilet? Get back out here, I've got a drink for you! 😊

I re-enter the bar in a daze. I'll pretend I have a headache, make an early exit. But as I approach him, I stop short. He's sitting there, his eyes naked with hope and longing. I don't want to go home. I don't want to read the piece. I don't want to read my messages. I don't want to face the music.

'You okay?' Sean rubs my back, tingles dancing down my skin.

'Can we – can we just go back to mine?'

Sean downs his pint, jumps up and grabs his jacket.

As we head into my road, I see Dominic is back.

He's reading a newspaper. It's too dark to see which one, but I'm certain it's the *Daily Mail*. I can't be in today's paper – the news has only just broken. No, he's just flashing me a sign that he knows.

And then, with a chill, I remember the figure that Romain and I saw, when we were kissing drunkenly outside my flat. Could it have been Dominic?

'I see that fecker's still hanging about,' Sean says loudly, but I sense he doesn't want to push it, not after the row we had that broke us up.

In my lift, he slings a warm arm around me. I'm going to have to tell him once we get in, I decide.

Sean greets my birds with ecstatic enthusiasm. Mimi dances on his shoulder. 'Murderer!' she sing-songs.

'Hey, you're still saying that?' Sean croons, smiling.

'I thought I'd trained her out of it,' I mutter.

As Sean plays with Mimi, I head into the kitchen. I suffer a masochistic urge to read the article in full on my phone, let each word sting me. But as the kettle boils, Sean appears in the doorway, smiling, holding up his phone. He tells me to smile and he takes a photo, then caresses it with his finger. 'You look gorgeous as ever,' he says. And I think, *I should tell him, right now,* but I can't bear to ruin the moment, to have him look at me with disdain instead of love. He walks over to me and takes my face in his hands, gently brushing his lips against mine.

'I've missed you,' he whispers.

'You didn't reply to my messages,' I reply, my voice raw with hurt.

'I know, I know. I'm sorry. I just needed time. I just felt like – I was getting hurt. I wanted to move in, to make a commitment – and you weren't there . . .'

'I'm sorry,' I whisper.

If only I could rewind time. If Sean had moved in, I would never have watched Mina that night, never have been found out, never have slept with Romain . . .

Sean guides me out into the living-room and we sink onto the sofa. I remember sitting on Romain's lap, shove the flashback away. Romain was just fucking; this is lovemaking. I feel the need to drown myself in him, to be healed by the loving touch of his hands, to love him in return. I close my eyes and let Sean press record on the video, sighing as he enters me, losing myself in the night and his beauty.

But as our climax breaks into stillness, I open my eyes and a sadness hits me: *I'm going to lose him. Within hours, he'll know.*

In the morning, I feel as though I'm waiting for a bomb to go off.

Sean's so tactile that it keeps making me laugh. I go to make the tea and he pulls me in for a kiss; I fill the kettle and he caresses my shoulder.

'Sit down, Mr Kelly,' I chide. He starts checking his phone

and I start to feel nauseous. Sean doesn't read the tabloids. But surely one of his friends is going to spot it and message him any minute . . .

'Hmm, interesting news story,' he mutters.

I drop the toast and he puts his phone down, laughing and shaking his head.

He tells me the story is about seagulls attacking tourists on Hastings beach.

I suddenly feel like crying. I almost want him to know, just to end this cruel waiting game.

'You okay?' Sean pats my hand and I nod, remembering to keep my smile bright.

'Can I come back tonight?' he asks tentatively and I nod sadly, knowing that he won't want to come tonight, or any night, once he finds out the truth.

CHAPTER FORTY-FIVE

Mina

Romain and I stand outside our front door. I barely slept two hours, my insomnia so severe I felt as though I was turning over and over on a raw spit. The tea tray I'm carrying makes my wrists ache. As I offer cups of Earl Grey to reporters, my smile comes unstitched. Romain is making a speech: 'It was just one kiss . . . I was inebriated, I admit . . . I have always been loyal to my dear wife . . . we're putting this behind us . . . we're stronger than ever.' Cameras flash around us, white afterburn squares sizzling on my pupils until I feel dizzy and sick.

We retreat back inside. Romain seems on the verge of collapse; he leans against the wall, closes his eyes, feels for my hand and squeezes it tight. Lucas's words sing through my mind: *How long are you going to play at this charade and come be with me?*

Two days later, we're led to a wrought-iron table outside the Maverick, a newly opened restaurant in Mayfair, a heater flaring orange beside us.

Romain pulls out my chair for me and I thank him ostentatiously. The waiter brings a menu; I eye up dishes such as chargrilled sea bass or rotisserie Suffolk chicken. I'm aware of Romain casting self-conscious glances at the other diners. Yesterday we had a drink at a bar near Grosvenor Square and a few people snapped us on their phones. Romain revelled in it. It reinforced an image of us as a couple who've bravely weathered a crisis.

'Are you sure we can afford this?' I ask Romain. 'With the vineyard issues, and everything?'

'I think we can scrape it together – we do have savings,' Romain says.

I nod, returning to the menu. *Bastard,* I say silently. The words blur and I'm back in that secret room. Listening to him tell Alice that he exaggerated, perhaps even fabricated, the financial crisis to manipulate me. Seeing him thrust into Alice, drowning in animal hunger for her. I think of every time he's rejected me, said he's busy with work, feigned a headache, gone to sleep. Yet – when I sought relief in an affair, he didn't want to stop and wonder, *Why?* Why might my wife be looking at other men? No: he just decided to punish me.

Bastard.

'I'll have the salad, then the squid,' Romain tells the waiter.

'The same for me,' I say, passing the menu back. I look at Romain. 'I think we also need to scrape together enough to bring Baba back.'

'Oh, I'm not sure if we can afford her,' Romain declares.

'Then you can do the washing-up, darling,' I reply.

'Fine, fine,' Romain gives in, not wanting a fight in public.

He picks up his phone, scanning social media. The scandal has devastated him. His popularity was just picking up. The #PublishingJourney, which turned him into a cultural star, is now being used to slay him. The fact that he and Alice made a video in her flat, just before they were photographed kissing, was terrible timing. The tabloids have had a field day with headlines such as MP MENTORS WIFE'S ASSISTANT

IN BED and articles laughing at how he has 'certainly taken her on a publishing journey'. On Twitter, there are endless retweets and nasty memes about how Romain has favoured #TeamAlice. Romain's been reprimanded by the Party leader and warned he's on 'thin ice'. Now he's terrified of being deselected before next year's election.

Before I set Alice and my husband up for a fall, I sought out Alice's stalker, Dominic. I asked him for a chat, took him to a local café. He sat there, twitchy, wary, fiddling with his phone; I got the impression he was in poor mental health. I knew it was a risk, using him, that there was no guarantee of any success, but I took the plunge all the same: 'Romain will be at Alice's flat tomorrow night. You might want to be there.'

He sat up then, bright and animated. Here was the moment he'd been waiting for.

'You could take photos and sell them straight to the papers. I should imagine you'd get in the region of thirty K, maybe more.'

'The police are on to me, they've told me to stay away.'

'It will be dark. Find a hiding place, be discreet. Look, I'll give you five hundred pounds. It's all I can afford.' I'd already asked Lucas for a loan, without disclosing why.

Dominic looked hungry, then shadowed by suspicions: 'Why the fuck would you want to help me?'

'You warned me,' I reminded him. 'That night you came up into Alice's flat, you told me I should watch out for her. Well, you were right. She betrayed me.' His eyes gleamed then, and I knew he'd take the bait.

Of course, there was no guarantee they'd be foolish enough to kiss in public. My biggest hope was they'd get drunk, so I told Romain to take a Chateau Soisy-le-Vicomte that I knew was his favourite: open a bottle of that and he'll down glass after glass. I lit a match not knowing if the flame would catch, but it did; and the fire has spread further than I'd ever imagined. I'm still jittery that I could get burnt.

The blackmail emails have abruptly ceased. I have no idea why. It could be a sign that Dominic was my blackmailer, that he backed off when I fed him the scandal. But what if one of my Feeld lovers spots the piece, recognises me, declares we've been together? Still, how could they prove it? I never handed out my mobile number. I can claim that my identity was stolen, that I'm shocked to see my photos used on a fake profile. And yes, I'd be on CCTV, going in and out of Alice's building, but so what? She was my employee. My friend. It would prove nothing. I hope.

There's one part of my plan that hasn't gone as expected. I thought it would set me free. That Romain would admit he wants out. I've tried three, four times, to sit him down, to suggest that it might be over, but the moment I even mention *divorce*, he slams me down. Closes the conversation. Sometimes he even cries. He insists we have to stay together. I'm horrified by his determination to cling on.

Because I can't end this marriage alone. Romain always has the last word. He has to agree that we're over.

Now I watch the waiter pour me a glass of white and I raise my glass to my husband.

'Lovely evening,' I say.

'Gorgeous.'

The hard part has been staying away from Lucas. I miss him so much. I ache for his touch. In order to even text him I have to hide in the bathroom. I imagine what Lucas might say, if my Feeld flings were to come out. The press, the public are in sympathy with me, but I'd soon go from martyr to slut.

Not that I'm much enjoying being the poor middle-aged

martyr either. At least Alice gets to play the sexy, villainous temptress. She's the woman with the power, the home-wrecker, the seductive destroyer of worlds, whereas I'm being shown as the passive victim. If my affairs did come out, at least I'd be the one with the power, but the press loves caricatures, not contradictions.

A text on my phone, and I have to repress a smile. It's from Aimee: My dad is such a cunt!

'To our marriage.' Romain chinks his glass against mine.

I think there's a reporter at the next table.

I lift mine and chink his.

The happy couple.

The next morning I get into work and note that Alice's desk is still empty. She's been on a leave of absence from work. I've been in sporadically. Charles has said briskly that he doesn't want to 'take sides'.

Despite everything, I feel an unexpected pang: I miss Alice's energy, her enthusiasm.

As for Sarah – she's gone from being sullen and moody to looking exhilarated. She's having the time of her life this week: she's in gossip heaven, her office rival's been felled, and she's back as my main assistant.

'The papers have been ringing again,' Sarah says. 'People are saying there's more juice about to come out about Alice!'

'Well, if they ask us for a quote, we simply say no comment,' I say firmly, noticing Sarah's disappointed expression.

'Okay,' she says. 'Whatever you say. I'm on TeamMina, as you know. But I do think it's good if more dirt comes out, since Alice is getting *some* support.' I half imagine she'll be producing graphs and pie charts next. 'TeamAlice are saying it's wrong to slut-shame her, that Romain is a predator.'

'Well, let's just put it behind us,' I say stiffly, aware of more people coming into the office, of eyes on me, insidious whispers.

That evening, I'm glad to see that Baba's back. She gives me a hug, saying she's so sorry about the papers. I feel touched; if only my own mother could be that supportive. Whenever she calls, she adopts a told-you-so tone. She never wanted me to marry Romain and now she's finally been proved right.

At dinner, I tell Romain that Baba nearly lost her flat when he suspended her so suddenly.

'We should give her a bonus,' I insist. 'She's still in rent arrears.'

'I'll check the budget and see what we can afford,' he replies firmly.

He always has to make the final decision.

Once, I found that so sexy: that he was firm and decisive. Is this where my marriage went wrong? Once upon a time, he was my mentor. My father only ever taught me about Christian values and piety. When I married Romain, moved to London, mixed in high society, he taught me about the real world. I tasted caviar for the first time. A voice coach helped me to lose my northern accent for a well-to-do London one. I relished the way he shaped me into adulthood.

But, as I grew up, as my twenties turned into my thirties, resentment crept in. I developed my own opinions, ideas. I started to say no, disagree, answer back, haggle. Is that why Romain stopped wanting me? When I watched him with Alice, I saw how much he relished controlling the situation, dominating her sexually.

'Have you seen this video of Aimee?' Romain asks.

It's up on Twitter. Aimee's looking very drunk and she's

reeling about on a pavement outside a nightclub, saying, 'My sister has a bastard for a husband . . . My *sister* . . . ha-ha . . .'

'Oh God,' I say. I've been phoning Aimee on a daily basis, warning her not to speak to the press. But I know that she could break at any time.

'We need to face the fact that the – Aimee – *issue* – could come out,' Romain says. There's fear in his eyes. 'She could go to the papers . . .'

'She won't,' I assert.

'So you are in touch,' he complains. 'I knew it.'

'She's my daughter,' I fire back. 'We've exchanged a few texts. If we cut her off, she's more likely to feel hurt, to retaliate. This way, I can keep an eye on her.'

Romain rubs his fingers up and down the stem of his wineglass. 'But getting involved with Aimee is never safe. Do you want us to lose everything?' His voice shakes. 'We can weather one storm, but not another.'

I nod miserably. A buzz on my phone. Lucas is getting more and more hurt by my public assertions that I still love my husband, that I want to stand by him.

'We're good together, you and I,' Romain goes on, reaching across to caress my hand.

I pull away. I can't stand anymore of this bullshit. 'Romain, we're not good together, not anymore,' I burst out, trembling.

Romain gazes at me, his eyes glinting with pain.

'Why keep pretending? So you get your seat next time? I'm sure you can find yourself another trophy wife . . .'

He stands up and walks around the table and for one surreal, sick moment I'm scared he's going to hit me. But then I realise he's holding out his hand. I take it in confusion; he draws me up, pulls me into his arms, so tight it hurts. He showers kisses over my neck, murmuring softly, and the past rushes into the present: all our good times together, our history, the chemistry we once had. I feel an ache inside and I curl my arms around him too, pressing my cheek against his chest—

But then an image sears into my mind: I picture him with Alice again, driving into her, his face blazing with desire.

I try to tug away. Romain fights me, draws me back to him.

'We have to stick together,' he insists in a quiet, intense voice. 'We've always been loyal to each other, haven't we . . .? When you killed that boy, I stayed with you . . .'

'I didn't—' I break away in shock, seeing the threat in his eyes. 'I didn't *kill* him . . . God, Romain.'

'You made a decision to let him die,' Romain says. 'I never walked away when you were in trouble. I might have made a mistake with Alice, but it's nothing compared to what you did, Mina – I mean, come on.'

Romain touches my face and suddenly his caress feels like a threat: *Stay with me and I'll keep your secrets; leave me and I'll expose you.*

I suddenly feel like breaking down, wailing, howling. I'm kicking against my marriage, trying to destroy it, to find freedom and air. And yet I only feel more trapped than ever.

CHAPTER FORTY-SIX

Alice

Two Years Earlier

The morning after being arrested for stealing first editions from Julia, I slip into Chesterton House as someone comes out. I spent the night in the graveyard of St Mary Abbots Church, hiding behind a cracked gravestone, sleeping restlessly, freezing cold, scared Dominic might come looking for me. There's no way I can go to our squat. After three years of friendship, of fighting the world together, it's over between us.

As I knock on her front door, I feel sick. Julia changed her mind, dropped the charges, but she might well call the police again.

The door opens. She starts, and I'm shocked to see the fear in her eyes. She thinks I'm here for revenge.

'I just wanted to say sorry,' I gabble. 'Dominic was the one who wanted me to steal and I feel really bad about it and I'm sorry. I've loved reading to you and cooking for you and looking after you. It wasn't a con in the end, even if it started out like that . . .'

Julia looks tired. She glares at me and I start to back down the hallway.

'Wait,' she says.

My heart leaps as she opens the door. As I venture in,

I'm wary, wondering if I might find Dominic present, sneering away.

'I'd like some tea,' Julia demands, sitting down. 'Leave the door open, please,' she adds, as I go into the kitchen, and I blush with shame.

As I make the tea, I feel the pressure of the moment. She's giving me another chance, perhaps, but how do I convince her?

I carry the tray in and sit down opposite her.

'I'm sorry,' I begin. 'It's just – I ended up homeless a few years ago and it all started when I was a teenager and my mum—'

'I don't want to hear any sob stories,' Julia snaps. 'We're all responsible for our decisions in life.'

Easy for you to say, I think, *when you live in a place like this.* When you're poor, fate overwhelms you; it's money that gives you free will.

'The only reason I'm letting you back in here is because I can see Dominic had you under his thumb.'

I feel a bit humiliated and nearly protest – but then I see I'd be falling into a trap. Instead, I nod and look a little pathetic as though yes, Dominic has dictated all my decisions.

'He was always such a troubled child,' Julia muses. She trails off, eyeing me warily. 'Sometimes I get tired of the persona, the lie. I go into my hallway, I chat with Jean, my neighbour. In her head, she's completely fooled that I'm one of them. But I'm not, you see. I'm like you, Alice.'

She laughs and before I can dig any deeper, she pushes a book in my direction and asks me to read. I'm desperately intrigued but the situation feels so delicate that I obey her and read aloud. Julia doesn't seem to be taking much in. I finish the chapter, then set the book down, waiting.

'I see much of myself in you, Alice.'

'What – what d'you mean by that?' I ask nervously.

'How do you think I came to be in the possession of this flat?' she asks, her eyes bright, her voice high.

'Dom said . . . Well, he was educated at private school, so I figured you were . . . wealthy.'

'I grew up much like you, Alice. That was the hand of cards that life dealt me. My childhood was one of wanting. It was the fifties, a time of austerity, rebuilding after the war. And then came the sixties, which made it worse. I wanted dresses, I wanted fine things, I wanted a car. I got married in my twenties, as you were expected to do in those days. We kept trying for a baby for years before I gave birth to Dominic. I eventually grew tired of playing at being housekeeper and cook and whore. We got divorced. And there I was: a single mother, on benefits, living in a high rise in Crouch End.' She shudders. 'One day, due to a clerical error, my social security was cut off. And we were hungry. And when you have a young child, you must feed them – instincts take over. You do as you must . . .'

'You . . .' I've got the wrong end of the stick: I think she's talking about prostitution. But Julia says: 'I taught Dominic.'

'What . . .? You mean you homeschooled him?'

Julia laughs. She picks up a Duchy biscuit from the plate. 'You're not a fool, Alice. What do you think?'

As it dawns on me, I feel shocked. 'Oh.'

'We'd go walking together. Looking at houses. Seeing weaknesses. Watching people. When you have a child, a cute child, they're the perfect alibi. Everyone is distracted by them. And children are useful. They can climb through windows . . .'

I know I shouldn't judge Julia. I know the taste of that

kind of desperation – I've been there myself. But: *what kind of mother was she?*

'And then I met Timothy.' She sighs, swallows some biscuit. 'I was in my forties, he was fifty-five. I studied him for months. He had this glorious flat in Kensington, he was the most eligible bachelor. He had a fetish for women who were very submissive and sweet. Dominic was nine, now. I taught him to speak nicely. I tarted myself up. I "bumped into" him one day in Kensington Gardens. And I nabbed him!' Julia has a triumphant look on her face, the sort she gets when we're playing cards and she slams down an ace.

'Of course,' she sighs, 'I was so busy keeping my eye on the prize, I didn't stop to think, *Why is a man who owns a flat worth millions a bachelor?* Because he was a complete shit, of course.'

In my nerves, I laugh in shock, for Julia normally bans swearing. She smiles grimly.

'A shit,' she repeats. 'I was living in luxury, but I'd find myself with a black eye if I put too much milk in his Darjeeling. All these first editions.' She waves her hand at the bookcase. 'Guilt books, that's what they are. He'd give them to me once he'd calmed down and the shame came. Why d'you think I'm partially sighted? Because he once hit this eye – the left – so hard I was blind in it for several weeks, and my cornea never fully repaired.' She exhales. 'And as for Dominic . . . I thought that, despite everything, I'd done the best for my son. At least Timothy was paying for a splendid education. But Dominic was miserable. The other boys could smell he wasn't one of them. He told me he'd been happier when I was sending him into houses to steal. And those scars on his head – oh dear, they were the result of him hitting adolescence and clashing with Timothy . . .' She trails off.

'Oh my God,' I say, wide-eyed.

'So, in the end, we had to get rid of Timothy. What else was there to do?'

'What . . . what do you mean?'

'It was Dominic who said it first. He was fifteen. I thought, *What sort of monster have I created?* But he was right.'

'Did you . . .?' I trail off, stunned.

'In the end, nature took care of him. Timothy had a heart attack. I woke up to find him gasping for breath. So instead of calling an ambulance, Dominic and I went for a long walk around Kensington Gardens. When we returned, he was dead. On the day of Timothy's funeral,' she skips ahead, 'I had to stop myself from behaving as though it was one big celebration. Dominic kept laughing and I had to tell others he was hysterical. God – the relief. But . . .' She sighs. 'What we went through. Maybe it was worth it. I did get this flat, and it's heaven to be here, and to wake each day not worrying about the bills. I love these fine things in life – these biscuits, my books, my view. But Dominic – I lost him.' There's a catch in her voice. 'He didn't know himself anymore. He ran away at the age of eighteen, hung out with drug addicts and down-and-outs, pretending he was poor too.'

A silence. Her clock ticks; traffic passes on the road outside. She suddenly reaches for my hand, squeezing tightly.

'I don't want you to go,' she says. Her voice is full of lonely anguish, just as it was that first day we met in the library. 'I don't want to spend my last days alone.'

'Of course I'll stay,' I whisper, squeezing her back.

And so, for the next two years, Julia became the mother I'd lost, and in turn, I fulfilled the loss of her son. I moved in as her live-in carer. We ate together, played cards together; I read to her. Once we even created our own theatrical version of *Jane Eyre*, acting different roles, to an audience of nobody. Her confession had opened up our relationship, allowed for a certain honesty; after that, I felt I could tell her anything.

For all her history, I found Julia to be the wisest and kindest person I had ever met. She said that money changes people: for some it corrupts, for others it creates an insatiable hunger for more, but it had brought her contentment and grace. Mindful of her past, she gave to charity. She blessed me with gifts. She taught me how life worked, what to value and what to ignore. With Dominic, all my emotions had been basic, primal; with Julia, they were delicate and beautiful. Finally I had found a place called home, the place I had craved.

Only Dominic was the rub. For Julia refused to see him or forgive him, declaring that he was no longer her son. On the few occasions that he tried to visit the flat, often bearing gifts, she'd become hysterical, and he'd be forced to leave.

He was furious that I was still there. He couldn't believe that I was staying out of sincerity; he tried to persuade Julia that I was just nurturing a con of my own. I was now his nemesis, the woman who'd stolen his mark, his plan.

Julia would defend me but I could always see a little doubt on her face after he'd left. And I would reassure her, again and again, that I didn't want to be in her will. That wasn't my game or my goal.

And I meant it. When Julia passed away, it broke my heart. I was in mourning when I was summoned by her lawyer, Mr Wentworth. When the lawyer read out that I was the sole heir of the flat, I was delirious with shock. Elated and terrified. My mind was like a pendulum, swinging from *Dom will go mad* to *I've won the fucking property lottery.* I holed myself up in Julia's flat, now my flat: and a day later, the buzzing started, as Dominic realised he'd been cut out.

CHAPTER FORTY-SEVEN

Alice

I gaze at my reflection in the bedroom mirror, fingering my smart new grey trouser suit. This afternoon, I'm going back into the office for the first time in a week. My stomach is frantic with butterflies.

I've spoken to Charles a few times on the phone. He was more sympathetic than I expected him to be. 'I don't want to pick a side,' he declared in a diplomatic tone. 'I can imagine this is all terribly stressful, but I'm sure that in a week or two, people will have moved on.'

But will they? I wonder. Every time I have a conversation with anyone I work with, there'll be a constant subtext, looks of embarrassment, questions in their eyes. Nobody will see me for me. I've become a caricature, a femme fatale, a conniving slut.

I don't even know how Mina has reacted. I haven't had a single call or message from her. There have been times when I've wanted to shout out across London: *Mina is the one having an affair, not me!* The photo of her in the *Mail* made her look wan instead of powerful, as though she's some poor wifely victim. In more cynical moments, I wonder if this was her game all along, if she wanted to hide her affair behind my fake one. Even if she and Lucas do get exposed, it'll look as though I ruined her marriage first and she sought solace elsewhere. But then I think: *Surely Mina wouldn't go that far?* She and Romain have been together over twenty years. And how could she have known we'd be photographed?

I don't trust any supposed quotes from her in the papers. I've read things that that I've apparently said, from 'My bitch of a boss deserved it' (attributed to a 'close friend' of mine) to 'Can my mentor ever forgive me?' In truth, I've refused to give a single statement or answer a single buzz on my door. My neighbour Jean has been incredibly supportive in briskly ushering away any journalists who've ventured up to our floor. I thought she might judge me, but she offered tea and comfort, even if it was clear that all she wanted was the gossip.

It's nearly nine and I'm going to be late.

A message on my phone. I'm half terrified it's work telling me not to come in, that I've been fired. To my relief, it's Sean.

Good luck today.

It's been the one comfort in the dark of the last week: Sean has been there for me. Yes, he was shocked, and hurt, and when I told him the full story, he reacted in horror, telling me that I had to change jobs. But he's been loyal to me, and I love him for it.

The reporters have been diminishing by the day but I'm still dreading there might be a handful outside.

When I head out into the open air and see there's nobody, relief swims through me: *Maybe I can get through this.*

Then I see Dominic. Standing by a wall, smirking. And I feel a rage burning up inside me. A few weeks ago, I thought I'd won this battle. And now here he is, back on top, making my life hell.

I stride up to him and see red. I curl my first into a ball. He cowers in shock.

Then I see someone watching, holding up their phone and I quickly back away.

'Just give me half,' Dominic says. 'Sell the flat, give me half. That's fair and square. Then I'll leave you alone, let you get on with your life.'

'What life?' I laugh harshly. 'You've already ruined it.'

'Half. You'll never see me again. Come on, I'm sick of all this too. I just want justice . . .'

I turn and walk away from him.

I get off the train at Blackfriars. I'm not far from work but I can feel my steps slowing.

A buzz on my phone. It's from Sean. Sorry to send bad news, but have you seen this?

I spot a bench overlooking the Thames and hurry to it, brushing away crisp autumn leaves. I sit down and click on the link.

'*Oh shit*,' I murmur.

Just when I thought it couldn't get any worse.

I sit, stunned, watching a gull yank a fish out of the water, which wriggles in its beak as it flies away.

My phone buzzes and I jump. It's from Sarah: Charles is wondering if you're coming in this afternoon.

I message her back: Sorry, I'm feeling really sick. Think I have food poisoning from some dodgy fish I ate last night.

I look at the article again.

Oh, Julia, I say to her in my head, aching for her to be alive again, *I think I'm had. I really am going to have to give up this job, sell your flat, start over.*

Dominic's won.

CHAPTER FORTY-EIGHT

Mina

I stroll into the White Hare feeling nervous. I'm used to heads turning the moment I enter a place. I've become a walking headline personified: the Wronged Wife.

I've taken the day off work today, which I'll admit coincides with Alice's return. Plus, I wanted to meet my daughter. Aimee refused a private meeting; she was determined to meet in a bar, her addiction calling the shots. So I picked the quietest pub I could find, in a sleepy part of Surrey. I'm relieved to find the place is virtually empty, except for an old man sitting with a pair of springer spaniels by the door, engrossed in *The Times*.

Aimee's sitting in a booth at the back. She's wearing a black silky dress with a tear in the lace sleeve, and as I lean in, I smell gritty scents, sweat and smoke. I hug her tightly, trying not to wince at the bottle of wine before her. She pours me a glass. I set it to one side.

'Is Romain here?' she asks.

'First things first,' I say firmly. 'Have you got Lucas's gun?'

Aimee admitted to stealing it from Lucas's friend, on a whim, but promises she hasn't used it. She passes it to me under the table, wrapped in a carrier bag; I slip it into my handbag.

'Thank you,' I tell her. 'I'll give it back to Lucas.'

'Is Romain here?' she asks again.

'I'm sorry, darling, he couldn't make it,' I say. She looks crushed and my heart aches for her. Romain ranted and raved when I told her that Aimee wanted us to meet her boyfriend, Michael, declaring he'd only turn out to be some drug addict who would drag our reputation down even further. He only gave me permission to come on the grounds that we need to stop her blabbing to the press.

Though I loathe Romain's cynicism, I know he's right. I'm also terrified that Aimee's going to break. There's so much at stake, and I'm not sure I can face another round of headlines, of scandal, of statements, of neighbours gossiping and colleagues being sympathetic. I'm scared that Aimee wouldn't be able to handle it either. Romain's already concocted a horrible contingency plan: if it comes out, we'll deny it and send her to rehab abroad.

'Michael's late.' Aimee looks agitated as she keeps checking her phone. 'Are you and Romain going to get a divorce? Because he's behaving like a total bastard, isn't he?'

'We're staying together.' I repeat the assurance I've said a hundred times over the past week, to friends, family, the press. The words sound less convincing every time I say them.

'What about Alice? Are you going to fire her? She's a total slut.'

'Aimee!' I'm surprised by her vitriol. 'I'm not sure what we'll do about her.'

'But she's horrible, she tried to steal Romain from you.'

'It's not all that black and white,' I say uncomfortably.

Aimee checks her phone again. 'Where is he . . .?'

Michael's now twenty minutes late, he's not got in touch with my daughter, and suddenly I sense this get-together is not going to go well.

'Michael and I – we've got you a present, but I wanted to wait til he gets here . . .' Aimee tries calling him. And again. And again. She goes to down the rest of her wine and I stop her.

'Fuck him,' I say. The shock of my words makes her laugh. 'I mean it, Aimee. You don't have to drown your sorrows. You find someone better.'

'But he's so perfect . . .' Aimee reaches for her glass and once again, I pin it to the table, giving her a firm look. 'Well – here's the present we were going to give you.' She pulls it out of her canvas bag and I feel touched to see she's wrapped it up in gold paper. It's been many years since Aimee last bought me something.

I unwrap it: it's a first edition of *David Copperfield*, and I can't help mulling that I saw a similar book on Alice's bookshelf. Still, it's such a sweet gesture.

'It's beautiful—' I break off, realising that Aimee's crying.

She tries to speak through her tears and I realise she's saying, 'I'm sorry.' I tense up. *Oh God*, I think. *This is it. She's spoken to the press*. It was inevitable; we couldn't buy her silence forever—

'It was Michael's idea, not mine . . .' she whispers. 'To demand money. That's why he's not showing. We – we had this argument last night and I said we should pay you back—'

'You don't need to pay us back,' I say gently, in relief: so Aimee's just feeling guilty about all the money we're sending her, to pay for her silence.

'No – but – you don't get it. Michael found out about your affairs, and I was upset – I didn't realise that Dad was fucking around too. I thought you were being a bitch, I'm really sorry. Michael said we should make you pay, so we sent the emails . . . asking for money. You were supposed to stop, but you didn't.'

My head swims. I reach for my wine and down it. Aimee laughs in horror, and then, as I gaze at her in fury, her tears return.

'So,' I say. 'Let me get this straight. You and Michael are the ones sending me blackmail emails?'

'Yes,' she sobs. 'It was us.'

My own daughter. Not Alice, whom I was convinced was the culprit. Not Sarah. Nobody at work, no enemy from my past. But: Aimee.

Anger rears inside me. I almost feel like I could slap her.

Then I look at her. I notice, through the tear on her dress, there's a red mark on her arm, a new tattoo of a snake, that looks raw, in danger of becoming infected. I notice how thin she's getting. This is where my daughter's ended up, and I've played a part in that. I start crying myself.

'Well, I deserved it,' I say.

'You didn't.' Aimee reaches for my hand, clutching it desperately. 'At first I thought that you deserved it. You and Dad, you didn't even want to see me. But then you suddenly changed . . .'

I dab my eyes with a napkin. 'But darling, who is this Michael? How did you find out about me?'

I have visions of Aimee hacking my computer, sneaking into the house and checking my laptop.

'He – he was watching Alice's flat. And he had me watching sometimes. I borrowed a key from your coat pocket once. And we saw what was happening – I know you and Lucas used to go in separately . . .' Aimee reaches for my napkin, blows her nose.

At the mention of Lucas, I tense up.

'Do you have a photo of Michael?' I ask Aimee. When she hesitates, I say: 'Look, I just want to see if it's someone I know.'

Aimee taps in her code and passes over a photo. Even though I suspected as such, I still gasp. He's wearing a suit and looks slick compared to that dreadful cagoule he normally adopts. But it's definitely him.

'Aimee – this isn't Michael, it's Dominic. He—'

'He changed his name,' she interrupts me. 'He didn't like Dominic. He got a new job in the City and he wanted a new start.'

'Aimee, he doesn't work in the City. He's feeding you stories. He's Alice's stalker – and—'

'He's not her fucking stalker.' Aimee's eyes flash in anger. 'She's just pinned that label on him so people don't take him seriously, but she's a fucking snake who stole his inheritance. You shouldn't be in her flat, you should just fire her and tell her to go to hell.'

Oh God. I want to drive over to Alice's flat, find him, slap him, put my hands around his neck. And to think I used him too, that I sought him out for help, and he smirked at me, and took my money, knowing all along that he was abusing my daughter. No wonder he hasn't turned up for drinks. Meet the parents? Dominic must have been silently laughing himself sick when Aimee invited him to meet us.

'Aimee, this man is toxic,' I say, but Aimee's shaking her head. I realise that the more I attack him, the more she'll defend him. I let out a breath and pour myself more wine. *Fuck,* I think. I might be setting a bad example, but I need some alcohol.

'So what else did Domi—Michael ask you to do?' I ask. 'Aside from blackmailing me and putting me through hell?'

'I'm really sorry. I want to pay you back.' Aimee swings back to sorrow again. 'But Alice, she deserved everything she got.'

'What do you mean by that?' I ask sharply.

'Michael wanted her to get fucked up and she deserves it,

after what she did to him. He got me to mess things about in her flat.'

'Mess things about? Like *what*?'

'We moved her books around. Played thrash metal to freak her neighbours. Taught her parrot to say, "Murderer." Michael told me he once set her video camera off at night. Just stuff to scare her – don't look at me like that, she deserved it.'

'And he thought *I* deserved to be blackmailed, remember?'

Aimee turns to her wine. And suddenly I reach for her, pulling her in for a tight hug, but fear comes over me, of how out of control everything is.

'Darling.' I push her hair back from her face. 'Does he know who your real mother is?'

'No.' Aimee shakes her head.

'You're sure?'

'I didn't tell him. I don't ever want to tell anyone – you've made me feel like it'd be the crime of the century if I do. You're so ashamed of it coming out!' Aimee wails.

'It's not that, it's never that!' I cry. I lower my voice: 'You know that I love you. And we will announce it, in good time.'

'You promise?' Aimee pleads, and I lean in and kiss her cheek.

'I do,' I tell her. 'But knowledge is power, and if you give that power to him, then he owns you. You understand? You keep it secret for now, and you stay strong.'

Aimee nods and laces her fingers into mine. We sit there, drinking together, and I feel a fierce, protective love flow towards her, laced with unease. She's so vulnerable, and I want to shout at the world to leave her alone, to stop anyone ever harming her. If Dominic was here right now, I'd kill him with my bare hands.

CHAPTER FORTY-NINE

Alice

Bloody Heather Perkins.

My greatest fears have come true.

She's today's news. A photo of her in the *Daily Telegraph* in a powder-blue suit, looking anguished, with the headline ALICE SMART STOLE FROM ME. This cuts even more than the affair piece, somehow.

Will Charles ever let me come back to the office once he sees this? And where will it all end? If Dominic did sell those photos, what's to stop him going for the jugular, calling up the papers and creating another headline? I can just imagine it: FEMME FATALE STOLE MY INHERITANCE AND MURDERED MY MOTHER. People are ready to believe anything about me now.

After sitting on the bench by the Thames in a daze for too long, I start to shiver in the autumn chill. I get back onto a train and head for Golders Green. I stand by the trio of ash trees near his flat, waiting for Dominic to leave. I've got to finish this war between us. The moment he tried to push me onto the tube tracks should have been warning enough of how serious he is. I've got to be smarter. One step ahead. I have to know what he's planning next.

An hour passes. Then I spot him.

Frustration fills me as I watch him *entering* his flat. I could've gone in and got out by now. At the sight of him, I feel a rage prickle over my skin that verges on violence.

I'm tired, and I'm hungry. Dom probably won't re-emerge for a while; I walk up the road and enter a cheap café, buying a sausage roll. I'm about to exit when I see Dominic strolling past and I quickly backtrack, pretending that I need more napkins. He strides past, his hood up, looking intense.

I hurry back to his flat. I just want it to be quick – if his phone's there I'll steal it and take it home. I don't care about the repercussions.

I don't need to force the front door. It's closed, but on the latch, which is worrying – maybe Dominic has just popped out.

I need to work fast.

I hurry to his desk. There's a new fake ID in progress; Dominic's photo on a passport, with the name MICHAEL MILLS.

But – no phone. I check the sofa. Run into the bedroom. Nothing on the bed, or on the floor, where I found it last time.

There's the sound of a car pulling up outside. Then I hear voices, the sound of the front door opening.

Shit. Déjà vu: I look round the bedroom helplessly for somewhere to hide – but there's nothing I can do but stand behind the door, pressed against the wall.

Dominic seems to be mid-argument with someone.

'I want my money,' the man is saying. His voice is familiar, European, accented. I frown – is that . . . *Lucas*?

'I don't have it right now,' Dominic is protesting. His voice is cool.

'You're supposed to be working for *me*. I thought we had

an agreement. You watch the flat. You report back. You were not supposed to be taking photos.'

'Yeah, I know, but I did everything you asked, I gave you all the intel—'

'And how much did you get for selling those fucking photos? Maybe you can give me that, hey?'

So Dominic did sell the photos to the press: no surprises there. But who – who is he speaking to? I tiptoe to the edge of the door. All I can see is fragments: a man in a dove-grey suit, a wave of dark hair.

I freeze in shock.

What the fuck is Romain doing here?

I need to move back to a safe place. They'd only have to turn, and they'd see me. But I can't stop staring. Romain *knows* Dominic. When? How?

I quickly dive back behind the door.

'Okay, okay,' Dominic snaps. His voice rises to a shout. 'I'll give you a share. I got thirty K, okay? From *The Sun*. But I had debts, bills – I don't have much left. It was Mina's idea, anyway.'

'Mina's idea? What?' Romain asks.

'She told me you and Alice would be having sex. She wanted me to sneak in – she even gave me a key. But I was like, *Nah, it's too risky, I can't just walk in there, it's a crazy idea*—'

'Hang on.' Romain sounds incredulous. 'You're now trying to claim that – *my wife* – approached you and made this offer? Really?'

'I'm serious – you fucking ask her, get her to admit it herself. She wanted to fuck you over, mate.'

'Mate?' Romain sneers. 'I'm not your mate. Mina would never do that. You're lying.'

'Don't shoot the messenger.' Dominic's cocky again. He's always thrived on conflict.

Roman is silent. I risk another glance. His shock mirrors mine: did Mina really set this up?

'But Mina – wouldn't . . .' He trails off.

'She gave me five hundred pounds cash,' Dominic says.

'She can't have, she has no money. I removed that luxury from her life.'

'Well, I don't know where the fuck she got it, but she did. I've got . . .' Dominic goes to his desk, pulls open a drawer, lifts some papers. 'I've got fifty, here, alright?'

Romain takes it, counts it, pockets it. 'This is a farcical sum. It's not nearly enough to compensate me. You've destroyed my career. My reputation. One year before an election. Do you understand what you have done?'

'What your wife has done,' Dominic protests, but he sounds pathetic now, a little scared.

'You can pay me back by working for me for free,' Romain demands.

'Sure,' Dominic backs down. 'I'll carry on watching, okay.'

So Romain was employing Dominic to watch my flat?

But Dominic was there before I ever started my internship. It was his way of torturing me . . .

Then I think back to that night, when Mina first promised me a real job and Romain drove me home. He approached Dominic; at the time I thought he was protecting me, seeing Dominic off. Now I wonder if he saw an opportunity . . .

'I want you to be available to do what I want, when I want it,' Romain carries on in a bullying tone, as though he's addressing a peasant.

'Yes, sir,' Dominic mocks him.

I risk another look and see that Romain has suddenly gone for Dominic, is pressing him up against the wall, Dominic's

T-shirt twisted in one hand, his elbow against Dominic's throat, and he's pushing hard, squeezing, and I can't bear it—

'No,' I gasp. 'No.'

Romain turns. 'Who's there?'

I dart back to the wall, press myself against it, trembling all over.

Romain comes into the bedroom. He scans it, kneels down, checks under the bed. I'm a foot away from him, staring down at his back, the expensive cloth of his suit rippling across his shoulder blades. For a moment I think I've got away with it. But then he turns and sees me behind the door—

'Alice!'

He takes my arm and tugs me into the living-room. Dominic frowns at the sight of me.

'What the fuck are you doing here?'

'Well?' Romain asks. 'Is this what's going on? Are you planning on sharing your thirty thousand pounds with Alice?'

'What?' I cry, incredulous.

Dominic laughs, incredulous too. 'I have no idea what the fuck she is doing here. She must have broken in. I've got nothing to do with the woman who killed my mum and stole my flat.'

Romain looks at him, then me, and I'm numb with shock that he thinks we're in cahoots.

'Were you recording us?' Romain demands. 'Where's your phone?'

I take it out of my bag, hand shaking, and pass it over to him. It's buzzing – I see that Mina is calling me, for the first time in a long time. I'm desperate to answer it, to tell her what I've seen, to ask her to call the police. But then I think, *She's not my friend, she set me up*, and I lose my nerve, and Romain's hand is curled around mine, prising the phone away. He asks for the code and I tell him, and he puts in his pocket.

I swallow.

'Alice, we need to have a chat,' he says. He nods at Dominic. 'Thank you for inviting me here. I'll do what I can to help you buy your flat from the council. I do my best to help all my constituents.'

It's such a lame attempt at covering up that Dominic laughs. I'm not laughing. Romain is guiding me out into the hallway. His car is parked on the kerb, on a double yellow, ridiculously glossy on such a grim road; a few local teenagers are eyeing it up. He tells me to get into the front. I think about making a run for it, and he quickly glides to my side, opening the door, pushing me in. Then he's in his seat and I hear the click of the locks.

PART V

Police Report: Interview with Jean Winters

4 October 2024

DS Matthews: Can we resume focus on this evening, and when you first felt concerned about what was happening next door?

Jean Winters: It was when the lights went down. That was odd. I knew then that something was wrong.

CHAPTER FIFTY

Alice

I sit in the car in a fog of fury. So Mina – my boss, my mentor, my champion of diversity – set me up. For a moment, doubt assails me: what if Dom's just winding Romain up? But no: it was all so perfectly choreographed. Over the past few weeks, I've kept mulling on the fact that Dominic was backing off, leaving me in peace after the police warning – and then he just happened to turn up on the exact evening that Romain and I were together.

I never dreamed Mina could be so ruthless. God, I'm naive.

And as for Romain – I flick him a look – he's no better. He's had Dominic watching my flat, *paid* him to do so, not even caring about the impact on me. He's Mr Control Freak. He wanted every drop of intel on his wife he could get.

This is all about them. Their marriage. Their Machiavellian games. Their reputation. Their #PublishingJourney facade. I'm just a pawn.

I reach up and give Romain a harsh slap on the cheek. It's not sexy this time. I'm seriously fucking angry.

The car swerves and a horn toots behind us.

'I deserved that,' he says softly.

I realise that he's heading towards Kensington. 'This isn't a good idea, us being seen together,' I point out.

'Let's just get you home safely.'

Anger surges through me again. The moment I get home, I'm not calling Mina back. No: I'm damn well going to post another #PublishingJourney video. And this time I'm going to tell the world *everything*.

I cringe as he pulls up by my apartment building. The reporters might have given up, moved on to their next prey, but someone could well spot us, snap us.

As we enter the lobby, Felipe, the doorman on duty, looks up from his desk with a double take; I'm sure he's read the recent tabloid scandals. I give him an awkward grin.

'Look,' I say to Romain as we reach the lifts, 'you can go. I don't really want to discuss this anymore. Can you please give me back my phone?'

'I will. But first we need to talk,' Romain insists.

'I have a headache. And really, it's fine. I know Dominic can't be trusted, so whatever business you have with him – I don't care. As for Mina and what she's done to me – well . . .' I shake my head, fighting my rage. 'I just want my phone, thanks.'

'Alice,' Romain says in a warning tone. When I glare at him, he cajoles me: 'Please – just give me five minutes? That's all I ask. It's so important that we understand each other. Then I will return your phone. I promise.'

The lift seems to take forever to get to the fifth floor. We stand inside with folded arms.

I reluctantly let him into my flat.

'Murderer!' Mimi greets us, calling out from her cage.

I watch Romain saunter in with his usual arrogance, as though this is his flat and I'm the guest, and I snap.

'You should know that Mina set us up to sleep together,' I say savagely. 'It was her idea. She was watching, by the way.'

'She *what* . . .?'

For a moment I relish the shock on Romain's face, the crack in his cool. And then I just feel shame, as I remember how I felt that night, how dirty the sex was.

'Wait – where did she watch us . . .?'

'There's a secret room in my flat – with a spyhole—'

'*Where?* Show me. Show me right now.'

'Actually, I just want you to go,' I reply.

'Show me.' Romain's voice quietens to a hiss and fear prickles over me. I slip behind the TV and unlock the door. He follows me and glances around, peers through the peep-hole, shakes his head.

Then he turns to me, his expression hardening.

'So you were in on this?' His voice is like a whip.

'Mina insisted,' I cry. 'She said I'd lose my job.'

'So that was the only reason you slept with me? You were forced to?' He sounds hurt now, his ego frail.

'No,' I admit. 'I mean – I did – want you – but God – between the pair of you, I've had enough. And before you start having a go at me, let's not forget that you *paid* my stalker to spy on my flat.'

'But that's where I helped you, Alice,' Romain cuts in.

'Helped me?' I laugh in outrage.

'Dominic was always going to stalk you,' he says. 'He wants this flat and he's prepared to do anything. Once I started paying him, I had him in the palm of my hand, see? He could report on you, but he couldn't hurt you. Those were the rules. Remember what happened with on the tube?'

'You were there? You saw that?'

'Of course I didn't. But he told me about it, and I told him to stop. I told him he was going too far. I kept him on a leash.'

My anger rises. Romain's tone is so reasonable, but I swear this is all manipulative bullshit.

'You didn't do any of this for me!' I cry, my voice high and choked. 'If you actually cared one drop about me, you would have told me about this whole scheme. Do you realise how many nights' sleep I lost over Dominic, with him out there, watching me? None of this has been for my benefit, only for *your* benefit, because that's how it is with you and Mina, it's all about what *you* can gain. You're so selfish: you lie to your wife about a financial collapse, you pretend I came onto you when it was you who started all that and, to top it all, you can't even bloody acknowledge your own daughter. You're a hypocrite. If you ask me, you deserve to lose your seat at the next election.'

I exhale, shocked at my own outburst: I hadn't meant to let slip that I knew about Aimee. Romain flinches. He's silent for a moment, but manages to hold his smile.

'Well, Aimee's really none of your business,' he says lightly, as though I'm some hack interviewing him. 'It's not a subject I'm prepared to discuss.'

I cross my arms. Enough, I think, enough. Suddenly the room feels very claustrophobic. I turn to go, when Romain's tone changes:

'I still want you, you know.' To my shock, he moves closer, stroking my face with trembling fingers, and I realise his whole body is shaking. I try to push him away, but he gently brushes his lips against mine. I jump, the electricity sparking between us again, irresistibly, and step backwards.

'Alice – I wanted this flat watched because I stopped trusting Mina. She doesn't listen to me anymore, doesn't respect me. We've been falling apart for years, to be honest.' He swallows. 'Perhaps divorce is inevitable. Think about what that could mean for us . . .'

'You can't be serious . . .'

'Do you really have something special with Sean? As special as we have?'

'It's different.' I'm trapped in the corner now. 'Sean's not obsessed with power and control and his reputation.'

Romain's expression grows sullen. He retreats, and I let out a shaky breath.

Then I hear the door close behind him.

The key turns in the lock.

'Romain?' I rattle it. '*Romain?*'

CHAPTER FIFTY-ONE

Mina

Charles enters my office and sets a newspaper down on my desk. I gaze down at the pictures of Heather Perkins and Alice. At the headline: ALICE SMART STOLE FROM ME.

'It's an impossible situation,' he says. 'If we fire her, it's an embarrassment; if we let her stay, it's a mess . . .'

Guilt sobers me. I was so furious when I found out that Alice had been watching me that I took revenge. She became the perfect weapon to use against Romain. I was bitter that she inspired a desire in him that had entirely died out for me. But anger blinded me to foreseeing the full consequences. I didn't mean for Alice's bad publicity to spread this far.

'Alice told me all about Heather Perkins,' I say, sticking up for her. 'I looked into it thoroughly. It was a misunderstanding and Heather is being entirely unfair. When Alice is ready to come back, we should give her another chance.'

Charles looks surprised, then shakes his head as though I'm playing the martyr.

After he leaves, I sit at my desk feeling awful. Alice was supposed to be smeared, not destroyed. Romain has recently hired a PR firm to help limit the damage to his reputation. It strikes me that they might even have decided to plant bad stories about Alice to mitigate any harm to him. The thought makes me feel sick. I resolve to speak to Romain. I can help fight for Alice to keep her job, though I wonder if it would be possible for us to work together, for her to ever forgive me if she knew what I'd engineered . . .

Towards the end of the day, Sarah comes into my office carrying her notebook.

'Are you okay?'

Everyone keeps asking me this. They make me feel as though I have a terminal illness or something.

'I'm fine,' I snap. Then, seeing her recoil, I say: 'I'm sorry. I'm just stressed.'

'Are you and Romain going to divorce?' Sarah blurts out. She realises that she's been inappropriate, and goes to apologise, but I cut in.

'It's fine, Sarah. At least you've asked me face-to-face. The rest of the office are all speculating behind my back.' I sigh. 'I don't know.'

'It's just . . .' Sarah hesitates. 'I felt I should tell you – about that time I went to Alice's flat, after you first rented it . . .'

'Yes?' I ask, my heartbeat speeding up.

'Well, it was Romain who asked me to go.' Sarah looks sheepish. 'I'm sorry I denied it. I just felt – kind of awkward. He collared me on my way to work, and he asked me to go, to see if you'd left – ahem – any underwear, or an earring, and to text him the outcome. So I went – but I couldn't find anything. I didn't want to go, but when Romain asks you to do something . . .'

'He can be so very persuasive,' I hear myself saying in shock.

'Yes! Exactly. And now it's all out in the open – well, it's rather ironic, really. Because it turned out he was the one – I mean, it's always the jealous types who turn out to be the cheaters,' Sarah muses.

'And – did Romain give you a key?'

'He did, yes, he had a spare.'

'Thank you so much for telling me.' I'm conscious that when I'm most stressed, my politeness reaches levels of royalty. 'It's so very kind of you.'

'I'm sorry I wasn't honest with you earlier.'

In a daze, I give Sarah some task and she leaves my office. I sit there, stunned.

Before the big media crisis, Romain's lost libido had led me to believe that he didn't care, that his love for me had hardened into indifference. When I watched them together, he did confide in Alice that he thought I might be having an affair – but it sounded to me like a vague speculation, a way of justifying his own betrayal.

I shouldn't have been fooled. Romain always has to stay in control. If he was getting Sarah to investigate me back in the Feeld phase – then he probably knows a lot more than I realise.

Disorientation hits me like vertigo. I don't understand what my husband's playing at. He doesn't want to divorce, yet he's punished me by lying about the vineyard. I don't know if he wants revenge or he wants to save our marriage or what the hell he's up to.

I think of our past. Of the bloody secrets that bind us. A dread fills me.

I close my eyes and I'm back there. Back in Otley, back when I was seventeen years old, back on that night when I saw Chris for the very last time . . .

It's evening. We're sitting in his car, parked by the graveyard, the twilight imbuing the trees and stones with an eerie blue glow. I'm telling Chris that it's over. He keeps asking me if Romain's behind this, and I say no, no, even though it's a lie: Romain has insisted on this break-up. Chris's blue eyes glint with pain. He starts driving. Faster and faster. I tell him to slow down. I tell him I want to get out. He screeches to a halt, yells at me to *fuck right off*. I stumble out and watch as the car shoots off, speeding into the night, towards the woods.

I start walking. I'm in a little babydoll dress and I'm shivering. I call Romain. He needs to find somewhere private; I overhear him making an excuse to his wife. 'I broke up with Chris,' I tell him, my voice shaking. Now I've done as he asked, maybe he'll leave his wife.

'Good girl,' Romain replies warmly. His voice is so seductive that I want to tell him I'll do anything for him, anything—

BHAM!

At first I wonder if I've heard a gunshot. I spin round. Then I see a ball of gold furling up into the night sky. Romain asks what's up. And I suddenly click: *it's Chris*. And I babble to him in tearful shock: 'Oh my God, it's my fault, he was upset, we've both been drinking I have to go—'

'No,' Romain cuts in firmly. 'Now, listen to me. You do not go and seek him out. You were never in the car. I have a reputation to maintain.'

'But – but – *Chris*—'

'It's happened, Mina. The car's on fire. He's gone.'

'But – I can't – I can't . . .'

'You have to make a choice, Mina.' His voice becomes urgent and fierce. 'This is one of those moments when life tests you. If you're going to be with me, you walk away now, you never saw anything, you never heard anything. You said goodbye to Chris at the graveyard. I can't be involved in this, you see? In teens drinking and crashing cars. I'm already taking too many risks, being with you, and I cannot survive – I cannot survive,' he repeats, his voice harsh with stress, 'if you go to him. You head back to your friend Sue's house. You say you popped out to the graveyard, but now you're spending the evening with her.'

'But there'll be CCTV, it'll show me in the car before he . . .' I sob, seeing yellow flare into the dark.

'I have a friend in the force, Howard. He can take care of any details we need help with.'

'But – he might still be alive – I can't just leave him to die.'

'I'll organise a 999 call,' Romain says. 'I can be anonymous. It can't come from you . . .'

And so I stumble and sob my way back down the road towards Sue's house, the cottage where her parents live. I'm picturing Chris, his skin seared, body turning black, and I vomit into the grassy bank. I shake myself, wipe my sour lips, force away my fear as I repeat Romain's instructions. I go to her front door, knock. She lets me in, picks up immediately that I'm not right, asks what's wrong, and I reply that I'm just anxious about exams. We chat, do some homework, watch a bit of trash TV. I keep telling myself that it's OK, Romain will call 999, but the horror still screams through me: that every second of delay might be the difference between life and death for Chris. I've lied to Sue and my father preaches that lying is a sin and I'm terrified that I'm going to be struck down by a thunderbolt on the way back to the vicarage. That Chris is gone, that I've lost him, my boyfriend with blue eyes who always has a cheeky joke to tell, is not something I can even take in. Some part of me is convinced that he must have run from the car, that he's safe and well and watching his dad's Fiat become ashes in drunken embarrassment.

I shake myself, coming back down to earth. To my office, my laptop, the surge of colleagues leaving the office, heading home. I try to force the memories away, briskly checking my diary for Monday's schedule. But I can never cure the afterburn of regret, forever scorched in my heart since that night. After the announcement of Chris's death came the grief, came the trip to Scotland, dragged there by my mother. Romain wouldn't take my calls. I was still in mourning for Chris. And I was pregnant too. I remember Sue coming to visit me and telling her I was carrying a baby. She promised to always protect me, to keep my secret safe.

Back home, I open the front door feeling on edge.

To my relief, there's no sign of Romain. No sign of his red box. No doubt he's at the Commons. Baba's cooking us a delicious Italian meal. She's been so sweet since the scandal, fretting and fussing that I'm losing weight, feeding me her most nourishing dishes. I do something I know that Romain will disapprove of, given he believes in a separation between employer and staff: I insist Baba eats with me, giving her half my meal.

My phone pings with a message from Lucas.

I was wondering if you could bring the gun over? I don't like the idea of it floating about! It's not safe.

I hesitate. I know the gun story is just an excuse. Lucas wants to drive our affair towards a conclusion. I can't delay making a choice much longer. I feel love burn in me, a hunger for Lucas's kisses; and then fear constricts me again, wondering what Romain might do if I walked out on him. The betrayal, the damage to his reputation, a probable deselection – he'd never forgive it. Revenge would be served, cold and fatal, somewhere down the line.

I head upstairs to my study. I remove Lucas's gun from my top drawer and slip it into my handbag.

I'm on my way to Lucas's in an Uber when Romain calls. I pick it up and hear the urgency in his voice.

'Mina – could you please come over to Alice's flat?'

What the hell's he doing there? I wonder in shock. I tried calling Alice earlier, feeling it was time to finally have a talk about everything, but she didn't pick up.

'I'm on my way to a launch party,' I lie nervously. 'Romain, I think you should get out of there, if the press see you—'

'Darling, it's urgent. I'm afraid we have something of a situation on our hands.'

CHAPTER FIFTY-TWO

Alice

How long have I been trapped in the secret room now? Maybe half an hour, maybe an hour. I've tried shouting to Romain, cajoling him, banging on the door, but he just ignores me.

I've tried calling out. I went to the window, looking down into the quiet side street, willing someone to walk by. Finally, a drunken gang of lads appeared, but when I hailed them, they simply blew kisses and catcalls, then staggered on.

Now I get up and press my eye to the peephole.

Romain's sitting at my dining table, chin in his hands, gazing out of the window.

'Murderer!' Mimi sings at him from her cage.

'Be quiet,' he snaps, and my heart contracts: he'd better not harm my darling birds.

He goes back to plotting. His eyebrows are drawn; he's clearly working out his next move in this game of chess. And I have to calm these waves of panic and work out his game plan, if I want to get out of here alive. Romain's reputation is everything to him, that's why he's flipped out. I just need to reassure him, maybe even seduce him . . .

'Romain,' I call softly.

Silence.

Buzz-buzz.

Romain stands, goes to the intercom. 'Come on up.'

I stiffen: *who's this?* A little while ago, I heard him make a call and pressed my ear to the door, desperately trying to hear, but he must have shut himself in a bedroom.

Now I have visions of a policeman, or even an assassin, some guy hired to do away with me—

I hear Romain opening the front door and Dominic bursts into the room. What the fuck?

'So, now what?' Dominic demands. 'I hope you've brought me here to fucking apologise. It's not my fault, you know, that I had to sell those pictures. You promised me legal help, you said you'd make sure I got this flat back, and then – nothing, no lawyer, it was all bullshit.'

'Dominic! Calm down, okay? I just want to clarify something.' He hesitates, his tone becoming cautious: 'Do you know about Aimee?'

'Aimee? Yeah, she's mine,' he replies defiantly.

'I'm sorry?' Romain, like Mina, becomes more polite the more stressed he is.

'My girlfriend, right?' Dominic looks amused.

'Your girlfriend?'

'Uh-huh. She was helping me spy on this flat.'

'And you didn't feel it might be appropriate to inform me of your connection?'

Dominic shrugs. 'My love life is my business.' He can't resist a chance to put down an ace: 'And she's your daughter, yeah?'

'That's what Aimee claims?' Romain says.

'She does,' Dominic says. 'But don't worry, your secret's safe with me.'

Romain falls silent; then he smiles his awful smile.

'Aimee's an alcoholic – you can't trust a thing she says. She comes up with all sorts of ideas as to who her father might be. But look: I have a little gift for you, that I think you'll enjoy.'

I hear the key turn in the lock and the door swings open and then Dominic's shoved in—

We gape at each other in shock.

The door slams.

The key turns in the lock.

Now we're locked up together.

CHAPTER FIFTY-THREE

Alice

I press myself against the wall, terrified. Dominic hammers at the door, so hard he eventually has to stop. He winces in pain as he rubs his raw knuckles.

He turns on me. 'What the fuck is he playing at?'

'I don't know!' I cry. 'He just shoved me in here, now you.' I glare at him, warning him that he'd better not turn on me, trying to hide my terror. Romain clearly put him in here to beat me up, a cruelty that shocks me despite everything he's done so far.

Dominic is about the same height and weight as me, but he's vicious. I start to shake at the thought of having to fight him; I order myself to use my anger as fuel, to be prepared to lose my humanity, because if I don't, I might not survive this.

'For fuck's sake!' Dominic pummels the door again, then kicks it. 'Jesus! What is he playing at? His lordship puts you in here, then me. Clearly we're supposed to fight like a pair of fucking dogs! Like entertainment for the posh cunt. I don't think so, do you?'

I shake my head numbly, in relief.

'If he wants to play divide and rule, I'm not up for it.' Rummaging in his pocket, Dominic pulls out some chewing gum, softens it in his mouth, then smears it over the peephole.

He slumps to the floor, then drags his palms over his face. It's a gesture that's so familiar, that I've seen him do dozens of times, in those breathless moments after we robbed a house, after we ran from the police, that I feel an unexpected affinity with him.

Then I shake myself. Our friendship is long gone and Dominic can't be trusted; his mood might change at any point.

He turns to me and hisses, 'What's his game?'

'I don't know,' I hiss back. 'You're the one working for him.'

'If you hadn't fucked me over, I wouldn't have to,' Dominic cries.

Silence. We both glare at each other.

'You're the one who shopped me to Julia over that book,' I point out. 'You got me arrested.'

'Yeah, I know.' Dominic shows some regret. 'I stopped trusting you, but yeah, I got paranoid. I made the wrong move.'

I'm not sure how sincere his regret is, but I force a wary smile. Dominic is right: if we're going to beat Romain, we need to transcend our grudges, work together.

'So you found this place,' he says, his eyes flitting from walls to window. He rubs his palms over his face again. 'Mum blocked it off. Timothy's the one who put in the fucking peephole. He used to put me in here, then beat Mum up. I was fourteen years old and he knew I'd have to watch, cos if I didn't, my imagination would create something far worse.'

He suddenly looks close to tears, and I frown, feeling sympathy for him despite our enmity.

'Timothy and Romain – two of a kind,' he says. 'I knew I shouldn't have got caught up with him. A fucking MP!'

'But it might stop him harming us,' I say in a low voice. 'He won't want the scandal.'

'How fucking naive is that?' Dom laughs at me. 'He'll be friends with all the cops, we don't have a chance.'

He starts to peel up the carpet, clearly looking for anything he might use as a weapon.

'There's nothing,' I say, 'I already looked.'

'We need a plan, Alice,' he says in a low voice. 'We need a plan.'

And suddenly the lights go out.

The single bulb in the room dies. The room is plunged into shadows, edged with amber from the dim light of a streetlamp at the bottom of the side street. Dominic gets up.

'It must be a power cut,' he says. 'What the fuck is he playing at out there?'

'You shouldn't have covered the peephole,' I hiss, getting up and trying to peel the gum off. 'Now we can't see him . . .'

But it's pitch black in the living-room now, anyhow: no hope of gauging what he's up to.

Dominic kicks the door again, then sits down. We sit in silence for a while, exhausted and nervy. There's a sour taste in my mouth from a lack of food and drink. I think I can hear Romain pacing and fear shivers over me. *What is his game?*

'This flat,' Dominic says. 'If I help you now, if I save you, then you have to promise to sell it, give me half . . .'

I roll my eyes.

'You know I haven't been able to because Julia put a clause in her will,' I tell him. 'I can't sell for a period of two years.'

'I thought you were making that up.' Dominic sounds spiky again.

'No. I was being honest.'

'Really?'

'Really. Julia used to say she wasn't going to put me in her will because money just brought a fresh set of troubles. I never expected it, you know.'

'Yeah, I know,' Dominic concedes.

'I loved her,' I say fiercely.

Dominic gazes at me, eyes wide, and then nods sullenly.

Silence. We wait, we watch, we listen.

I open my mouth and close it.

There are memories that I want to share with Dominic. I couldn't tell him the truth, not once I'd heard the will; it would've been too dangerous. But I wish he knew what it had been like. Those last few weeks, when Julia became so frail, her skin like paper, her bones protuberant, and every tiny act of eating or drinking took monumental effort. As her lungs grew weak, the hospital issued her with an oxygen machine and she had to wear a mask that was attached to it. She complained it made her feel as though she was under-water. Once or twice I would leave her bedroom and come back in to find she'd taken it off, see her gasping desperately for air. I told her off and she looked meek. On the third occasion, I realised that she was trying to speed up her end. I burst into tears.

'It's all very well for you,' she complained between stolen shallow breaths. 'I'm stuck in this broken body and I'm tired. I've had my time, Alice, I've had a good life, but I don't want to carry on in this pain. Now, take the pillow and give me my peace.'

It took several more days before I was persuaded. I took the pillow and pressed it over her face, but I lost my nerve at the last minute – and she berated me, begged me. And then, finally, I obeyed her, saying a prayer for forgiveness, pressing down hard until her body stopped shuddering and fell still. A horror came over me. But then the pillow slipped away and the look on her face was a redemption and my tears turned to joy: all the tension knotted into her features had gone, leaving an expression of euphoric peace. For some time, I sat with her, holding her stiff hand, telling myself that I had done the right thing.

But it made me a murderer, even if I had killed out of love.

I've wanted to tell someone. Sometimes Sean, sometimes Dominic. He sensed something, saw a fragment of a letter Julia once penned where she was asking me to kill her, and he misunderstood it, twisted it.

But now I feel that, when we get out of here, I'll tell Dominic. He should know. I'm tired of this war. Maybe I have been selfish, unfair. Maybe I should have found a way to sell the flat. He was the one who first saved me from life on the streets—

'So what's the plan?' Dominic's whisper cuts into my thoughts, dragging me back to the horror of the present, this tiny room and the man pacing in the room next door.

'There's two of us,' I whisper. 'If he opens the door, we pretend to reason with him, then we go for him.'

'You kick his balls, I'll go for his eyes—'

The turn of the key in the lock.

We both stand up.

And then we recoil.

Romain has taken out one of the knives from my kitchen block. He brandishes it at us.

'I want to speak to Alice,' he says.

CHAPTER FIFTY-FOUR

Mina

Be careful.

I eye up the message from Lucas. I know he feels hurt that I've deserted him for Romain, but I promised him I'd be quick and come to him. I have a bad feeling about this he replied. Maybe I should come with you. I laughed him off, saying it was fine, and yet an unease tickles me too.

Why does he want you to go to Alice's flat? Maybe they're going to announce that they want to be together Lucas texts.

Maybe, I think. It would solve everything, set me free, and yet the sad wrench inside me surprises me. My marriage would be an official failure, after two decades together.

The Uber pulls up outside Alice's building. The air is crisp and chilly, the twilight darkening and deepening into night. I'd been dreading that I might find Dominic hanging around. The very thought of him fills me with disgust; I wouldn't have been able to stop myself berating him for putting his hands on my daughter.

But there's nobody about. No press, either, thank God, just a resident on their mobile on the path outside, going on about an electricity issue. Alice's buzzer didn't seem to be working. I try calling Romain but to my surprise, he doesn't pick up.

The lobby is empty. Stepping into the lift, with its crystal-rimmed mirror and creamy carpet, sends a frisson through me, associations of anticipation, sexy underwear, new perfume on my wrists, tingling with guilt.

I jab at the button. But the lift just sits there.

I decide to take the stairs. By the time I reach the third floor, the pull of muscles in my thighs is painful.

I push open the door to the fifth floor, step into the main hallway, to find it in darkness.

Shit.

I can hardly see. I wave my hand around, wondering if they're on some sort of timer.

I'm here I message Romain.

I rap on Alice's door.

Silence.

A sudden noise, from behind the door – did I hear a scream? I rap again – and then the door opens and Romain is standing before me, holding up his phone.

The eerie glow lights up his face. There's a look on his face that I haven't seen in a long time, a mixture of terror and a cold determination to control that emotion all costs. It takes me right back to that night in Otley, when I was seventeen years old and police sirens were screaming and the crash was still a shock in my heart. The way that Romain lectured me, instructed me, told me how he was going to fix everything. A flurry in my heartbeat; I suffer the dangerous potential of a panic attack and reach for the doorframe.

'Why's it so dark?'

'The electricity – it just cut out,' he replies, his breath warm against my face. 'It must be the whole floor. Come in, darling. We need to talk.'

He looks behind him and it's then I notice the wound on his face, a slash across his cheek, the blood still fresh.

'What happened to your face?'

Romain doesn't reply. I step in – hear a thud, a voice calling. I stop.

'What's going on?' I ask.

The voice thins into a scream: 'Let me out! Let me out!'

Romain closes the door behind me, then shines his mobile at me, making me squint.

'As I said, we have a situation.'

An urge grips me, to fling open the door and *run,* but Romain takes my hand and grips it tightly.

'Mina, we have to stick together. It's your assistant who's caused all this trouble. We have to work out what we're going to do about her.'

'Alice? Is she the one calling? Is she—'

'Listen: you need to know the facts. She asked me to meet her here,' he says in a low voice. 'I said no, it was too risky, but she kept phoning, pleading, said it was an emergency – I gave in . . .'

I hear another cry, and I shiver: what the hell is going on?

'She was ranting away. I tried to calm her down. She hurt my face—'

'But where is she? Is she okay?'

'In the secret room. I had to put her in there. Alice has committed a crime, Mina.' Romain's voice is so pious it reminds me of my father giving a sermon.

'What crime? Romain – what's – going on?' The oceanic darkness is disorientating, collapsing a sense of space and time.

'Alice's flat is now a crime scene.'

'Then we need to leave,' I hiss, tugging his hand, his wedding ring cutting into my flesh.

'No: we can't. We have to clean up. You've used this flat, previously.'

What does he mean? Is he referring to . . .?

'Come,' Romain pulls me forward, ignoring my resistance. His mobile turns the hallway into an chamber of reflected light.

As we enter the living-room, Alice's cries start up again. She bangs against the door of the secret room like a caged animal. There's a feeling of chaos in the room; there are things scattered across the floor; my heel bangs against a book, which skids away from me.

Then Romain's mobile highlights a figure, slumped over the sofa, and I hear myself let out a scream.

CHAPTER FIFTY-FIVE

Mina

'It's okay,' Romain says softly, rubbing my arm. 'Mina, it's okay.'

'Oh my God,' I hear myself saying, over and over.

He tries to hold me, but I struggle away: 'We can't go through this again. We have to get out of here, now, right now—'

'We have to be smart,' Romain asserts, in a cool voice.

As I pull my mobile out of my handbag, Lucas's pistol glints up at me and I quickly push it down, hiding it.

Romain's hand curls over mine and under the fluorescent glare, I see the blood streaked across his knuckles.

'Mina!' Alice suddenly cries. 'Mina – is that you? It's me, he locked me in here, with Dominic—'

'SHUT UP!' Romain suddenly breaks, his voice rising. 'JUST SHUT UP!'

She falls silent.

I'm shaking violently. Romain tries to stop me, but I push him away and I use the light from my mobile to confirm what I dread: the dead man is Dominic. Alice's stalker. I want to touch his skin, to see if there might be any hope, a beat of life, a whisper of breath, but I curl my trembling fingers away, dare not put my prints on him. Bruising is patterned on his neck in clusters, like pinky-grey flowers. One eye is half closed; the other stares right at me, glassy and unblinking. I swallow back a sob. My breathing starts to come hard and fast and Romain, recognising I'm on the verge of a panic attack, holds me tight. He smells of sweat and blood and something else, something terrible that I can't place—

'It's awful.' Romain's voice breaks too. 'Oh God, it was awful . . .'

'But . . . how . . .?' I hold the phone up near his face.

'Alice did this,' he whispers. 'It's my fault, I put them in a room together . . .'

'But why? Why on earth did you do that?'

'Alice was going crazy, going on about Aimee being our daughter, trying to blackmail us, so I had to put her in the room. Then suddenly Dominic turned up, accusing her, accusing me, acting crazy. He said you'd paid him to take a photo of me, to set up the story—'

I let out a choked gasp.

'I didn't believe him, of course. But he was getting out of control too, and he heard Alice calling and demanded I open the door. I let him go in. I shouldn't have, I know, I made a terrible mistake . . .'

'But did he attack her? I can't imagine that Alice would—'

'I don't know what went on. I just heard kicking and screaming and I panicked. I opened up the door and Dominic was lying there . . .'

'So you moved him out here?'

'He wasn't dead then. I tried to resuscitate him. Alice came at me, tried to stop me – that's when she scratched my face and I fought back and put her back in the room . . .' Romain splays his hands in front of my mobile, the fluorescence highlighting the streaks of blood, the red rimmed beneath his frayed nails.

'It was too late. I couldn't save him. I tried so hard, Mina – it was just – horrifying – to see . . . him gone.'

He's lying, a voice whispers. *Alice wouldn't – she wouldn't –* and then I think of her past, her harsh upbringing, her homeless period. I've lived a life of privilege. I can't understand what she might be capable of.

Romain senses my hesitation and a look of anger darkens his face.

'I'm your husband – and you don't believe me?'

'No,' I reply quickly. 'I believe you, I believe you.'

'Do you?' His tone is almost accusatory.

'I do,' I assure him. 'But we should call the police.'

'No,' he fires back. 'Imagine what Alice might say to them.'

'But the forensics will prove she did this, surely?'

'Not what she might say about me, Mina. What she might say about *you.*'

'*Me?* But I . . .' I glance at Dominic's still body and the desperate urge to get out of here overwhelms me – but as I step forward, Romain blocks me.

'You're the one who hired Dominic. Alice found out. Now you have a reason for murdering him – Alice might say it was all your idea.'

Is he threatening me?

And he knows about me hiring Dominic: *shit.*

'The CCTV will prove when I entered the building,' I manage to say.

'The electricity is down, the CCTV is down. There is no proof.'

'Alright,' I concede. 'I did hire Dominic to go to the papers. I . . .' I ought to say *I'm sorry* but even now and here, something inside me kicks against him. I fall silent.

Romain's face is wrought with devastation.

'You think I'm your idiot husband. I suppose you and Lucas are laughing at me all the time.'

Another curveball, which leaves me speechless. I thought he might have found out about the Feeld affairs, but not Lucas.

I should have known. I've been too lost in love and lust. Romain has spent his life perfecting the art of being one step ahead.

'How could you? I gave you everything, Mina: a beautiful house, luxury, money, status – and then you threw it all away. You destroyed my reputation, got me into the tabloids – *how could you?*'

'You – you stopped wanting me,' I fire back.

'I didn't stop,' he says, but his tone falters and I know he's lying. 'I just had to teach you a lesson.'

'A *lesson*! I'm not a schoolgirl anymore. I've grown up, and that's what you never seem to understand.' I let out a shaking breath and come back to the surreal horror of the present. 'This is madness. We have to call the police.'

But Romain keeps on and on, lost in emotions that have no doubt been churning in him for months. 'If you hadn't hired Dominic to betray me, then he might be alive now.'

'You can't put that on me!' I exhale. 'And as for me wrecking your reputation – I didn't force you to sleep with Alice. It was a test.'

'I slept with her long after you started fucking young men.'

I gaze at Dominic and I think of the power he would have over us, if he were still alive, knowing my secrets, knowing Romain's, and I shake my head: 'We have to call the police.'

'We have to be smart,' Romain asserts, his tone sharpening. 'We have to trust each other. We have to come out of this without any smears.'

We stare at each other and despite all the hurt, fear binds us. If we're going to get this, we have to unite.

'What's our story, then?' I ask.

'We can tell them that we arrived here together, we came in, we found the body, and as we put Alice into the secret room, she tried to fight me. That's our story. Are we agreed?'

'Do we really need to lie?' I ask nervously.

'Alice is a young thirty-something; I'm a white man in his fifties. I'm guilty before they even arrive. You know the way the world works now. It's going to be my word against hers. We need to be on the same page, Mina.'

As he gazes at me, I feel his plea: *I was loyal to you once, I got you out of a messy situation. Now pay me back, be loyal to me.* Panic is erasing the present; it's as though we're back in the past. Back in that moment when I was walking away from Chris and called Romain and he told me, fiercely, that I had a choice, that I had to choose him.

'Hurry up then,' I say quietly. 'Wash away the blood. Then we call the police.'

'Oh, Mina.' Suddenly Romain pulls me in close. He holds me tight and I feel how badly he's shaking and then his lips are on mine. He kisses me deeply, desperately, with a passion I haven't felt in years. 'We're in this together.'

CHAPTER FIFTY-SIX

Mina

Romain is washing his hands. I stand in the doorway of Alice's bathroom, watching him claw his nails deep into the soap, and I imagine her blood and Dominic's blood sluicing away. I feel sick. I turn away.

Using my mobile as a torch, I creep back to the living-room. There's a horrific energy in the air: the silent echoes of screams, an evil that's almost visceral. I keep fighting the urge to examine Dominic again. I can't quite believe he's really dead. I step closer, and then a little closer, and with my phone I illuminate his lifeless eyes, staring back at me, glassy as a doll's – and I'm so horrified that I drop my phone and curse.

I kneel down, picking it up. The times says 8:03. Romain in the bathroom, Alice in the secret room, Dominic dead. The surrealness of the moment hits me: just three hours ago, I was in the office, feeling bored, wondering what Baba might cook for dinner. And now – this.

I edge towards the secret room. Alice is still very quiet.

Dominic, the stalking, his relentless, ruthless pursuit of her flat: she must have finally snapped. I can understand that rage, though I can't understand how far she took it.

I try to look through the peep-hole. But it's covered with a white gummy mess; I can only see Alice in fragments.

An amber glow from the streetlamp bleeds into the room. There's blood on the carpet. Red handprints on the walls.

Alice is sitting with her knees hunched up. She's injured. Her hair is streaked, matted with blood. One of her eyes is bruised, the eyelid crushed. Her cheek is scratched. She's visibly shaking.

There's a knife lying on the floor, shiny with blood.

Sensing me, she jumps up, so that her face is close to the peephole. I step backwards in horror, grab the edge of the TV.

Panic quickens my breath. I sink down, put my hands over my ears, my heartbeat pounding; I tell myself to *calm down, calm down*, but all I want to do is run. The room swims, becomes a black blur, a circle of hell.

'Mina?' I hear Alice say. 'Are you okay? Breathe in for two, out for three . . . Can you let me out, Mina? Please? I'm hurt.'

Despite everything, I find myself obeying her instructions, and my breathing starts to soften. The darkness thins; details emerge. Aimee's face appears before me, evokes a fierce love. I cling to it for solace. It gives me strength. We can't go to prison. I have to get it together, be strong, get through this for Aimee. We're just starting to bond for the first time in years. She needs me to be her mother.

'Mina?' Alice asks.

I go back the spyhole, frowning.

'Your husband is a psycho. He killed Dominic. You have to call the police.'

I draw back in shock. She's in denial, I think numbly. And then, as horror dawns: *So now she's going to try and pin it on us?*

'Alice,' I tell her, 'if you don't own up to what's happened, it might make it all the worse. I can back you up to the police, tell them that Dominic never left you alone, that you were driven to it out of desperation—'

'I didn't kill him!'

Maybe she's in shock. Maybe she was so overwhelmed with emotion that she can't face it, can't remember what she's done.

'Do you think I even have the physical strength? Dominic and Romain – they argued about you setting us up, getting Dominic to take the photos – and then about Aimee – and Romain said he knew too much and – he—Oh God . . .'

'Alice, Romain isn't capable . . .'

'I'll be next, don't you see? If you don't call them now, it's going to be too late.'

I hear the shower stopping. He'll be out any minute; I want to press pause and think everything through slowly, but there's no time—

Romain is my husband. I know he can lie and cheat and he's smart and conniving – but murder? I gaze at the silhouette of the slumped body again. No, Romain could *never* . . .

'Mina, please listen to me.' I hear Alice's voice behind me. 'I tried to stop him, do you see? I hurt his face, but I was trying to stop him . . .'

Is she just a brilliant actress? Is this how Heather Perkins felt before she was conned by her? This tug of doubt, this sympathy, this . . .

'Romain hired Dominic to watch the flat,' Alice cries. 'He knows about your affairs. I didn't know about any of that until now. I'm sorry . . .'

I stiffen. So Romain has been using Dominic too? I open my mouth to fire back that it's ridiculous, but—

If I think about it – oh God – it all makes sense. Otherwise, how did he find out about Lucas? I was too shocked to even compute, but he only hired Sarah that one time, and so . . .

I think of poor Aimee, dragged into it too by Dominic; Romain can't have foreseen that.

'When?' I ask. 'When did he start?'

'I honestly don't know . . .' Alice's voice is ragged. 'I was at Dominic's flat – I wanted to know what was going on – and suddenly Romain turned up. I couldn't believe it myself, Mina. I can see why you might find it all hard to take it – but I swear, I swear, I am telling you the truth.'

I step closer as though in a trance. I need to look Alice in the eye.

The key to the secret room sits in the lock. I twist it. Is this madness, going in? Will she attack me? I swallow, turn the handle, enter, my heart beating.

Alice stares at me in shock. I kneel down and gaze into her eyes. She's telling me the truth, I know it, I can feel it.

You have to make a choice Romain once said to me, on that night that Chris died. But I didn't choose. I did as he instructed. I was a teenager. I had no idea what I was doing. He acted through me, yet I've lived with years of guilt, a guilt that has caged me, left me feeling like I owe him, that the debt binds us.

'Mina!' I hear Romain calling.

I turn around in shock.

He stares at me.

He knows I know.

'You hired Dominic too,' I say, forcing strength into my voice.

'I had to. You were about to bring us both down. I had to know what was going on, Mina. But I didn't harm him.'

'But how – how could Alice – fight Dominic?' I cry, the fog clearing. 'And then you?'

'Mina – he was out of control.'

'So you're saying you . . .'

'He knew too much. He could have gone to the papers

about your affairs next. He could have told them about Aimee. Our reputations would have been trash, our lives over.'

A long silence, as I try to digest the truth, but I can't, it just sits in my stomach in a ball of pain and horror.

He steps forward, calling my name.

I spin round, go to close the secret door—

But he's too quick. He runs, lunges at me, dragging me out of the secret room, and I fight him, but he throws me, and I feel the floor coming up to meet me, smashing against my ribs, knocking the breath out of me. My handbag tumbles; my mobile spins and slides. I gasp for air, my lungs aching. The gun – I see its silver edge poking out of my bag—

Romain enters the secret room and I hear Alice cry out—

I jump up, picking up the gun, cocking the trigger, knowing that this is my choice: he will kill Alice, and I will have to play along with fake stories to the police and bribes to cover us, and he will play it beautifully, tell the world that she was a deranged, over-sexed working-class intern who wrecked our middle-class calm—

And I enter the room and see him on top of her, animal in his fury, his violence, his hands around her neck—

And I scream, 'STOP!'

Romain looks back at me in shock—

Alice gasps for air; she seizes the moment and punches him—

And as he goes for her again, I pick up the gun, my whole body on fire with panic—

In the distance comes the sound of sirens—

But they won't come in time, it'll be too late—

And my finger pulls the trigger, and I feel the jolt, and hear the whizz of the bullet as it slices through the air—

EPILOGUE

Alice

One Year Later

'I'm so proud to be here celebrating the launch of *Playthings* . . .'

I break off and smile at Lucas. He's standing next to me in Daunt's bookshop, hardbacks of *Playthings* piled high on a table. His friends and family are gathered before us. They beam at Lucas. But every time they look at me, I see the question marks behind their smiles.

They're here to celebrate Lucas's debut, but they're also curious. They've read the headlines. Seen the TV reports. Gossiped about the scandal. I come with baggage now. At least I'm no longer the femme fatale; what came after was so horrific, it eclipsed that tabloid tattle.

It's been a year since that night, which ended in Dominic's death and Romain's arrest. I still remember sitting in the ambulance. A paramedic had put a blanket around my shoulders, wrapped a band around my arm to check my blood pressure. I watched Romain being bundled into the police car, blue lights scything over his face, blood dripping from his ear where Mina had shot him, grazed his earlobe. There was a haughty look on his face, as though the police officers were fools and would soon be apologising to him. I don't suppose he ever really believed that Mina would betray him by telling the police that he had lied. I was interrogated by officers in my hospital room. I could hardly get the words out, terrified that my past would colour their perspective, but a forensic analysis of the room, of Dominic's body, proved that Romain had killed him.

For all his wealth and power, Romain is now sitting in Belmarsh Prison, awaiting trial. Sometimes I imagine him gazing out of his cell, his tiny square window, imagine his restless fury, and I shiver.

'. . . and so please – everyone – please do buy the book and get it signed,' I hear myself enthusing, coming back to the present. 'And now let's all raise our glasses to Lucas Chamila!'

Everyone bursts into applause. Lucas beams and blushes. He sits down at his signing desk, a long queue snaking before him. His girlfriend, Priya, rubs his shoulder, smiling down at him.

I glance over at Mina. She looks stern, tired, but when she catches my eyes, she smiles to show she's proud of me. And I feel a rare burst of joy. I am an editor. I've just made my first launch speech. I've got my dream job.

And I think back to when I was a hungry intern, when I stood in a bookshop for my first launch party, listening to Mina make a speech. I remember how I invited her back to my flat in the rain. How desperate I was to impress her. I've come so far since then.

As the party wraps up, Mina shakes Lucas's hand and congratulates him. We share an Uber home.

Since Romain's arrest, his vineyard has suffered a plummet in profits, given how badly he's damaged their brand. Mina ended up moving out of her Mayfair home, which is being sold. I've seen online pics of its white walls scrawled in graffiti. He's become a caricature: the rotten MP, a symbol of corruption now, a sociopath who abused me, who killed a vulnerable man. And sometimes I want to say, *It was all a lot more complicated than that* . . .

Mina's renting down the road from me. We pull up in Notting Hill, outside a small house. The front door opens and golden light spills out. I see Aimee in the doorway. She's a different person since rehab. She's in therapy now and is studying drama at RADA; she lives with Mina all the time.

She's had to forgive Mina for being an absent mother for so long. Just as I've had to learn forgiveness too, for all Mina's past manipulations. But I know that, if it were not for Mina, I'd have suffered the same fate as Dominic. I remember the squeeze of Romain's hands on my neck, darkness swimming through my mind, my body kicking and then falling slack – I was so close, so close. Mina saved my life that day, and it's something I'll never forget.

As Mina waves goodbye, she gives me a secret smile, and I grin back at her.

The Uber driver heads on, dropping me off outside Chesterton House. He looks up at the block with a flicker of recognition – 'Isn't this where that shooting happened? And that psycho MP killed that guy?'

I stiffen, wondering if he recognises me. But I realise he's not trolling me; he's just curious.

'I think so,' I reply.

'You'd think that rich people would be safe in a place like that.' He shakes his head. 'It just goes to show – anything can happen to any of us.'

I enter the building quickly, head down, give Felipe a quick smile and then dive into the lift up to my flat.

I shrug off my jacket and greet my birds. 'Lucas, Lucas,' they chatter back, which makes me smile; they listened to me practising my launch party speech earlier. My flat still has a slightly acidic smell, from another coat of fresh cream paint. I open a window and pull the curtains closed.

All okay? Sean texts me.

It was such a great launch! I send him a photo.

So proud of you! Sean texts back, and I smile – God, I miss him, but he'll be back from his work trip tomorrow.

I head into the bathroom, gazing at my reflection as I wash my hands. A scar on my cheek, from Romain's attack on me when I tried to fight him. I run my finger over it.

And then I go to the kitchen, and take a bottle of water, and pick up a throw from the sofa, and I sidle into the secret room.

For weeks after that terrible night, I was unable to enter it at all. I'd put the key in and curl my fingers around the handle, but I couldn't push open the door. I'd be back there, locked inside whilst I heard Romain and Dominic battle it out; gazing through the smeared peephole, Dominic gasping his last breaths as Romain strangled him; hammering the wall whilst I screamed at him to *STOP*. And then, one day, I just did it: I turned the key, I walked in before I could think about it. And I saw: it was just a room. The darkness I suffered was all inside me; that's what I needed to deal with. I opened the window. My hand trembled. I tore up the carpet. I started to repaint it. With every fierce stroke of my brush, I tried to paint away the bad memories.

I go to the peephole.

I stand and watch.

It's delicious, the suspense of not knowing who'll come in first.

The sound of my front door opening. Lucas enters.

He's wearing a baseball cap and he flings it onto the sofa. To avoid more scandal, Mina and Lucas have had to become very discreet. Lucas's close friend, Priya, has been happy to play the role of an on/off girlfriend for now, to help distract people and dispel speculation.

He's humming, clearly on a high after his launch.

There's the sound of a key in the door.

Mina enters, looking beautiful and exhilarated.

They kiss passionately and then hug tightly.

'I'm so proud of you,' Mina beams.

'I wanted to kiss you all night.' Lucas sounds drunk and sad. 'I mean, I loved it all but – it seems like we're doomed to end up being a secret forever . . .'

'Soon,' Mina promises. And I wonder. If it's not just about her reputation or the headlines their love affair might create, but if she prefers the deceit and the danger.

She glances around the room and Lucas frowns, looking worried.

'I haven't checked to see if we're safe,' he says. 'But I don't think Alice would . . .'

'Oh, no, Alice would never,' she agrees, and I see her flash a quick smile at the peephole.

It's a secret pact we've made.

Mina says she likes me watching. She got angry when she found out I'd done it without her permission, but now she says it makes her feel sexy – and safe. Someone is watching her, watching over her. Nobody will ever truly understand what we've been through when we shared the darkness of that night, a trauma that has bonded us forever. I love to see her taking solace in Lucas, in his youth, in his kisses. These are the ways we're trying to rebuild our lives, our ways of fighting back against the dark: love and sex, books and beauty.

Mina flashes me a secret smile, and then reaches up to kiss Lucas, drawing him down onto the sofa . . .